Praise for Anne Emery

Praise for *Lament for Bonnie*
"You know you are in the thick of a good mystery novel when you start becoming suspicious of characters you consider shady in the parking lot of your very own town. Anne Emery's latest, *Lament for Bonnie*, will leave readers spooked and wary of their surroundings." — *Atlantic Books Today*

"*Lament for Bonnie* is a good mystery in this entertaining series set in eastern Canada." — Glenn Perrett, All Things Entertainment

"The author's ability to say more with less invites readers along for the dark ride, and the island's Celtic culture serves as a stage to both the story's soaring narrative arc and a quirky cast of characters, providing a glimpse into the Atlantic Canadian communities settled by Scots over two hundred years ago." — *Celtic Life*

"The novel is ingeniously plotted." — Reviewing the Evidence

Praise for *Ruined Abbey*
"The eighth in the series, this winning mystery stands on its own . . . fans of Emery's earlier works will enjoy seeing Father Brennan in the bosom of his feisty Irish family." — *Booklist*, starred review

"True to the Irish tradition of great storytelling, this is a mesmerizing tale full of twists that will keep readers riveted from the first page to the last." — *Publishers Weekly*, starred review

"This is a really tightly plotted historical with solid characters and the elegant style we expect from Emery." — *Globe and Mail*

"Suspenseful to the final page." — *Winnipeg Free Press*

Praise for *Blood on a Saint*
"As intelligent as it is entertaining . . . The writing bustles with energy, and with smart, wry dialogue and astute observations about crime and religion." —*Ellery Queen*

T0037619

"Emery skilfully blends homicide with wit, music, theology, and quirky characters." — *Kirkus Reviews*

Praise for *Death at Christy Burke's*
"Emery's sixth mystery (after 2010's *Children in the Morning*) makes excellent use of its early 1990s Dublin setting and the period's endemic violence between Protestants and Catholics." — *Publishers Weekly*, starred review

"Halifax lawyer Anne Emery's terrific series featuring lawyer Monty Collins and priest Brennan Burke gets better with every book." — *Globe and Mail*

Praise for *Children in the Morning*
"This [fifth] Monty Collins book by Halifax lawyer Emery is the best of the series. It has a solid plot, good characters, and a very strange child who has visions." — *Globe and Mail*

"Not since Robert K. Tanenbaum's Lucy Karp, a young woman who talks with saints, have we seen a more poignant rendering of a female child with unusual powers." — *Library Journal*

Praise for *Cecilian Vespers*
"Slick, smart, and populated with lively characters." — *Globe and Mail*

"This remarkable mystery is flawlessly composed, intricately plotted, and will have readers hooked to the very last page." — *The Chronicle Herald*

Praise for *Barrington Street Blues*
"Anne Emery has given readers so much to feast upon . . . . The core of characters, common to all three of her novels, has become almost as important to the reader as the plots. She is becoming known for her complexity and subtlety in her story construction." — *The Chronicle Herald*

Praise for *Obit*
"Emery tops her vivid story of past political intrigue that could destroy the present with a surprising conclusion." — *Publishers Weekly*

"Strong characters and a vivid depiction of Irish American family life make Emery's second mystery as outstanding as her first."
— *Library Journal*, starred review

Praise for *Sign of the Cross*
"A complex, multilayered mystery that goes far beyond what you'd expect from a first-time novelist."
— *Quill & Quire*

"Snappy dialogue, a terrific feel for Halifax, characters you really do care about, and a great plot make this one a keeper."
— *Waterloo Region Record*

"Anne Emery has produced a stunning first novel that is at once a mystery, a thriller, and a love story. *Sign of the Cross* is well written, exciting, and unforgettable."
— *The Chronicle Herald*

POSTMARK BERLIN

THE COLLINS-BURKE MYSTERY SERIES

Sign of the Cross
Obit
Barrington Street Blues
Cecilian Vespers
Children in the Morning
Death at Christy Burke's
Blood on a Saint
Ruined Abbey
Lament for Bonnie
Though the Heavens Fall

POSTMARK BERLIN

A Mystery

ANNE EMERY

Published by ECW Press
665 Gerrard Street East, Toronto, ON M4M 1Y2
416-694-3348 / info@ecwpress.com

Cover and text design: Tania Craan
Cover image and author photo: © Mick Quinn/mqphoto.com

LIBRARY AND ARCHIVES CANADA CATALOGUING IN PUBLICATION

Title: Postmark Berlin : a mystery / Anne Emery.

Names: Emery, Anne, author.

Series: Emery, Anne. Collins-Burke mystery series ; 11.

Description: Series statement: The Collins-Burke mystery series ; 11 | Previously published in 2020.
Identifiers: Canadiana 20220213852

ISBN 978-1-77041-702-1 (softcover)

Classification: LCC PS8609.M47 P68 2022 | DDC C813/.6—dc23

ALSO ISSUED AS:
ISBN 978-1-77041-387-0 (hardcover)
ISBN 978-1-77305-465-0 (PDF)
ISBN 978-1-77305-464-3 (ePUB)

The publication of *Postmark Berlin* has been generously supported by the Canada Council for the Arts which last year invested $153 million to bring the arts to Canadians throughout the country and is funded in part by the Government of Canada. *Nous remercions le Conseil des arts du Canada de son soutien. L'an dernier, le Conseil a investi 153 millions de dollars pour mettre de l'art dans la vie des Canadiennes et des Canadiens de tout le pays. Ce livre est financé en partie par le gouvernement du Canada.* We acknowledge the support of the Ontario Arts Council (OAC), an agency of the Government of Ontario, which last year funded 1,737 individual artists and 1,095 organizations in 223 communities across Ontario for a total of $52.1 million. We also acknowledge the contribution of the Government of Ontario through the Ontario Book Publishing Tax Credit, and through Ontario Creates for the marketing of this book.

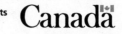

PRINTED AND BOUND IN CANADA

PRINTING: FRIESENS   5   4   3   2   1

MIX
Paper from responsible sources
FSC
www.fsc.org   FSC® C016245

CHAPTER I

Father Brennan Burke

A loud rapping on the door jolted Father Burke from the fog of sleep. What time was it? Where was he? His cell in the Crumlin jail! The screws were murdering his sleep again. No. Merciful God, no. His room at the parish house? He looked around, bleary-eyed. Hadn't he already woken up? Somewhere else? He sank back into sleep. The rapping again, even louder this time. Christ. His head was pounding, his stomach was queasy, and that racket at the door wasn't helping matters. "Fuck off!"

"Open this door. Now!"

Jesus, Mary, and Joseph, was that . . . Oh, God, not the . . . Sure, it was indeed the bishop. Archbishop, to be precise. And Father Burke was in for a belt of the crozier. He bolted from the bed, pulled on a pair of trousers and a shirt, and rocketed into his bathroom. He didn't care if it was the Pope himself; the man would have to wait.

Brennan Burke would not greet anyone, human or divine, without first brushing his teeth.

He made a quick job of it and then lunged for the door. He yanked it open, and there was His Grace, the Most Reverend Dennis Cronin, looming in the doorway like the wrath of God. His handsome face was suffused with anger, his blue eyes as cold as the dusting of snow on his coat. Brennan stepped back to let him in. Just before he closed the door, he saw *that one* lurking in the corridor, taking it all in. Mrs. Kelly, the housekeeper, had never approved of Father Brennan Burke. Every time he saw her, she had a puss on her. Now she could hardly keep the triumphant smirk from her normally prissy lips. Brennan gave the door a good hard slam and turned to face his superior officer.

"Where in the hell were you all night, Father Burke?"

"All night? What time did I get here?" Brennan asked stupidly.

"How do you think it looks to the people of this parish, this diocese, to see one of their priests out in public helping himself to lashings of drink and carrying on and singing at the top of his lungs . . ."

Whatever Brennan had done, he knew he hadn't done any bad singing; his music was always top notch. This was not, however, the time to debate musical quality with his bishop.

". . . and then passing out drunk, staying the night somewhere other than the rectory of Saint Bernadette's church?"

"I, em . . ." Brennan began, though he had no idea what he was about to say.

Didn't matter; the bishop overrode him. Advanced on him and raised his voice. "You!" he said, stabbing a finger into Brennan's chest. "You are acting like the very worst stereotype of an Irishman!"

That got to him. "What exactly do you mean by that, Bishop?" he demanded.

"I mean the stereotype by which many people define us to this day. Next month when you're out and about, take a look at the Saint Patrick's Day cards displayed on the shelves. What is the constant theme? Besides the leaping leprechauns and the pots of gold, what do you see? Jokes about the drink and the drunks. That's us, the way much of society still views us. And little wonder, with the likes of you out there acting the maggot."

"Dennis, for Christ's sake . . ."

"What did the *London Times* say about us during the famine? What were our habits? 'Sitting idle at home, telling stories, going to fairs, plotting, and rebelling.' Disraeli called us 'this wild, reckless, indolent, uncertain, and superstitious race!' That's what they thought of us. And, it hardly needs saying, they all assumed we were *drinkers*. Do we want people to think we're still good for nothing but fighting, fucking, and getting drunk?"

It was rare old times indeed when the bishop let fly with the F word; that said it all about how wound up he was. If Mrs. Kelly still had her twitchy ear up against the door, imagine the state of her, hearing His Grace say fuck.

"I don't have to spell it out any further for you, Brennan, what was and still is said about our people. And here's you, acting it out for all to see. You've only been back in the city for a few days, and how have you been spending those days? Hungover from boozing it up night after night. You're a disgrace."

To my race, Brennan finished silently. Brennan wasn't the type to let somebody walk all over him, wasn't the type to remain silent in the face of aggravation. He came from a family whose ancestors, and whose members still living, had taken up arms to fight and die for Ireland. They were Fenians, Irish Volunteers, IRA men. The Burkes had no need to be lectured on what an Irishman should be. He never thought he would live to see the day when somebody would accuse him of letting down the side for Ireland. But he spoke not a word. It was, at long last, time for him to turn the other cheek.

Because he deserved it. He fully deserved a bollocking from his bishop. He was guilty. He'd been legless with drink, and not for the first time.

"And so, because you drank yourself senseless, you weren't here for our parishioner Meika Keller. She came looking for you here at ten o'clock last night. Said you had agreed to see her."

What? What was he saying? Meika Keller? Had she been talking to Brennan recently? Yes, of course. It was just . . . when? Yesterday, wasn't it? He tried to clear his head.

"What did she say to you?" the bishop asked now.

"Say to me? When?"

"For the love of God, Brennan, wise up here. What did she want to talk to you about?"

"I don't . . ." It was coming back to him through the haze now. The woman had been chatting with him at Saint Mary's University, where she was a professor and Brennan a part-time lecturer. As Meika was leaving the campus, she asked if she could come and speak with him. Could she meet him that night after a charity event of some kind that she had to attend? That would have been last night. "What time is it?" Brennan asked now.

"It's too late, Brennan. That's what time it is."

"No, no, I'll see her. Just let me . . ."

"Was it a confession she asked for, Brennan? At least tell me that."

He tried to reconstruct the conversation with Meika Keller. She was usually cheerful, witty, full of personality. She had always struck him as unflappable. Yesterday, though, her manner was different. There was something on her mind and it must have been serious, if she wanted to meet Father Burke at ten o'clock at night.

"I'm thinking yes, Dennis, she may have wanted to see me in the confessional. Well, I'll track her down now and apologize and hear what she has to say. Maybe help put her mind at rest."

"No, you won't, Brennan."

Something in Cronin's manner gave Brennan a chill. "What is it, Dennis?"

"At seven thirty-five this morning, Meika Keller's body washed up on the beach at Point Pleasant Park."

It was a chilly, grey morning in Halifax when Detective Sergeant Piet Van den Brink had stood on the shore looking out at the Atlantic Ocean, as if the rolling surf could bring in the answers he needed to explain the presence of the body lying at his feet. A man out for an early morning run in the park had spotted the woman at the water's edge; he had dashed to his car in the parking lot and called the police on his cellular phone. Since then, the technical work had all been completed, the body and scene examined and photographed, evidence gathered and bagged, and Piet took one last look and scribbled a few more observations in his notebook. Lying on her back on the rocky beach was a woman who appeared to be in her early forties, slim, with light-blond hair matted with seaweed. What struck Piet as immediately significant was her clothing. She was wearing a gold necklace and a black dress in a pattern with white lines in it. Over the dress was a black jacket, which had come partly off, leaving her left shoulder bare.

"How would you describe that dress?" Piet turned to his partner, Detective Sergeant Ailsa Young. "What would you call that pattern? Not plaid, but what? Checkered?"

"Windowpane check, I'd call it," she replied, and Piet made a note in his book. "Dressed for an evening out. And not an evening in the water."

Not that anyone would go for a swim in the waters off Point Pleasant Park, night or day, in the month of February. Piet was shivering with the cold even in his heavy winter coat and gloves. He had always liked Point Pleasant, which covered the southern tip of the Halifax peninsula with one hundred and eighty-five acres of trees, trails, a two-hundred-year-old Martello tower, and a number of ruined fortifications. Piet found it fascinating that the city continued to pay the local representative of the British Crown, the lieutenant governor, one shilling per year in rent for the site. Water surrounded the park on three sides: Halifax Harbour to the east, the Northwest Arm with its yacht clubs and pricey real estate on the shore to the west, and the Atlantic Ocean to the south. The temperature of the water in February wouldn't rise much above one degree centigrade.

Monty Collins

Monty Collins couldn't wait to see the last of his client. The guy, Bowser, had just had a meltdown in the courtroom, after the judge found him guilty of aggravated assault. Bowser had insisted on a defence of mistaken identity, which didn't have a hope of success, given that he and the victim had known each other for years, had a long-simmering grudge against one another, and were seen together the evening of the fight. Monty had tried over and over again to change his client's mind, advised him to agree to self-defence as a strategy, or to explore a plea bargain with the Crown, all suggestions the client had dismissed hands down. Of course, all of that was utterly predictable from a guy who had fired his Legal Aid lawyer, one of the best trial lawyers in the province, and then fired his second lawyer, claiming they were no effing good. Then it was Monty's turn. After the verdict, Bowser had screamed at Monty in front of the prosecutor, the judge, and the courtroom gawkers. The judge bellowed at Bowser to shut up. The accused man's uncontrollable rage would no doubt leave an impression on His Honour for sentencing time. The prosecutor and a couple of the other lawyers present commiserated with Monty on the way out of the courtroom. "We've all been there, buddy. And you've got a file full of CYA letters to produce if need be." Cover-your-ass letters, showing how Monty had given all the right advice, and the client had not taken heed. Oh yeah, the file was full of those.

Monty was the only criminal defence lawyer at Stratton Sommers. He knew that his partners tolerated turkeys like this case only because

Monty attracted righteous or high-profile cases as well, which brought fame and fortune to the firm. When he got back to the office just before noon, he found his senior partner, Rowan Stratton, standing in the reception area with some of the other lawyers.

"Ah, Monty. Just back from court?"

"Yeah. Don't ask."

"I shan't. We've just heard some very sad news. Perhaps you've heard it as well. A woman was found dead this morning on the beach at Point Pleasant Park."

"No, I didn't hear anything."

"She's been identified as Meika Keller."

"Christ! Does anybody know . . . ?"

"Nothing yet, as far as I have heard."

Monty knew Meika Keller to see, though he had never met her. Her name was frequently heard in connection with fundraising events for the symphony, theatre, and charitable organizations. She was a university professor and a patron of the arts.

"Did you know her, Rowan?"

"I've seen her with her husband at various charity wingdings. He is Commodore Hubert Rendell, Commander Canadian Fleet. Only knew them to say hello. Shame, really; the family lives a few blocks from us. Moved in a couple of years ago. Emscote Drive. Inherited the Rendell house after a death in the family, so the commodore left his dockyard Navy house and moved into the old family homestead. Well, excuse me, chaps. Must be off."

The lawyers drifted back to their offices, and Monty reflected on what he had just heard. Emscote Drive was one of the most exclusive streets in Halifax's tony south end. Residents like Meika Keller and Hubert Rendell could look out their windows and see their sailboats tied up at the yacht clubs on the other side of the Northwest Arm. An old poem came unbidden into Monty's mind, by E.A. Robinson. Monty only remembered bits of it, about a man who was "richer than a king, and admirably schooled in every grace." He knew how it ended: "Richard Cory, one calm summer night, went home and put a bullet through his head." Simon and Garfunkel's version was going through Monty's head as he wondered what — or perhaps the question was *who* — had propelled Professor Meika Keller into the waters of the frigid Atlantic. He made his way into his office and opened his next criminal file, involving yet another client who lived as far as you could get, geographically and socially, from Emscote Drive.

Brennan

It all came back to Brennan when he was left alone in his room to brood over the death of Meika Keller and to agonize over whether he could have prevented her death had he not been out on a rip with his brother Terry. Terry was a commercial airline pilot flying out of New York; he had made no effort to pretend he just happened to be assigned a flight to Halifax instead of Frankfurt, Rome, or Zurich. In fact, he hadn't been assigned a flight at all; he had taken a handful of unused vacation days and flown to Halifax as a passenger. "I'm here to check up on my big brother. Are you doing all right, Brennan?"

Was he doing all right after spending eight months in prison in the North of Ireland is what Terry meant. Brennan didn't care to dwell on the series of events that had landed him in the Crumlin Road Gaol and then the H Blocks, or on the distress his family had suffered on his behalf.

When he had finally been released, he had spent a few days with cousins in Belfast, getting himself re-accustomed to living in the outside world. From there, he had flown to New York to spend another few days with his immediate family at their home in Queens. His father Declan, a former IRA man, was ready to set fire to the British and Irish governments' *Framework for Agreement* and launch a rocket attack on counties Antrim and Down in revenge. And his normally serene mother, Teresa, was nearly as fierce as her husband in her condemnation of the "justice" system in Belfast that had railroaded him into prison.

Brennan had arrived back in Halifax ten days ago. Terry had been away on overseas flights for most of the New York visit, so he was making up for that now. Brennan had done his best to reassure Terry that he was recovering from his ordeal, and they had headed out for supper and a pint at O'Carroll's. It was quite the session of beer as Brennan recalled it now; his brother had termed it "drinking for Ireland." And, yes, there was singing. The Burke brothers had given their fellow drinkers a few ballads and rebel songs, including a heartfelt rendition of "Our Lads in Crumlin Jail." Nobody in the pub, including a couple of judges who were regulars in the place, had complained; in fact, some in the crowd plied them with drink and asked for more. Then what happened? They rolled out of the bar and stumbled to Terry's hotel room, where they had a nightcap or two. There were twin beds, and it seemed now that Brennan had passed out for a while on one of them. What time had he made his way back to the parish house? Was the sun coming up?

And it had all cost him the opportunity to minister to one of his parishioners, a fairly recent convert to Catholicism, a professor of physics, a woman who had asked for a nighttime consultation with her priest. Brennan had been so gilled by ten o'clock that Meika Keller had not even entered his mind. She would be in his mind and on his conscience forever now.

It was time for him to say his noontime Mass, so he went about his showering, shaving, and dressing with splitting head, sick stomach, and heavy heart. He opened his door and what did he see at the end of the hallway but the faded blond head of Mrs. Kelly bent over a sponge and bucket. He wondered whether he could get past without having to acknowledge her, as she worried away at a nonexistent stain on the baseboard of the corridor wall.

"Oh, Father!" she cried out in feigned surprise. He nodded at her and walked past. But, appearances to the contrary, she was too quick for him. "Did those two girls get home all right, I wonder?"

Girls? What girls? He kept on walking. He wasn't fool enough to play into her hands by asking what she meant.

He managed to rise to the occasion and sing the old Latin Mass without sacrificing the quality of the worship. His confession of guilt during the *Confiteor* was especially heartfelt today: *Mea culpa, mea culpa, mea maxima culpa.* And he prayed fervently for the soul of Meika Keller and for her family. Today's celebration of the Eucharist was even more precious to Brennan because Terry was his altar boy. They both greeted the parishioners afterwards and satisfied the curious by telling them that this was Father Burke's brother. Some saw a resemblance; others did not. Terry had chestnut-coloured hair and bright blue eyes, while Brennan had black hair with strands of silver, and black eyes, but there was a similarity in their faces, several people agreed. What brought Terry to Halifax? Well, he had just touched down for a visit. There were a few cracks about the sky pilot and Father Burke having his own shuttle to the Man Above, and foolishness like that, and Brennan tried to enjoy the innocuous churchy humour and put his worries aside.

But when he and Terry had left the church and were on their way over to the parish house, there was the bishop coming out of the house towards them. "I need a word with you, Brennan," he said. Brennan nodded, introduced his brother, and waited. "About last night."

"Yes?"

"There was drink taken, as we know, and ballads sung, but was there something else?"

"I don't know what you mean, Bishop." And he didn't, but it had him concerned.

Archbishop Cronin looked from Brennan to Terry and back. "Was there perhaps some female companionship to round out the festivities?"

Women?! What was Cronin on about? Brennan's memories of the night before were dimmed by the tide of drink, but . . . he remembered the insinuating remark directed his way by Mrs. Kelly. And, it would seem, directed to the bishop. Was it something other than piety that inspired Mrs. Kelly to get up every morning for the early Mass? Was gossip being exchanged along with the sign of peace? Brennan recalled some of the singing in the bar, and there were women in the group around him and Terry and the musicians, but apart from that . . .

Terry took over the controls and brought the imperilled conclave to a safe landing. "If you heard something about two women leaving the bar at the same time Brennan and I did, Your Grace, I can assure you they went one way and we went the other. They were part of a big group who were enjoying the music and the banter, and when the place closed, they came out with us. I put them into a cab — Casino Taxi, I believe it was — and sent them off home. Brennan and I then walked over to my hotel and chatted there for a while, catching up on family news."

Thank God and Saint Brigid, the patron saint of beer, for brother Terry and his clear head. Brennan was able to picture the scene then, the two women getting into the cab and waving goodbye.

The bishop said, "All right. Glad to hear it. At least that's one thing we don't have to worry about today."

The encounter left Brennan seething. A parishioner of Saint Bernadette's, a lovely woman who had spent many of her non-working hours raising funds for charities and for the arts, had been found dead in the water. And Brennan would wear the sackcloth and ashes for letting her down, following what seemed in retrospect to have been an urgent request. If he had done the right thing instead of going out and getting langered, she might still be alive. That was the evil sufficient unto this day. Not whether Father Burke and his brother had been out at a local bar for an evening of *ceol agus craic* — music and fun — with a group composed of a representative sample of the population, that is, women as well as men.

Brennan walked into the parochial house followed by his brother and caught sight of Mrs. Kelly scuttling out of view. He pointed her out to Terry and said, *sotto voce*, "That's the informer, right there."

"We'll bring one of the boys over from the old country," Terry said. "Have her kneecapped."

When they got to his room and closed the door, Brennan lit up a smoke, took a much-needed hit of nicotine, and proceeded to tell Terry all about Meika Keller. Terry did his best to defend his brother. "You can't take the entire weight of this on your shoulders, Bren. You couldn't have known. If you'd sensed anything that dire, it would have stayed in your mind. You wouldn't have forgotten it. So it must have seemed fairly routine to you."

"I appreciate your efforts here, Terry, but I'm gutted about the whole thing. And I deserve to be."

"So, who was she?"

"A physics professor at Saint Mary's University here."

"That's where you teach your courses."

"That's right. A course in philosophy and, now, the Irish language. Or Jailic, as it is called by the lads locked up in the place where I had so much time to practise the more colloquial elements of the language."

"Thank Christ you got something out of your time in the clink."

"Yeah, and they were good enough to keep me in there till my cuts and bruises healed. Sustained at the hands of the police and the warders." He took a deep drag of his cigarette and blew the smoke out with a sigh. "Meika was a brilliant woman. Originally from Germany. Started coming to Saint Bernadette's three or four years ago. Her husband was a churchgoer, an Anglican, but Meika was not. Not until she began to take seriously the implications of statements like that of Galileo, that 'the universe is written in the language of mathematics.' And of her fellow German physicist, Einstein, who did not believe in a personal God who concerns himself with the doings of the crowd of us here on Earth but did believe in 'Spinoza's God, who reveals himself in the lawful harmony of all that exists.' She'd been told about the music here at Saint Bernadette's and came to Mass to hear our choir." Brennan thought back to some of their conversations. "I remember talking to her and the two of us exchanging quotations about mathematical laws, harmony, music. She said she understood what the mathematician J.J. Sylvester meant when he said, 'May not music be described as the mathematics of the sense, mathematics as music of the reason?'"

"She was a deep one. Like yourself. Any time you get launched on this subject, I tell myself I have to read more!"

"Either that, or listen to more music. Meika was a big opera fan, I know that. Do you know the name Fried Habler?"

"If he flies for Lufthansa, I may have met him. But if, as I suspect from the direction of the conversation, he's an opera singer, I've never heard of him. That's no reflection on him, but I've never been to the opera in my life."

"He's what's known as a heldentenor. Sings the big beefy roles, heroic roles, such as those in Wagner. And Habler looks the part, a great big good-looking fella with a mane of salt-and-pepper hair, and an enormous laugh. I saw him just after I got back to Halifax. Dal here has an opera program, and —"

"Dal?"

"Dalhousie University. There are half a dozen universities in Halifax, Dal and Saint Mary's being two of them, both in the south end of the city."

"Right, okay."

"So, Habler sang with some of the students at the Dal Arts Centre. He was brilliant, and the students were superb as well. Meika Keller's name came up at the reception following the performance."

"What was her connection?"

"Well, for one thing, she's a big fundraiser for the symphony, and they perform regularly at the Arts Centre. So most of the people at the reception knew her or knew of her. But the reason Habler mentioned her was that he had gone to school with her in Germany, in their hometown of Leipzig, before he'd made a name for himself in Vienna. So, they got reacquainted when he was selected to spend the year teaching opera students at Dal and at the University of Toronto. He commutes between the two and sings with the Canadian Opera Company. He said he phoned home to Mutti — to his mother — about seeing Meika Keller. Said he had known Meika as Edelgard, but she had never liked that name. One of the advantages of growing up was that you could change an unwanted name. He told us that Mutti was pleased to hear he was meeting nice German friends here in Canada."

"So, did he invite her up on stage with him, 'my long-lost pal,' that sort of thing?"

"He probably would have, but she wasn't there on that occasion."

"Missed a big event like that?"

"She was away; she had decided to go for an opera fix in Milan and Vienna. He said he wanted to think that seeing him again recently had rekindled her love of opera — that was his preferred interpretation, not that she fled Canada after he turned up here. And he belted out a couple of lines from 'Rondine al Nido': '*Sei fuggita e non torni più*.' 'You have fled, never to return.'

"So, a few laughs. There was more, but I missed it because someone else in the crowd started talking to me. I did hear him say the reunion between the two school friends had made the news back home in Leipzig, and his mother had faxed him the clipping. It was a nice, cozy little event."

"How well did you know her?"

"Just enough to chat with after Mass, talk about music, that sort of thing."

"Had she ever, well, I know you can't reveal anything . . ."

"No, she never came to me for confession. If she went to some other priest, I've no idea. I'll go see if Mike O'Flaherty is in, ask if he had any contact with her. Make yourself at home. There's some . . ."

"I'll not get into it yet." His brother knew exactly what there was some of in Brennan's cabinet.

"All right, back in a minute."

Monsignor O'Flaherty was not in his room, so Brennan went downstairs but there was no sign of him there either. He was not going to ask Mrs. Kelly for the whereabouts of Michael O'Flaherty. He would not have asked her for directions to the fire escape if the building had been firebombed.

When he got back to his room, he found he had missed a phone call. "We're invited to a hooley," Terry announced.

"How did we manage that?"

"Your pals Monty and the MacNeil are having a house party on Friday. To give everyone a bit of cheer in the depths of winter, she said. And she was kind enough to include your little brother in the invitation." He peered at Brennan. "What's wrong?"

"Nothing." He lit up another cigarette, drew the smoke into his lungs and took his time letting it out.

"Doesn't look like nothing."

"No, I just . . ."

It was beyond Brennan's capabilities at that point to make something up. And he wasn't going to use poor Meika Keller to excuse his reluctance. The truth was that Brennan had not seen Monty and the MacNeil — she being Monty's wife, Maura — since his return to Halifax a week and a half ago. Had not seen them since the ill-starred venture they had embarked upon together in Belfast. Maura had called when her daughter, Normie, reported Father Burke's reappearance at Saint Bernadette's Choir School, but he had deflected Maura's invitation to dinner with the excuse — and there was nothing dishonest about it — that he was overwhelmed with work, catching up on his duties at the church, the university, and the choir school.

Brennan had been reluctant to face people and their inevitable questions upon his return to Halifax. And his first appearance at the choir school was a mixed blessing. One of the many things he had agonized over while lying awake in his prison cell was the fear that he might never see the children again; they would have been long gone from the school if he had served the six-year sentence he had been handed. So, seeing them again was a joyful experience for him. But he had then faced the task of explaining what had happened, that he had been tried and convicted of a number of offences, and that justice had finally been done when the Court of Appeal overturned his conviction. It was a particularly emotional scene when he saw little Normie Collins. Normie had a heart of gold, and she was in tears when she met him in the school corridor. She kept saying, "I didn't know! They didn't tell me for the longest time! I'm so sorry about what happened to you!" Brennan knew that Maura and Monty would have sheltered their daughter from the appalling news as long as they could.

Maura had made another call after her initial effort, and Monty had made one, too. Brennan had trotted out his over-work story again, but he suspected that they didn't buy it. He suspected that they knew he was avoiding them, because of the Flanagan case. Monty had taken on a client when they were all in Belfast the year before. The lawsuit was a righteous one; Brennan had no quarrel with that. But Brennan found out that Monty had been warned that there was more to the case than Monty realized, and that it could have repercussions for Brennan and other people he knew in Belfast. And indeed it did have repercussions. All of it, the show trial in the Crumlin Road Courthouse, the beatings, the unbearable months in prison, all could have been avoided if only Monty had listened to those warnings. But he hadn't; he had simply brushed them off.

Maura did say that the next time she issued an invitation, she would not be taking no for an answer. So now he'd be seeing them all. Terry had accepted the invitation for Friday night, and Brennan was not going to make obvious his disquiet by refusing his old friends' hospitality.

CHAPTER II

Piet

There was very little about the body of Meika Keller to indicate anything other than drowning as a cause of death. There was swelling
around her mouth and a cut on her lip, and there were some scrapes on
her hands, but nothing close to a fatal injury. Something might come
up in the autopsy later. Right now it was time to talk to the family. Piet
and his partner drove to the city's south end and turned into Emscote
Drive. Ailsa Young eyed the large brick colonial house with white shutters and trim, and the other substantial-looking houses on the street,
and as he parked, she said, "Doesn't fit my image of a high-crime area."

Piet merely nodded and got out of the car. They walked up to the
front door and rang the bell. They were met by a short, heavy woman
with thick grey curls. She did not identify herself, but she led the two
detectives into the living room. Despite the deep-red walls and dark
furniture, the room was bright with winter light coming through the
big south-facing front window. Piet stood in the archway and looked

in at a tableau of a family in grief. They were not huddled together but spread throughout the room as if each person was grieving alone. The husband, Hubert Rendell, was a prosperous-looking man in his mid-fifties, but there was nothing confident in his appearance today; his face was grey, expressionless. He rose from a large brown tufted-leather armchair to greet the new arrivals. A young guy, presumably the son, sat glowering on the chesterfield, hunched over with his elbows on his knees. He was muscular and had light-brown hair cut with military precision. At the far end of the room, curled up in a cream-coloured armchair, was the daughter. She had the same colouring as the brother, and she had long wavy hair. Her face was wet and her eyes red from weeping.

Ailsa Young stood a respectful distance away from Rendell and said, "Commodore Rendell, we are very sorry for the loss you and your family have suffered." Her glance took in all those who were present. "We have a few questions. We won't keep you long."

Rendell introduced the woman who had let them in as Mrs. Beasley, the family's housekeeper. His daughter was Lauren and the son Curtis. "Meika of course was their stepmother."

Step. What happened to their mother?

Rendell answered the unspoken question. "My first wife, Edwina, and I divorced in 1978." That would have been when the son and daughter were just little, if Piet was correct in estimating their ages to be in the early twenties.

"Mrs. Beasley was just on her way out."

"Sure, Mrs. Beasley," Piet said. "Could we get your contact information in case there is anything you can offer about what happened to Ms. Keller?"

"Oh, I don't know anything. I wasn't even here when the tragedy happened!"

Nobody knew exactly when the tragedy happened or rather, Piet corrected himself, the police didn't know. Yet. All he said to the housekeeper was "We understand. We'll take your address and phone number just in case." When he had the details, and she had left, Piet turned to the family once again.

As tactfully as he could, Piet asked to speak with each member of the family individually. Hubert Rendell led them into a large, airy room that was a combination den and library on the side of the house facing the shoreline. He did not invite them to sit, so Piet and Ailsa stood before him, a few feet apart from one another.

"Last evening, and the days leading up to it," Piet asked the commodore, "did you notice anything unusual about Ms. Keller?"

"I will give you two answers to that. If it had turned out to be a normal night, with us attending an event and waking up as usual the next morning, I would have remembered nothing about her mood or demeanour."

Piet wondered what it took for the woman's husband, even though he was used to being in command, to stand there, ramrod straight, and answer questions about his wife's last night on Earth, as if he were giving a briefing to a superior officer.

"There was nothing so obvious that it would have stuck with me. But because of what happened, I looked back and thought, in retrospect, that she had been preoccupied about something. Yet it did not make a huge impression on me and, as I say, nothing about it would have been memorable."

"But, as things turned out, you recalled something. What can you tell us about that?"

"She wasn't snappish or anything; it was just that her mind was elsewhere at times. You know, there were a couple of speakers at the dinner."

"Dinner?"

"A dinner and silent auction for the symphony; it was held at the Lord Nelson Hotel."

"Right."

"There was a bit of wit and humour in the speeches, and it seemed to go right over her head. Then she'd notice people laughing, and she'd laugh along. Playing catch-up, that sort of thing."

"Was she the kind of person who would have told you if something was bothering her?"

"She was not a person to be yapping on and on about minor troubles. She figured people had very real, sometimes unbearable, trouble in their lives, and she was not going to be heard complaining."

"But what about something serious? She would confide in you?"

"I would have thought so. I mean, we communicated fairly well during our marriage." His voice faltered, and Piet saw the man's lower lip tremble; he looked away from the detectives.

They gave him a moment to recover, and then Piet asked, "Was there anything medical she might have been concerned about? Illness? A recent diagnosis or anything like that?"

"Not that I know of. And she had not said anything in the last few days about any problems or concerns. In fact, the only thing I remember that bothered her in any way, and it was something very minor, was that her holiday pictures hadn't turned out."

"Oh? Where did you go for your holiday?"

"I didn't go. She went by herself. A spur of the moment thing after she reconnected with the opera singer Fried Habler. You know who I mean?"

"I can't pretend I know anything about opera. Fiddle music is more my style. Guess you could say I went native after my family arrived here from the Netherlands."

"Nothing wrong with fiddle music, Detective."

"But I've seen Habler's name in the paper."

"Yes, well, he and Meika were in school together in Germany, and he is here for the university term, splitting his time between Dal and the University of Toronto, giving master classes. So, she saw him, and after that, nothing would do but she had to take a little opera-seeing trip to Europe."

"Where in Europe did she go?"

"Milan and Vienna."

"When was that?"

"She flew out on Friday, January twenty-sixth, and returned on the thirty-first. A short jaunt but enough time to squeeze in three or four nights at the opera."

"And when she returned, you say she was all right except for her pictures?"

"Yes. I mean I noticed that something was bothering her or making her a bit edgy. Not that she didn't enjoy the trip, the nights at the opera. She did. But she took her film in to be developed and they told her there was something wrong with it, and none of the photos turned out."

"All right. Now, you attended the symphony dinner last night. Then what?"

"We were invited out for drinks after that with another one of the officers from Maritime Command, him and his wife, but Meika didn't want to go. So, we made our excuses and came home. I had a nightcap and retired early. I was in bed before ten o'clock. I'd had a tiring few weeks at work. Meika had been teasing me about my inability lately to stay up at night. She called me *Opa* — Gramps. In an affectionate way, I hasten to add. She was going to stay downstairs for a while to read. Or so she led me to believe." Rendell reached a hand out as if looking for support.

"Take a moment now. There's no rush."

"I just . . . I had no idea . . ."

"When did you discover she was not at home?"

"I awoke at half past six. She wasn't here, but I didn't think much about it. I'd slept right through the night. When you've slept in a submarine and a destroyer, or a sailboat in rough seas, you can sleep through anything. And there was nothing to disturb my rest that night because, of course, she never came in. When I woke up, I assumed she had gone in to work early, which she sometimes did. It was nearly eleven when I got the news."

"I'm sorry, sir. This is terrible for you, we know. But we have to ask these questions."

"I know that. I understand."

"Did Ms. Keller ever say anyone was bothering her? Had she felt threatened in any way?" Rendell shook his head. "No?"

"No."

"Did she ever give you the impression that she was interested in, or involved with, someone else?"

"Never."

"What do you think accounted for her death, sir?"

"I have no earthly idea. All I know is that I will not have a moment's peace until I find out what took her away from me." He turned and walked out of the room.

✝

Lauren Rendell could hardly speak, she was crying so hard. Piet and Ailsa waited her out. After a few minutes, she calmed down a bit, and Ailsa asked, "Now, Lauren, do you live here or out on your own?"

"I still live here. I'm going to get my own place after I've worked a bit longer. Saved up some money of my own. I don't want Dad to have to pay for a place for me. Even though he would. And Mum — Meika — always said she liked having another woman in the house."

"What can you tell us, Lauren? Have you any idea what might have led to her death?"

"I don't know! I can't imagine her walking into the sea and drowning herself. She had a wonderful life here with Dad, with us. Everybody loved her at Saint Mary's, and she was highly respected for all her fundraising and support for the symphony and other arts organizations. It just doesn't make sense."

"So, she never confided any troubles to you? Health problems maybe?"

"No, nothing."

"Anything personal that had her upset?"

"No."

"Family disagreements or anything like that?"

"Definitely not. We all got along great."

Ailsa was gentle as she ventured onto sensitive terrain. "Now, Ms. Keller came into your life when you were how old?"

"Well, I was three when Dad and my mother divorced. And he started seeing Meika a year later, I think it was."

"A difficult situation for a little girl, her dad and mum splitting up."

"Yes, of course it was."

"Have you always lived with your father? Or did you divide your time . . . ?"

"Always with Dad. My mother was more concerned with herself than with us. People think 'big bad witch' when they hear 'stepmother,' but, believe me, Meika was a godsend. She didn't rush us, didn't pressure us or get in our faces when Dad first starting seeing her. But we took to her right away and fell right in love with her! Same with my brother. She treated us as if we were her own. It's unbearable that she's dead!"

"I'm so sorry, Lauren," Ailsa said. Then, in a lighter tone, "Now, if your family is anything like mine, there may have been a few little clashes between mother and daughter, mother and son."

"Oh, yeah, just the usual. But even that was for our own good. You know, arguments about boyfriends, about our future plans."

"Right. Is there a boyfriend in your life these days?"

If Lauren thought this was off-topic, she didn't show it. But she didn't offer anything beyond, "I'm kind of seeing somebody now. Nothing too serious."

"And about your future plans?"

"Mum — Meika — thought I should be doing something more with my life than working in a wine bar. She thought I should be with the Royal Winnipeg Ballet."

"Oh, you're a dancer?"

"I took ballet for years. I was pretty good at it. But, well, I didn't want to leave . . . didn't want to leave my friends here in Halifax. And I started making really good money at the bar, and, well, I guess I'm not very ambitious. Meika thought I could be doing more. And I know she was right. If only I could tell her I was wrong!"

✝

Curtis wasted no time on preliminaries. "There is no way in the world my stepmother killed herself. No way. She was the most level-headed person I know. Wouldn't happen. And whenever you catch who did this, you'd better have him in protective custody, because I can't promise I'll be able to control myself."

"I understand how you feel, Curtis. I'm sure we'd all feel the same way," Piet said. "Now, do you live here or out on your own?"

"I've got a place on Tobin Street."

"So, from what you say, sounds as if you were not aware of any concern Ms. Keller had, anything bothering her?"

"No."

"Are you aware of anybody she might have been worried about? Anybody who might have wished her harm?"

"Nobody I'm aware of, except of course . . ."

"Except?"

"No, nothing."

"It can hardly be nothing, Curtis. That was a spontaneous, heart-felt reaction there."

"I just meant, you know, the divorce. But that was what? Eighteen years ago."

"The divorce would have been your father's doing, not your mother's?"

"As they say, it takes two."

"But?"

"But it was a long time ago. And my mother isn't even here. She's in Toronto. She has her own life. There's nothing in all that ancient history that has anything to do with this."

"What about family quarrels here in Halifax? Every family has disagreements."

"If you mean Meika and Dad, forget it. They got along great. And me and Lauren got along great with her, too. Meika was protective of us for sure, so sometimes she'd tell us if she thought we were going down the wrong path."

"Can you give us an instance of that?"

"Nothing too exciting. She thought that I should be making more of my life than being an able seaman. I should be pushing for promotion. Same with my sister. Well, not promotion, but she should be joining one of the big dance companies. Ballet and all that. But at least Meika had nothing to worry about with me in the romance department. She loves — *loved* — Jesus, it feels disloyal saying it that way. She loved my girlfriend, Anita. We're getting married next year."

"Congratulations. So, Ms. Keller was happy with your choice of a mate. Was she happy with your sister's choices?"

Curtis shrugged and said, "Mother-daughter stuff? I don't know."

"You never know what little detail, however insignificant it might seem, will help us get to the bottom of this."

"I have no information at all that would explain this."

"Well, if anything comes to mind, Curtis, anything at all, get in touch with us, will you?"

"You can bet on it. And you can be sure I'll be trying to find out what the hell happened. If I come across anything, you'll be the first to know."

Detectives Young and Van den Brink thanked the Rendell family, offered their condolences again, and left Emscote Drive for the residence of Mrs. Beasley in the Harrietsfield suburb. You never knew what a housekeeper might have seen or heard in the family home. Piet tried to shoo away the phrase "What the butler saw," as he waited with his partner on the front step of the modest, vinyl-clad bungalow.

"Oh!" Mrs. Beasley was clearly taken aback by the arrival of the police on her doorstep. "I'm sure there's nothing I can tell you that will help you solve the killing."

"Perhaps not, Mrs. Beasley, and we won't keep you for long. Could we come in for a few minutes?"

"Oh, yes, of course. You'll have to excuse the look of the place. It's, well, it's not south-end Halifax!"

"I don't live in south-end Halifax myself," Piet said.

She led them in to a living room where brightly coloured quilts were draped over the worn dark-brown chesterfield and armchairs, and she offered them tea or coffee. "No, thanks, Mrs. Beasley," Ailsa said, "but it's kind of you to offer. Now, when we first arrived, you said 'the killing.' Is there something that makes you think this might be more than a drowning? Apart from the fact that it is winter, of course."

The woman was protesting with outstretched hands before Ailsa completed her question. "No, no! I just, you know, the unexpected death, and the police coming . . ."

"I understand."

They sat down, Mrs. Beasley on the edge of her seat. "I can't imagine that anyone would want to hurt her. But to think of her doing . . . well, taking her own life, that's just as unbelievable."

"I'm sure it is," Ailsa agreed. "Can you think of anything odd or out of place in the family's life recently?"

The woman shook her head.

"Phone calls or visitors that seemed to disturb Ms. Keller?"

"No, nothing."

"Now I'm sure you are loyal to the Rendell family, Mrs. Beasley."

"Oh, yes!"

"But if you noticed anything distressing lately between members of the family, any arguments or strain, you needn't feel as if you are telling tales out of school. It may be something like that which can lead us to an explanation of Ms. Keller's death."

"Everybody got along great, though. I never heard him and her so much as raise their voices to one another. And the kids — well, Lauren and Curtis aren't kids anymore, both of them grown up now — but they loved their stepmum. And she doted on them. She was certainly a protective kind of mother, especially with Lauren. You know, worried when she'd stay out late, warning her not to get into a car with somebody who was drinking. That kind of thing. I think she figured Curtis could take care of himself. Maybe because he was the boy, and in the Navy."

"Right. So, nothing else you can think of then?"

"No. Except maybe, but no . . . That's all over now."

"What's that?"

"Well, a boyfriend of Lauren's was a bit of a . . . a drinker. What do they say now? A party animal! But I don't think he ever hurt her, or anything like that."

They thanked Mrs. Beasley, reassured her that her conversation would not be relayed back to Commodore Rendell, and headed back to the police station.

"Nothing much there," Piet said.

"No," Ailsa agreed. "I think Meika Keller was loved by her husband and stepchildren, and we haven't learned anything that would account for a suicide, let alone a homicide. If Rendell took her out on their boat for a late night sail and threw her overboard, we haven't come up with anything remotely like a motive. And the two kids. I don't see anything there. Boyfriends? Gold-digging future in-laws? It would be stretching things to find a motive there."

"Except that if you're a guy who marries into the Rendell family, you will eventually share in a nice inheritance. The house on the Arm, the boat, the money. And if the mother is standing in your way, trying to force you off the board, why not eliminate her now?"

"So, the guy gets Meika out of the way now, then he'll hold the commodore's head under water at a later date? We won't be making any arrests based on that scenario, Piet."

"No, we've got nothing to go on there."

"And if it wasn't suicide, how did the killer get her out there? She would hardly have gone for a swim with him at midnight in the first week of February. The water would be barely above zero. So how did he do it?"

"That's what we have to find out. We'll check to see if any boats were out late at night."

CHAPTER III

Brennan

Brennan and his brother had a couple of shots of whiskey on Friday evening before they set out on foot for the Collins-MacNeil family's wood-shingled house on Dresden Row. A light snow was falling, and the golden light shining in the windows offered a warm welcome to guests. Brennan ushered Terry in ahead of him to be greeted by Maura MacNeil. They had met on a couple of occasions before, and the MacNeil said she was delighted that Terry was in town. Then it was Brennan standing before her, looking down at her lovely soft face — deceptively soft; a tongue-lashing by the MacNeil would leave you in shreds — the face that had sustained him during those months when he was in prison and she was still in Ireland. Visiting hours were what he had lived for; he well remembered how bereft he had been following her last visit, before she got on a plane to fly home to Halifax. Bereft. Inconsolable.

Her big grey eyes looked up at him, with none of their customary mischief. She made no effort to mask her concern. Did he still look like the bruised and battered convict he had been in Her Majesty's prisons in the North of Ireland?

"Brennan, you look as if you're thirty days into a hunger strike," she said, drawing him into her embrace. He wrapped his arms around her and held her, then broke free and attempted a smile.

He looked over and saw Terry's eyes on him. He finally came up with something to say. "I've at least had a shave since you saw me last."

"Oh, Brennan," she said, "of all the things you endured in there, I figured the 'hygiene procedures,' or lack of them, would be the thing that would do you in."

"How well you know me, *acushla*." Brennan knew he had a reputation for being fastidious. He still had nightmares, and probably always would, about his first day in the Crumlin jail when he found out he'd be lucky to get two showers a week. A week! And then he'd caught sight of the unspeakable thing on the floor of the cell: a chamber pot. The fact that he had to share a cell with another man was bad enough, but to have to be in someone's presence when . . . He drove the thought from his mind and said, "Have you something a class up from prison-made potcheen, my dear?" *Poitín* was home-distilled liquor, often made from potatoes. The stuff they managed to make in prison had nearly done his head in.

"We have it all, and you know where to find it."

Brennan led Terry in the direction of the drinks cabinet in the dining room, stopping to greet the two oldest children on the way. Brennan introduced Terry to Tommy Douglas, Monty and Maura's oldest son. It had been more than a year since Brennan had seen Tommy; he would be twenty-one or twenty-two by now. He looked like his father, with blondy hair and sky-blue eyes. He was a student in university and was in a band called Dads in Suits. Terry got into conversation with him, and Brennan turned his attention to the daughter of the house.

Normie was twelve years old, red-haired, bespectacled, and angelic. He had noticed that she'd been rather quiet at school since he came back, not that she had ever been loud or disruptive. She was friendly and courteous as always, and her work was top of the class, but he'd had the impression that something was bothering her. And what he seemed to be seeing now was the putting-on of a brave face. "Hi, Father!" Her voice was bright, her eyes wide, and her lips turned up in a smile. "How are you?"

"Grand, grand, Normie, just fine. And yourself?"

"Great!"

He leaned down closer and said, "Is everything all right with you, Normie?"

"Yes, everything's really good." The same bright-eyed insistence.

Brennan was not at all convinced, but he was not about to spoil the party for her by getting into it now. Nor did he want to dwell on what had happened to the choir school during his involuntary absence from the place. He had been invited to spend a year directing a choir in Rome, which had not triggered any upheaval here at his school. But then events spiralled out of control in Ireland, and if a certain judge in the Crumlin Road Courthouse had had his way, Brennan would have been held behind bars in Belfast for years. Well, nature may abhor a vacuum, but power thrives on it. A cabal of meddlers at the choir school — some of the more high-strung parents, devotees of a local business mogul styling himself as W. Langston Soames — had set themselves up in positions of authority at the school. A coup d'état. Well, Brennan would devise a way to overthrow the lot of them. But for now, he would put all that aggravation aside. He headed to the sideboard and poured himself a good measure of Jameson, threw it back, and then poured another.

And now here was Monty.

"Brennan," he said and clapped a hand on Brennan's shoulder. "I don't even know where to begin, after what you've been through."

Brennan shook his head and raised a hand to ward off any discussion of the events in Belfast.

But Monty continued. "And of course I was no help to you, being more than twenty-five hundred miles away when your ordeal began. Bad timing, to put it mildly."

Putting it mildly was putting it all too mildly, in Brennan's view. He couldn't help feeling the way he did, angry and betrayed. Monty had brushed off the late-night warning that his Belfast lawsuit could have serious implications for Brennan and other members of his family over there. Worse still, as Brennan had heard from one of the Burke family's IRA associates, when the man had given Monty the warning, Monty had even laughed and made a joke about it.

And here they were now, face to face. Well, Brennan wasn't about to let on how badly the whole thing had affected him, was not about to whinge at him, "You *laughed at me.*" He was not about to *show weakness* in front of Monty. He knew the MacNeil would have only one word to say about his determination to brazen it out: *Men!* Nor was Brennan going to allude to any of this in front of Monty's children or his guests.

But Monty spoke up again. "I know we always think we 'can imagine' what somebody went through in prison, lawyers perhaps most of all, given what we've seen of our clients. But of course we can't even come close. I am so sorry about what happened to you, Brennan."

Brennan merely nodded in response. Monty's words struck Brennan as a lawyerly expression of regret: he was sorry for what had "happened to" Brennan, not for any part Monty himself had played in the debacle. But Brennan admonished himself: who was being lawyerly now? They stood in silence for a few seconds, and then Tommy Douglas walked by and waved. "I've got a gig at Gus's."

Dads in Suits were playing at the old north-end Halifax pub. Everyone wished him luck, and this opened the way for Monty and

Brennan to make small talk about music. Sports came up then, and they speculated about the fortunes of the Quebec Nordiques hockey team, which was now the Colorado Avalanche, of all things.

Oh, good timing at last. One of Monty's fellow lawyers hailed him from across the room, and he excused himself. Then Brennan spotted little Dominic, the youngest child at four years of age. Black of hair and dark of eye, he had been conceived when Monty and Maura were living separate and apart. On more than one occasion, people had made a jest about the child looking a lot like the family's parish priest, Father Burke. All in fun, of course, but Brennan knew Monty had not found it the least bit amusing in the early days of the child's life. That was all behind them now, though. Monty loved the little fellow like his own son and had recently made the adoption formal.

Dominic had known Father Burke all his life, and he gave him an uproarious greeting. "Father! Father!" Brennan put his whiskey glass on the coffee table and held out his arms. The little boy flew across the room and crashed into Brennan, who lifted him high in the air and wiggled him around. The child laughed with delight. Then Brennan put him down and said, "Dominic, do you remember one time I told you I have a brother who flies airplanes?"

"Yeah!" There was nothing in the world Dominic loved more than planes. He had an entire fleet of toy aircraft, and his parents had to keep a close eye on him to keep him grounded.

"Well, here he is. My brother, Terry."

Dominic stared at Terry with eyes wide and mouth agape. Then, "Do you really fly planes?!"

"I do."

"Wow! Can we go in one now?"

"Not right now, Dominic, but some day we will. Have you ever been up in a plane?" Terry knew the answer to that.

"Yeah! I flew all across the ocean. And back again." He spread his arms out like wings. "And they let me look in the front!"

Brennan had heard that the crew on the Air Canada jet returning from London to Halifax, after the Belfast trip, had invited the little lad into the cockpit before take-off.

"I have planes in my room! You have to see them!" He took Terry by the hand and pulled him up the stairs to inspect the fleet.

Brennan went for another glass of whiskey and engaged in some idle chat with a couple of the lawyers, and then helped himself to another drink. He was feeling pleasantly lit by this time, though he was still a long way from langered. Somebody cranked the music up, and a few couples started to dance. He sat watching, nursing his whiskey. Terry came down from the skies with an ecstatic little novice pilot by his side. "He flies this one! Terry does! Seven-four-seven!" Dominic waved the little plane around for all to see. Then he broke away and yanked his sister by the arm and boasted to her about his contacts in the aviation industry.

Maura MacNeil was standing with her best friend, Fanny, unconsciously swaying to the music as the pair of them talked. Brennan had the urge to get to his feet and take a turn around the floor with the MacNeil, but, before he could decide yes or no, Monty came by, took her hand, and danced her around the room. They did such a fine job of it that others merely looked on from the sidelines. Brennan, too, watched the show until he glanced over and saw that Terry's eyes were on him, again.

What Brennan needed was another drink but he did not want to dip any further into his hosts' supply. He made a mental note to bring a quart of Jameson over on his next visit to replenish the stock. But now he got up and walked over to Terry, cut off whatever his brother started to say, and announced, "Time to hit the road. Go to O'Carroll's for a jar or two?"

"Whatever you say."

"Good. We're off."

They said a few quick goodbyes and hit the pavement, walking from Dresden Row to Morris Street, then down to Lower Water and turning left. The falling snow shrouded a giant container ship making its silent way out of the harbour to distant seas.

When they got to O'Carroll's on Upper Water Street, they saw the same musicians they had sung with on the fateful Tuesday past. Terry and Brennan greeted them, ordered pints and glasses of whiskey, and settled in for the *ceol agus craic*. After his second pint and a whiskey, Terry felt called upon to give the room a song. Brennan felt called upon to affect complete ignorance of whatever his brother might be trying to imply. The song was the Tom Jones version of "I Who Have Nothing." All about the fellow on the outside looking in, while his love goes dancing by with a man much better placed to give her anything she wants in this world.

Monty

The party last night was a good time enjoyed by all, none more so than little Dominic, who had done a bit of networking and made a connection with a man who could further his planned career in civil aviation. Terry Burke was everything an aspiring pilot could hope to be: a man who flew jumbo jets around the world and who could keep people's attention with announcements from the cockpit or tall tales around the bar between flights.

His brother Brennan was a little subdued, though. It was the first time Monty had seen Brennan since the action-packed semester in Belfast, and Monty had been more than a little apprehensive about seeing his friend after all Brennan had been through. Brennan was a bit cool to him, Monty thought. There was no doubt that Brennan had had a very rough time in Belfast. But no one had spelled out to Monty at the time how the case he had taken on in Belfast could possibly have had consequences for Brennan and the other members of the Burke clan in the North of Ireland. As far as Monty had known then, the only controversial episode Brennan had engaged in over there had been done in collaboration with Maura; they had disguised themselves as American tourists and entered a bar in Loyalist East Belfast to try to spot a man connected to a series of bomb attacks committed decades earlier. The subject of their investigation was as serious as anything could be — the bombs had killed more than thirty people — but from what he heard from Brennan and Maura after their bit of theatre, their performance had been nothing short of hilarious. No wonder Monty had laughed and made a wisecrack when an IRA man confronted him late at night on a Belfast street and told him, without offering any details, that Monty's legal work could pose serious problems for his friend. All Monty could picture was the Reverend Father Brennan Xavier Burke, BA (Fordham), STL (Pontifical Gregorian), STD (Angelicum), dressed down as a redneck American tourist. And, sure, he had laughed.

Brennan

Brennan said goodbye to his brother Saturday morning and then said his early morning Mass. The sacrament gave him some consolation, but that feeling of peace was short-lived. When he was in the kitchen afterwards, having breakfast and reading the paper, Mrs. Kelly came flapping over to the table. "Father Burke! Father Burke!"

He looked up. Her face was flushed and her eyes gleamed with excitement. Malice, more like. She attempted to arrange her features in a funereal expression as she said, "There's someone here to see you. That poor, poor soul! The commodore! In the parlour."

Brennan rose without replying and walked into the sitting room. He put out his hand to Hubert Rendell, but Rendell didn't take it. The two men faced each other silently for a long uncomfortable moment. Then Rendell's eyes went to the far corner of the room, and Brennan turned around, just in time to see the arse end of Mrs. Kelly scurrying out of view.

"Commodore Rendell, I don't know where to begin to —"

"Let's begin with the night of Tuesday, the sixth of February, when she asked for your help and you didn't bother, or didn't remember, to show up for the meeting."

The man's cold anger, his icy calm, struck Brennan more forcefully than any amount of red-faced agitation or shouting could have done. Brennan was guilty, no point in trying to plead otherwise, so he merely said, "All right."

"Now Meika didn't even tell me this herself. Which suggests to me that whatever was troubling her was something grave. Well, it obviously was, wasn't it? Given that she walked into the sea and kept walking, after being stood up by her priest and confidant."

Brennan hadn't thought it possible to feel any worse than he already did about Meika Keller, but this pasting from her husband made him realize there was an infinite vein of guilt to be mined. All he could do was stand there and take it.

"The only reason I heard about this planned meeting at all was that our friend Vicky Latimer, another professor at Saint Mary's, called me to say she had overheard Meika speaking to you at the university and asking if you could see her later that evening. Vicky kind of teased her about going to see a priest. 'Going into a dark room with a handsome bachelor and telling secrets,' she said to Meika, or something like that. Meaning the confession box, I take it. But Meika told her it was 'spiritual guidance, the usual Catholic stuff.' She sort of indicated the building around them, the McNally building, when she said 'Catholic.' You know, building named after a bishop. 'Nothing scandalous,' she said to Vicky. That's the way our friend remembered it. She thought no more about it. Until, of course, she heard the news the next day. So. Father Burke. What was it my wife wanted to talk to you about?"

"She didn't say what it was. Just could she come speak to me after a charity event she was attending that evening. She thought she'd be free by ten o'clock, so we agreed on that time. She would come here to the parish house."

"Which she did, apparently. And was told by the housekeeper that you were nowhere to be seen."

"I am truly sorry."

"Yes. So. What was she like when you saw her at SMU, when she made this request?"

"She was concerned about something, no question," he acknowledged.

"Oh, I think we can agree on that, Father Burke."

"But she gave no indication of what had her troubled."

"That would be typical of her, I suppose. She was a strong woman, not one to be skittish or complaining of this or that little thing. Well, she had to be strong to get out of Communist East Germany in 1974. Escaped through a checkpoint in the Berlin Wall."

"Right, I knew that. She didn't tell me about it, but I heard it somewhere. How did she manage that? Thousands tried."

"She has this little scar. You may have noticed it above her left eyebrow. That's a souvenir of the day she escaped. Meika never liked to talk about it, always wished she could forget it all. She had worked for months, and paid dearly, to get false papers giving her nationality as Belgian — papers for her and her daughter, Helga — and giving a date when she had supposedly entered East Germany. When her contact finally produced the papers for her, it took her weeks to steel herself to approach the border. She would start out, come close, and then lose her nerve. But finally the day came. Up she went to the guard post at the checkpoint, clutching her little girl's hand and trying to look as if she didn't have a care in the world. The guard scanned the documents and the photos, looked up, and glared at her. She nearly had heart failure. Finally, the guard let them go. She started the long walk across the bridge over the railroad tracks, the bridge from east to west, fighting down the temptation to run for her life. She nearly made it. Then they opened fire on her. A woman and a five-year-old child! Someone had caught on that Meika wasn't who she claimed to be; there was something wrong with her identity papers. She took off at a run. Tripped and fell, and that's how she cut her forehead. But thank the Lord she got her feet onto the ground of the French sector of Berlin."

"What a terrifying ordeal for her," Brennan said. "She must have had nightmares ever since."

Hubert raised his voice for the first time. "If you think she took her own life because of that ordeal, I can assure you she would not have done that! So —" He turned his head away from Brennan and fell silent. Then, after a long moment, he regained his stony composure and said, "It was twenty-two years ago. She got out from behind the Iron Curtain and made a new life for herself here in Canada. But of course, as you may know, her daughter did not survive the trip."

Oh, God. "What happened to the child? Was she injured during the escape?"

"No, nothing like that. The plan was to get out of East Berlin and stay in West Germany until Meika could arrange to immigrate to the United States. But Helga had been sick, weak — under-nourished, I expect — and died before Meika could complete the arrangements and book a flight across the Atlantic. A very painful subject for my wife, as you might imagine. So painful that, as I later heard, she did not talk about it at all for the first couple of years she was in this country. Just kept it inside her. By the time I met her at the end of the 1970s, she was able to speak of it, but just barely. Anyway, Meika came to Canada instead of the U.S., got to Toronto, earned her master's degree and PhD in physics, and then came to Halifax to teach at Saint Mary's. She is — was — when will I ever get used to the past tense for my wife? — she got deeply involved in the arts and music, and her charitable works, charities for children, and lived a beautiful life."

"I know. In the short time I knew her, I admired her greatly. Commodore Rendell, I regret with all my heart that I failed to see her Tuesday night."

"I'm sure you do."

It wasn't an hour before Brennan had company again. And if Mrs. Kelly had been wound up over the arrival of the widowed naval commander, she was positively feverish about the appearance of two plainclothes Halifax detectives in the doorway. She bustled around them, offering tea and cake, coyly asking if they were allowed to indulge while on duty, but Brennan led them up to the privacy of his room.

When they were inside with the door shut, the detectives greeted Brennan. He knew one of them, Detective Sergeant Piet Van den Brink. "Hello, Father Burke. Let me introduce you to my partner, Detective Sergeant Ailsa Young. Ailsa, this is Father Brennan Burke."

Brennan knew Van den Brink from various ecumenical Christian gatherings over the years. He was one of the representatives of what Brennan thought of as the Dutch Reformed Church, but which was actually the All Nations Christian Reformed Church. Van den Brink was in his early forties, tall and slender with blond hair and light-blue eyes that appeared to scan everything and miss nothing. Brennan knew he had come to Canada from the Netherlands in his late teens. He spoke with a fairly strong Dutch accent.

If Piet Van den Brink looked typically Dutch, his partner looked as if she had just sailed in from Scotland, with her strong facial features, short curly dark hair, and deep blue-grey eyes.

Piet began the questioning. "You know why we're here, Father."

"Yes, I do. It's dreadful what happened to Meika Keller. As you obviously know, she and I saw each other at Saint Mary's late on the afternoon of that Tuesday, the sixth."

"Yes, that's what we heard. Can you tell us what happened?"

"It would have been around five o'clock, when each of us had finished teaching for the day. She asked if she could come and talk to me. We agreed on ten o'clock, after a charity event wrapped up that evening. A fundraiser for Symphony Nova Scotia. She came to the parish house at the agreed time, and I was not here. I had . . ." There would never be a time when this would not be an excruciating admission. "I had gone out with my brother, who was visiting from New York. We went out for a few scoops, at O'Carroll's, and I completely forgot about Meika." Brennan stopped and took a deep breath. "I let her down on the most crucial night, the last night, of her life. All I know is that she was concerned about something. I have no idea what, because I didn't show enough concern about one of my parishioners to remember to show up for the meeting. You can probably imagine how I feel about that."

"Yes, I can imagine how it feels for you, Father. But we are all human and we all make mistakes. There are many things we forget to do, all of us, and usually there is nothing catastrophic as a result. Your fault is no greater than it would have been on any other occasion of forgetting."

"Thank you, Piet. Officer. But it doesn't feel that way."

"I know."

Detective Sergeant Young nodded in what appeared to be sympathy with his distress.

Brennan wasn't sure how much the police would be willing to reveal, but he ventured a question anyway. "Did she . . . is it known how she died?"

"Actually, we know very little so far, Father. A man jogging through the park spotted her body in the water. The shallow water at the beach. The witness had a cellular phone and called us. It appears that the cause of death was drowning, but of course it will be up to the medical examiner to determine that."

"Yes, right."

The detectives then asked how long Brennan had known Meika Keller, and he went over the history with them. He repeated that she had been concerned about something that night, but that was the only time he had ever seen her worried or distracted. "And then I left the university and came back here. And, well . . ."

Van den Brink said, "That was the last you saw of her. So, the last person to see her alive, as far as we know right now, was your housekeeper, Mrs. Kelly."

Brennan fought down the unworthy thought that the best thing that could happen in this terrible situation would be the sight of Mrs. Kelly dragged out of the parish house in handcuffs and charged with the murder of Meika Keller. He immediately sent up a silent Act of Contrition for this low and unworthy imagining.

"We'll go down and have a word with her."

"Of course, yes."

"An excitable person," Van den Brink said.

"She is that."

Piet

Excitable indeed. Piet remembered a line he had heard. Perhaps back when he was learning English in preparation for his family's immigration to Canada, and he had compiled a list of common sayings and proverbs. *No man is a hero to his valet.* Well, poor Father Burke was no hero to his housekeeper. The woman knew nothing more than that Meika Keller had come to meet Burke and that it fell to the housekeeper to deliver the bad news that Father Burke was not there. Piet wondered whether Meika Keller got a regretful "he's not in" or whether she got the joyous glint in the housekeeper's eye that was all too apparent to the detectives. However it was imparted to Meika Keller, it was the only piece of evidence the housekeeper had to offer. Yet she endeavoured to keep the police in attendance as she made various broad hints about Burke, with a hand gesture meant to signify "drinking" and another gesture to denote the aiming of a gun, when she tried to spin a line of gossip about the priest's family in Ireland. Piet and Ailsa finally got away, leaving the woman vibrating with excitement in the kitchen.

"Well," said Ailsa when they were back in the car, "we have one in favour of suicide in that house, and the other hoping — guiltily perhaps — that it was a homicide."

"Brennan Burke's a good guy. Can hardly blame him for hoping it wasn't suicide after he failed to show up and listen to whatever she wanted to unload on him."

"True. And the housekeeper! She loathes Burke for some reason; she'd love to see him fall on his face over this."

"That would make her day, no question, though 'loathe' might be too strong a word. But she strongly disapproves of him, no mistaking that. I've met him a couple of times at church events, Catholic-Protestant gatherings. He likes his liquor, and that didn't serve him well on this occasion, but he's a good man. Good priest, from everything I've heard."

"Maybe her nose is out of joint because he never invited her along to O'Carroll's!"

O'Carroll's. The name of the place brought back a painfully embarrassing memory for Piet. It was Saint Patrick's Day, two years ago. He had been to a conference the day before with representatives of several of the Christian denominations in the province, Brennan Burke among them. They got to chatting, and Brennan mentioned Saint Patrick and a get-together at O'Carroll's for the event. Piet, against his better judgment and against all the teachings of his strict old pastor back in the Netherlands, decided to attend. And it was a fun evening. At first. Brennan was there along with some other local Irishmen, and there was a band playing the traditional music of their culture. They were rousing tunes and everyone was singing along, even Piet after a while. After a few drinks, to be more accurate. It never ceased to amaze him the capacity some people had for alcohol. Unfortunately — why was it unfortunate? Why not fortunate? — Piet had no such capacity. He was not a drinker; he came from a long line of non-drinkers, their attitudes formed by the ultra-strict church they had attended in the old country. His fellow cops needled him about it, and people teased him about being from "sin city." Amsterdam, they meant, with its world-famous red-light district, cannabis cafés, and all of that.

"All of that" was precisely why Piet's father had packed up the family and left Amsterdam for Pictou County, Nova Scotia, where there was a strong Presbyterian community of upright, hard-working Scots so much like the upright, hard-working Dutch of whom the Van den Brink family was an exemplar. Piet's father had known all about Pictou County because his sister had been a war bride. She had met her Canadian soldier husband at the time of the liberation of the Netherlands. The Canadians were much loved by the Dutch, none more than Major Donald David MacKenzie, who took Jozefien Van den Brink for his bride. Given the background, an avoidance of alcohol had been instilled in Piet since birth. And he had seen the effects of it on family life and human behaviour: violence and crime. The few times he had broken out of his teetotalling lifestyle and had a glass of beer or hard liquor, he had not enjoyed it. Didn't even like the taste. Not even, if he was honest, the taste of Heineken. And on the night of Saint Patrick's in 1994, he had become violently ill after four glasses of Guinness stout and some kind of Irish whiskey. The only thing that saved him from complete mortification was that he had made it to the toilet before losing the contents of his stomach. He had slunk out of the bar after that, never mentioning the incident.

Piet shook off the humiliating memory and returned to the present. He looked over at Ailsa and thought, as he so often did, how lucky he was to have her as his partner. When he first made detective, he had been teamed up with a guy he couldn't stand — a rigid, humourless older cop who barely offered a word of conversation when they were on duty together. Ailsa was the opposite of that. She and Piet were around the same age, early forties, and her conversation wasn't limited to the job. They soon discovered that they both had teenage children, and those children had strong views about their respective cultural backgrounds. In Piet's case, not surprisingly, his son Luuk wanted nothing to do with the stern, self-denying lifestyle his family had brought with them to Canada. Ailsa's teen daughter, on the other hand, was mortified that her mother barely knew a word of Gaelic, and the young girl had taken up the language and Highland dancing with great enthusiasm. So Piet and his partner were never short of topics for conversation.

Turning his mind to the subject at hand, the Keller case, Piet reflected that he had not been entirely forthright with Father Burke, telling him that the medical examiner *would* determine the cause of death. In fact, Piet had received the autopsy report late Friday afternoon. The medical examiner confirmed that the cause of death was drowning, but the other injuries were noted in the report: abrasions and some broken skin on the hands, and swelling of the lips. There was a laceration — a cut — on the lower lip, left side, which would have bled to some extent.

Ailsa mentioned Burke and said, "He's in for some anguish on this one. Everything points to suicide. *So far.* It looks like a drowning death. But those injuries to her hands and her mouth . . ."

"Defensive wounds possibly, the marks on her palms, but more likely the kind of scraping of the skin that might have come if she'd been handling rough material. Rocks perhaps somewhere on the shore. Maybe she tumbled about and cut her lip."

"But, of course, we don't know yet whether she went into the water of her own accord or whether someone pushed her in. What we need is a witness, somebody to say he saw her at the park or on the shore somewhere else farther out. She could have jumped or fallen, or been pushed, into the water from a cliff, or one of the islands. The outer harbour is what, eight kilometres?"

"Something like that, yeah."

They pulled in to the long, low red-brick police station on Gottingen Street and parked, but neither of them made a move to get out of the car.

Ailsa said, "Meika Keller's arrival in this country came after quite a terrifying scene in Berlin. Escaped through one of the checkpoints. She and her wee daughter were shot at as they fled. I wonder if something in her past in Germany might have reared up again. Unlikely, I know, but . . ."

"Long time ago, though, Ailsa. Hard to imagine anyone holding a grudge after all this time, especially now that the old regime has collapsed."

"I know. But I asked Constable Fraser to check with her family and the people at Saint Mary's to see whether she had received any worrisome calls or letters, that kind of thing. Let's get in there and see if Fraser turned up anything on that score."

Constable Archie Fraser reported that there were no letters or calls to the victim's home or office from Germany or anywhere else overseas. She did not have a cellular phone.

"Now we know," Piet said, "that Meika Keller and her husband were boating enthusiasts. Well, the husband is commander of the naval fleet, after all! Though someone had to explain to me, Archie, the meaning of the name of his yacht. The *Busman's Holiday.* I understand that it means a holiday that is much like one's own workday. But anyway, there were no ghost ships floating in the harbour that night with no one left on board. Unless you came up with anything there?"

Fraser shook his head. "Apart from the big tanker that's always here, the fire tug and other tugs, coastal defence vessels, you know, the regular ships we always see, there were no unusual vessels in the harbour. One of the frigates was in, the *Charlottetown,* I think. But there was nothing that went out from the Squadron, I mean the Royal Nova Scotia Yacht Squadron, where Keller and Rendell have their sailboat, or from any of the other clubs or marinas. Though somebody could have had a boat tied up at home and gone out for a late-night winter cruise — we can't rule that out completely."

CHAPTER IV

Piet

At home the next evening, Sunday, Piet got a call from the station. "Sir, we received a tip over the phone. Possible witness to an incident involving Meika Keller." Half an hour later, Piet and Ailsa Young were sitting in the Cole Harbour apartment of Carl Dickson, a twenty-one-year-old university student who had something to tell them about the night of February 6.

"I'm sorry I didn't call you guys sooner about this, but, well, the girl I was with that night, Jeanine, she was away and she just got back, and I wanted to compare notes with her. To see if what I remember was accurate and all that. I didn't want to go off half-cocked and call you if it didn't have anything to do with . . ."

"Don't worry about that, Carl. Why don't you just tell us what happened?"

"I was with a couple of my buddies at Peddler's Pub on Tuesday night, and we got talking to a bunch of girls at the next table. I was

47

really hitting it off with one of them. It was funny because when the night started, I was kind of pissed off. My buddies and I have this thing where one of us is the designated driver, and we did this on rotation. And that night it was supposed to be Da — one of the other guys, but he'd started drinking right after supper. So, it was me as the driver again. But it turned out great because of this girl at the next table, Jeanine. Anyway, it was getting late and I wanted to take off with Jeanine, but I'd promised these other guys a lift home. But they let me off the hook and said they'd get a taxi. So, I got to drive her home."

"What is her last name, Jeanine?" Piet asked.

"Sorry, sorry, I'm telling you all this stuff you don't need to hear. Mercer is her last name. And she lives on Francklyn Street."

"Okay, go on."

"So, I'm driving her home. We go from downtown and through the south end, down Tower Road and over the railroad tracks, then right on Pine Hill Drive, and all the time I'm thinking I want to stop the car before we get to her parents' place, you know. Not to do anything, just . . . I wanted to talk to her and see if I could arrange a date before I got her home. I made a left onto Francklyn and slowed right down and stopped. She told me she lived at the far end of the street, but I wanted a bit of time for us to chat. I'd already lit up a smoke without even thinking she might not like it. Bad move on my part."

The young guy was taking his time getting to the point, but Piet didn't rush him. What you wanted was the witness's own story, in full. You never knew what you might miss if you interrupted or hurried him along.

"Jeanine didn't like that a bit, me smoking, so I butted out the cigarette and rolled down the windows and tried to wave the smoke out, cursing to myself. It was freezing cold, but I figured that was better than the smoke. She had a warm jacket on. Anyway, sorry, here's the point. With the windows open, I could hear two people hollering at one another. I looked over and saw a car parked on the property of the theology school; it was stopped in the driveway beside the college, facing the water. The driveway on the left of the school if you were facing it and the water. And this blond lady got out of the car and left the door open and started running. Then a man freakin' launched himself out of the car, driver's side, and took off after her, yelling at her to come back. Jeanine and I watched what was going on. The guy turned and saw us and he put up his hands, as if to say, you know, 'Nothing to see here, folks. It's a minor spat, and I'm harmless.' And he got back into his car. So, I drove Jeanine down to the end of the street.

"When I heard about that lady, Meika, being found on the beach and saw her picture in the paper, I remembered this weird scene. The lady I saw was kind of slim, not skinny, but nowhere near fat, and she was blond and had really nice clothes on. I mean it may be nothing, not related, but I figured I should call you guys just in case."

"You did the right thing, Carl. We appreciate it. Now, what happened after that? You drove Jeanine home . . ."

"Yeah, and of course my mind was on her. On Jeanine and wondering how we'd be leaving things when I dropped her off. Turned out her folks were home, and the living-room light was still on, so, well, we stayed in the car for a few minutes and made a plan for a date the next week because she was going up to Fredericton for a few days. She just got back today. Anyway, that night, she got out of the car and went into her house. I turned around and drove back along Francklyn. I noticed that car; it was still there."

"Was there anyone inside, could you see?"

Dickson shook his head. "Nobody there."

The car there, and nobody in it. The man had returned to the car but then got out again. Where did he go?

"How many minutes had passed between the time you left for Jeanine's house and when you drove by and saw the car again?"

"Less than ten. Seven or eight minutes maybe."

"You didn't see either of the two people at that point? The second time?"

49

"No. And I felt kind of weird, kind of guilty, driving away from there. I was wondering if the woman was all right, after the hollering and that. But — I know this doesn't sound very good — I didn't think about it again till two days later; that's when I heard about her death. But what could I have done, really? I wouldn't have known where to look even if I'd stopped and got out. If I'd started running through people's backyards, somebody probably would have called the cops on me. The police."

"Don't worry about that, Carl. You're helping now by giving us this information."

"And I remember thinking that the couple lived nearby and that's why they'd parked their car at the theology school — you know, had permission to park there. It's a rich part of town; maybe they had too many cars for their driveway!"

"Sure. What time would this have been, when you saw the car with nobody in it?"

He paused to think it over. "Midnight or so, a little before maybe. Sorry I can't be any more clear on it."

"No, that's fine. Now, can you tell us anything about the car?"

"Yeah. Because of the yelling and all that, I did take in what kind of car it was. There was enough light from the street lights for me to see. A black, late-model Volvo. And I noted the tag number. I'm studying math and computer science, so I guess I tend to notice number patterns. Didn't write it down at the time but . . . I did today." He reached into his pocket and produced a scrap of paper with the licence number.

Well! This was going better than Piet had expected.

"But by the time I got home to Cole Harbour, I'd pretty well put the whole thing out of my mind. The only thing on my mind was Jeanine. But then two days after, I heard the news. Even then, though, even today, I thought if I called you, I was afraid I might, you know, come off as an asshole. One of those nosy types that want to butt into a big story and make themselves sound important."

The detectives assured young Dickson that was not the case; they thanked him and left. As soon as they got back to the station, they phoned the Mercers and arranged to speak with Jeanine at the family home on Francklyn Street. Jeanine gave the same account of events as Dickson had, except of course she had not known that the black Volvo was still in place when Dickson left the neighbourhood.

Monty

Just before eleven o'clock on Monday morning, Monty got a call from the police station, telling him the police had a man in for questioning, and the man had asked to speak to Monty Collins. Twenty minutes after that, he walked into the station on Gottingen Street and was informed that the man's name was Alban MacNair. He was being questioned about the death of Meika Keller.

Detective Sergeant Piet Van den Brink greeted Monty and told him that he and his partner had gone to MacNair's home in Armdale at seven thirty that morning, following reports that MacNair had been seen in the company of Meika Keller in the late-night hours of February 6, 1996, the night before her body was found on the shore at Point Pleasant Park. The witnesses said they had seen the two of them together in a car parked beside the Atlantic School of Theology, which overlooks the waters of the Northwest Arm. The witnesses saw Meika Keller open the door of the car and go running. And the man had got out and started after her. There was an argument of some kind. Monty would ask for more details later on; for now, he was anxious to meet the man who might become his client.

"He's in number three," the cop said and opened the door to the interview room. The room was maybe ten feet square with high ceilings, bare walls, and two doors, one for the lawyer, one for the client if he was being held in custody, which this man wasn't. Yet. Each of the doors had a window of reinforced glass. There was a metal table affixed to the wall. The client was sitting at the table; he gave Monty a long look when Monty sat down across from him and introduced himself.

The man was an Army officer, Lieutenant-Colonel Alban MacNair. Even sitting in the police station, where he had been for three hours, Lieutenant-Colonel MacNair had the bearing of a military man. He sat upright and alert in his seat. And he had been savvy enough to bring in a lawyer at the questioning stage. Not many of Monty's criminal clients had the foresight to do that. MacNair appeared to be in his late forties or early fifties with a salt-and-pepper crewcut and a direct gaze from dark grey eyes. But the tension was evident from the first word he spoke to Monty.

"I did not kill anyone. Make this go away."

"I'll do all I can to help you, Lieutenant-Colonel MacNair. I know how stressful this must be for you."

"You have no idea unless you have sat in my place in a police inter-rogation room for something you didn't do."

With a quarter century of experience in the criminal justice system, Monty had seen countless clients in exactly MacNair's place in here, but he let that pass.

"First of all, tell me what happened this morning."

"They came and accosted me in front of my wife and our son, and a couple of neighbours who were getting an early start to their day."

"What did the police say when they arrived at your door?"

"Established my identity and requested that I come in to the police station. For questioning. About the death of Meika Keller! I didn't want this going on with my family there, so I agreed. And here I am." He looked around the room with disgust.

Now for the most important question of all. Monty did not ask whether MacNair had "given a statement." In Monty's experience, clients denied having made a statement and then, in many cases, went on to reveal that they had gabbed away half the night to the inves-tigating officers. A *statement* to the layman was a formal thing; of course, he or she hadn't given a *statement*. That rarely meant the client had been sensible enough to exercise his right to remain silent. "What did you say to them?" he asked his client now.

"I told them they were barking up the wrong tree, that I hadn't laid a hand on Meika Keller."

Not that he didn't know her, not that he hadn't been anywhere near her, just that he hadn't touched her.

"They say they have a witness who saw you with her on the property of the Atlantic School of Theology late on the night of February sixth, just hours before she was found dead on the shore on the south tip of the peninsula."

Monty was well aware that the Atlantic School of Theology was only a minute's walk from Emscote Drive, where Meika Keller lived. Like the roadway running alongside the theology school, Emscote ran down from Francklyn to the Northwest Arm.

"What can you tell me about that?"

Monty watched as MacNair weighed one disastrous course of action against the other; he considered the fate that might befall him if he was caught in a lie versus the fate that might be his if he blurted out the truth. Monty sought to help him make up his mind. "If this goes further, if charges are laid, and I put on a case for you based on fiction or on an incomplete picture of what happened, that case will be demolished in the courtroom."

"Yeah, I know. Don't lie." He started to speak again but nothing came out.

Monty prompted him. "Let's start with the night she died. We'll go back in time later. So, the night of February sixth."

"I saw her at a fundraising dinner and auction for the symphony."

"You're a classical music buff, are you?"

"No. I mean, some of it I like."

"But you're a fan of Symphony Nova Scotia?"

"What is this, cross-examination by my own lawyer five minutes after we meet?"

"I'm just trying to get an understanding of the events that brought you and Ms. Keller together that night."

"Sometimes I go to those things; sometimes I don't. That night I did. Even if I don't know everything there is to know about Beethoven, it doesn't mean I wouldn't support fundraising for something as important as a local orchestra."

"All right. So, you saw her at the fundraiser. You spoke to her there?"

"For a few minutes, yeah."

"What did you talk about?"

The client steeled himself for whatever it was he didn't want to say. "Meika and I had a little flirtation going. Nothing too serious, but . . ."

But she had either committed suicide or been murdered. An accident under the circumstances of this case was highly unlikely.

"I mean, nothing had happened between us yet. Ever."

"When did this begin, the flirtation?"

"Last few months or so."

"Where did you see each other?"

"Public events at Stad, or Windsor Park." Military facilities here in the city, two of several addresses that made up Canadian Forces Base Halifax. "Or charity events like the one for the symphony."

"When did you meet her for the first time?"

The direct gaze faltered. Monty could see him considering his answer. "I honestly can't remember the first time. Years ago. She was married to a military man, so we came into contact. Don't know when exactly."

"How often were you alone with her?"

"Only a couple of times."

"Where?"

"Chatting in my car, or hers."

"Like the night of her death." No response. "What happened that night, Lieutenant-Colonel MacNair?"

"She came up to me at the symphony dinner, said she wanted to speak to me in private. I knew I wouldn't have the opportunity till late that night, because . . ."

"Because?"

"My wife and I had plans to drop in on her sister after the dinner. I knew we'd be tied up at the dinner till well after nine, and then with my sister-in-law for an hour or two, then home to Armdale. After that, I'd have to come up with some reason to go out. Best to wait till my wife went to sleep. Nothing was going to happen, you understand."

Monty understood perfectly well.

"So, with all that —" There was a shout and a bang outside the room. MacNair jolted in his seat and whipped around. But if somebody had been thrown up against the wall, the drama could not be viewed from inside the interview room. Monty waited for the rest of the story. "Uh, right, so I told Meika I could meet her at eleven thirty at the earliest. I figured she'd say forget it, make it another time, but she agreed."

"All right. What was the arrangement?"

"She picked a place close to home. The college there, overlooking the Arm. She walked over from her house, and I was there waiting in the car. She got in."

"And then?"

"We just talked."

"What about?"

"Local events, my son's scholarship to McGill, just . . ." He wound down.

"She knew she had only limited time with you alone, so presumably she told you what was foremost in her mind?"

MacNair took in a big breath and expelled it with force, then said, "Meika wasn't satisfied with the way things were between us. She wanted more. Wanted to get past the talking and flirting stage."

"She wanted things to get more intimate."

"She wanted a commitment, which I was in no position to give."

"Was this something you wanted as well?"

"She was a beautiful woman, a wonderful woman. Who wouldn't want more? I'm only human, after all. But I love my wife. I love my family. I was not about to do anything that would endanger my marriage."

The words sounded right, but there was something in his client's demeanour that didn't seem to match the forthrightness of the speech.

"Sir, I hear what you are saying. But *if* in fact you were having an affair with Ms. Keller, that would obviously cause you problems with your wife and family. But it would not, by itself, land you in prison for the rest of your life. We have to keep things in perspective here."

"Collins, I've asked you here to act as my lawyer. You come highly recommended. But if you think I'm a liar and you think there was something else going on, how in the fuck are you going to be my advocate if I get charged and this goes to court?"

"I'm a much better lawyer if I find pitfalls in my cases at the outset rather than during the trial. Believe me when I say I have seen countless cases come crashing to earth when the defence lawyer gets sandbagged in the courtroom, when the Crown prosecutor brings out something before the judge and jury that the client hadn't told his lawyer. Whatever the true situation is, I can work with it, as long as there are no surprises."

"She started giving me hell because I was 'leading her on' and would not commit to a relationship or a future, and she got wild and hollered at me and then she got out and slammed the door."

"What did you do then?"

"I . . . I got out of the car, shouted at her to come back, and started to follow her. Then I was afraid someone might hear me, somebody in one of the houses. Sound travels over the water. So . . ." He looked ashamed then. "I went back to the car, started the motor, and drove away."

"Which direction did she take off in?" Monty knew that area of the city. She could have gone through backyards of the houses or the college, or she could have gone up to Francklyn Street, or down to the shore.

"She went behind the houses. In a southerly direction. I figured she was going home. Emscote Drive is only about two hundred metres away."

"You would have seen her if she was headed home, then."

"Yeah, but then she zigzagged around somewhere and I lost sight of her." Monty said nothing, and his client added, "I was pissed off, and I just left."

That was, as far as Monty knew, the last time she had been seen alive. But one thing he did know: if it was an accident, if she had gone down to the water's edge and fallen, she would have washed up right there on the western side of the peninsula, not over and around the tip of Point Pleasant Park. In order to come in where she did, she would have to have been out in the open water of the Atlantic.

There were only three possibilities: (1) Meika was so distressed over the situation with Lieutenant-Colonel MacNair that she ran all around the southern tip of the Halifax peninsula and swam out into the winter surf and took her own life; (2) MacNair somehow got her into the depths or the surf of the Atlantic Ocean, threw or pushed her in, either in a rage or in a move calculated to keep her from threatening his marriage and his family life; or (3) someone else came into the picture between midnight and seven thirty-five that morning, a random killer or someone who coincidentally had a motive to kill Meika Keller. Monty knew which of those scenarios a jury would find most likely.

CHAPTER V

Brennan

Brennan was feeling the morning-after effects of his Monday night, this time drinking and smoking alone in his room. Not the best condition for a man morally required to attend an event at which he would be most unwelcome: the funeral for Meika Keller. Although she had adopted Saint Bernadette's parish as her own, it was no surprise that Commodore Rendell did not choose Father Burke's church for his wife's funeral. It was in fact held at a chapel on the naval base, CFB Stadacona, in Halifax's north end, and the chapel was Saint Brendan's. Appropriate for a naval chapel to be named for Saint Brendan the Navigator, who, according to legend, had travelled far from his native Ireland in the sixth century in a leather-hulled boat. Some even maintained that he had made it all the way to Newfoundland. Most people scoff at the idea, but then they had also scoffed at the story that the Vikings had landed in Newfoundland, until their settlement was uncovered in the 1960s.

Well, wherever the Irish saint had sailed to, he was honoured as a navigator in places far from his home in County Kerry.

But that history would not be enough to distract Brennan today, any more than would the magnificent building he saw on the base. He was told it was Admiralty House, a neo-classical building in stone with rows of multipaned windows, three dormers, and side chimneys. He would love to have gone in there to explore the interior, but he was called to a much more painful duty. Monsignor Michael O'Flaherty, God bless him, not only offered to accompany Brennan but came up with a ruse to keep a desperately keen Mrs. Kelly from attending the funeral. Mike told her that the bishop might drop by with a cousin who was home from Boston. Brennan knew that the cousin had been in town for a week already and was planning to stay until after Easter, but it was not technically a lie to say he and Cronin might drop by.

The church was jammed with mourners, and there was an easel at the side of the altar with a large photograph of Meika, standing atop a hill somewhere, a pack on her back, her hair blowing around in the wind, a big smile on her face. Brennan and Mike sat near the back of the chapel, sang along with the hymns, walked up to the altar with all the rest of the mourners for Communion, and then listened to the words of remembrance delivered by family members and friends before the final commendation. According to the rules governing Catholic funerals, these were to be short pieces highlighting the faith of the person who had died. Brennan had never stuck to this format; he let the people say whatever they felt moved to say, and the priest here at Saint Brendan's was obviously cut from the same cloth.

Brennan felt as if he was taking a lash of the whip every time a poignant memory was evoked. There was a young musician who had failed in her attempts to join the symphony orchestra as a clarinet player. She met Meika at a fundraising event and ended up telling her the whole sad tale. "Meika said, 'Come to me at Saint Mary's on Monday and bring your clarinet.' So I did. I went to her office and she nodded her head at me and said, 'Play it.' I felt a bit self-conscious, but I played her a couple of pieces. It didn't go all that well, so I stopped and sang the notes to put them in my memory and played them again on the clarinet. When I finished, she said, 'No wonder you have not been accepted into the orchestra.' And I wanted to run out the door and keep on running. I was mortified! Then she said, 'You are not doing justice to it.' I could hardly bear to ask but I had to. 'Not doing justice to what?' The composer, the instrument? 'Not doing justice to your voice. Your voice has a dark, rich timbre; a magnificent contralto. You should be in the Halifax Camerata Singers or in the opera program at Dal.' I thought I was too old, but she shook her head. 'I will introduce you to the people you should know.' I had sung in a couple of choirs at school but never thought I was any good because I couldn't reach the high notes! So I had put all my effort into the clarinet. I took lessons for years, so I thought I should be making something out of that. But Meika set me on the right course. I'm singing Cornelia, wife of Pompey, in Handel's *Giulio Cesare* in Vancouver next month! Thanks to Meika!" She smiled, then teared up, and said, "God bless you, Meika. I miss you and will never forget you!"

There were other uplifting stories, and some that were heart-scalding, and then the two Rendell children got up, grown children, Lauren and Curtis. Lauren stepped up first; she was a short, slim young woman with long wavy light-brown hair. Her face was ravaged with grief. She held a sheet of paper in her trembling hands. She started to speak but couldn't manage it. She tried again, and her brother took hold of her arm to steady her. But she fell weeping into his arms. Hubert Rendell got up and escorted her back to her seat. Then he rose again and passed the page to Curtis. The young man, with his military bearing and strong features, looked as if he would fill his father's shoes someday.

Curtis began to read his sister's words. "When I was eleven, I was starting to become self-conscious about my hair." He put his hand up and ran it back over his short-cropped brown hair, and there was gentle laughter in the church. "Even though it was a nice colour of blond back then." He looked upwards and made a face as if to say *Where are those golden locks now?* And again there was laughter. "It was thick and curly and I couldn't do a thing with it." Curtis looked up from the paper and said, "Story of my life." And the congregation loved it. "One Friday at school, we were all to come dressed as a character from a book. I wanted to be the girl from an old book I loved, *National Velvet*." Curtis raised his hands in a gesture that said *I'm a natural for the part*, then returned to the reading. "And of course I didn't have a horse, so the next best thing was the jockey's cap that my grandfather had found for me. But my hair wouldn't cooperate. So Mum — Meika is Mum to me, always — did my hair up in beautiful, elaborate braids and said I now looked like a little German girl and I would go as Gretel in *Hansel and Gretel*. And she took a pair of our curtains and somehow sewed them into a costume that looked like a German style of dress. Except Mum, well, she was so smart at science and all kinds of things but not sewing. But I loved my braids so much, I didn't even care about the sloppy seams in the dress. And I had great fun playing Gretel at school.

"But the point of this story isn't about my hair. The point is what Mum said to me while she was doing the braids. She said —" And here it was Curtis's voice that faltered. He cleared his throat and said, "'You know I had a little girl. I used to braid her hair like this.' Dad had told us that she had a daughter who had died, and her name was Helga, but Mum — Meika — never talked about it. And I was a typical young girl, full of insecurities, and I blurted out, 'Am I your little girl now?' But even at that age I knew enough that a child who died could never be replaced by another, and I was anxious and worried about what she would say. But what she said to me that day has stayed with me my whole life, sustained me my whole life, and it always will. She said, 'You are my little girl, Lauren. I love you as if I made you myself. Don't you ever, not for one minute, ever doubt it.' And Mum, I love you as if you made me yourself. I will never stop missing you."

Curtis stepped down then and took his sister's hand, and she stood with him facing the congregation. Curtis looked up and said, "Mum, the loss of you is so great that I won't even try to put it into words. But you're up there, and you know. I see your face before me every night before I go to sleep. And we will find whoever put you in that water, whoever took you from us and took your life from you!"

Brennan looked over at the photo of Meika, her yellow hair blown about by the wind, and he pictured that same hair being tossed about by the waves, the face under the water, her eyes wide open and locked on Brennan's own. When the Mass was ended, he slipped away like a criminal desperate to avoid detection.

✝

Back on his home turf, Brennan struggled to turn his mind away from the grief over the woman's death, the mortification over his neglect of her on the final night of her life, and his persistent hangover, and he concentrated instead on one of the joys of his life: his choir school. To be working with bright young students; fostering their appreciation of the greatest, most sublime music ever composed; hearing that music sung in the clear, ringing tones of their young voices was heaven on earth to Brennan. But somebody was having trouble with her music theory. Brennan was looking over the tests the students had written last Friday, and even allowing for the difficulty of the subject, the performance of Normie Collins was far below her usual high standard. Brennan wanted to talk to her but didn't want to alarm her. Normie was a sensitive child, to the point that she sometimes had experiences of second sight. Brennan had met her spooky old great-grandmother in Cape Breton, who had the same ability. Brennan tended to dismiss out of hand most reports of people who claimed to have "psychic" visions, but with Normie it was genuine, he knew. Just as were his own occasional experiences of that kind. Normie's nature was such that she was far too ready to find fault with herself, and she was constantly on guard against hurting the feelings of others. Brennan had known her since she was just a little girl, when he first met Maura MacNeil and Monty Collins. Well, he had to speak to her, but he would put her mind at ease right away. The students in the upper grades had a practice session in the auditorium; he would come up with something then.

When Father Burke strode into the auditorium, there was a mad shuffle of papers, and young voices fell silent, as everyone affected a pose of the hardworking student going over his and her music sheets before the rehearsal. "Good morning, Father," several of them chanted. One of the boys tried to be subtle as he shifted a large piece of paper under his desk. Richard Robertson. This will be good, thought Brennan, knowing Richard's standing as a wit and a wag. So, Brennan reached back for a phrase wielded by prissy schoolmarms against students from time immemorial. "Have you something to share with the class, Richard Robertson?"

"Uh, I've already shared it, Father. They told me it's not worth wrapping today's mackerel catch in, so . . ."

"Ah, now, you're too tough on yourself, lad. Let's have a look."

Richard's face was the colour of a boiled lobster. But he knew resistance was futile. He pulled out the paper, on which was drawn an excellent likeness of Father Burke looking imperious in a Roman collar and black soutane. His expression was stony. Even so, he looked much better in the portrait than he felt this morning. It appeared that Richard had started to draw a conversation bubble before he was interrupted. Brennan would love to know what words the talented young artist had intended to put in his mouth. But, for now, he'd give the talented young artist a ribbing.

"Have you not kept up with modern art, Robertson?"

"Um, I don't know."

"Here, let me show you the modern, 1990s way to draw a face."

"Okay."

Brennan went to the board and drew one of those ubiquitous, supremely annoying smiley faces you saw everywhere these days. "Isn't that better now?"

The kids all laughed, and Richard said, "Thank you, Father. I'll change it right away."

Brennan leaned towards the young fellow and said, "I'm only after blackguarding you, Richard. Your picture is brilliant. Don't change a thing. And tell Mrs. Moretti —" the art teacher "— to make sure you get to do heaps of portraits this term. I'll be happy to model for you any day of the week."

So, he had them laughing. But the laughs would be short-lived. They were about to rehearse Anton Bruckner's sombre setting of the "Christus Factus Est."

"Turn to the Bruckner."

"Scary," Richard muttered.

"Scary indeed," their instructor agreed. "There's nothing more harrowing than the events of Good Friday. Jesus taken prisoner and executed in the most brutal fashion. Translate that first sentence for me. What do the words mean?"

He looked out at the assembled students, and they recited the words, "Christ became obedient for us unto death, even unto death on the cross." The austerity of the Latin, the D minor key, and Bruckner's ominous opening chords, with the melody line staying on the low D for the first two and a half measures, made it even more harrowing. *Christus factus est pro nobis obediens usque ad mortem.* He always got chills whenever he sang or heard it.

And so did Normie by the look of it. She was susceptible to the moods induced by music, all the more so with a piece as haunting as this one. They sang it through until the choirmaster was satisfied, and then he told them he would be back in ten minutes for Victoria's "Popule Meus."

"Get your books out and read over your parts. Normie, could you come and help me for a minute?"

"Yes, Father." Always self-conscious, she avoided the curious eyes of her schoolmates as she left the auditorium.

He led her into an empty classroom and gently closed the door behind them.

"Am I in trouble?" the poor little thing asked him immediately.

He smiled at her. "Sure, when have you ever been in trouble, Normie?"

"Maybe I just never got caught."

"Ah. That must be it. Well, you've not been caught this time either."

"It's my theory test, isn't it?"

"I know you're a whiz at music theory, so I was a little surprised at your Circle of Fifths." That was the Circle of Fifths showing the keys, their signatures, and the number of sharps and flats for each.

"I'm sorry. I know it! I just made a mess when I started putting the sharps in and then I . . . Can I do it again?"

"Don't be worrying about one little test. No need to do it again. I know that you know all the keys. I'm the one who's worried here, and I'm worried about you, *acushla*."

"How come?"

"I've a feeling that you're not your old self at all. Is something wrong?"

"No." He waited, and then she said, trying for casualness, "It's always sad to sing about Jesus being . . . taken prisoner, and then the way they . . ."

"But is there something else? Can you tell me about it?"

Her voice was shaky as she began her confession. "I failed, and you got hurt!"

What on earth? "What do you mean, Normie?"

"If it wasn't for me being a failure, you would have been safe."

A lifetime of hearing people's woes and their transgressions was no help to him here. "I'm not sure what you mean, Normie, but I'm sure you weren't a failure in any way. And certainly not in any way that affected me."

"It's about what happened to you!"

"To me?"

"They never told me! Even after we made that poster for you."

She must have meant the poster his students had made at the end of the last school year in anticipation of Brennan's return from Belfast: when he was supposed to touch down in Halifax briefly and then head over to Rome for a year to direct a choir at Sancta Maria Regina Coeli. Which he never got to do, because he was arrested and imprisoned on *terrorism* charges in Belfast. Not knowing what had befallen him, the choir school children had made him a poster showing a choir of angels singing for him in the Roman church, with the Halifax kids' faces pasted in over the angel bodies. Except for Richard Robertson, who was portrayed as a little devil. Brennan treasured that gift from his students in spite of how things had turned out for him.

"I love that poster, Normie. You know I have it framed and hanging in my room. And I think maybe you were the operating mind behind that lovely gift."

"It's true. I was. Which shows even more how stupid I was."

"How on earth were you stupid, little one? I don't understand."

"I only found out later what happened to you over there."

"Right."

"But I should have known about it."

"I'm sure your mum and dad didn't want to upset you. It's scary stuff being thrown into a jail over there. I don't recommend it!"

The dear little soul was weeping by this time. Brennan couldn't take it. He got up and went around to her, gently lifted her from the chair and held her in his arms. They stood like that and he let her cry it all out. Whatever it was.

Eventually, she said, "You know all about my *gift*. That I have the sight."

He gingerly released her and settled her back in the chair.

"I know that," he told her.

"Well then, how come I didn't see what was going to happen to *you*? I *failed* and you went to jail on account of it!"

How could the child possibly look at that series of events and somehow conclude that she was responsible? He knew she had an overdeveloped conscience, always worrying about whether some little remark, or even the expression on her face, might hurt somebody's feelings. But this! "Normie, darling, there was no failure on your part. And you aren't responsible in any way for what happened to me."

"But don't you get it? If my sight had been working right, if I hadn't just been thinking of myself and all the fun I was having in Ireland, I would have had a vision of what was going to happen, and I would have warned you and you could have got away."

"No, no, that . . ." He just didn't know what to say to her.

"You have something like that yourself, don't you, Brennan, I mean Father?" She tended to call him by his first name at home and his title at school. "You see things."

"I do. Sometimes." With him, it was the occasional ecstatic moment during Mass or during the performance of a particularly ethereal piece of music. He felt at those times that he was in unmediated communion — he knew he was — with the Divine. And there were a few instances when he had seen into the soul of a person, had seen or felt pure evil behind the eyes of a fellow human being. But the kind of visions Normie sometimes had, seeing beneath the surface of an event, or even foretelling the future, well, he had never considered himself gifted, or cursed, in that way.

"So, you know it's real," she said to him now. "And I didn't have any vision at all, any idea, of what was going to happen to you over in Ireland. And I should have. So, I was too selfish to notice what was happening to you. I could have saved you! But I didn't."

"Normie, my love, I got into trouble because I did something stupid. Nothing violent. I didn't hurt anybody. But something dumb that I shouldn't have done. I did it to save a member of my family over there. And then I ended up in a kangaroo court, and —" Her tear-stained eyes grew wide at that. "That's just an expression meaning a bad court, one that doesn't do justice."

"So, the judge was bad!"

"The judge wasn't the greatest, for sure, but the whole criminal justice system over there was bad. Well, your dad could explain that."

"I don't dare ask him. Mummy and him fight about it. Argue about it, I mean."

"Ah." He had no idea what she was getting at there. Perhaps best not to know.

"Why do you think I didn't see what was in the future for you then?"

"We don't know how these things work. They are mysterious forces. Nobody can say why they 'work' sometimes and not at others. I had no foreknowledge of it myself! You were a hundred miles away from me, living in Dublin, remember. But no matter what, you have to understand that there was no failure by yourself! Do you believe me, Normie?"

"I have to! God speaks to you and listens to you!"

"Ah, I only wish that was true, darlin'. Most of what comes out of my mouth is not what God would say or ever want to hear."

CHAPTER VI

Monty

A week and a day after Meika Keller's body was found, the police and the Crown prosecutor decided that there was sufficient evidence to have Lieutenant-Colonel Alban MacNair arrested and charged with first-degree murder. Monty was with MacNair for the arraignment in Halifax Provincial Court on Spring Garden Road, and he managed to schedule a bail hearing in the province's Supreme Court for the following day; if that went well, MacNair might have to spend only one night in a cell. He was apoplectic as he looked ahead to that night, which Monty could well understand. He did his best to calm his client's fears, reassured him that there was a fairly good chance that he would be granted bail, and then he left to confer with the Crown attorney about whatever new information he had to justify the arrest.

The Crown is obligated to provide the defence with its evidence and the identity of its witnesses in a criminal case, and there was no delay in receiving the information that had been gathered so far. The Crown prosecutor was Bill MacEwen, a lawyer Monty had known for years, and they had been adversaries in court on many a case. But beyond the walls of the courtroom, they had an easygoing relationship. Now, in the Crown's office in the Spring Garden Road courthouse, MacEwen provided Monty with a "can say" statement given by the young fellow and his girlfriend who had witnessed the shouting match between MacNair and the victim on the night of February 6. So much for MacNair's insistence that he had quickly given up on Meika, returned to his car, and driven away. The witness, Carl Dickson, had left the spot where MacNair was parked, and when Dickson drove by again a few minutes later, MacNair's car was still there, sitting empty.

"And there's more," Bill MacEwen told Monty. "Blood on MacNair's right-hand glove." A shouting match, and now blood. Things weren't looking good for the lieutenant-colonel. "The outside of the glove, Monty, before you ask. It's in the lab for analysis. And now we come to the phone calls."

Ask not for whom the bell . . . All Monty said was "Yes?"

"Police looked at the victim's phone records, at home and at the university. Found nine calls to her office at Saint Mary's from MacNair's number at work. The calls were made over the course of two days just prior to her death, that is the fifth and sixth of February."

Why in the hell, Monty wondered, would the man make repeated calls to her from his own office number? Whatever had him agitated, it would strengthen the hand of the prosecutor in proceeding with a first-degree murder charge, on the assumption that MacNair was worked up about Meika Keller and his actions were premeditated. Monty would make the opposite argument: whatever MacNair wanted to reach her for, he obviously had no intention of harming her, or he would not have taken the risk of having the phone records discovered. Monty would make the argument, but would anyone believe it? Could Monty make a convincing show of believing it himself?

70

Blond hair, blue staring eyes: this is what Brennan saw as he tried to shut his mind off and sink into a dreamless sleep. Meika Keller's face looking up at him, expressionless, from her watery grave. That's the way it had been for Brennan the two nights following her funeral, so he found the days exhausting.

But he had a welcome distraction Thursday evening. He was sitting in his room with a glass of whiskey in his right hand and the telephone receiver in his left, talking to his brother Terry, who was back home in New York City. After a bit of catching up on family news, though, Brennan got on to the subject of the woman who, as he saw it, died on his watch.

"I'm asking myself whether whatever happened to Meika Keller had its genesis in Europe."

"Unlikely, wouldn't you say? Didn't you tell me she left Germany in the mid-1970s?"

"She did. But I remember something a little odd. It was when I first met her, when she started coming to Saint Bernadette's. This would have been three years ago, maybe four. You remember All Souls' Day, good Catholic lad that you are."

"How could I forget? We used to be up all hours on Halloween night stuffing ourselves with candy till we made ourselves sick, then had to get up in the morning and go to Mass because it was a holy day of obligation."

"Close but no licorice cigar and no pillowcase full of treats for you. That's All Saints' Day you're thinking of. November first. That's why the night before is All Hallows Eve. So. All Souls is the next day, November second. Some call it the Day of the Dead."

"You have no one to blame but yourself, Father, for being so lax with your little brothers, not teaching them how to find God in this world of terror and turbulence."

"I'll try to make it up to you. And, in return, you'll teach me how to find the landing gear in the workings of a seven-forty-seven."

"Somehow I suspect that would result in the pair of us finding God at the very same instant in time."

"You're probably right. Anyway, back to my point here. Many of the churches, including mine, have a Book of the Names of the Dead. People can inscribe the names of family members or others who have died, and we pray for them on November second and throughout the month."

"Yes, I've seen those."

"Well, when Meika was new to the church, I saw her writing a name in after Mass. And I decided to write in the name of a young fella I knew from my prison ministry here." It hit Brennan yet again that he had been ministering to inmates in the local prison for years, and yet, when he himself was incarcerated in Belfast, it had taken him an unconscionable length of time before he had risen to the occasion and started ministering to his fellow prisoners. They had been more helpful to him than he had been to them. Another failure on his conscience. He returned to his conversation with Terry. "The lad I'm talking about, in the correctional centre here, was not a bad fella at all, just the product of a very difficult life like so many of the others there. He was stabbed to death by another inmate. So I went over to the book to write in his name. And a few names above it was the name Meika had inscribed. I can't recall the name now, but I remember it was German, and I made a comment to her at the time. There must have been something about it that struck me enough to mention it. Maybe something unusual, can't remember now. I greeted her and said whatever I said about the name. And thinking back on it now, it seemed she was a bit unsettled."

"But you're looking back on it knowing what happened to her last week. So that may be colouring your impression of it."

"Sure, I know, but then I asked her where in Germany she had lived, and she said Leipzig. Then she appeared sort of flustered and said, 'But I moved around a lot. I left Germany long ago.' Something like that. I knew she had escaped from East Berlin, but I didn't mention it. At the time of this encounter with her, there was a delegation from our archdiocese making arrangements to go over to Germany and to Poland early the following year. Some German and Polish people living here and hoping to establish contact with people there, especially those who had been behind the Iron Curtain, as they say. Invitations would be given out for a return visit, Germans and Poles coming to stay in Halifax. So, I told her that. Thought she might be interested, but no."

"That's a stretch, I'd say, Bren. You can't necessarily draw any conclusions from that."

"I know, but stranger things have happened. Thinner threads than that have bound events together."

"I suppose so."

"Wish I could bring back that name." He polished off his whiskey and then said, "I can."

"You can what?"

"Find the name. We still have the old books. They're all in the sacristy. I'll dig it out when I get back."

"Back from where? The Midtown?"

Brennan had been avoiding the old drinking spot that he had so frequently attended with Monty Collins. He wondered if the tavern's accounts had taken a hit. To Terry, all he said was "O'Carroll's. I'm meeting a couple of the lads there."

"Well, don't be skulling pints till the wee hours without me there as your guardian angel."

"Your concern is noted."

"You don't know from concern!" his brother said then, in a strong outer-boroughs New York accent. "Your family is worried sick! Call your mother! Your brother Patrick is considering taking a month's leave to go up there and tend to you. And that man is a doctor!"

"The blessings of God on you, Terrence." There was nothing jocular in his tone of voice. He knew that his family, Terry included, were worried about him. Well, he'd make sure he didn't get sozzled tonight.

Monty

Following a bail hearing in the Nova Scotia Supreme Court on Friday morning, Lieutenant-Colonel Alban MacNair was released on a $100,000 surety with conditions, including staying within the jurisdiction and having no firearms in his possession except if required as part of his military duties. This was not a feat of exceptional court work on Monty's part; it was not out of the ordinary for a murder suspect to be released pending his trial. Now Monty wanted to test the waters, so to speak, with respect to the strength or weakness of his case. One thing he did not look forward to was hauling Father Brennan Burke into his office for a grilling about the incident Detective Sergeant Van den Brink had mentioned; the day before she died, the victim had asked Burke for a tête-à-tête and he had failed to show up. Things were already tense between Monty and Brennan following the fiasco in Ireland; he could imagine Brennan's frame of mind if Monty started asking about the night Meika Keller died, with the obvious intent of making the case for suicide. But Monty would put that off for a bit. First, he wanted to talk to somebody else who knew Meika, and he knew just who to ask. Monty had played hockey in his university days with a guy who now taught chemistry at Saint Mary's. They saw each other once in a while, though it had been a year or more since they'd been able to sit down and have a chat. He called the department at the university and left a message for Professor Don Phillips.

Monty heard from the prof an hour later and explained the purpose of his call. Don said he could make time for lunch, so the two of them agreed to enjoy a beer and a meal at the Lower Deck before heading back to work. A cold rain was falling, and a brisk wind was lashing water up over the wharves when Monty reached the waterfront, but the atmosphere inside the bar was warm and the beer was golden as he sat down to wait for his old linemate. When Don arrived, they placed their orders, then reminisced about their hockey and drinking days, talked about the Colorado Avalanche and the Florida Panthers, and expressed amazement at how far hockey had travelled from its great white northern home. And they caught up on their recent family events and work lives, before Monty got to the primary goal of the get-together.

"As I told you, Don, I'm representing the man accused of killing Meika Keller."

"I'll be grown up about it and say I know you have a job to do, but Jesus."

"Some people are much less gracious about the job I do."

"And I know he's innocent until — *unless* — proven guilty."

"That's right. It's my job to make the Crown do *its* job and prove guilt beyond a reasonable doubt, or my guy gets acquitted. And I have to say there's lots of reasonable doubt here."

"If you say so."

"What I'd like to find out, if you'll bear with me, is what she was like."

"She had a brilliant, clear, logical mind, and a facility for getting the most difficult concepts across to her students. Her specialty was particle physics, the study of the fundamental particles of matter. She was always willing to give the students extra time."

"How did she get along with people? The students? Other faculty members?"

"We're not playing 'blame the victim' here, are we, Monty?"

"No, just trying to get a handle on what factors might have been at play in her life."

"That lack of precision wouldn't get you very far in her physics department."

"I'm sure you're right."

"Meika was a wonderful person. Always courteous, friendly, not prone to displays of ego even when she was brighter than ninety-seven percent of the people in the room, whether the classroom or the faculty lounge. Everyone was horrified when they heard about her death."

"What about her personal life? Did you know her outside the office?"

"She and my wife, Ellie, played tennis together. So, I sometimes saw her outside the university. Ellie was devastated when she got the news."

"So, Meika's personality? Can you tell me anything more about her?"

"Always on an even keel. She had strong opinions on certain things. Social justice, academic bullshit, students getting wasted at night and wasting time the following day. But she was never a scold, just quietly and persuasively made her views known."

"Ever show signs of a temper?"

"Did she provoke somebody into killing her, you mean?" Monty raised his hands in a noncommittal kind of shrug. "I never even heard her raise her voice, and never heard anybody else say she'd got worked up into a temper or a snit. That wasn't Meika. If she disagreed with you, she let you know it, but she made her case in a quiet, cool, rational manner. Remember she got herself out of East Germany. Kept her cool crossing from East to West Berlin and into a new life over here. And if you were in an argument with her and you were right, she would concede with a simple 'I see that you are correct.' She was — well, we used to tease her about it, in a good-natured way — we'd say, 'Meika, you are so *disciplined*.' You know, making a little joke about her being German. And she would thicken her accent and say '*Jawohl!*' So, no, if she ever lost her temper, none of us saw it happen. None of us heard about it happening off stage either."

Which left Monty to wonder about the scene described by Alban MacNair, Meika "hollering" and slamming the car door and stalking off into the night. Then, again, passion moves people in unpredictable ways.

The Crown's office provided Monty with some more information late that afternoon. The police had gone door to door and questioned residents of Francklyn Street. Two of the people living near the theology school had heard some shouting between a man and a woman but had no information beyond that. People farther from that scene and therefore closer to the southern tip of the peninsula had heard nothing and had no information to impart.

Of more interest to Monty was the transcript of the police interview with the woman's husband, Commodore Hubert Rendell. Monty sat at his desk and read the transcript. Meika Keller and her husband had attended a dinner and auction for Symphony Nova Scotia. She seemed to be preoccupied throughout the evening; she had turned down an invitation to see friends afterwards, and the couple returned home. Rendell went to sleep at around ten or before and thought nothing was amiss when she was not there at six thirty in the morning because she often went to work early. She had recently met up with the opera singer Fried Habler, having known him back in Germany, and shortly afterwards, she embarked on an impromptu excursion to Europe to take in a couple of operas. She took some photos and they did not turn out.

The police obtained a second statement from Rendell after the MacNair incident came to light. After the preliminaries, the police got to the night of, or before, her death.

"Did you think there was something going on between your wife and Lieutenant-Colonel MacNair?"

"No, I did not."

"But, as you know now, she was seen with MacNair not far from your house the night she died."

"I have no idea what that was about. I wish to God she had confided in me about whatever problem she had with him."

"What can you tell us about Ms. Keller's acquaintance with Alban MacNair?"

"It was MacNair who introduced me to Meika, actually. There was a dinner at the Army mess, you know, at Royal Artillery Park."

"When was that?"

"A year or so after my divorce from my first wife. The divorce was in 1978."

Monty restrained himself from being distracted by the reference to a first wife and got back to the transcript. "You were at the dinner by yourself then, or . . . ?"

"Well, with some of the other men and their wives, other naval officers, fraternizing with the Army. We were all in a group. I saw MacNair there, and we greeted each other."

"How long had you known Alban MacNair at that point?"

"Forever. I was Navy and he was Army, from an Army family going way back, but we would see each other at various events. Of course, I frequently left port to carry out my responsibilities, and he was posted to other parts of Canada and other parts of the world, but we would see each other during our times here in Halifax. I would call him an acquaintance, not a friend."

"Were you on unfriendly terms?"

"No, just not close at all. And I have to say I always found him peculiar with regard to Meika."

Oh, Christ, thought Monty.

"In what way?"

"Just, well, not completely at ease whenever we were in the same room together."

"They had a relationship before she started seeing you?"

"Whatever they were to each other, it had ended long before she and I met at RA Park. He was married to Connie."

"And you're not sure what accounted for the awkwardness, if I may put it that way."

"Right. If he was carrying a torch for her, the feeling was not reciprocated by Meika, though she was always cordial to him."

Exactly the opposite of what Alban MacNair had told Monty.

"So, you and Meika began seeing each other after that initial meeting and eventually married."

"Yes, we married a year or so after that. Year and a half."

"And your children lived with?"

"They lived with me."

That was fairly unusual. Most often, in Monty's experience, the children lived with their mother. The police hadn't pursued it.

"You and Meika would see MacNair from time to time at military events in the city?"

"Yes, though as you likely know, MacNair had a number of overseas postings, and he spent a considerable amount of time at the Army base in New Brunswick — Gagetown — before he returned to Halifax last year."

"And he acted odd or peculiar in Meika's presence."

"In my view, yes."

"Had they seen each other recently? I don't mean the night of her death, but recently otherwise?"

"Not as far as I know. Not as far as I *knew*, I should say."

Monty picked up the phone and called Bill MacEwen. They greeted each other, then Monty said, "I just read through the transcript. This will come with more of your disclosure, but I'd like to ask you a couple of questions now."

"Ask away."

"Can you tell me something about the opera singer, Habler, and his relationship with Meika Keller?"

"They went to school together in Leipzig. And in fact she was not Meika Keller back then."

"Oh, I didn't know that."

"Yeah, she was Edelgard Vogt-Becker. Changed her name after she fled East Germany. Habler didn't get out until the wall came down and Germany was reunified. He went to Vienna and signed up with the Vienna State Opera. He came to this country just after Christmas to do master classes in the music department at Dal and also at the University of Toronto. When he arrived here, he met up with Meika — for the first time since they were in school. He gave a little spiel about their reunion at a reception some weeks after they met up. Meika wasn't there on that occasion; she'd gone to Europe. But apparently it went over well. People who knew her were pleased to hear him speak about her with such affection. And he had Meika and her husband over to his place one evening for dinner. So that's the story on Habler."

"You say she went to Europe?"

"Yes, a short trip. Left here January twenty-sixth and was back on the thirty-first. Just an opera excursion, Monty. Inspired, I assume, by meeting up with Habler again. Take in a few performances and then fly home, and back to work. Nothing dramatic for her on European soil this time."

"Quite a dramatic life she had before, though, leaving East Germany under stressful circumstances, being shot at during her escape."

"Yes, and her daughter died not long afterwards, while they were still in West Germany."

"The poor woman, going through all that. I assume the police have given consideration to the possibility that something from her past came back to haunt her? After Habler went public with her new identity and location?"

"It's not a new identity and location. She's been in this country, as Meika Keller, since 1974."

"New perhaps to those who had known her in Germany."

"She left Germany twenty-two years ago. We're not in the business of chasing phantoms, Monty. We're confident we have the right man. Look at the evidence. She and MacNair together, overlooking the water the night she died, him chasing her behind the houses, being away from his car for at least seven or eight minutes, and we don't know how much longer after that. And the spate of phone calls. That says *stalker* to me, and of course we know he was particularly aggressive on the night of February sixth."

"That's not the way he explains the relationship."

"Well, he's not likely to portray himself in an even worse light, is he?"

"Still, it's pretty thin. No evidence at all connecting him to her actual death or her presence in the water."

"I don't see it that way."

"I know. Well, thanks for your time, Bill. Bye for now."

Brennan

Brennan had headed off to O'Carroll's the previous evening after talking to his brother on the phone, and it was one o'clock the next morning when he made his way through the slushy streets to the parish house; the Book of the Names of the Dead didn't even enter his mind. He had only one thought in his mind: to have one more drink for the road to oblivion. He had a smoke, downed a glass of Jameson, performed his ablutions, and collapsed into bed. But oblivion didn't come; Meika Keller's face, nearly translucent under the shallow waters, her blue eyes riveted on his own, made its appearance in his mind, in his conscience, and it felt like an eternity before the image faded and he drifted away into sleep. He was jolted into consciousness a few short hours later by the sound of a vacuum cleaner being dragged along the corridor and banging against his door. His throat was dry, his stomach sick, and his mood murderous. The hallway did not have to be vacuumed at half seven in the morning. *That one* was trying to make a point again, in her far from subtle way. He tried to get back to sleep, but it wasn't going to happen. And, besides, wasn't there something he had to do? He was going to look up . . . the Book of the Names of the Dead, that was it. He raised his head, painfully, and pulled his body up out of the bed. He scrabbled around his desk and found a couple of oatmeal cookies, which he wolfed down with a glass of tap water. Then he brushed his teeth and had a shower. Didn't bother to shave.

He left his room and walked on silent feet into the hallway. There she was again, still bent over her noisome and utterly unnecessary labours on the floor. He started to walk past her, and she leapt a foot off the ground, then whirled around clutching her heart. "Oh! Father Burke! You scared me!" The woman would be frightened of the Lamb of God. He ignored her and kept going.

He went downstairs, out the door, and crossed over to the church. He entered the sacristy, where Monsignor O'Flaherty kept the books in a cabinet. What year was it when he saw Meika Keller entering a name? Four years ago? He had forgotten the name, but he knew he would find it just above the name of the young prisoner who had been murdered. That happened in 1992 or 1993, Brennan remembered; he had been invited to speak at the funeral. He reached into the cabinet and brought out the books. Ah. There it was, in 1993. Dwayne Brandon Gowly. But the name a few spaces above it on the page, which had been written in by Meika Keller, was now unreadable. It had been scratched out, scribbled over with black ink. He couldn't make out even one letter. At some point, someone had decided that a certain name, a certain person, should not be remembered.

CHAPTER VII

Monty

Monty suspected that the Crown attorney was right, that Monty was chasing phantoms on behalf of his client. And those phantoms, if that's what they were, gave him no rest over the weekend. He kept returning to the notion that the evidence against Alban MacNair was patchy enough that the Crown would have difficulty establishing guilt beyond a reasonable doubt. But a murder case always sat more comfortably with Monty if he could come up with a competing theory about the death of the victim. And in this case of course he had one. Suicide. Meika Keller's body had floated in on the tide and landed on the beach at Point Pleasant Park. But what drove her to such a desperate act? People who knew her, including her husband, were adamant that nothing had happened to plunge her into a state of depression. But if she had been despondent over MacNair's rejection of her advances, would she have masked her anguish, leaving her family oblivious? She was out of sorts after her trip to Europe, but her husband said this was because her holiday photos had not turned out. It did not sound as if she had been noticeably distressed about anything. There was no medical crisis, no failure in her career, no sign of anything like that. She was, by all accounts, a brilliant professor of science, popular with the students and faculty. She was a tireless champion of the arts, particularly of music, and her charitable and fundraising work was appreciated and acknowledged publicly and often. He recalled seeing her name in connection with fundraisers for the IWK children's hospital here in the city.

If there was nothing in Halifax that could explain her death, was there something in her past? Something in Germany? Well, he'd been over this ground before. She had met up again with a schoolmate from the old country, the renowned operatic tenor Fried Habler. He had relayed the news to people back home in Leipzig. That city of course had been on the eastern side of the border when Germany was still divided. Had the reunion with Habler set off a chain of events that came to a deadly climax on February 6 in Halifax?

Meika's phone records had been checked and yielded nothing but bad news for Monty's client. Nine calls to the victim's office from MacNair. None to her office or home phone from Germany or anywhere else in Europe. Meika did not have a cellular phone. Computer checks showed that she used her workplace computer solely for her work. She and her husband had recently set up an electronic mail — email — account; both had access to it, and Hubert Rendell gave investigators the password. There was nothing questionable in the messages found. There was no indication one way or the other whether either of them had a private email account. Rendell said that, despite her background in science, his wife had shown little interest in the new world of information technology. Had there been any regular mail at the house, letters or packages, which might have caused concern?

Monty could hardly call the commodore on behalf of the man accused of killing his wife and ask whether some third party had been sending her letters. But the police must have checked this. So, on Monday morning, Monty sought to enlist the assistance of his adversary once again. He called the Crown's office and left a message for Bill MacEwen. Bill returned his call half an hour later.

"Bill, sorry to bother you again."

"No problem, Monty. What can I do for you?"

"Don't tempt me like that, Bill, lest I suggest that you drop these unfounded charges against my client and call a press conference to announce that honourable and courageous decision on your part."

"No, I probably can't accommodate you there, you shyster. So, if there's nothing else . . ."

"There is something else."

"Kind of thought so."

"You told me about the phone records and the computers, but what about the mail? Did the police get anything on that?"

"Nothing there. They asked Hubert and, more to the point, they asked the housekeeper. She works mornings Monday to Friday, and she's there when the mail arrives. Of course, at first, she claimed she never looks at the family's letters, never even notices the envelopes, but eventually she came clean and said she sorts it out into separate piles for each member of the family. So, of course, she eyeballs everything that crosses the transom. Nothing strange or threatening. Nothing foreign apart from some flyers about opera productions in Italy and at the Met in New York. There were letters from a couple of acquaintances in the United States. Those people were called and found to have nothing useful to add." Before Monty could ask, MacEwen said, "And it was pretty much the same situation at her workplace. The person who receives and distributes the mail at Saint Mary's said she never noticed anything unusual. There were mailings that seemed to be mass-produced, from physics departments at various universities and think tanks in this and other countries. She did not recall any personal letters from Europe. And she did not recall Ms. Keller ever appearing alarmed after mail time — or at any other time, for that matter."

"All right. Thanks again, Bill."

"There's nobody on the radar except Alban MacNair, Monty."

After lunch that afternoon, Monty's secretary, Tina, stepped in to say he had missed a call from a Mrs. Kelly, who was supposed to come to the office ten minutes from now. "She said there has been an unavoidable delay. The bishop arrived, or at least that's what she said."

Monty laughed.

"Who is Mrs. Kelly?" Tina asked.

"She's the priests' housekeeper over at Saint Bernadette's church. I've got her as a witness. Meika Keller stopped in at the church the night she died."

"Oh!"

"And it would throw Mrs. Kelly right off course, the bishop arriving unannounced." Monty had seen her fluttering around Archbishop Dennis Cronin on several occasions. "That's fine, Tina. I'll see her when she gets here."

Monty returned to his regular preoccupation, trying to think of something he could produce that could get this case dismissed far short of a trial. He might have some luck at the preliminary inquiry, which would be held for the purpose of determining whether there was enough evidence to send the case to be tried. All the evidence was circumstantial, which was often the situation. There was no direct evidence linking MacNair to Meika Keller's death. The only witnesses were those who had seen her earlier that evening. Well, all right, late that night. A few hours before her death.

And here was one of those witnesses now. Mrs. Kelly, the house-keeper, was ushered into his office and now stood, uncertain, in front of his desk. He rose to greet her. God love her, she had certainly dressed for the occasion. Monty had seen her countless times at the rectory in a housedress and apron, her faded blond hair sometimes held back by a kerchief.

Now she was decked out in her best go-to-Mass-on-Sunday ensemble. She had on a fur coat of a kind Monty had not seen since his aunts had worn them decades ago. It smelled of mothballs, and Monty suspected she had taken it out of storage especially for this occasion. And, perhaps looking ahead, for the trial. She had on a pale-blue felt hat that Monty would have described as a tam except that it rose up in sort of a crown on one side. He could see stitches, and he had the impression that it might at one time have had a veil attached. Monty helped her off with her coat and hung it on the coatrack. Her hair had just been done in a Margaret Thatcher–style helmet, and Monty could smell the hairspray. Mrs. Kelly's dress matched the hat in colour and had a short jacket over it. She wore matching blue high-heeled shoes, in spite of the slushy weather outside, and completed the outfit with a blue leather handbag and white gloves. The outfit wailed "doesn't get out much" and Monty immediately chastised himself for being uncharitable.

"Mrs. Kelly, thanks for coming. Please have a seat. Would you like tea or coffee?"

"Oh! A cup of tea would be lovely. Cream and sugar if it's not too much trouble."

"No trouble at all." Monty buzzed Darlene at reception and ordered the tea.

"I'm sorry to be late, Mr. Collins! But His Grace came by just as I was about to leave. He was looking for Father Burke." Her lips compressed themselves into a thin line of disapproval. Darlene came in with the cup of tea and handed it to Mrs. Kelly, who thanked her profusely. She took a sip. "Lovely! Anyway, as usual, he was nowhere to be seen. Father, I mean. I don't know how many times His Grace has come looking for him, and nope, not there. Today, he said to me — the bishop said — 'Mrs. Kelly, I know he's a hard man to keep track of.' *You can say that again*, I felt like saying to His Grace, but of course I didn't say a word."

"Of course."

"But anyway, it was 'Mrs. Kelly, whenever you see him, ask him to give me a call.' And then he thanked me and left."

Monty let her ramble for a few minutes and then got down to business. "Now, Mrs. Kelly, did you know Meika Keller?"

"Oh, I only saw her at Mass from time to time. But she usually went to the Latin Mass with all that high-falutin' music." Father Burke's Mass, she meant. "She was really nice. Not the kind that would go on and on talking your ear off, but friendly anyway. Real smart, taught science at the university. The things women can do nowadays!" Monty was grateful that his wife, Professor MacNeil, was not on hand to hear that.

"So, other than the times you saw her at Mass, you hadn't known her well?"

"No, not well, God rest her, the poor soul." She made a sign of the cross. "Should never have happened."

That was stating the obvious.

"Now, on the night of February sixth, she came to the rectory?"

The woman's face was animated as she leaned forward and said, "Oh, yes! She came up to the door and I answered, and I invited her in. And she said it was very important that she talk to him."

"Him?"

"Father."

"Burke."

"Yes." Again, the lips clamped down with churchy disapproval.

"So those were her words? Very important to talk to Father Burke?"

"Well, I'm not sure of her exact words."

"Try to remember." *Try to be a witness I can use.*

"I think it was 'Excuse me. Is Father Burke in? I'd like to speak with him.'"

"All right. And what time was this, do you remember?"

She said then, excitement once again creeping into her voice, "This is just like being on the witness stand in court!"

You have no idea. Monty kept that to himself. "The time?"

"It was ten o'clock exactly. We have a grandfather clock in the parlour, and it chimes the hours."

"And what did you say when she asked for Father Burke?"

"I hated to tell her —" In Monty's experience, when someone says "I hate to tell you this," it means they are bubbling over, can't wait to tell you whatever it is "— 'No, I'm sorry, I don't think he's in his room, but I'll check for you.' Of course, I knew he'd gone out as usual and hadn't come back. Anyway, I told her to have a seat in the parlour and I'd go up and check. And sure enough, knock, knock, anybody home? No! Not there. *Again.*"

Monty couldn't help himself. Things were strained between himself and Burke following the events that had unfolded in Belfast, and there was no question that Monty hoped to use Burke's truancy to his own advantage in this case. But he couldn't help coming to his old friend's defence. "Is Father Burke on duty that late at night, generally? I mean, his schedule begins with Mass two or three mornings a week at seven thirty, and he serves other Masses, and has the lunch program for the poor and the homeless, and he works at the choir school, and the Schola Cantorum, and . . ."

"A priest is never off duty, Mr. Collins," she scolded him.

"Very well. So, he wasn't in, and you returned to Ms. Keller in the parlour."

Without being conscious of it, Monty assumed, she put a *we are sorry to announce* expression on her face and said, "I told her, 'I'm sorry, but Father went out for the evening and never came back.' Naturally, I didn't say to her that he was probably out *drinking again* with a bunch of his non-priest *cronies* at the Midtown Tavern or at O'Carroll's."

Monty was one of Burke's non-priest cronies at the Midtown, and good for him if he had pals at O'Carroll's as well. God knows, he needed a break from this woman and those like her, who thought priests had to be in their collars, rosary beads at hand, twenty-four hours a day.

Just for the sake of mischief, Monty said, "Sorry, did you say you did tell her he was out drinking or did not tell her?"

"I certainly did not! Somebody has to preserve the dignity of Saint Bernadette's church and rectory."

"What did Ms. Keller say when you told her Father Burke was not available?"

"Oh, it was awful! She looked heartbroken. She said, 'But he told me he would see me here at ten o'clock.'"

"Then what happened?"

"She said she would wait for a few minutes, but then she gave up and ran out of the building."

"Ran?"

"Well, she didn't run exactly, but she didn't waste time hanging around. She went off out the door."

Monty knew he'd be leading the witness into temptation here. "What was her expression like? Her mood?"

"She was upset! It was obvious that something was bothering her, and for some reason, she thought *he* was going to help her. But of course he stood her up. Didn't even bother to come home."

"And you could tell she was upset how?"

"The expression on her face. Disappointed, let down. Worried."

"Anything else you can tell me about that night?"

"That night was like so many other nights, I'm sorry to say, Mr. Collins. Especially since he got back from Ireland. We all know what he got himself into there! With his relatives. A bunch of terrorists, and him in the middle of it all!"

"He is not a terrorist, by any stretch of the imagination, Mrs. Kelly. The Court of Appeal overturned the wrongful conviction against him and released him."

"Yeah, right, he got off." She tried to affect the tone of someone who has seen it all, heard it all. "It's gotten to the point where I'm scared to go to sleep at night."

"What's got to the point? What do you mean?"

"Well, if he did that stuff over there, what might he do here? Especially after a night of guzzling beer and whiskey!"

"Now, Mrs. Kelly, I just explained to you. He was acquitted, after the Court of Appeal reviewed the trial judge's decision."

But she just sat there with a smug look on her face. If there was one thing more gratifying than Father Burke fucking up while on the booze, it was Father Burke being thrown into prison on charges relating to terrorism. Monty had his doubts about whether, in the event of a trial, he should call this person to the stand. He wanted her testimony of a distraught Meika Keller leaving the church with her problems unresolved, a Meika Keller in the frame of mind to take her own life. But he did not want a witness who would be dismissed as an embittered, vengeful person, the classic disgruntled employee, with an all-too-apparent grudge against Father Burke and his lifestyle, a witness whose credibility would be compromised for precisely that reason.

CHAPTER VIII

Brennan

From what Brennan had been able to discern, the evidence against Lieutenant-Colonel Alban MacNair was sketchy. Brennan felt that he himself was in a state of sin, hoping the man was guilty. Hoping the man could be facing a life sentence in prison, just so Brennan could absolve himself of responsibility for his failure to meet Meika Keller on the night of the crisis that ended her life. Of course, this was despicable on Brennan's part. And even if her death was not a suicide, he still might have prevented it if he had done his duty as a priest and a man, and not gone out on a rip and forgotten all about her. If she had been afraid of someone and had a history with that person, that may have been what she wanted to discuss with him. Brennan understood all this. But whatever the case, he wanted to know. He felt an obligation to know. If MacNair had killed her, that would, presumably at least, be determined at his trial. A trial, however, was a long way off.

If the lieutenant-colonel was innocent, someone else was out there. Getting away with it.

One conclusion was inescapable: something had set Meika off. And this led Brennan to wonder what had prompted her to take an unscheduled trip to Europe. Fried Habler at the opera students' reception had implied that her interest in opera had been rekindled by their reunion, making her long for the opera houses of Milan and Vienna. But maybe there was some other explanation for her sudden departure. At the reception where Brennan had seen Habler, the singer had mentioned that the press back home had reported on Edelgard's renewed acquaintance with Habler, and her new incarnation as Meika Keller. Could this connection have given rise to some other link with her German past? Brennan knew it was a stretch — not to mention a desperate hope — but if there was something else that accounted for her death, and if it wasn't MacNair, Brennan wanted to understand it.

He decided to talk to Fried Habler. The newspaper stories might be a good hook to hang the conversation on. He called the Dalhousie Arts Centre on Monday morning and asked for Habler, only to be told that he was in Toronto and could be reached either at the University of Toronto or the Canadian Opera Company. He left messages at both places and heard back from Habler just after noon.

Brennan introduced himself, told Habler he had heard him sing in Halifax, and congratulated him on a magnificent performance. There was nothing phony about his enthusiasm; Habler was as good as any operatic tenor Brennan had ever heard. They talked about opera for a minute or two before Brennan got to the point.

"I knew Meika Keller. She was a member of my parish here in Halifax. In fact, as painful as it is for me to confess this, she had asked to talk to me about something the night she died, and I was unable to meet with her." Brennan could not bring himself to confess the reason he had missed the rendezvous, though he knew Habler might eventually hear the sordid tale. "So, I let her down when she needed me most, and I feel compelled to try to understand what led to her death."

"Perhaps you are punishing yourself too severely, Father Burke. You could not have known. The chances were that you would have had another opportunity to speak with Edelgard. With Meika. She herself would say it was mathematically unlikely that you would never see her again!"

Unless, Brennan reflected, she was planning to take her life, in which case there was a one hundred percent certainty that he would never see her again.

"Thank you, Mr. Habler."

"We could dispense with formalities, if you wish. Please call me Fried."

"And I'm Brennan. I was wondering about that news story you mentioned, in the Leipzig paper."

"And not only in the Leipzig paper."

"Oh, is that right? I realize that it may not shine a light on what happened, but I'd like to see it if possible. Do you still have it?"

"Of course. It is in German, naturally."

"That's all right. I can read German." Brennan had learned German along with Italian while studying in Rome twenty years ago.

"Oh! I will be returning to Halifax this week. Perhaps some time we can get together and have a little session of German conversation!"

"I'd like that."

"But, for now, I can fax the news article to you."

Brennan gave him the fax number for Saint Bernadette's. Then he asked, "So what role are you singing now?"

"I am very pleased to say I shall be singing Tristan."

"Congratulations! I know you'll be up to the challenge."

"I hope to be equal to it. It is the opportunity of a lifetime."

"Who will be the 'wild Irish maid'?"

"Do you have anyone in mind, Brennan?"

"Oh, either of my two sisters would make Tristan earn his Tristan chord."

"Perhaps I shall meet them someday! But in the C.O.C. performance, I shall be singing to Silke Frandsen's Isolde. She is excellent."

"She is indeed. I would love to see a performance. You never know."

"If you are in Toronto and are able to come, I will be happy to secure you the best seat in the house!"

"Thank you, Fried. I'll let you get back to the helm. And thank you for the fax."

The fax came through, a short piece in the *Leipziger Volkszeitung*. There was nothing about Edelgard's life in Germany apart from the fact that she had attended the same school as Habler and that they had both stood out as talented students, he in music, she in science and sport. The Dalhousie University music department would be pleased with the prominent play given to the department in the write-up of Habler's stint in Canada. Symphony Nova Scotia was mentioned as well, and Edelgard Vogt-Becker's generous support of it.

Later that day, after listening to his grade six students sing parts of Antonio Vivaldi's *Gloria*, Brennan thought again about the piece in the Leipzig paper, specifically the references to music and the friendship with Fried Habler. The article mentioned Edelgard's position as a professor of physics in Halifax, but it did not specify her place of employment. Perhaps the writer thought she and Habler were both associated with Dalhousie; it was not clear one way or the other. It occurred to Brennan that if anyone back home in Germany wanted to contact her, the person might call or write to her at Dal or, if unsure, might get in touch with Habler and ask for her address or number. Or might try to reach her through Symphony Nova Scotia. It wouldn't hurt to check.

He was acquainted with some of the members of the symphony orchestra, so he made a call to one of them, and she said she would ask around. It wasn't long before he heard back; there had been no phone calls or letters for Meika Keller. So, he would try Dal. It was a fine, sunny day, so he left the parish house and walked to the campus of Dalhousie University, where the architecture ranged from Georgian-style elegance to brutalist modern. A stark example of the latter group was the Arts Centre, a massive structure dominated by precast concrete with local stones embedded in it. Fortunately, he found the interior warmer and more inviting, with open spaces and several auditoriums. And, dear to Brennan's heart, great acoustics in the Rebecca Cohn Auditorium. He had attended a good many concerts here over the years, and he was familiar as well with the offices of the music department. He was on his way to see one of the music profs he knew, when he saw a man washing the windows of the box office. Good, this would save him from having to cobble together a story for the prof.

"Excuse me." The man gave his window a final swipe and turned to Brennan. "Could you tell me who distributes the mail here? I have a —"

"That would be Dorothy. Wilson. That's one of her duties here. Little lady with big hair. She's upstairs. Try the fourth floor." He pointed a finger upwards and returned to his work.

"Thanks."

Brennan headed up the stairs. He wasn't long in finding her, a short woman with masses of long, curly grey hair tied back in a ponytail.

"Excuse me. Mrs. Wilson?"

"Yes?"

"I'm sorry to be bothering you like this. I'll only keep you a minute. I'm Father Brennan Burke. Meika Keller was one of my parishioners."

"Oh, yes. Mrs. Keller. That was a terrible thing."

"Yes, it certainly was. Of course, we know the police have a man charged in connection with her death."

"A colonel in the Army! I don't think he did it!"

"Hard to know. Now, as I say, she was a member of my parish, and her death has hit me hard."

"Oh, I'm sure it has!"

"And she left me with some questions, some things we never had a chance to talk about." He wasn't about to say why they never had a chance to talk. "One of the things I've been wondering about, in light of the arrival of Fried Habler on the music scene here at Dal, is whether someone might have heard about her connection with him — there was a little story in the newspaper in her hometown — I was wondering whether someone might have taken note of that and tried to contact her here. The news article didn't mention Saint Mary's, so . . ."

"You're wondering if anything suspicious came in the mail for her, from Germany!"

"Well . . ."

"Of course, if anyone sent her a mysterious letter, she would be the only one who would have opened it. We don't open other people's mail here!"

"No, no, I didn't mean to suggest that."

"The only thing that I remember coming for her was —"

"Yes?" Brennan's hopes had got the better of him, the better of his manners. He apologized for interrupting and said, "Please go on."

"A postcard, that's all it was; not a letter in an envelope. And it was 'care of Herr Habler.' So maybe somebody did follow up on the news story, but, whatever it was, there was nothing secret about it, because it was just a postcard and the message was there for all to see. All who speak German, anyway, including Professor Habler. I never thought of it again until I heard about her death."

Christ. Brennan's hunch had been sound enough; something had come for her here. But it was only a postcard, not a secret missive in a plain brown envelope. Even so, it could turn out to be evidence, a matter for the police.

"Did the police come by and ask about messages?"

"No! Maybe they didn't think of us here since she worked at Saint Mary's. Oh, God, should I have reported it? But there was nothing to it anyway."

"A postcard from where? Leipzig?"

"No, it was from Berlin. I would not have known because it just showed a great big building. But the postmark was Berlin. You know, it's fascinating some of the places we get letters or postcards from here. Well, they don't come for me! But the music professors, they seem to know people all over the world."

"What did it say, or . . ."

She laughed. "I don't speak German. It was just a few lines, written to 'Frau Keller.'"

"Did you notice the name of the sender by any chance?"

"Professor Habler might know. He was in Toronto when it arrived, so I waited till he came back, and I gave it to him to pass along to her."

Wunderbar. Habler would know what it said.

"Thank you very much for your help."

"You're welcome, Father."

"Professor Habler is in Toronto again, I know."

"Yes. He's due back on Wednesday and has his master class from two to four in the afternoon. You know, I never had a clue about opera at all, even though they teach it here. But Professor Habler is such a nice guy, a real character, that I started peeking in at some of the rehearsals here. I think I'm becoming an opera fan!"

"Good. I imagine he'd be pleased to hear that. I'll come by and ask him about the postcard on Wednesday."

CHAPTER IX

Monty

Lieutenant-Colonel Alban MacNair arrived at Monty's law office on Wednesday morning and handed Monty a thickly stuffed envelope. A copy of his record of military service. Monty put it aside on the desk.

"Thanks for bringing this, Lieutenant-Colonel MacNair. We will want to put your character in evidence. Unless there is some reason not to."

"What in the hell do you mean by that, Collins? 'Unless there is some reason.' I would like to think my character will speak for itself."

"Things that speak for themselves are not always good news in a courtroom. There is a legal term, used mainly in civil litigation, *res ipsa loquitur*. The thing speaks for itself. It generally means that some act or circumstance, by the very fact of its existence, is evidence of the fault alleged in the trial."

"I'll say it again. I think my character will speak for itself in a court of law. Unless you can get this bogus murder charge dismissed before we have to go to court."

"There is nothing I would like better. But your evidence, that you were trying to discourage Ms. Keller's ambitions for a relationship and that you left the area near the waters of the Northwest Arm without causing her any harm or putting her in danger, that evidence is contradicted at least on the face of it by the evidence of the witness who drove along Francklyn Street seven or eight minutes after first seeing you there and saw that your car was still in the same place. Without you in it."

"His timing is off."

"So, it will be your word against his. If we put you on the stand."

"Of course you're going to put me on the stand!"

"But, Alban, your story does not sound credible even to me, and I want to believe you. It will sound even more hollow to the Crown prosecutor, who is trying to put you away. And by the time he gets through with you on cross-examination, how do you think it will sound to a jury?"

"What is it about my *story*, as you put it, that has you so hostile?"

"I wouldn't say hostile; I'd say concerned. What bothers me is the timing. And those multiple phone calls to the victim's office. That, to a jury, will give the impression that you were stalking her. Why make all those calls, in rapid succession, to a woman you are trying to avoid? It doesn't ring true."

Despite the military bravado the Army man tried to impart, there was no question that he was on shaky ground and he knew it. Monty could see the tension in the hands that gripped the edge of the desk.

"So, what about those calls, Alban?"

The client took a deep breath and blew it out. "I got a bit fed up. With her putting the pressure on me. I tried to call her to talk it out. And I didn't get any answer. Or she pretended to be busy and had to hang up. As I say, I got fed up with this, and I was determined to get her to talk to me."

"Nine calls?"

"I know, I know. It doesn't look good, but it was just frustration. I wasn't stalking her! And I did not hurt her."

Monty wasn't any more impressed than the Crown would be, or the jury. But the calls were there, and Monty would have to put the best spin he could on them when it came time for the trial.

Now, on to other evidence, which was equally if not more damaging. "All right. Moving on," Monty said, looking directly into his client's eyes, "what would account for her blood on your glove? And yes, the lab results are in. It was her blood."

MacNair was ready for this one. "It was icy. She slipped when she was . . ."

"When she was?"

"Running away. She fell. I got to her and helped her up. I must have touched her."

"Touched her where?"

"Jesus, I wasn't thinking of all this at the time, cataloguing it for future reference! But I think she cut her face when she fell on the ice. Cut her mouth. I must have tried to wipe the blood away."

Maybe it happened the way MacNair said it did, or maybe not. Monty had no way of knowing. "She also had injuries to her hands."

"Oh, yeah? Well, maybe I held her hand when she was getting up. Got blood on myself then."

"But it was so cold that you had gloves on. Wouldn't she have gloves on, too? How could blood have got on you if her hands were covered?"

"I don't fucking know, Collins! I just told you; I didn't memorize my actions, didn't know I'd be facing a murder charge, for Christ's sake."

Monty pictured his client on the stand, losing his temper and presenting the jury with the image of an angry man. A man who might have lost his temper and somehow caused the death of the woman who had him so enraged.

"Let's get back to the question of character, Alban. If we put your character in issue, that is, if we portray you as a sterling citizen with no criminal history, as a person who would never commit a crime like this, that opens the door to the Crown to bring in evidence of bad character. If you have any prior criminal convictions —"

"The only thing I have is a breathalyzer conviction here in the province, and that was ages ago."

"Lost your licence then."

"Yeah. My wife wasn't too happy with me, but I was away a lot that year anyway. It was back in 1979 or so. I haven't had a drink since some time in the 1980s. Who cares if they bring up an old breathalyzer offence? No juror in his right mind would say that makes me a killer."

"All right. You're a career Army man, I take it? Went in right after completing your education?"

"Yes, I am and I did."

"So, this will be the record of your entire adult career."

"You got it."

"I'll take a few minutes to skim through it here."

"Go ahead."

The lieutenant-colonel was born in wartime and was now fifty-two years old. And his record was indeed an impressive one, with timely promotions and glowing testimonials. This was all to the good. Much of his time on Canadian soil had been served at the big Army base in Gagetown, New Brunswick. He was now on the staff of LFAA, Land Force Atlantic Area, here in Halifax. He had taken part in a number of peacekeeping missions: Egypt, Cyprus, Croatia. He had been posted to Canadian Forces Base Lahr in West Germany in the 1970s; he was part of the 4 Canadian Mechanized Brigade Group. The worst that was said of him earlier in his personnel record was that he occasionally drank to excess, but never while on active duty. There was nothing recent relating to alcohol. There was a reference to a letter placed in his record for a breach of some kind. But he continued with his duties after whatever it was. Monty did not see the letter among the documents in front of him.

Nothing violent, except perhaps in the line of duty as a soldier. If, *if,* these were the only blots on his copybook, his character should not be a problem. He looked across the desk at his client. "I see you served in Germany, Alban, at Canadian Forces Base Lahr."

"That's right."

"I don't suppose you ran into Meika Keller while you were there?"

"She's from Leipzig. I was in Lahr. Look at a map, Monty."

"I know people in Montreal, in Calgary, in Vancouver, Alban. I don't have to tell you to look at those distances on a map."

"I was in Lahr, West Germany, as part of our NATO commitment during the Cold War. East Germany was cut off from the West, remember?"

"That's a 'no,' I take it."

"Correct."

"I had to ask. I've looked through this, and it certainly appears to be a shining testimonial. But is there anything I should know, anything that didn't make it into the official file?"

MacNair broke eye contact with Monty for a second, then reverted to his customary direct gaze. "No, just what's there."

"Now there's one thing . . ."

"The letter on file."

"Right. What was that about?"

"It was about the unification of the forces. My outburst about it would have been a minor thing if it had taken place in-house, so to speak, but I made the mistake of talking out of school. I went on a bit of a rant in the presence of some civilians, including politicians. That's just not done. It earned me a Report of Shortcomings in my pers file. Personnel file. It was just before I got posted to Germany, early 1970s. I come from a long and, may I say, distinguished line of Army officers. My great-grandfather, grandfather, father, uncles, my brother. World War I, World War II, Korea. An Army family. And none of them, myself included, were happy with what Hellyer did in the 1960s. You know what I'm talking about."

Monty did. The Royal Canadian Air Force, the Royal Canadian Navy, and the Canadian Army were stripped of those illustrious identities and unified into one organization, simply, the Canadian Armed Forces. Paul Hellyer was minister of defence at the time. Monty remembered the resentment the policy had engendered in the three services. The merger may have made sense in terms of a unified national defence policy, and the elimination of duplication in services and expenses and all of that, but Monty knew how wildly unpopular it was among the soldiers, sailors, and airmen.

MacNair said, "Anyone with even the slightest knowledge of the military and of history knows there is a long tradition of loyalty and pride in one's own branch of the services. And those traditions help keep morale up among those of us who are sent out to fight and die for our country, and that feeling should have been respected. Imagine what a Navy or an Air Force man thought of getting into a *green* uniform and having Army ranks foisted upon him! Fellows I knew in the Navy called the new uniform the 'bus driver's uniform.' Some called it the 'unibag,' comparing it to a garbage bag. They refused to use the new ranks. No sergeants here, folks. Some admirals quit over it. None of us liked it, no matter what branch of the forces we were in. Some of the damage has been undone over the years, but we're still a long way from what we were. In the glory days!"

"I understand."

"So anyway, with all this being forced on us against our will, I was sitting with a couple of Navy buddies at a feel-good session held here in the city with senior ranks and politicians, and things got a little heated. I gave voice to my opinions on the matter in front of the wrong people. Hence the report in my file."

"This is a military town, Alban. The jury's not going to hold that against you."

"Well, then, I'm clean, counsellor."

"Glad to hear it. Now, I'm getting ahead of myself here, looking to the trial."

"Christ, I can't even stand thinking about it."

"I understand. But it never hurts to plan ahead. So, I'm wondering about character witnesses. We have the written record, which is good, but it's also helpful to have the jury see and hear someone testifying to your sterling character."

What Monty didn't say was that he wanted to speak to people who knew MacNair, to help Monty himself assess the character of his client. He wanted to get some idea, if he could, of the kind of man MacNair was. Was he or was he not, in the estimation of those who knew him, the kind of man who would, somehow, get Meika Keller out into the surf of the Atlantic Ocean and drown her?

"So, Alban, who do you suggest I speak to as a potential witness to tell the court what a jolly good fellow you are? A man who would never commit the kind of crime you are charged with here."

"How many do you want?"

"For now, a couple will do. I take it you have any number of people who would give you a glowing reference."

"I'd like to think so. Colonel Bryce Simmons would be one. Deputy Commander of Land Force Atlantic Area. He's chief of staff."

"Sounds good."

"My family and Bryce's have been friends since I was a Cub Scout." He thought for a few seconds and said, "And Lieutenant-General John Joe Patriquin. He's Air Force."

"Patriquin, great! My father knew him."

"Is that right?"

"Yeah. They didn't serve together, but I know they've met at gatherings of some of the veterans who served in England, or flew out of England, during the war."

"What was your father's war service?"

"Intelligence."

"Oh? That sounds intriguing."

"Yes, he was one of the codebreakers at Bletchley Park. He was a grad student in mathematics here in Halifax, left here for Cambridge to do his PhD, and was recruited to work on the German codes. Came back after the war and taught at Dal, eventually becoming head of the math department."

"Sounds like a clever fellow, your dad."

"True enough. So, good, I'll speak to Lieutenant-General Patriquin and Colonel Simmons about testifying to your good character."

Brennan

Brennan made a phone call to Fried Habler at the Dal Arts Centre at four thirty on Wednesday afternoon.

"Ah, Brennan. How are you today?"

"I'm fine, thank you, Fried. I was wondering if I could have a word with you. It's about Meika Keller."

"Yes, certainly. I am just about to leave my office now, but I have an idea. Do you enjoy drinking beer, Brennan?"

"Is the *Papst katholisch?*"

"Is the . . . oh, yes, I understand. Very good. Well, I have a fine selection of German beers at my house. I have a dinner engagement later in the evening; otherwise I would invite you to have a meal at my place. But if you would care for a glass or two of beer, you would be most welcome."

"That sounds like just the thing, Fried. Just tell me where and when."

"Let's make it six o'clock. I am renting a little cottage-style house on Clyde Street, number fifty-four seventy. A light-blue colour. I shall be waiting for you there."

"Perfect." And perfect for another reason as well. Brennan could stop in at the revered Clyde Street Liquor Store, and pick up some cans of Irish lager and stout to replace the German beer that would be consumed during the visit.

Right on the dot of six, Brennan was standing at the door of a small shingled cottage with two five-sided Scottish roof dormers. Fried Habler opened the door, and Brennan complimented him on his residence.

"Thank you, Brennan. Yes, I am very happy in it. And do you know why I chose this one over other possibilities? Because this area of the city with all these beautiful wooden houses used to be known as Schmidtville. And this was Rottenburg Street."

"I didn't know that."

"I suspect the German name fell out of favour sometime, perhaps earlier this century!"

Brennan laughed. "Maybe so. Though they did keep Gottingen Street. And Dresden Row." Where Monty and family lived, a short walk from here. "Whatever the case, it's the Clyde Street Liquor Store I patronize, not the Rottenburg Street Liquor Store."

Brennan handed him his brown paper bag, which contained four cans of Harp and two of Guinness. Canned Guinness was not a patch on the Guinness that was lovingly poured from the taps of a proper Irish bar, but the canned Harp wasn't bad at all. Habler tried to wave away the offering, but Brennan insisted.

"Come in, come in."

He followed his host into the living room, which was notable for antique furnishings and an impressive new sound system, with rows of compact discs stacked beside it in neat columns.

"*Ein Pils? Ein Kölsch?*"

"A Pils will do me just fine, thanks, Fried."

Habler filled two frosted steins with beer and handed one to his guest. "*Prost!*" he said, and they both took their first sip. Brilliant stuff, it was. Brennan pulled out a pack of smokes and raised an eyebrow at his host.

"You go ahead, Brennan. I won't join you." He tapped his throat. "Have to keep the instrument in tune."

"An example I should be following, Fried," he said, then laughed as he lit one up anyway.

They chatted about music, Brennan's Palestrina and Victoria, and Fried's Wagner, about the demands of a choir director trying to keep the bar raised high in the age of new Catholic schlock, and of a heldentenor trying to meet the challenge of the most heroic roles on the operatic stage, where the bar had always been set at high C.

Then, on the second glass, it was time to ask about Meika. "Fried, you know about my interest in the death of Meika Keller, and you know the reason for my interest."

"Yes, I do."

"I don't imagine anything I learn will serve to ease my conscience about being unable to meet her — failing to meet her — but I feel compelled to find out whatever I can about her death. Learn what I should have learned the night she died. So, I've done a bit of asking around and I discovered that she received a postcard from Germany not long before she died. Before she embarked on what was apparently an unplanned trip to Europe."

"You are correct. She did receive a postcard. It came from Berlin, and the person who distributes the post at the Arts Centre gave it to me. That is the way it was addressed, to Frau Keller through me."

"Right. Do you remember when it arrived?"

"I am not certain of that, because it came when I was in Toronto. I saw it when I returned to Halifax, and that would have been the week of twenty-second January. Yes, I was back at the Dal Arts Centre on Monday, so the twenty-second. I got the card and gave it to Meika Keller that day. I am sorry that I have not retained a memory of the date it was posted." He shrugged. "It was not significant at the time."

"No, I understand. Did you hand it to her personally?"

"Yes, I did."

"How did she react?"

"Unfortunately, Brennan, the weather was frightful that day, snow and rain, so I put it in an envelope when I took it to Saint Mary's. I handed the envelope to her; she thanked me, and we chatted about other things. She did not open the envelope in my presence." He hesitated, then said, "Of course, because it was a postcard, I could not stop myself from reading it before placing it in the envelope."

"We would all do the same."

"But there was nothing in the message that would cause any alarm. It said, and I am translating from the original German, 'Congratulations, Frau Keller!' And I think I am remembering correctly, or I have the general idea anyway. It said, 'I always wished I had your talents for sport and for science. Alas, I am talented only at reading and researching. But good for you! I must go; the scoundrel is here. Yours, L.'"

"Do you know who L is?"

He shook his head. "No, I do not. And the printing was in block letters, so I could not tell you whether it was a man or a woman."

"I don't suppose you know who the scoundrel is."

"No. The word is *Schlingel*. Scoundrel or rascal, that sort of thing."

Brennan didn't want to put Habler on the spot by asking if he had reported the postcard to the police, but he could come at it from another direction. "Did the police speak to you, as somebody who knew Meika Keller?"

"They did. They came to question me. They knew I had recently become acquainted with her again. They wanted to see whether I had an alibi for the night she died!"

"And did you?"

"Yes, you may be confident that you are not sitting in the house of a killer! It was not much of an alibi. I was home in bed. If Commodore Rendell told the police I could not be reached that night, that is the reason."

"Meika's husband tried to reach you?"

"Yes, I found a message on my answering machine when I woke up. I had not even heard the phone bell ringing."

Brennan looked around the room and did not see a phone.

Habler saw him looking and said, "The telephone is in my bedroom." Brennan waited. "I was unconscious. I had passed out from drinking too much of the rum that is so popular here! I am not used to it. So, I was here, asleep. And did not hear the ringing."

"You say Meika's husband left a message?"

"Yes, a message from Commodore Rendell, looking for his wife and sounding quite angry. Not an operatic anger, but that cold kind of anger some people have. Asking where she was, and was she with me! He demanded that I pick up the phone, as if he thought I was in the house ignoring the call."

"What time was that?"

"Oh, it was fairly late. Just before midnight, I believe it was."

"Did you tell the police about his call?"

"I certainly will if they come back again and ask me."

"Now, they're not likely to ask you if they have no reason to think he might have called you. Maybe you should let them know."

"Well . . ."

"Well?"

"Where I come from, Brennan, one does not go looking for trouble by contacting the police. They have not approached me after that quick first visit, so I am making the assumption that they have no concerns about me. If they come, of course I will tell them honestly that I had been drinking and had passed out."

Brennan gave this some thought. He had been known to pass out on more than one occasion, but he was fairly sure that any time a telephone had rung on a table beside his bed, he had heard it. But then again, if he hadn't heard it, and nobody later said they'd tried to ring him, he wouldn't necessarily know the phone had rung and he hadn't heard it.

"But, Brennan," Habler said, "back to this postcard. If she kept it, the police must surely have found it. Would they not search through all her things at home and at her office?"

"I would expect so."

"Yes, in my experience, police are very thorough! Even so, I do not see how they would be able to connect the mild words of that card to her death."

"No."

Brennan changed the subject then, back to music and the roles Habler had sung over the years, and what he hoped to do in the future. They lingered over a couple more glasses of the outstanding German beer, exchanged some witticisms in the German language, and then Brennan got up to leave.

"I know you have dinner plans, Fried. I won't keep you any longer."

"If I did not have the plans, I would be happy to stay in and talk music and drink beer with you, Brennan. You are a man very well versed in music. Have you ever thought of taking the stage yourself? I have heard you in your church, and it is easy for me to imagine you singing Puccini or Verdi."

"Oh, I'm content to remain a humble parish priest, Herr Habler."

The man let loose with a great Pagliacci laugh, which brought forth a bark of laughter from Brennan.

"When is your next performance?"

"Before *Tristan* begins in April, I have been invited to do a little afternoon concert in Lunenburg. A selection of pieces in German. Much of the population there is German, I understand, or of German ancestry."

"That's right. When are you singing there?"

"This Saturday at the Central United Church. Fine acoustics, I am told."

"I'll see you there."

"That pleases me very much, Brennan."

"And I intend to have a meal there after. If you're free, I'll treat you to a good, hearty Lunenburg supper."

"Excellent."

Brennan headed for the door and said, "Thank you for the hospitality today. And for the information on that postcard from Berlin. Not much there, I guess. The police have a local man in custody, so a little note of congratulations from the old country would not be of much interest to them."

CHAPTER X

Monty

Monty completed his work week with two character witnesses for Alban MacNair. On Friday afternoon, he met with Colonel Bryce Simmons at RA Park across from Citadel Hill in the centre of the city. Royal Artillery Park was established in the early 1800s when Canada was still a British colony. The uniformed chief of staff stood waiting at the door of the long low white building that housed the Army mess of the 5th Canadian Division. He introduced himself and shook Monty's hand and then gave him a little tour. There was the Air Force room; Monty looked in and saw the walls decorated with photographs of the great old war planes. Next Colonel Simmons pointed to the Army mess, with its elegantly papered walls, rounded arches, and formally set tables. Two of the tables ran lengthwise along the room, with a head table perpendicular to them. "You'd better be able to hold your liquor, quite literally, if you're invited to dine in there. You're not permitted to get up from the table until the head table gets up first.

Woe to the fellow who enjoys a few too many glasses of wine and then feels the need to relieve himself. Sorry, soldier, not till the brass at the top of the room get up to take a leak."

Monty laughed. "I'll keep that in mind."

"It's not so formal downstairs in the bar."

The bar was named after a Halifax tradition that is over two hundred years old: every day but Christmas, a cannon on Citadel Hill fires a one-pound charge of black powder at exactly noontime. The Noon Gun Room was panelled in dark wood, and photographs and guns from various eras were mounted on the walls.

"Beer?"

"Please."

Simmons walked over to the bar. "Two brew for us here, Shirley."

"Keith's, sir?"

"Yes, please. You know me well, Shirley."

The colonel brought the glasses to a table, and he and Monty sat down. The Deputy Commander of Land Force Atlantic Area was a film-version image of a military commander. He had an angular face, cropped greying hair, and dark eyes. He was tall, fit, and tanned, as if he had just come back from directing operations in a theatre of war close to the equator. He would be a godsend on the witness stand. Another man rose from a nearby table and came over to join Monty and Colonel Simmons. Simmons introduced the newcomer as Everett Cunningham, from the Assistant Judge Advocate General's office. Monty found it slightly amusing that a lawyer from the AJAG office would be sitting in on the interview, but he merely welcomed the lawyer and directed his attention to Simmons and his friendship with Monty's client.

"Thanks for seeing me, Colonel. I'm pleased to be meeting with you, and I'll be seeing Lieutenant-General Patriquin as well, to gather evidence of Alban MacNair's good character."

"Put me on the stand first! Patriquin will be a hard act to follow. I can't claim anything like that rescue he pulled off in the Sinai Desert!"

"I look forward to hearing all about that, but I know you'll make a good impression yourself, Colonel."

Simmons had nothing but praise for Alban MacNair.

"He was under my command in Croatia. An excellent soldier, a great man for logistics. Disciplined, forward-thinking, loyal. And a good fellow to have around. But I'd known him for years before we served together."

"All good then?"

"All good. Sure, Alban is a bit of a partier. Or he was. We have to keep an eye on that sort of thing."

"Drinker?"

"MacNair liked his liquor, but it was never a major problem. It certainly never affected his work. And in fact, he gave up the booze a few years ago."

"Oh?"

"Yeah, Christmas party at my place — 1987 or '88, I think it was. I'd been joking with my wife about stocking an extra bottle of rye for Alban, but when he showed up at the party, he said he was off the stuff."

"How about women? Any trouble there?"

"I never knew MacNair as a skirt-chaser, not any more than the rest of us. He had girlfriends, of course, but then he got married and settled down. Nothing ever came to my attention about misbehaviour on that score. Not that I would necessarily have heard about anything private."

"He mentioned an incident where he was disciplined by his superiors. He was a little outspoken about unification of the forces, as I understand it."

Simmons gave a hoot of laughter. "We all had something to say about that! But, yeah, he went out of bounds by mouthing off about it in the presence of civilians, and that went into his pers file. But nobody here in Halifax held it against him. The flak came from up the line in Ottawa."

"So, it was just words with MacNair? He didn't act out his frustrations in other ways?"

"What kind of ways? He didn't set fire to the Department of National Defence or anything. Just ranted about it and was disciplined for that. He never said or did anything, to my knowledge, that would suggest the kind of crime he's charged with, and you can sign me up as a witness to say so."

The AJAG lawyer obviously had no objections, and the three men parted company on a friendly note.

†

An hour later, Monty was sitting across from Lieutenant-General John Joseph Patriquin, D.F.C., in the living room of Patriquin's home on the Bedford Highway. The view out his front window was of the Bedford Basin, where enormous convoys of ships had assembled before heading out across the Atlantic during both World Wars. Patriquin served in the Royal Canadian Air Force in World War II, was awarded the Distinguished Flying Cross for his wartime service, and was decorated again for his actions during a peacekeeping mission. Now in his mid-seventies, he was of medium height, stocky, and white-haired. He and Monty asked after each other's families, then Patriquin said, "And now you're representing Lieutenant-Colonel MacNair. A dreadful situation. Dreadful that the woman died, of course, but also that Alban MacNair has been charged. Unbelievable."

"Exactly. So, tell me, sir —"

"John. If you start 'sirring' me, I might start giving you orders!"

"Very well then, John. I wouldn't be competent to carry them out. So, tell me how you know Alban MacNair. He had various postings overseas, but I don't imagine you served with him in any of those places, given the age difference."

Patriquin laughed. "I was of a different era, true. But our postings in West Germany overlapped for part of a year. As you would know,

I'm sure, he was with the Army at Lahr in the 1970s. I was at the Air Force base, Baden-Soellingen, in 1974."

"Would you have seen him then, even though you were on different bases?"

"The bases were fairly close to each other, near the border with France, and I recall seeing him a couple of times. Once I think was a NATO exercise. Not much time for socializing on that occasion, but there was a golf tournament and I'm pretty sure we had a drink at the nineteenth hole. More than likely!" Patriquin laughed, then said, "MacNair served in Egypt and so did I, though our times there didn't overlap. He was later. But I'm well aware of his career and his advancement since then."

What was it Monty had heard about Patriquin's role in Egypt? The Suez Crisis? "John, I should know this, so please excuse my ignorance. My father once told me about some daring deeds of yours during our peacekeeping mission in the Suez. What's the story on that?"

"Not much more of a story than hundreds of others in uniform could tell you. You know what the crisis was all about: the president of Egypt, Nasser, nationalized the Suez Canal in 1956. The canal had been built and run by the Suez Canal Company, a company owned primarily by French and British investors. Well, I shouldn't say they built it; Egyptian labourers did the heavy lifting. It should have come as no surprise that Nasser nationalized it; it's in Egypt, for God's sake. But it linked the Red Sea with the Mediterranean, provided a shortcut between Asia and Europe, and was the lifeline for Arab oil going to Great Britain. The Brits were wild. The prime minister at the time, Eden, apparently said England could not allow Nasser to 'have his thumb on our windpipe.' They, along with the French, wanted to take it back by force. The French were even more militant about it. They were having their own troubles in North Africa, with Nasser supporting rebel forces in Algeria. So, England and France, along with Israel, wanted to mount a military action to get the canal back in, well, Western hands."

"War again, only eleven years after the end of World War II. And smack in the middle of the Cold War."

"Right. And the funny part, if you can call it that, was the attitude of the Yanks. For all their adventures on the soil of foreign countries, they were dead set against the use of force in this instance."

"They were the cooler heads this time around."

"Yeah, except they didn't prevail. Israel sent paratroopers in on October twenty-ninth and, two days later, the Brits and the French started dropping bombs on Egypt. They sent an ultimatum to Nasser and launched an armada. The Americans were furious. So were we. Apparently Prime Minister St. Laurent sent a blistering telegram to the British PM. Party politics came into it here: the opposition portrayed the Liberal government as being disloyal to Britain. But in fact, the government was trying to keep our allies, the U.K. and the U.S., from falling out over the whole thing. And the Soviets were playing a double game, offering to cooperate with the United States while at the same time threatening nuclear — yes, nuclear! — bomb attacks on Britain and France! Well, anyway, good old Mike Pearson stepped in and got UNEF off the ground. This was the first UN peacekeeping force; earlier forces had just carried out monitoring operations. A Canadian general, Burns, got the command. And Pearson got the prize."

That was Lester B. Pearson, nicknamed Mike, secretary of state for external affairs at the time and later prime minister. He was awarded the Nobel Prize for Peace for his efforts.

"Great story about Pearson," Patriquin said. "President Johnson was up visiting from Washington, and of course the Secret Service was on hand to protect Johnson. One night up at Pearson's cottage retreat, one of the Secret Service men sees Pearson and says to him, 'Who are you?' And Pearson says, 'I'm the prime minister of Canada, I live here, and I'm about to go and have a leak.'"

"Love it. He was quite a wit."

"As was his wife, Maryon, I seem to remember. But, anyway, yeah,

Mike Pearson, Nobel Prize winner for promoting the peacekeeping force in the Middle East."

"You won some accolades yourself, John."

"Oh, well, I was over there. It was us, Norwegians, Danes, Brazilians, Yugoslavs, a contingent from India, some others as well. There was a big flap early on; the Egyptians didn't want us there, because they figured the locals wouldn't be able to tell us apart from the Brits. They really put their foot down about the Queen's Own Rifles! But anyway, I arrived in the spring of '59. I would be flying reconnaissance missions over the Sinai desert in one of the Otters. Otter aircraft. Jesus, the heat over there! You hear about the desert, but you really have to be there to experience it. It's well over a hundred degrees Fahrenheit. I didn't know how I'd be able to function in it. And it's hell for flying, too. Sometimes the engines can barely get enough power to lift off. And landing: you'd have these shimmering heat waves that would throw you off. And the runways were miniscule; God help you if you overshot them, because they were surrounded by minefields."

"That's it — the story I heard about you had to do with minefields."

"Right. I injured myself in a rough landing on the less-than-ideal terrain there. Hit my head and got a cut on my face near my right eye; it swelled up and the doctor was worried about my vision. I didn't think it was affected, but they wouldn't let me near the controls of a plane. But I couldn't bear sitting around doing nothing. Well, one of the Royal Dragoons came down with 'Gyppo gut.' That's what we called the horrendous form of dysentery you'd get from drinking the local water or eating food that wasn't prepared by our people. But you could get it even if you were careful. Anyway, one of our soldiers was sick, so I talked my way into a ground mission, reconnaissance mission, and got into the Jeep, and we headed out on patrol.

"Now this was the springtime and that means you have a desert wind bringing in the intense heat from the south and whipping up the sand to the point where it's a freakin' blizzard. Sand gets into everything, every part of your equipment, your planes, your vehicles, yourself! You can't see. And that's what blew up while we were out."

"And to think we complain about snow."

"Give me snow any day. Eventually, it melts. Anyhow, on this particular day, we were out on patrol and we could barely see the hood of the Jeep. I don't know whether you ever heard this, but the Bedouin people sometimes helped our men out on recce patrol. The Bedouins often knew where the landmines were. And for a modest fee — cigarettes, for example — they would tell us where they were. And then a soldier would get out of the Jeep and use a mine probe to locate them. But some anti-tank mines were made of plastic and couldn't be detected. So, the local people would go out into the sand and dig them up."

"Taking an awful chance there."

"Well, they knew that the weight of a man was not enough to set the mines off. But if you got to a place where a Bedouin didn't venture out, you could assume there were anti-personnel mines out there."

"That speaks volumes about poverty, doesn't it?"

"And nicotine addiction. Well, that day we were rolling along, and a couple of Bedouins emerged out of the swirling sand by the side of the road. Offered to help with the mines. All fine and good. The two of them said there were anti-tank mines nearby and they started off to retrieve them. All of a sudden, shots rang out. We were pretty sure the Bedouins weren't the targets; we were. But they were helpless out there in the sand with the bullets whizzing by them. We saw one of them go down; he'd been hit. They were civilians, and they'd been helping us. Couldn't leave them out there. So, I went out."

"What about the soldiers on patrol with you?"

"I'm sure any of them would have gone out."

Monty wasn't sure of that. Some may have, some may not. And the patrol itself had to be protected.

"The other Bedouin and I picked up the casualty, ran back to the Jeep —"

"Through a minefield."

"Well, what could we do? And they'd walked out that way; maybe they knew there weren't any anti-personnel devices in our path. We dodged the bullets pretty well and —"

"Pretty well or successfully?"

"Bullet grazed my arm. No harm done. We got back to the vehicle and took the wounded man to our hospital."

"Did he make it?"

Patriquin shook his head.

"That got you a Medal of Bravery, and rightly so."

"Well, yeah. But that's not what I'm remembered for in the minds of the United Nations Emergency Force."

"No?"

"I was known over there and known to some veterans even today as not the Desert Fox . . ."

"No, that honour belongs to Field Marshall Rommel, and him alone."

"Exactly. I was the Desert Pox!"

"Should I even ask?"

"My wife did. The men regularly sent letters home, and didn't one of them talk about me being the Desert Pox, and didn't the story eventually get around to my wife, Irene. She thought I'd caught a dose of the clap, like so many other guys, after a wild weekend in the fleshpots of Beirut. Problem was I *had* been in Beirut. No women for me, but way too much booze. So, when I returned from Beirut, I slept like a dead man. When I woke up, I had an ugly red rash all over my face, arms, and hands. Was it something I ate? Was I bitten all over by something in my bed, and I was too drunk to feel it? There are scorpions and sand vipers — some of those snake bites could kill you. And spiders you've never seen the like of. Whatever it was, I was known from that day forward as the Desert Pox."

They shared a laugh over that, and then Monty said, "So, what will you be able to say on behalf of Alban MacNair when this goes to trial? Or is your reputation so spotty that you'll do more harm than good for my client?"

"Oh, I think I can present myself as a credible witness."

There was no question about that, Monty knew. He pictured the hero of the desert sands in his uniform on the stand, bolstering the reputation of his client.

"Where even to begin?" Patriquin said. "A good soldier, a hard worker, a patriotic Canadian, a great family man, not a violent sort, and — you may not want to use this! — a fun guy at a party."

"Not inclined to, well, commit crimes of violence?"

"Absolutely not."

"What about moods? Fits of anger, that sort of thing?"

Patriquin was shaking his head. "Not that I ever saw or heard of."

"And women? Any concerns there?"

"I wouldn't know that, but I've certainly never had any reason to wonder about Alban's treatment of the fairer sex. Good solid family man, far as I know."

"Now, did you know Meika Keller, John?"

"Oh, sure. Used to see her at Forces events around Halifax. Please don't think because I'm more than willing to stand up for Alban MacNair that I'm in any way callous about her death. She was a woman everyone admired, as you can imagine. The dramatic escape from East Germany, and then all her accomplishments here. I didn't know her well, but I had great respect for her. There's no way in the wide world Alban killed her."

"What kind of relationship did she have with Alban, do you know?"

Patriquin was instantly wary. Hearing something he hadn't known about MacNair? "Relationship?"

"I just mean, did they know each other well? Get along?"

"Can't imagine why they wouldn't get along. But I don't think there was any kind of 'relationship' there. I never had any reason to think they were particularly close. He probably just knew her the way I did."

There was more to it than that, as evidenced by those nine phone calls, but it would not suit anyone's purposes to reveal that to Lieutenant-General Patriquin.

"All right then, John. I'll be off. Thanks very much for your help. If and when we get to the point of a trial . . ."

"I'll be more than happy to get up on the stand and tell the judge and jury what I've just told you."

CHAPTER XI

Brennan

Things had changed at Saint Bernadette's Choir School during Father Burke's prolonged absence from the school and parish. He had founded the choir school seven years ago, having moved from New York City to Halifax to establish the school at the invitation of some people he had met years before. He had also set up the Schola Cantorum, which attracted priests and laymen, nuns and others, from around the world, people who loved and wanted to preserve the traditional music of the Catholic Church. Initially, the children's school offered grades four to eight, but, as the years went on, many of the students and parents requested that Saint Bernadette's start serving the high school grades as well, so they wouldn't have to leave the choir school. Saint Bernadette's therefore expanded to include grade nine and later ten as the students advanced. Grades eleven and twelve would be added in the same fashion. For the first couple of years, Brennan had split the responsibilities with Sister Marguerite Dunne; she was the principal and Brennan the music director, but everyone knew it was Brennan who ran the show. When Marguerite moved on to do charitable work in South America, Brennan was the sole "higher power," as the teachers laughingly called him. Administration bored him, and that went double for meetings. His interest was in the students, the high-quality curriculum, and of course the music. The teachers were excellent at their class work, Brennan coaxed the music of the spheres from his choristers, and there was an accountant to handle the finances, so the place ran like a finely tuned orchestra.

Until Brennan was detained in Belfast. This emboldened a couple of hyperactive parents to catch the ear of the bishop and persuade him to implement a new system of administration. And to give the bishop his due, Brennan had been sentenced to six years in prison, so it seemed the school would be without its higher power for all that time. Fortunately, his spell in prison, as agonizing as it was, turned out to be a matter of months and not years. Anyway, in the course of events, a group of parents and a crowd of *bumbógs* — busybodies — in the parish appointed themselves a board of directors and installed someone called W. Langston Soames as chairman of the board. There were committees for this and subcommittees for that, and Brennan ignored them. He wasn't a committee man. Worse than all that, though, was the Soames family's delusions about the talents of its members. And even that, if left to the realm of community theatre or karaoke night at some suburban drinking hole, could be dismissed as a minor irritation. But it could not be dismissed when it manifested itself in Vivian Soames, wife of Langston, standing at the lectern during Mass, looking more than a little imperious with her ashy-blond hair puffed up and swept back from a pronounced widow's peak. Vivian Soames *acting* during her readings of holy Scripture, making dramatic pauses and gestures with her head, raising her voice, and preaching to the congregation.

There is something called objectivity in worship, in liturgy. The idea is that the Mass is a common prayer for everyone; it is not supposed to be an opportunity for attention-seeking by the priest or any of the other participants. Gregorian chant is a perfect example; the words and the tones are what we are to hear. The chant is done in a neutral voice; the priest or choir are not to illustrate their own individual vocal stylings to draw attention to themselves. All are to be subsumed in the collective worship of God. This is, or should be, the farthest thing from amateur theatrics and self-aggrandizing behaviour. Vivian Soames had obviously missed the lesson. Or she was so grand that she dismissed these edicts as having no possible relevance to her. And then there was the son. Chadwick Soames was new to the school, having begun grade eight in September. It was Soames family lore that the kid was "gifted" and that his gifts had not been recognized by the philistines operating the other schools the boy had attended and abandoned. So now Saint Bernadette's had the care of his soul. If he had one. The kid was an arsehole, his academic performance as abysmal as his attitude.

His attitude was on display Friday morning. As was his idea of what constituted a display of wit. The school choir was rehearsing the Mozart "Ave Verum Corpus" and young Chad was standing a little too close for comfort beside Kim Kennedy, Normie Collins's best friend. Kim was without question a lovely young girl, with a classically beautiful face and long blond braids. As the choir got to the words "*natum ex Maria Virgine*," Brennan was able to lipread the exaggerated way in which Chad said to Kim, "Virgin, eh?" His actions in crossing his legs and crossing his hands over his crotch removed any doubt that the context was "Virgin, eh?" rather than the prayer at the centre of the piece. Kim leaned away as far as she could and kept singing. Normie, who was standing in front of her, turned and gave Chad a look Brennan couldn't see. But it was met by the little bastard taking that opportunity to scratch his nose with the middle finger of his left hand. Father Burke would be having a word with Chadwick L. Soames following the rehearsal.

Brennan congratulated the choir on a job well done, and when they began filing out, he crooked his thumb at Soames, who affected to ignore him. So, Brennan moved to block his way out and said, "Stay behind."

"Sorry. Can't. I have to be . . ."

"You do not have to *be*. You are merely a contingent being whose existence might have occurred or might never have occurred."

"Huh?"

"Sit down over there and wait till the other students have left."

The parade of exiting choristers slowed as, one after another, the students turned to see who was going to have to answer for offending the higher power. When the last of them had shuffled out, Brennan closed the door and turned to his captive. "I never again want to see, nor do I want it happening out of my sight, any disrespect shown to any of the students of this school."

"What? I don't know what you're talking about."

"Yes, you do. Don't do it again. Or anything like it."

"I don't have to fucking be here!"

"Correct. I believe I made that point at the beginning of our discussion."

"I can just leave this stupid school and get my money back."

"You can indeed."

"And then, like, you lose my money!"

"And then, *like*, I'll get another student to take your place. Someone who appreciates the fine music here and knows how to treat his or her fellow students. If you know the sort of person I mean. But perhaps you don't."

"Oh, yeah? How many people have the money to come to this old place? It's like from another century!"

"Thank you. You are more perceptive than I initially perceived you to be. As far as replacing you, to understate things considerably, you are not irreplaceable. As for money, as you may have noticed, we have students here on bursaries, those who do not come from high-income families."

"Noticed? Can't hardly miss them. They're the ones with patches stitched onto their uniforms and their shoes all worn out and they come in on the bus! My old man says he's going to cut down on them coming here. Says the school's losing money because of them taking up space."

Brennan called, as he so often did, on Saint Monica, known informally as the patron saint of patience, and he refrained from calling down the wrath of God on the obnoxious individual slouching at the desk before him. As much as he would love to see the back of Chadwick Soames, he knew he couldn't boot him out of the school and off the grounds for the one offence Brennan had personally observed. He settled for saying, "I'll pretend I didn't hear that crass reference to money. And when I said that you are to show your fellow students respect, that applies to every student regardless of who he is. Or she is. And regardless of the student's background. For in this place, there is neither Jew nor Greek, there is neither slave nor free, there is neither male nor female —"

"You don't let Jews or Greeks in here?"

"Oh, God," Brennan pleaded, "give me strength." He put both hands on the desk where Soames was seated and leaned towards him. "Soames, there are Jewish and Greek students here, among so many others. I was quoting Saint Paul's letter to the Galatians, where Paul was making the point that there are no divisions between people, that whether a person was Jewish or Greek, male or female, slave or free, that didn't matter because all are equal, all are one in Jesus Christ. Paul's great, ringing declaration of equality. Paul, of all people, proclaiming the equality of female and male in Christ. And you've never heard of it." He raised his right arm and pointed at the door. "Go. And don't let the door bang you in the arse on the way out. Oh, and don't be skipping catechism class; you're surely in need of it."

✝

Brennan received news of more pleasant company coming his way when he answered a phone call at lunch time from his brother Terry.

"Paddy gave me a blast when I got home from Halifax."

"A blast for what?"

"This." At the other end of the line, Terry clinked ice cubes around in a glass.

"He gave out to you for enjoying a drink?"

"Not exactly."

"What then?" As if Brennan didn't know.

"For going to Halifax and drinking with you." Brennan made no response, so his brother continued, "He's worried about you, Bren. We all are. He's right that I shouldn't be, well . . ."

"Well what? Setting a bad example? Encouraging me to drink? You can tell him I need no encouragement, as he well knows, and that you are blameless."

"Well . . ."

"What did he think we'd be doing?"

As soon as the words slipped out, Brennan tried to imagine what his brother Patrick, the psychiatrist, would say in response to a question like that. A more loving man you would never meet. Brennan knew his brothers had his best interests at heart and were worried half to death. "I know, I know," he said then to Terry. "I'll have to cut back a bit on the drink."

"A bit?"

Brennan ignored that.

"And you'll have the opportunity to display that change in lifestyle for him, Bren, because he's heading off to see you, flying in later this very afternoon."

"Is he now?"

"He is. So, you'll have to scramble to come up with some wholesome activities to entertain him."

"No worries. He can be my altar boy for my Latin Mass tomorrow. I hope he's not forgotten his Latin."

"Being an altar boy is like riding a bike. You never forget the old lady next door growling at you for racing through her flowerbed and you never forget the old priest bawling at you to correct your Latin."

"Maith an buachaill." Good boy. "I'll look forward to seeing Paddy."

Terry gave him the flight number and arrival time, and he signed off.

Patrick Burke was a couple of inches shorter than his older brother, with sandy blond hair and bright blue eyes. He was a contrast to Brennan in demeanour as well. Brennan knew people perceived him, Brennan, as a bit austere. Haughty, perhaps. Patrick was warm, open, and friendly. Dr. Patrick J. Burke was exactly the sort of fellow you'd want to tell your troubles to. If you had any troubles. And if you were the sort of fellow who told his troubles to others. In this case, Brennan felt he had no choice, given how the Meika Keller case was with him every waking hour. And given that Patrick had not quite been able to mask his reaction at the sight of Brennan, bone-weary as he was from another sleepless night. So, on the drive in from the airport, he filled his brother in on Meika's death and his failure to be there for her on the last night of her life. He made no attempt to downplay the role drink had played in his failure.

Patrick's response was, as Brennan anticipated, compassionate and thoughtful. And he veered beyond the psychiatric to the philosophical when he said, "We have to look at cause and effect here. We tend to feel guilty when our actions have an adverse effect on someone when in fact we have done the very same things over and over with no harm done to anyone, and we never give our actions a second thought. All you did was go out for a meal and a drink with your brother, as you have done a thousand times before. Even with the addition of a promise and a failure to meet someone later, there is nothing innately evil or immoral or even careless about that. We all go for an evening out; we all forget things. It is only natural that the one time your actions are associated with — not causative of — harm coming to someone, then you feel guilty. Yet the actions themselves are no more blameworthy than they were on the countless other occasions you engaged in them. That's the formal side of it. What I hope is that I can give you some comfort with the *feeling* aspect of it. There I go again, with that word beloved of shrinks: *feeling*."

Brennan turned his head to his brother and nodded his appreciation. They drove in silence for a few minutes until they came to a lake to the left of the highway. Brennan said, "Doctor, every time I drive by this lake, I think of . . . dragons! What do you suppose that means?"

Brennan took a glance at Patrick again and was gratified to see a startled look on his face.

"I see it, too, Brennan. That can only mean one thing, since we were brought up together: our mother was an overpowering, frightening figure in our formative years."

Brennan laughed. Teresa Burke was the kindest, wisest, most loving mother anyone could hope to have. The Miller Lake Dragon was either a natural formation of wood or something carved or created to look like a dragon's head. Any time Brennan saw it, he was speeding by on his way to or from the airport, and he'd never taken the time for a closer look. They kept up the light-hearted chatter until they arrived at the parish house.

"Now," Patrick asked when they'd arrived and gone up to Brennan's room, "where are you going to take me for a bite to eat? I don't smell anything boiling down there." He pointed to the first floor.

"God between us and all harm!" Brennan intoned. "Yer one in the kitchen here would like nothing better than to slip deadly poison into my porridge and have done with me."

"Now, Brennan, are we getting a little . . ."

"Trust me on this one, Paddy."

"All right. Let me just make a mental note. *Direct future consultations to explore possible paranoid ideation.*"

"You'd be paranoid, too, if she was out to get you."

"Fair enough."

They had a lovely meal of moussaka for Patrick and scallop souvlaki for Brennan at the Athens restaurant. Brennan was happy to prolong the occasion with a couple of glasses of Greek wine. Happy to be with his brother and equally gratified to be missing a meeting of the board of directors who had appointed themselves chieftains of his school. A meeting on a Friday night! And if the timing wasn't bad enough, the subject was even more execrable: board chairman W. Langston Soames had it in his head that the school needed "rebranding." Brennan had barely listened when the man called him on the phone and began rattling on about the school's "brand." But he had tuned back in when the word "prestigious" came up; Soames wanted it in the "promotional bumpf" or whatever he said. Brennan explained in what he hoped was a patient tone of voice that it was up to others to use the word "prestigious" if it was applicable. "Prestige is something to be inferred by others, Mr. Soames, not implied by us." That didn't shut him up, though; nothing ever did. He went on then about a "communications subcommittee" that would report to some other fecking committee . . . Brennan sent up a prayer of thanks when the call finally ended. Yes, much better to be enjoying a glass of wine and catching up on family news with his brother than listening to a shower of *bumbógs* droning on and on at yet another time-wasting meeting.

When supper was ended, Brennan walked Patrick to his hotel and said, "See you in the sacristy for the morning Mass. If you have to put yourself into a hypnotic state to recall your Latin responses, please do so."

"No, I go to the old Mass in New York, so I'm well able for it."

"Is maith sin!"

"I didn't say I'm well able to be gabbing in Irish!"

"Noted. I'll see you in the morning. And after your sacramental duties, you and I are taking a little road trip to Lunenburg."

"Oh? Good."

"We are going to hear the great tenor Fried Habler in the mid-afternoon. But we'll go early and see the sights first. The old wooden buildings of the town are so well preserved that the place was recently named a UNESCO World Heritage Site."

"Great buildings are right up with great music for you, I know, Brennan. Ever regret that decision to switch from architecture to Holy Orders?"

"There are moments . . ."

"I don't doubt it. Anyway, I'm looking forward to the road trip."

Piet

Detective Sergeant Van den Brink was doing some weekend work at the station, going over his notes on yet another child sexually abused by her mother's boyfriend, when Ailsa came in and said, "I heard a strange story from a friend of mine in New Brunswick. I grew up with her here. She married a Mountie, Keith, and they're stationed in NB." She caught sight of his notebook and said, "Oh, sorry, Piet. I see you're busy here."

"The interruption is welcome." He looked with distaste at his notes. "Another mum's boyfriend case. I'd rather listen to your strange story, no matter what it is."

"And I'd rather talk about it than your case. Just tell me this, though. Is it a situation where the mother was completely in the dark, or does it fit into that other category of horror stories, the kind where the mother knew or suspected and yet —"

"Let's hear your story."

Ailsa looked at him and then said, "Right, here it is. My friend, Shauna, called me last night. Told me about a weird incident a few years ago at the flying club they have up in Moncton. They had to shut the place down, not let anybody fly. This coincided with the visit of some of the brass from the Department of National Defence in Ottawa going on a little goodwill tour of various military bases. It was

New Brunswick's turn to do the spit-and-polish routine for the Chief of the Defence Staff and his attendants. The first visit was to the base at Gagetown, which I'm told is one of the biggest military bases in the country. Anyway, the visit was to rally the troops. So, there was a big do there in Gagetown. Then the delegation went to Moncton to speak to the Air Force Association, or something like that. And the flying club grounded everybody. Shauna said she'd get more details for me.

"Now, here's the part that's of interest to us, in case you were wondering when I'd get to it! Late that night, an RCMP patrol car stopped a driver on Route Two outside Moncton on suspicion of impaired driving. Gave him the demand and got him to blow, and he was under the limit. They couldn't get him for point zero eight. He was alone in the vehicle, and his story was that he had momentarily lost his concentration while trying to swat a hornet or something, and he assured the Mountie that it would be steady as she goes from then on. Mountie didn't charge him with impaired driving. But he remembered this when he heard the recent news from here, and he mentioned it to Shauna's husband. Driver was Lieutenant-Colonel MacNair."

"Really! Well, that's interesting. Bit of a habit with MacNair. We know he had a breathalyzer conviction here in Nova Scotia back in the day."

"Right. Now the Mountie in NB remembered seeing some kind of emblem or souvenir on the front seat, something that was given to the people who attended the defence department get-togethers. And he made some kind of crack to the driver, MacNair, about standing on guard for the country and not *stumbling*, or whatever he said. Now there's not necessarily any connection between the roadside stop on the highway and whatever happened at the Moncton Flight Centre, but you remember MacNair's file and what we learned about him being pissed off at the brass, at the government when they lumped all the armed forces in together. Unification. Well, what Shauna heard was that somebody at the Moncton get-together was drunk and belligerent. Pretty thin, I know, in terms of making a connection. Even if MacNair was drunk and obnoxious to the brass, that may have had nothing to do with the planes being grounded. And even if he had something to do with that, it doesn't make him the kind of guy who kills women."

"No, you're right. It doesn't. But if it was him, it shows him to be a bit of a hothead."

"He was stopped on Route Two near River Glade, which is southwest of Moncton, about half an hour's drive. I looked at my notes and saw that he was stationed at Gagetown at the time. And you'd take Route Two if you were travelling west from Moncton to Gagetown."

"Feel like taking an unofficial drive out of province, just to look around and meet old friends? Even if it turns out to be nothing, we get a road trip."

"I do, but I'm going to be giving evidence in that armed robbery trial. So, it'll be a couple of weeks at least before I can get away." She started out of the room and then turned back. "Think you can have your child abuser convicted and locked up by then?"

"How about I take you to his cell to see him, Ailsa? By the time you get through with him, he'll be pleading to confess and be placed in protective custody."

"If I get anywhere near him, he'll need it."

CHAPTER XII

Brennan

Doctor Burke did a stellar job as Father Burke's altar boy on Saturday morning. Then they had a bite to eat and got into Brennan's car for the trip to the south shore. They turned off the main highway as soon as they could and drove along the Atlantic coast until they arrived in Lunenburg.

"First stop, the golf course."

Patrick turned to him in surprise. "You? Golf?"

"Of *course* not. You can decide whether that pun was intended, or was a Freudian slip, or . . ."

"Get on with it."

"Right. It's just that the best view of the town is from the golf course."

He circled around Lunenburg harbour so they could see the magnificent townscape from across the water. The brightly coloured wooden houses on the slope of the snowy hill made for a spectacular

136

view. Then they drove across and up into the town and parked the car. They walked up the steep town streets to a big white nineteenth-century wooden church on Cumberland Street. Central United.

Brennan and Patrick entered the lovely old church with its wooden beams and stained-glass windows. Priest and altar boy genuflected before taking their seats and then laughed when they caught themselves performing Roman rituals in the Methodist-United place of worship. The church was packed, and there was excited chattering as people took their seats.

"He's got a good turnout," Patrick remarked.

"He has. Not often the smaller centres get a big name like Habler. Let's hope he can join us for dinner. Here he comes."

The lights went down and the musicians appeared, followed by the opera star himself in a formal black suit, white shirt, and white bowtie. The applause was thunderous. He responded graciously, speaking to the audience in German and English, which he said was appropriate, given that "the town was named by an English king after a place in Germany, which was Lüneburg, because the king was the Duke of Braunschweig-Lüneburg . . ." He stopped to take a breath, then continued, "Because he was really German but, anyway, who can follow it all?" The audience laughed at the convoluted explanation, and Habler said, "It is easier to follow the plot of *Der Ring des Nibelungen!*" He told the audience that he would be singing some Wagner, and he noted that he and Wagner were both born in Leipzig, and both were opera nerds. Habler made no reference to aspects of the Wagnerian canon that had so pleased the people who took power in Germany in the 1930s. The concert repertoire included arias by Mozart and Strauss, a couple of folk songs, and some sacred pieces as well. His voice was magnificent, and the crowd was on its feet for a good five minutes afterwards, prompting a couple of curtain calls and encores until the people finally let him go.

Brennan and Patrick waited until Habler emerged and came over to them. Brennan complimented him on a wonderful performance and introduced him to Patrick, who offered compliments of his own. The Burkes invited him to join them for dinner. Habler said he had been asked to go and have a beer with some of the people who had organized the event, people involved in music in the town, but after that he would join them for the meal.

"There's a place on Montague Street," Brennan said. "They scoop everything tasty out of the sea, boil it up, and put it on plates for you. I can't remember the name of the place right now. There are several, but this one is quite far up the street on the water side, and it has a dining room with big windows overlooking the harbour."

"This is not a big city. Montague Street. I shall poke my head into all the places until I find you."

Brennan and Patrick decided to hoof it around town, up and down the narrow, hilly streets, to appreciate the architecture and the harbour view before darkness set in. Then it was time to eat. "There it is," said Brennan, pointing to Big Red's. They went inside and settled themselves at a table overlooking the water.

The waitress came by, a friendly looking woman who introduced herself as Betty. Brennan greeted her and said, "We'll be ordering a meal, and we'll have a bottle of German white wine with three glasses. We have a guest who'll be joining us a bit later."

She answered in what Brennan thought of as a typical Lunenburg accent, which sounded to him like a combination of Germany and New England. A lilting cadence with the letter R not pronounced. "Take all the time you need. If you'd like to wait and order when your guest arrives, that's fine. Or I can come back to the table right away and put your dinner onto 'er if you're faint with hunger and would rather not wait."

"Sure, we'll order now, Betty. We can have dessert when he arrives. Now, I'd usually go for a pizza and I know yours are brilliant, but this evening I'm going for the kind of creatures you bring up in pails from the shore down there. You, Patrick?"

"Fish for me, too."

So, they ordered bowls of chowder and heaps of scallops, lobster, and clams, along with great whacks of the renowned homemade bread. "And a bottle of the Riesling, please."

A man at the next table asked the Burkes where they were from, and Brennan gave a pocket history. "We were booted out of Ireland, wound up in Hell's Kitchen in New York, and now I've found sanctuary here in Nova Scotia."

Another patron asked Brennan how he liked it here, and the conversation went on until the chowder arrived. It was the best Brennan had ever tasted. The Riesling arrived, too, but they decided to wait for Habler before getting into it. Brennan's intake would necessarily be limited, given that he was the wheelman for this outing.

"Friendly town," said Patrick.

"And to think this place was settled precisely to counter the likes of you and me, Paddy."

"The likes of us in what way?"

"Catholics. The British were trying to establish their colony here, which of course meant displacing the local population. Sound familiar? They sent Cornwallis over, after he'd done such a splendid job exterminating the Highland Scots after Culloden. But the native people here and the Acadian French didn't take kindly to the new arrivals. They worked together trying to pick the new colonizers off, put the run to them."

"The way our ancestors did in the oul country."

"And not just ancestors." They exchanged a meaningful glance across the table. Several members of the Burke family had been fighting the British in Ireland in very recent times. Brennan's troubles in the North of Ireland were a direct consequence of that recent history.

They put those memories aside when the steaming platters of seafood arrived. And right behind Betty the waitress came Fried Habler. "Is this the gentleman you were waiting for?" Betty asked. "Well, I guess you didn't wait!" Her eyes went to the chowder bowls, scraped clean.

"Thank you, miss, thank you! Yes, these are my dinner companions," Habler said and joined them at the table. "Please bring me some of whatever was in those bowls, at your convenience. I am not in a rush."

"Certainly, sir. Coming right up."

Habler sat, and they chatted about the concert and the town. Brennan said, "We were just discussing the local history. Some of the battles here were named after priests who were allied with the native people against the British. 'Father Le Loutre's War' was one of them. I can't remember the other names. The Brits did here what they did in Ireland. Brought planters in, good Protestant stock to displace the locals, to populate the empire and make it work. But — and this may interest you, Fried — they weren't satisfied with some of the riffraff they'd dragged over from England. So, they decided to recruit a bunch of 'foreign Protestants,' Germans and Swiss. Thought they'd do a better job of it. And they did."

"Of course they did! They should have called us in right at the start."

When they had finished their last mouthful of shellfish and wine, it was time for dessert. "Blueberry grunt, lads?" Brennan inquired. "I see they have it as a special this evening. Not the most elegant name but very tasty. Blueberries, dumplings, whipped cream. Sometimes it has maple syrup." They hailed Betty and ordered three servings.

"You know what they say about guys who take to sweets in a big way, Bren."

"No, Doctor Burke, I do not," Brennan replied. But he did. He helped run a lunch program at Saint Bernadette's church for disadvantaged people. He hadn't missed the fact that people who were seriously addicted to drugs or alcohol went for the sweet stuff in the middle of the day. Fourteen cubes of sugar or loads of that whitener stuff, whatever it was that people put in their coffee. Just dumped it all in. Be that as it may, Brennan wasn't the only one to finish off every scrap of the blueberry grunt.

A group of people arrived then and recognized Habler, and they stopped by the table to chat. Betty came over with the bill and Brennan took it. Patrick grabbed it from him and paid for the meals. Brennan signalled to Habler that they would wait for him outside.

While they waited, Brennan's mind went back to the concert. The German composers, the pieces that had been selected. His mental wandering had an unanticipated benefit. Seeing all the German names written on the program triggered his memory of the name that had eluded him when he saw the scribbled-out line in the Book of the Names of the Dead. He had it now. The name Meika Keller had written in was Rolf Antonio Baumann. Why had she reacted to Brennan's acknowledgement of the name? Why had he acknowledged it in the first place? Then he remembered. It was just that the middle name was Italian, and it had brought to mind the composer Antonio Vivaldi, and he had made some kind of comment about that. But who had gone to the book and obliterated Rolf Antonio Baumann from the Names of the Dead? And why? Was it Meika herself who had erased him from the record?

A Baumann in her life, now dead, and a person who had sent a postcard just over a month ago, someone with the initial L.

Habler extricated himself from his admirers in the restaurant and joined Patrick and Brennan outside on Montague Street. They all pronounced themselves sated with food and drink and were about to part ways.

"Just before you go, Fried, I have another question for you about Meika."

"Oh, yes?"

"A name came up one time when she was at my church. Rolf Antonio Baumann. Does that mean anything to you?"

Habler thought for a moment, then said, "No, I'm sorry. I should tell you that I lost contact with Edelgard, with Meika, once we finished our secondary school, because I was given permission to go to Prague and study music there. Czechoslovakia was an East Bloc country of course. Even so, I had to agree to return home and teach when my studies were completed. But during my student years, I did not go home to Leipzig very often. So, she and I were not in touch with each other. By the time I returned to teach, she was no longer in the city. I never saw her again until we met here in Canada. Whoever she knew in Berlin is unknown to me."

"I understand. I guess the postcard is not going to open any doors for us."

"No." Someone pulled up beside them in a car, rolled down the window, and said to the singer, "*Wunderschön gesungen!*" Wonderfully sung! Habler waved and said, "*Danke schön.*" He turned back to Brennan and said, "I wonder, though, whether the police found the postcard after she died. And if they saw it, did they recognize the building that was shown on the front of the card?"

"I doubt it, unless it was the Brandenburg Gate or the Reichstag building."

"It was not either of those, Brennan. It was a gigantic building made of concrete with rows of windows and no pleasant architectural features. Nothing pretty for a postcard. It was in fact the headquarters of the Stasi. You know who I mean by the Stasi."

Brennan stared at him. "A postcard of the Stasi headquarters?!"

Brennan knew perfectly well who the Stasi were. The East German secret police. He tried to process what he had just heard. How likely was it that the police in Halifax would have recognized the building or even given it much thought? But wait, though, didn't postcards always have a description or an identification on the reverse side? Of course, they did. *Citadel Hill, Halifax, Nova Scotia.* "Fried, what was the full name of the secret police?"

"*Ministerium für Staatssicherheit.*"

Hard to imagine that on a tourist card. But then again perhaps a point was being made in the aftermath of German reunification.

"Was the building identified on the reverse of the card?"

Habler laughed. "No. Old habits die hard, I suppose. They were the *secret* police, remember. But no, I remember very well that there was not anything printed on the back of the card to identify the building. Not even a street address, or the word Berlin."

"So, this may have been a do-it-yourself postcard," Brennan said. "Here, people can have family pictures or other personal images made into postcards. Or put on key rings and coffee mugs for that matter. I assume the same technology exists in Germany."

"Oh yes, it was probably first in Germany! Or Japan."

"You're probably right. This person may have had the card specially made up."

Habler did not reply.

"Fried? Does this ring any chimes for you? Do you know of any role the Stasi might have played in the life of Meika Keller, when she was Edelgard Vogt-Becker, or in the lives of her friends or family?"

"As I say, I did not know any of her acquaintances after she left Leipzig. But I do know this: Meika would have made herself very unpopular with the state security apparatus by escaping to West Berlin. Other than that, I can offer no explanation." He said his goodbyes and started to walk away, then turned back. "You must remember, Brennan, that the Stasi played a role in the life of every person in the German Democratic Republic."

CHAPTER XIII

Brennan

Patrick, as a brother and a psychiatrist, was concerned about Brennan's drinking. But he was also a Burke. So, simply put, he wanted to enjoy a drink with his brother. In moderation. And he expressed an interest in revisiting one of Brennan's regular drinking spots, the Midtown Tavern — he had been there on a previous occasion — so they hiked over to Grafton Street after returning from Lunenburg. Brennan knew it was almost a certainty that Monty Collins would be there on a Saturday night. And he knew he couldn't avoid Monty, couldn't indefinitely restrict himself to casual greetings or short conversations, regardless of the hangover of bad feeling from the Belfast catastrophe. And sure enough, there was Monty with a group of people Brennan recognized as lawyers. Monty raised his glass in greeting, and the Burkes greeted him in turn. There was no room at the table for the newcomers, so Brennan and his brother found another place to sit. Dave the waiter came over with a Keith's draft for Brennan and recognized Patrick, though not by name, and welcomed him back to the beloved Halifax establishment. Patrick thanked him and said he'd have the same, so another Keith's arrived at the table. As always, the talk turned to the family in New York, his parents Teresa and Declan, Patrick's children, and Brennan's other nieces and nephews. After an hour or so, the cartel of lawyers got up and left, and Monty looked over at Brennan, who motioned him to his table.

"Good to see you again, Monty," Patrick said, "and good to be in the Midtown again. Grand old spot, this is."

"Exactly," Monty agreed. "You get a drink, you get a steak. You don't get braised tofu drizzled with raspberry-infused anything."

"I can understand the attraction. Will you join us?"

"I will. But, just so you know, the coal miner's daughter is due to arrive here any minute now. She kindly offered to be my designated driver this evening."

"Does the verb 'offer' have an included meaning close to 'insist' by any chance?" Patrick asked.

"You are a scholar of the subtle shades of meaning in the English language, Doctor Burke. I commend you. And if your skills are as keen in the realm of human behaviour, which I believe they are, you may recall a formidable quality behind the mild, gentle demeanour of the lady of the house. In fact . . ."

"Well, if it isn't the Father, the Son, and the Holy Ghost." The speaker was none other than the gentle lady herself, coming in the door and bearing down on their table. "I'm not sure I'm fit for such sanctified company."

"Sure, aren't you a saint yourself, though?" Brennan replied. "Saint Oda of the Magpies, I'm thinking."

"Who?!"

"Do you not know the saints of your ancestral home?"

"Apparently not."

"Well, your lesson today is Saint Oda of Scotland who, it happens, was forever being annoyed by flocks of magpies, until the birds herded her into a lovely space in the woods, perfect for prayer and contemplation, and she realized the magpies had been sent to her by God."

"How in the hell did you come up with that?"

"I sure as hell couldn't make it up."

"You made up an Irish saint who turned water into beer!"

"O ye of little faith. Saint Brigid of Kildare did indeed perform that miracle. There is even a blessing for beer in the *Rituale Romanum*. Would yez like to hear it? *Benedic, Domine, creaturam istam cerevisae, quam ex adipe frumenti producere dignatus es: ut sit remedium salutare humano generi.* Shall I translate for those who have not had my advantages? Bless, O Lord, this creature beer, which thou hast deigned to produce from the fat of grain: that it may be a salutary remedy to the human race."

"Brennan, you never fail to amaze me," his brother said. "And I'd say you are now the man to beat if our Terry is to retain his preeminence as the barroom raconteur of the Burke clan. How can he compete with that?"

Brennan signalled to Dave to bring another round, including one for the blessed lady who had just joined the party. Patrick's mild blue eyes caught Brennan's own, and Brennan caught the meaning, and it wasn't a shared veneration of the patron saint or her product. It was more Aristotle than Brigid: *Moderation in the bodily pleasures.*

The conversation continued in a cordial vein, with no references to Irish history more recent than the sixth century. But eventually the Keller case crashed the party. Patrick was telling Monty and Maura how much he enjoyed seeing Lunenburg, which led to the Fried Habler concert. Monty said, tongue in cheek, "Herr Habler, where were you on the night of sixth February, 1996?"

"Wherever he was," Brennan said, "he was probably resting his voice in preparation for five long, taxing hours of Wagner."

"Now there's another first for me in my career, first time I've heard that alibi."

"From what I hear, Monty, your client MacNair wasn't resting his voice the night Meika died. He was seen having a row with her not too far from the seashore late that night."

"Brennan, if he had pushed her into the water of the Northwest Arm, she would have floated back onto the shore there, not onto the southern tip of the peninsula at Point Pleasant Park. Somehow, she ended up in the ocean. *Went into* the ocean of her own accord is my take on it."

"Hard to imagine, though, isn't it? Someone wading out into the frigid waters of the Atlantic and then putting her head under and waiting to drown. I know people do desperate things to take their lives, but would she be able to maintain her resolve long enough to stay out there, or would a basic survival instinct kick in and drive her back to the beach? People tend to use quicker methods like jumping into very deep water from a great height. They often die of a broken back before they can drown."

"So, what do you think happened, Brennan? You think my client got her out there. How? He shanghaied somebody's boat, she went along with it, they went out to sea, and he tossed her overboard? We know there was no boat found floating in the water that morning with nobody left aboard. And nobody has reported seeing my client hauling a boat back onto the shore or wrestling it onto the roof of his car for the journey home. The Rendell family has two kayaks, but they were still in their boat shed the next day, and there was no sign that they had been moved at all over the winter, so Alban MacNair didn't avail himself of one of those."

"If she did it all by herself, counsellor, how did she get out there? Did she take a boat out and then set fire to it, a Viking funeral kind of thing? That may not have happened even in Viking times. And it didn't happen here. Nobody saw a fiery ghost ship out there, no burnt wreckage came ashore, and she had no burn marks on her."

"I'm not suggesting a flaming ghost ship, Brennan. She got herself out there somehow."

"Maybe she took a ship out of dock and scuttled 'er." Brennan made a ritual out of lighting up a cigarette and avoided the eyes of his psychiatrist after this latest flip remark. But, he knew, the eyes of the Man Above could not be so easily evaded. And his own conscience would come back to haunt him at bedtime yet again, he knew, in the form of Meika Keller's lifeless face.

"Right, Brennan," Monty replied. "Or a German U-boat came up and sank her. There's one out there, we know, U-190. It sank one of our ships during the war, surrendered when the war was over, and our Navy made quite a ceremony of bombarding it from the air, sinking it, in 1947. But maybe clever German engineers got down there and patched it up."

"Tell it to the judge, Monty," his wife counselled.

"I think I'd be sailing a little too close to the wind with that story, my dear. So, I say we stick to reality, if possible."

"Humour me for a minute here, Monty," said Brennan, "and consider the argument that it was not a suicide. If it wasn't that and it wasn't MacNair, do you think her history in East Germany might account for what happened?"

"What? *Ve haff vays of dealing with people who escaped across the Berlin Vall twenty-two years ago?* You're seeing a commie plot in this after all these years?"

"Maybe *you* should be, since you are searching for fanciful ways of explaining away your client's aggressive behaviour hours before she died."

"Boys, boys, boys!" Maura cried out. "Why can't we all get along? Why don't we all just discuss things in a courteous manner and come to a consensus? How many times have I said it? If only women ruled the world, fighting and warmongering would be a thing of the past."

"I've a two-word answer to that, MacNeil, if you'd care to hear it."

"Not an obscenity, I hope, Father?"

"Two words: Margaret Thatcher."

But in fact Brennan *was* thinking of a commie plot. Well, maybe not that exactly. But . . . "I take it you know about the postcard from Germany?"

Brennan had oft been told he had a poker face. So did Monty Collins, Q.C., barrister and solicitor, who had become all too accustomed to surprises going off like bombshells in the courtroom. But Brennan had come to know him well, and he knew that the postcard had just arrived as another unwelcome surprise. And Monty was man enough not to pretend otherwise. "Tell me," is all he said.

"A postcard arrived for her at Dal."

"Dal, not Saint Mary's."

"Right. I knew that the story of the Meika Keller–Fried Habler reunion had made the news back in Germany. Habler's is the big name and he's teaching part-time in the music department at Dal."

"So, you figured someone might contact her through him."

"And someone did."

"What did it say, do you know?"

"I have the German written down, but I can tell you what it said. 'Congratulations, Frau Keller! I always wished I had your talents for sport and for science. Alas, I am talented only at reading and researching. But good for you! I must go; the scoundrel is here. Yours, L.' Initial L."

"Do we know who L is?"

"Not yet."

"What about the scoundrel?"

Brennan shook his head.

"A scoundrel doesn't sound like someone threatening. More like a humorous reference. So, I'd say there's nothing sinister about it. A simple note of congratulations."

Brennan leaned forward and said in a mock-conspiratorial voice, "That's what they *want* you to think."

"Who would 'they' be in this context, I wonder?"

"I don't know, but the picture on the card might raise a few eyebrows."

"Oh?"

"The building depicted on the card was the headquarters of —"
Brennan pronounced it in the German way "— the Shtasi."

"What?" Monty had abandoned his courtroom *sangfroid* as had
Professor MacNeil. Patrick Burke's eyes went from one to the other,
but he maintained a professional silence.

A few seconds went by and then Monty said, "Maybe *ve haff vays*
after all."

"Who did you talk to about the card, Brennan?" Maura asked.
"Fried Habler?"

Brennan nodded yes.

"Did he have any idea what it meant, the mild wording and the
ominous photograph?"

"He didn't."

"And no idea who sent it?"

"No."

Monty asked, "When was it sent?" He picked up his glass of draft
and took a sip.

"I don't know the date but the postmark was Berlin, and Habler
passed it on to Meika on January twenty-second."

Monty put his glass on the table and stared at Brennan.

Maura looked at her husband. "Wasn't that around the time she
took off on an unplanned trip to Europe?"

Monty answered, with obvious reluctance, "Yeah. She left four days
after that, on the twenty-sixth." To Brennan, "You're sure of the date?"

"I'm sure."

Monty

Monty blamed it on the beer. He'd gone way over his usual limit
at the Midtown. He'd poured almost as many glasses of draft down
his neck as Brennan had, and that could hardly be a good thing.
Monty was no stranger to the hops or to the places where the final

product was served, but it was rare that it brought him down like this, rare that Monty fell prey to alcohol's properties as a depressant. There was no question that Brennan's presence had worked on him, bringing with it unwelcome memories of the shambles in Belfast. But Brennan's experience there could hardly be laid entirely at the feet of Monty. And now this fixation Brennan had with the Keller case and some dastardly deeds he imagined had occurred in Germany. All to assuage his own guilt about standing her up when he was out boozing at O'Carroll's.

"Do you think Brennan's losing it these days?" he asked Maura when they were back in the house on Dresden Row.

"What exactly do you mean by that?"

"This crackpot idea he has about Berlin." Monty wondered if his wife could hear the effort he had to make to push his words out and pronounce them right. He slowed down, tried to sound sober and rational. "I can understand him being desperate to fashen — fasten — onto something other than suicide, but come on! He thinks there was some kind of plot hatched over in Germany to do away with her? What does he think she was — a Nazi? A commie? A rocket scientist being wooed by both sides in the Cold War?"

"You don't have to be so snarky about it. Maybe there was something over there, something that led to her death. She received a postcard referencing the secret police; four days later, she jetted off to Europe."

"Oh, come on, Maura. The woman left Germany more than twenty years ago, and she died . . . she died right here in Halifax. I suppose it's understandable that Burke is desperate for somebody else to blame since he stood the poor woman up on the night she needed to speak to him, the very night she threw herself into the sh . . . the sea." Monty could hear the slur in his voice; he sounded every bit as sloshed as he felt.

Maura gave him the kind of look a slurring drunk deserved, but she stayed on topic. Sort of. "Brennan couldn't have realized how serious her trouble was, whatever it might have been, or he would have remembered. Who knows? Maybe he has women wanting to meet him alone at night several times a week! The Roman nose, the Irish mouth, the wavy black hair, those black, black eyes. Anyone as tall, dark, and devastatingly attractive as he is must have to fight them off!"

"*Devashtatingly* attractive?"

"You're pissed, Monty. You can hardly pronounce your words."

"Do *you* find him devastatingly attractive, Maura?"

"I don't think about him like that. I'm married to you. And he's a priest. But I see the way other women look at him and —"

"Maybe they wouldn't feel that way if . . ." He managed to stifle a belch. "He is one of the most brilliant and talented men I have ever met. He has a doctoral degree from Rome, he speaks several languages, he sings like Pavarotti, he can coax the music of the *heavenzh* from his choirs, he was selected to direct one of the greatest choirs in the city of Rome, and how does he end up? *Shtaggering* home at two in the morning, hungover some mornings in the classroom, with a coup being planned against him by the board of directors at his own school. So maybe all his female admirers would look at him differently if they could see that. Though I suppose if the ladies are looking for a spectacular Irish flameout, then he's their man."

"*What* did you say?! What did you just call Brennan? Spectacular Irish . . ."

Monty tried to slough it off. "Oh, never mind. It's just a phrase I heard or read somewhere. I didn't mean . . ."

"This is not like you, Monty. Not like you to be nasty. Sober the fuck up, and limit yourself to two brew from now on. You obviously can't handle it. I never, ever want to see you like this again."

With that, she turned and headed for the stairs. Monty thought he heard the scrambling of little feet on the floor above. But maybe he had just reached the point where he was having alcoholic delusions. He wanted to kick himself. Maura should have booted him in the arse. She was right; this wasn't like him. He hated displays of jealousy.

Not that he was always immune to it himself, but he rarely stooped so low as to let it show. And even more rarely did he lower himself to the point where he made cutting remarks about a friend. He knew there was something else working on him: the guilt he felt for his own failures in Belfast. What happened to Brennan over there was partly the fault of Monty himself. But now all he wanted to do was put his head down and fall unconscious. And then wake up and realize that this was nothing but a nightmare, not a real-life tawdry scene between a piss-drunk man and his disgusted wife.

CHAPTER XIV

Piet

Shit! Piet Van den Brink was not normally a man to use foul language, but, on this occasion, it was justified. And it was directed at nobody but Piet himself. It turned out that Meika Keller had received a postcard from Berlin, not at her home or her office at Saint Mary's, but at the music department at Dalhousie University. It had come care of the opera singer Fried Habler. Piet had never thought of going around to other universities asking whether mail might have come for the victim at those places instead of her own workplace. Why would he have thought of it? But Father Burke had thought of it. He must have reasoned that once the Keller woman's reunion with Habler had made the news in Germany, someone might have contacted her by way of the singer. Obvious now perhaps, but only in hindsight. Hindsight for Piet, anyway. Not so for Burke. The call had come in that morning from a Mrs. Wilson, a woman who worked at the music department at Dal and who distributed the mail. She admitted that she had waited a few days — a week, to be precise — after the priest's visit, unsure of what she should do. Never mind that she had not thought to call the tip in when the news first broke about Meika Keller's death. But, she explained to Piet, she had thought no more about the card until Father Burke showed up, asking whether anything had arrived in the post from Europe following the news about the Habler-Keller reunion. And then, Mrs. Wilson said, she figured Fried Habler would have revealed it to the police if it had been at all significant. But, whatever her reasoning, she had phoned the information in today.

Piet had reassured and thanked her, and he was immediately determined to know what the victim's husband had to say about this postcard. But Piet would have more control over the interview if he didn't go in blind, without knowing what the postcard said. It was time for another visit with Fried Habler. A call to the Dalhousie Arts Centre netted him the information that Mr. Habler was teaching a class but would be back in his office just after eleven thirty.

Piet and Ailsa were waiting outside the singer's office when he returned from his class. His surprise was a couple of notches down from operatic, but there was no question that he was startled. But he gave them a cordial welcome. "Come in, officers, come in! I am sorry I have only two chairs, but I will stand if you both would like to sit."

"No, no, you sit and make yourself comfortable. We can stand."

"Ha, ha. I don't know how comfortable I can be with two police officers facing me! But then, after all, this is not Germany in the bad old days!"

Or the Netherlands in the bad old days of the Nazi occupation, Piet said to himself.

"So, how may I assist you today?"

"Mr. Habler," said Ailsa, "we wanted to ask you about the postcard Meika Keller received last month."

That brought on a big smile. Of pleasure? Relief? Was he expecting to be asked about something else? Having no idea what that might be, the detectives had nothing on which they could base their questions. So, Ailsa got on to the subject at hand. "Can you tell us when the postcard arrived?"

"Yes. It arrived here a couple of days before I returned from Toronto on the twenty-second of January. The woman handed it over to me on that day, the twenty-second, and I immediately took it to Saint Mary's University to Professor Keller."

Four days before she went off for an unscheduled trip to Europe.

"What was written on the card?"

"You assume that, since it was a postcard, I read it, and you are correct. It was in German, and said —"

"Sorry, Mr. Habler. I'll write it down."

"I'll write it," Piet offered and took out his notebook and pen. "Go ahead."

"It said, 'Congratulations, Frau Keller! I always wished I had your talents for sport and for science. Alas, I am talented only at reading and researching. But good for you! I must go; the scoundrel is here. Yours, L.' That is, the letter L."

Piet wrote out the words. "Do you know who the sender was?"

"I have no idea who he was. Or she was. I could not tell from the handwriting, or printing I should say, whether it was a man or a woman."

"The reference to 'the scoundrel'? Any idea about that?"

"No."

"Did Ms. Keller read it in your presence?"

"No, it was snowing and raining, and I had placed it in an envelope. She took it from me, thanked me, and that was all."

"Where was it sent from?"

"Berlin."

"I see. What picture or scene was on the card? Something in Berlin, I imagine?"

"Ah, that it is where it becomes most interesting. It was a picture of the former headquarters of the Stasi. I am sure that you, as police officers, know what I mean by the Stasi."

"Goede hemel!"

Ailsa looked at him, uncomprehending, but Habler caught his meaning and said, "Your words say 'Good heavens!' but your face says *'Godverdomme!'*"

Piet had to laugh. "Yes, God dammit! You have some Dutch, I see, Herr Habler." Of course, the Germanic languages were often mutually understandable. "So. The Stasi. Do you know why someone would send such a card to Meika Keller?"

"I cannot imagine. I honestly do not know."

"Is there anything else you can tell us? Anything at all that comes to mind since we spoke to you before?"

He shook his head. "No. I do not know anything that would help you identify the killer."

"Well, if anything comes to mind, however insignificant it may seem, give us a call."

"I will. Certainly."

✝

When Piet and Ailsa returned to their car, Piet called the station to phone Hubert Rendell at his office to tell him they were going to drop by for a minute. You couldn't just walk in to the office of the Commander Canadian Fleet, so Piet figured a phone call would speed things up at the security gate. He then drove through the city towards the dockyard.

"What do you make of that postcard?" Ailsa asked him. "Well, I guess we got your reaction in your native tongue!"

"Yeah, that was quite the surprise: a card showing the headquarters of the East German secret police! A frightening image, and a friendly message on the other side of the card. What's with that?"

"We could run it through our heads all day, coming up with hypotheses, and be none the wiser at the end. Let's see what the husband has to say."

157

They arrived at the waterfront and cruised along beside the naval facilities lining the western shore of Halifax Harbour. There was a mix of red-brick and newer buildings, and several light-grey Navy ships were tied up at the jetties. There was a brisk wind, and whitecaps had formed in the water. The detectives parked their car and walked to the gate, where they were met by a member of the commodore's staff, who led them through the dockyard to the commodore's quarters. They went inside, and Rendell rose to greet them. He thanked their escort and invited Piet and Ailsa to sit.

"Can't beat the location," Piet said lightly, "prime waterfront property."

"You wouldn't have said that if you were here in '17," Rendell replied in the same vein.

Piet knew, as did every resident of Halifax, that a large part of the city's north end was obliterated back in 1917 and thousands of people killed and injured, when two ships collided in the harbour. One of the vessels, the *Mont Blanc*, was an ammunition ship loaded with explosives destined for war-torn France. The *Mont Blanc* caught fire and drifted to Pier 6 on the Halifax shoreline where it erupted in a massive explosion.

"It doesn't get much worse than that," Piet said, "ramming a ship loaded with TNT."

"The ramming was unintentional, but you're right: it doesn't get much worse than that. And in fact it didn't, until 1945. This was the biggest manmade explosion in history until the atomic bomb."

"I think I read somewhere that the American scientists studied the explosion here when they were developing the bomb."

"Yes, they did. Oppenheimer and the other American scientists studied the Halifax Explosion when making their calculations. Our misfortune was in fact a reference point: *Time Magazine*, in writing of the bomb dropped on Hiroshima, stated that its explosive power was seven times that of the Halifax Explosion."

"The people of Halifax must have thought they were under attack by the enemy."

"Indeed, they must have. And then there were the fireworks on the other side in '45. Other side of Bedford Basin." He pointed roughly north. "After the second war. Bedford Magazine blew up, ammunition depot. Much of the city was evacuated. But luckily it didn't spread beyond the site, except for a lot of shattered windows and cracked plaster. Anyway, quite the show, exploding ammunition lighting up the sky."

"So, again," said Ailsa, "the people must have thought they were being attacked. Thought the war had started up all over again."

"Maybe so. Well, we like to think we have enough safeguards in place to avoid a repetition. So, you're probably safe here today. Now, what brings you to my door on this occasion?"

"We received word," Ailsa said, "that Ms. Keller received a postcard from Berlin only a few days before she took her trip to Europe."

The commodore visibly tensed in his seat but said nothing.

"What can you tell us about the postcard, Commodore Rendell?"

"I didn't see any postcard."

"This wasn't something she showed you? 'Look, I heard from an old friend in Germany.' That kind of thing?"

"It couldn't have been all that important to her; she didn't mention it."

"Did your wife stay in touch with people she knew over there, in Berlin?"

"No. That part of her life was over."

Piet didn't know what to make of that. Surely, there would be nothing odd about hearing from a friend or family member, even after two decades out of the country. "I know her escape from Berlin was a traumatic one," Piet remarked, "but did she lose all contact with the people there?"

"She may have been in contact with people in her first years here in Canada, but I don't know. By the time we met, she had established herself here as a Canadian. A new beginning."

"Are you curious about what the card said?"

He didn't look like a man who wanted to hear whatever was written to his wife by someone in her past. But he was going to hear it. Piet opened his notebook and read, "'Congratulations, Frau Keller! I always wished I had your talents for sport and for science. Alas, I am talented only at reading and researching. But good for you! I must go; the scoundrel is here. Yours, L.' Just the initial L, name not spelled out."

Rendell gave a shrug. "Sounds harmless enough."

"Did your wife ever mention a 'scoundrel,' someone annoying or perhaps amusing in her time over there?"

"Nothing comes to mind. It just sounds to me, Detective, as if somebody heard about her meeting up again with Habler, heard about her success here, and sent her a congratulatory note."

"Yet she didn't mention it."

"I told you she did not."

"The photo on the card did not quite match the tone of the message."

"Is that right?"

"The building shown on the card was, until the wall came down, the headquarters of the secret police. The Stasi."

Rendell made a dismissive gesture with his left hand, as if that was the sort of thing he heard every day. But, surely, it was not. He merely said, "Somebody has a strange sense of humour, I guess."

"Don't you find it significant that she took an unplanned trip to Europe just days after getting this card?"

"She took an unplanned trip to Europe after meeting Fried Habler; he got her keyed up about seeing some opera over there." He looked at his watch and said, "I'm sorry, Detectives, I can't be of any help to you on this. Now, if there is nothing else, I have a fleet to run."

"Well," Piet said to his partner as they walked along the water-front, "we don't know any more than we did before we left dry land."

"Don't we? Didn't you get the impression that the news of the card was not really news at all?"

"Possibly. And he doesn't want us to know even that, for some reason. Or he honestly thinks it was of no importance. And honestly believes she went to Europe for the sole reason of catching an opera or two. And maybe he's right."

"Maybe. After all, the man we have charged with the murder was not in Germany, did not set foot outside Halifax, during the weeks leading up to her death."

The detectives followed up by asking Rendell's son and daughter whether they knew anything about the card; Lauren and Curtis said they had never seen or heard about it. News of the postcard was just one more distressing revelation in the saga of the family's loss.

Monty

What, if anything, could Monty make of the fact that Meika Keller had received a postcard just before she took her trip to Europe, a card depicting the headquarters of the secret police in East Berlin? Monty pushed away the memory of his over-consumption of alcohol at the tavern and his contemptible behaviour afterwards in the presence of his wife. He focused his mind on the postcard. At the very least, he could present evidence of the card at trial and suggest that it repre-sented a threat to her. And that, given the timing so soon before her death, this raised serious doubts about the guilt of Alban MacNair. The lieutenant-colonel's military service records showed that although he had been stationed in Germany in 1974 — in West Germany obvi-ously, not the East — the last time he had been posted there was 1978. And his attendance records confirmed that he had been here in Halifax every working day of this year, which sometimes included weekends. So, if there was some twist to this that had its origins in Germany, MacNair had nothing to do with it. The Crown of course would argue that if the postcard had constituted a threat, surely she would not have run directly into danger by going to see the sender of the card on her trip to Europe, and that the card, regardless of the image, had no relevance in the case. The case was against MacNair, who had made persistent calls to her, had been in a shouting match with her a few hours before her death, and had her blood on his glove.

Monty decided to see what his client had to say about this newest development. MacNair's eyes fastened on Monty as he took a seat in the law office, wondering no doubt, *What now?*

"Did Meika ever talk about contacts she still had in Germany?"

The client's gaze intensified. "What do you mean?"

"Do you know whether she stayed in touch with people over there?"

"Not as far as I know. Clean break from the place was my impression. Why?"

"The police have found a postcard that was sent to her from Berlin."

"Is that right?"

"Aren't you curious about what it showed?"

MacNair shrugged. It was of no interest to him.

"It showed the headquarters of the secret police."

There was no hiding his reaction then; this hit home. A hesitation and then, "Sent by somebody to taunt her? Saying 'we can still get you'? All these years later? How fucked up is that?"

"The message on the card said something about talent, 'I wish I had your talent,' and it was sent to her via the opera singer Fried Habler."

This took a moment to register, then MacNair snorted with laughter.

"There's something funny about this?"

"No, no. Well, in a way, yeah. She talked about composing an opera."

"Oh?"

"About East Germany, what it was like there, her escape, all of that. She was as keen on opera as she was on science. I don't know if she ever actually worked on it, or just hoped to do it some day but well . . ."

"So, she may have been in touch with someone in the opera world over there."

"Maybe so."

"And the Stasi building. If she wrote about the East German regime . . ."

"The picture might have represented one of her themes or the stage setting or, well, I don't know."

As much as Monty would like to uncover a German rather than a Canadian angle to Meika Keller's death, as much as he was an opera buff himself, he was not about to drop everything and jet over to Germany in an effort to find — what? A temperamental diva or a mustachioed tenor going to operatic lengths to avoid being upstaged by a novice composer by the name of Meika Keller? He could, however, speak to Fried Habler to see if there was anything to MacNair's suggestion. But how could this help him? Monty knew it would almost certainly spell the end of any speculation about a plot conceived behind the wings at the Staatsoper Unter den Linden. But now that the suggestion had been aired, he felt he should make a token effort to see if there was something to it.

"I could have a word with Fried Hab—"

"No, no —"

"No? Why not? You just said there might be a connection with opera, so why not talk to Habler to see if she mentioned it to him?"

"I just mean that he wouldn't know. I doubt that her plan got to the point where she'd tell a world-class opera star about it."

Monty looked at his client. "But someone in Germany knew about it. Couldn't hurt to ask, could it?"

CHAPTER XV

Brennan

Brennan knew it was pointless to brood about all the aggravation that had come his way since his return to Halifax. His drink-induced failure to meet Meika Keller and possibly stave off her death; his shameful hope that her death was murder rather than a possibly preventable suicide; the rift between himself and Monty; and the bloodless coup that had resulted in the takeover of his school by meddlers and moneygrubbers. You'd think after what he had endured in the North of Ireland, anything else would pale in comparison. And well it should. He knew that, but still — to have to sit and listen to a bunch of pointless blather at meetings when he could be doing something useful? Or pleasurable? But he couldn't avoid the school's new, and completely superfluous, board of directors forever. So there he was, slouching towards the auditorium of Saint Bernadette's Choir School on a Monday evening to witness W. Langston Soames conduct one of his endless meetings. This one was close on the heels of the last one because Mr. and Mrs. Soames were flying out the next morning to spend a couple of weeks in an "acquisition" he had made in Florida. And, the meeting notice said, if anyone wanted to join them for a round of golf, a day at the pool, or a night of drinking piña coladas, they were more than welcome, exclamation point. All the parents had been invited to sit in on tonight's meeting. Brennan was exhausted from lack of sleep the night before, reliving the trauma of his prison cell all over again, seeing Meika Keller's eyes peering through the high slit of a window in his cell door. And the sight of himself this morning in the bathroom mirror: he looked badly hungover, though for once he wasn't. He paused in the doorway and recited to himself a verse from Isaiah: "Therefore I have set my face like a flint. And I know that I shall not be put to shame; he who vindicates me is near."

He entered in silence and sat at the back of the room. Once again, Soames was on about "the finances," how they'd been left to slide. Father Burke had not pushed the parents to pay their fees and he had allowed the admission of too many of the "let's just say disadvantaged kids" — children whose families could not pay the fees.

"There's a potential here," Soames said, "to go beyond the break-even point. This could be a profit-making endeavour, given the number of students from high-income families enrolled here. And I'm confident that we can attract more players, more parents from the higher tax brackets." It was all Brennan could do to tamp down his hostility to this obsession with the greasy till, rather than with the high quality of the academic and musical education, in which the school excelled. Now the man was on about a "paradigm shift"; he suggested that they "run it up the flagpole" and "dialogue" with somebody or other. Brennan felt his eyes closing. Now there was something about "investment vehicles," funds being structured some way or other, and section something of the Income Tax Act. Brennan was nodding off. Sleep beckoned like a mirage of a well-stocked bar glistening in a desert.

"Are we boring you with these practical matters, Father?"

He started and opened his eyes. "No, no. Carry on."

He tuned out the earnest speakers again until the vital subject of education found its way into the discussion. That got his attention. One of the parents was giving out about the material taught at Saint Bernadette's and rabbiting on about the "business worldview." Ah, Richard Robertson's old man. This was not the first time Murdoch Robertson had been pontificating about "business models," whatever they were, and how they should be incorporated into the curriculum. Brennan shifted in his seat and looked at his watch, wondering how much more of this horseshit he'd have to endure before he could lay his head on his pillow and escape into unconsciousness.

But then he heard Langston Soames say, "And why are we teaching our children, in this day and age, superstitious nonsense about the Shroud of Turin?"

"What?" Brennan asked.

"Oh, you're awake, are you?"

"What was that about the shroud?"

"I'm questioning why the religion classes at this school are still teaching our kids about this object that was revealed eight years ago as a medieval forgery."

"So, you think what we are teaching here is *pia stercora*."

"What?"

"You think it's all a load of pious crap. We teach Latin here, too, if you'd care to sit in sometime."

"I don't have time for Latin. You have heard of the carbon twelve dating that was done on the shroud in 1988, Father?"

"It was carbon fourteen."

"Twelve, fourteen, what's the difference?"

"The number of neutrons. Different isotope. But that's neither here nor there."

"Agreed, Father Burke. The testing found that the shroud dates from sometime in the twelve or thirteen hundreds, medieval times, not the time of Christ."

"Yes, that's what the tests showed."

"Right, so let's move on."

"No. You expressed concern over what we are teaching the students. I am telling you what it is exactly that we are teaching, in case the news hasn't been fully conveyed to you by your son. So, allow me to fill you in."

"Are you sure you're up to this, Father Burke?" That was Robertson again. "You look a little . . . tired."

Brennan didn't deign to offer a response. Instead, he gave them an education with respect to the shroud. "There are a number of reasons the test may have given inaccurate results."

Soames smiled. "Okay, let's hear them."

"Strict protocols were established to make sure the test met the high standards expected of science. There were to be several samples taken from the shroud itself, not just one area of the cloth. There were to be comparison samples, control samples, taken from other cloths. Seven C-fourteen labs were to participate. The testing was to be blind, meaning that none of the labs knew which sample they had been given, so no bias could creep in, one way or another. And the labs were not to confer with one another."

"Sounds good to me," Murdoch Robertson muttered.

"But these protocols were not followed."

"What?"

"The protocols were scrapped, for a number of reasons too tedious for us to contemplate here." The rivalries between groups of scientists and their labs, the potential for commercial advantage and fortunes to be made by the labs that had been part of the world-famous project, all of that would in fact be mother's milk to some of the people in this room, Brennan knew, but he didn't waste time explaining. "So, in the end, there was only one test done in one lab, and only one sample taken from the shroud. And it was cut from what may have been the worst possible part of the cloth, the top corner, which would have been handled by hundreds of people, countless times since the fourteenth century. Grasped by fingers in, shall we say, less sanitary times in hot, humid, carbon-dioxide-rich environments. Not to mention the fire in 1532, which scorched the cloth but did not affect the image in the centre of it. But still, effects of a fire on the material. There were cotton fibres mixed in with the linen as well, from repairs. If these were in the test sample, they would give a later date to the fabric. So, there are many reasons why the results may not be reliable.

"But let's leave aside the carbon test for now and look to history. There was talk of a sacred cloth in Edessa in southern Turkey in the first century. Then in the sixth century, such a cloth was found there. Up until that time, Jesus had been depicted without a beard, looking more like a Roman than a Jewish man in Palestine. That image changed in the sixth century to a look similar to that depicted on the shroud. Then there was what is known as the 'Hungarian Pray' manuscript, which dates from 1196 A.D. It depicts an object in the same herringbone tweed material as the shroud, and it shows a number of holes. A close-up view of the shroud shows holes in exactly the same pattern. So, we have historical evidence suggesting that it existed centuries earlier than the carbon fourteen date."

People had twisted around in their seats and were looking at Brennan with interest.

"There's more to it, but we'll leave that for now and move up to the year 1898. In that year, a lawyer and photography enthusiast named Secondo Pia was given the opportunity to take a picture of the shroud. When he developed his picture, he was gobsmacked to see that the image was actually a perfect photographic negative. The image of Christ was much more clear in the negative of his picture — that is, the negative of the negative being a positive. If the shroud is dated in the twelve or thirteen hundreds, here's what the forger had to do: he had to create a perfect photographic negative five centuries or so before the invention of photography."

This brought on excited whispers in the room.

"And there are also the archaeological facts about the Roman crucifixions. The nail was hammered in through the side of the heel, not the front of the foot, and through the wrists, not the palms. A medieval forger would have copied the standard image seen over and over in works of art: nails through the man's palms and the front of his foot. The shroud contains blood patterns — human blood, not paint — consistent with a wound to the side of the heel. And through the wrists, not the hands.

"And that leads us to the evidence of doctors and scientists in the United States. One of them, a doctor and forensic pathologist in Los Angeles, stated that the image is so clear that a pathology exam could be done on it. The angles of the blood flow show that the man's arms were originally held out, and there were abrasions on the back consistent with a heavy object bearing upon it, for instance, the beam of a cross. Marks on the head and forehead suggest wounds from sharp objects. These marks seem to indicate that it was not a crown of thorns but a cap of thorns covering the entire head. Historical evidence tells us that this was not the normal practice, so it appears that the cap was made especially for Jesus of Nazareth. Presumably, a medieval forger would have shown the better-known image, a crown or circlet around the forehead. One of the most interesting of the medical findings was the injury to the wrists. Not the hands as shown in so much of the art, but the wrists. One of the doctors explained that wounds like this would cause damage to the median nerves, which are used to enable the thumb to move back and forth. With damage to these nerves, the thumb would tuck in to the palms of the hands. Next time you have a chance to look at the image, you'll notice that the thumbs are not visible. The doctor described the markings on the shroud as 'clear and medically accurate.' So, the medieval forger would have to have been an expert in medicine and forensic pathology.

"Now I mustn't forget the evidence of a scientist from Switzerland, a police investigator who specializes in botany. Plants. He studied the shroud, and in addition to the pollens that reflected the cloth's time in northern Europe, he also noted pollens that are found only in southern Turkey — where, you will recall, something meeting the description of the shroud was seen in the first and sixth centuries — and other pollens found only in Palestine, in the areas around Jerusalem. How would a medieval forger know all that plant science and be able to go to the Middle East and gather all the appropriate pollens?"

Brennan was on a roll now, his earlier exhaustion forgotten. The parents and board were rapt with attention. He caught the eye of Bishop Cronin, and Cronin gave him a slight nod of the head.

"And now," Brennan told his audience, "we come to the rocket scientists. Permission was granted for scientific studies of the shroud, and some of the work was done at the Jet Propulsion Lab in California. The scientists there did image enhancement and something called frequency analysis. A medieval forger would have to have painted the image on the cloth with pigments of some kind, made from organic matter. The analyses found no pigments and no signs of brush strokes or other signs of a human hand having done the work. It was also studied at the U.S. Air Force Academy in Colorado by a physicist-cosmologist and a specialist in aerodynamics. They put the image into a machine, an image analyzer. It was called a VP-8 or something like that. And they compared it to a photo of one of the scientists, which was also put into the machine. The face of the physicist was distorted, but the face on the shroud was clear. A camera records differences in light, not distance from the object. The clear image of the face in the shroud could only have been produced if that image had been encoded with information about the distance from the cloth to parts of the face and body. In other words, it was a 3D image. Again, if the carbon dating is accurate, this was produced approximately five centuries before the invention of photography, and it is superior to it. One of the scientists gave voice to the opinion that it would be practically impossible for a forger, never mind one in the middle ages, to have produced an image like this."

This was met by a stunned silence. Brennan cast his eyes around the room and allowed them to rest upon Langston Soames. Then he said, "If any of the students told you that we talk about the shroud in class but didn't relay some of that information to you, you've not been getting the whole story."

One of the mothers put up her hand. "Father, how do these scientists think the image got on the cloth?"

"Scientists have tried to determine how an image could have been transferred to only the very surface of the cloth, without penetrating deeper into the fibres. The image is only forty or so billionths — yes, billionths — of a metre in depth. The theory is that what happened was a very brief flash of energy, lasting a small fraction of a second, powerful enough to imprint the image on the surface but not to destroy the cloth. A very quick burst of radiation."

There were a few gasps and intakes of breath at this.

"That is as far as scientists can go. Anything beyond that leaves the field of science and enters that of religion. So, let's hear no more about teaching superstition at this school."

A group of parents rose to their feet and began to applaud. Everyone else, apart from Mr. and Mrs. Soames and the Robertsons, followed suit. Brennan nodded in recognition and sat down. Good. Maybe Brennan had demonstrated that he wasn't just a muck savage when it came to academic standards. And he might be able to engineer a counter-coup, a Counter-Reformation so to speak, and return the school to the dignity it had enjoyed before he embarked on that ill-starred trip to Belfast.

CHAPTER XVI

Monty

Monty dropped in to the Dalhousie Arts Centre and made some inquiries. Yes, Mr. Habler was in his office, number 510. Monty walked up the stairs, found the office, and knocked on the door.

A booming voice invited him to enter.

"Good afternoon, Herr Habler. I was wondering if I could have a word."

"Certainly, certainly." He got up and bent over the guest chair facing his desk; he began scooping up papers and musical scores so Monty could sit.

"My name is Monty Collins, and I am the lawyer for Lieutenant-Colonel Alban MacNair."

Habler stopped moving and fixed his eyes on Monty.

Monty thought a bit of lightness would put Habler at ease, so he said, "I'm here with a question about opera. Have I come to the right place?"

Habler's shoulders relaxed a little, and he smiled. "Ah, yes, you have come to the right man."

"More specifically, I've heard that there might have been a bit of operatic composing done recently here in Halifax. I mean —"

Habler's mouth quivered and he moved back a little in his seat. The question seemed to have hit a nerve. Whatever it was, Monty decided to probe that exposed nerve. He had no idea, so he had to wing it.

"The story is making the rounds, so I thought I should get it straight from you rather than, you know . . ."

"You are thinking that Edelgard — Meika — was with . . . was with that group? She was not! What I have heard is that she was with the man you represent!"

What was this? Habler thought Monty was talking about the night Meika died. Why was the man so rattled?

Monty would see what else he could get. "So, the group that night . . ."

"That had nothing to do with her!"

"Then why do my questions disturb you?"

"I am not disturbed."

"Well, you certainly reacted to my question."

"Please explain why you are here, Mr. Collins."

Monty was unlikely to get any more on this subject. "I'm sorry, Mr. Habler, we seem to have got off on the wrong foot here. There was a suggestion that Meika Keller may have been composing . . ."

"Composing? Meika Keller?" He looked completely baffled then.

"The suggestion has been made that she was writing an opera about her time in East Germany, the repression there, her escape across the border."

This was met by amusement. Relief, more likely. Habler put on a big grin and said, "One would expect a lot of dark, bass notes in that! And some high shrieks from the soprano! But I should not make jokes about it, or about the long-lost German *Democratic* Republic. Or about Edelgard. Meika. God bless her."

"But she never mentioned it to you."

"No." Habler leaned forward then and said, "You are the lawyer for a Canadian Army officer who is accused of the killing. Why do the police think the Army man killed her?"

"Well, I can't talk about the case. Except to say they have the wrong man. My client is innocent."

Habler smiled at that. "Of course, that is what I would want my lawyer to say if the police accused me of a crime. But I read in the news, or I heard it somewhere, that the Army officer was with Meika the night she died."

"Lieutenant-Colonel MacNair and Ms. Keller had known each other for many years. Any time they spent together, nothing improper happened. And certainly nothing criminal."

"No, of course not! But I am thinking that if her husband telephoned Lieutenant-Colonel MacNair's home in the middle of the night looking for his wife, that call would not be welcomed by the lieutenant-colonel's own wife!" There was a trace of amusement again in the grey-green eyes that looked into Monty's.

"Called? What do you mean, if Meika's husband called . . . ?"

"I just mean that if he called me looking for her, he may have called every man she knew!"

What was this now? "Commodore Rendell called you?"

Habler's dropped his gaze.

"Mr. Habler?"

Habler still did not look up. But eventually he said, "Yes, he phoned, but I . . . didn't hear the phone ringing because I was so much asleep."

"Where is your phone?"

"It is in my bedroom, but, as I say, I was deeply asleep when it rang."

"How do you know it was Hubert Rendell who tried to reach you?"

"He left a message on my answering machine."

"What time was the message recorded?"

"It was just around midnight."

It was Monty's turn to try to mask his reaction. Hubert Rendell told the police he had gone to bed at something like ten o'clock or before and had slept through the night until six thirty the next morning. Now, Monty was hearing that he was awake and on the phone, looking for his wife at midnight.

"Mr. Habler. It is important that I hear that voice message from Commodore Rendell. Could I stop by your place at a time convenient to you and —"

"I am sorry, Mr. Collins, but the message is no longer available."

"Why is that?"

"Well, you know, I don't keep my messages."

"You erased it? Why?"

Because he didn't want the police to see him as someone Rendell thought of as a possible companion to his wife in the middle of the night? And what about his claim that his phone rang beside his bed and he didn't hear it? How could he not have heard it if it was in his bedroom? Was he home at all when the call came in?

Habler affected a shrug as if a message from a man whose wife had died in suspicious circumstances the night of the message was of no more importance than a call from a telemarketer.

"When did you erase the message?"

"When?"

"Yes. Was it before or after you learned of Ms. Keller's death?"

"You are making me sound like a criminal, Mr. Collins!"

"I'm sorry. I don't mean to sound accusatory. It's just that a message from the victim's husband would be a significant element of the case. What did Rendell say?"

"Oh, he was angry. He demanded to know if his wife was with me!"

"Angry."

"Yes, his voice was calm and cold-sounding, but he was angry indeed."

"What were his exact words, do you recall?"

"It was 'Mr. Habler, is my wife there with you? Have you seen her?' Then it was no longer 'Mister' but just 'Habler.' He thought I was ignoring him. 'Habler. Pick up the phone and speak to me.' And then a long silence and a click, ending the call."

"Mr. Habler, were you really at home when that call came in?"

"What? Are you asking me for my alibi?"

"I'm just trying to get a clear picture of who was where. I'm sure you understand."

"Yes, I do understand. You are representing the man charged with killing her and you are looking for other suspects!"

"I don't imagine you're in the frame for this, but I like to have all the information I can get so I can do a proper job at the trial."

"I . . ." He leaned forward then, hands clasped on the desk. "I had too much liquor to drink. I was passed out!"

"Where were you drinking?"

"At home. In my house."

"You were alone and you drank —"

"Yes."

"At first when I asked you about Ms. Keller and composing, you mentioned a 'group.' And I had the impression you were talking about the night she died. What were you talking about then?"

"There is no other information I can give you." He turned to a side table and began sweeping some papers into a pile and said, "I am sorry, I have to go and meet one of my students now. I am sorry to have to rush away."

And rush away he did, leaving Monty with more questions than he had had when he arrived. And not only about Habler. What about Commodore Rendell? He had told the police he had slept all through the night. He hadn't known until morning that his wife had not come home. Two men claiming to be sound sleepers and it seemed one had made a phone call and the other had missed it.

Now what was Monty going to do with this new information? Rendell, not Habler, was Monty's main concern. When a woman dies in suspicious circumstances, her husband or boyfriend — or former husband or boyfriend — was always the first to be suspected. And with good reason, given the high proportion of cases in which the man in her life was the culprit. And now Monty had caught the husband in a lie. So how could he best make use of this revelation? Save it for cross-examination when the husband was on the stand as a Crown witness? Raise suspicion against him in the minds of the jurors? Or inform the police about Rendell's jealous phone rant, which he had denied by stating that he slept through the night? No, putting the police on the trail this soon could very well backfire; they would almost certainly be treated to an agonized admission from Rendell — a convincing declaration that he had loved his wife, had been worried about her, and would never have caused her any harm. Even though, in Monty's long experience, love did not rule out murder; in fact, it was often the motive. Love, possession, jealousy. For now, Monty would keep the discovery to himself. But he would make a point of learning more about the bereaved husband of Meika Keller.

†

The Crown's office had a couple more items of disclosure for Monty. There was the family's denial of any knowledge of the German postcard. And there was a short supplementary statement provided by Hubert Rendell to the police.

"I just wanted to correct something I said earlier. Or add to it. You remember I said that Meika was troubled when she returned home from her European trip in January. It didn't have her down in the dumps, but there was something."

"Right."

"I asked her what was wrong and she said she was disappointed that the pictures she took of the trip didn't turn out. The photo supply place here in town told her the film had been ruined in some way, and there were no pictures."

"Yes, I remember that."

"Well, Meika always used the one camera. German camera, a Leica. Of course there were all the goofy jokes about Meika's Leica and all that. But anyway, my son decided to use the camera last week to take pictures at a party he attended. So, he borrowed the Leica. He noticed there was a film in it, with several shots left, so anyway he snapped his own pictures and dropped the film off at Precision Photo, and he just got them back. They turned out fine. But here's the thing: there were four other pictures on the same film, taken of Navy ships in the harbour, all lit up for Christmas. Before her trip to Europe. So as much as I hate to face this, she was telling me a fib about the film not working. As far as we know, she hadn't even taken the camera to Europe. Certainly hadn't taken any pictures over there. Whatever had her worried, that wasn't it."

"And you have no other idea of what accounted for her being upset."

"Not a clue. My take on it now was that I caught her worrying about something, and she came up with the film story on the spot to cover whatever was really bothering her. So I have something else eating away at me, the fact that she lied to me. And now I've got it in my head that MacNair had something to do with it!"

"With her being upset after the trip?"

"Well, you've got the bastard charged with her murder. Maybe you should check and see where he was the week of January twenty-sixth to thirty-first!"

"We've already done that, sir."

Monty saw with relief that there was a note clipped to the back of the statement, indicating that the police had confirmed that MacNair was accounted for all those days in Halifax.

He thought then of his conversation with Fried Habler, who had said Hubert Rendell left a message on his answering machine the night of his wife's death. Rendell had told the police he had slept through the night and did not know she was missing until he awoke in the morning. Why had he made that statement? Was there anything else the victim's husband had left out or misstated about that night? Monty knew he could not try to make a case against Commodore Rendell as the real killer. That would be seen as a desperate ploy to deflect blame from his client, and it would alienate the jury. And he could hardly interview Rendell himself. But when the time came and Rendell was on the witness stand, he could cross-examine him about his statement and this and any other inconsistencies — lies? in his statements to the police.

CHAPTER XVII

Brennan

Brennan had never been convinced that it was Albert Einstein who defined insanity as doing the same thing over and over, expecting a different result. But whoever had coined the phrase, he or she could have been describing the behaviour of one Brennan Xavier Burke. These days, it seemed, Brennan was the very embodiment of doing the same thing over and over and expecting not to be feeling like shite the next morning. Once again, he'd been at it to the extent that his hangover nearly had him destroyed. But he had work to do, so he heaved his ailing body out of bed, stood upright, felt everything in his stomach slop to the bottom, and made a beeline for the bathroom. Brennan was a man who couldn't bear sickness and couldn't bear the filth that came with it; that should have been motivation enough to change his ways.

He didn't feel much healthier when he met with his children's choir at nine that morning to rehearse their music for the season of Lent.

In fact, it was several days into Lent already, and Father Burke, priest of the Roman Catholic Church, had not given a moment's thought to giving up the drink for the penitential season. And, *O Domine*, what was this now? Was he seeing double? Had he reached the point in his downward slide that he was hallucinating? There were two little red-headed girls standing in the front row where there should have been only one, that one being Normie Collins. There were only a handful of redheads in the entire school, which was still an over-representation of gingers in the general population. This reflected the prevalence of Scottish and Irish families in the province. But on a global scale, they were the smallest visible minority in the world. Now he had two where there should have been one. He looked at the other choristers and was relieved to note that he was not seeing double with any of the rest of them. Ah. It was Kim, Normie's best friend. Either she was wearing a wig or she had dyed her light-blond braids a flaming orangey-red. They were twelve-year-old girls; he was a man. Discretion was called for here, and he affected not to notice.

He greeted his students and they replied with "Good morning, Father."

"Do yez all have the new piece I handed out, the Croce?"

"Yes, Father."

"Grand so. *O vos omnes, qui transitis per viam. Attendite et videte si est dolor similis sicut dolor meus.* Who can tell me what the words mean?"

Normie always knew her Latin, but Brennan did not want to call on her too often. Give the others a chance. And, for her part, she never put herself forward, afraid of looking like a show-off, which she was not. Unlike some of the kids who waved their hands in his face claiming they had it, and they had it all wrong. One of the lads in the back raised his hand.

"Alastair?"

"It means all you guys, or all of you, who pass by on the road, pay attention and see if there is any sorrow like my sorrow."

"That's it. Usually translated as 'if there be any sorrow,' but I'll leave that to your grammar teacher. Well done, Alastair."

Brennan looked at them all, raised his arm for them to begin, and noticed tears in Normie's eyes. A very sensitive little girl. Feeling sorry for Jeremiah and his lamentations or for Jesus on the cross, or something else altogether? Well, this wasn't the time to find out.

The choir of children sounded like angels out of heaven as they sang the achingly beautiful piece. Except for Chadwick Soames, slouching in the back row and singing off key, looking for all the world like someone who was above it all. Soames once again acting the maggot; it was all Brennan could do to be civil to him. "Chad Soames, sit up straight, sharpen your tone, and lower the volume, would you?"

"Yeah, sure, whatever."

"What?"

"Okay."

They sang it again. Soames clamped his lips together in protest, and that suited Father Burke just fine. Without Chad's flat tenor overriding the others, the sound was exquisite.

Chad Soames offended more than the lovely Renaissance music of Giovanni Croce. Brennan heard him when the kids were filing out. "What happened to you, Kimmie? Somebody set your head on fire?"

"Shut up!" Good for her. "Shut up" was a mild version of what Brennan would say to the little gurrier if he heard another nasty word out of his mouth.

Brennan caught up with Normie in the hallway and said, "Could you come in and help me with something, Normie?"

"Okay."

She went ahead of him into the classroom, and he followed and closed the door.

"What's the trouble, Normie?"

"Nothing," she claimed, avoiding his eyes.

"What is it, *acushla*? You were in tears in there. You'll tell me if there's anything aggravating you here at school, won't you?"

"But I can't — couldn't — tell you even if there was something. I'm not saying there is!"

"Why couldn't you tell me?"

"Because then I'd be a *tout!*"

So, there it was. Something here in the school, presumably someone, had her agitated. Now, how to reassure the child that she wouldn't be a tout — an informer — if she told him about it? It seemed she'd spent too much time in Ireland last year! Too much time with the Burke family, the "well-known republican family," for whom there was no form of life lower than someone who would inform on someone else to the authorities. Just when he was about to utter words of reassurance, she made her hand into the shape of a gun and pointed it at her knee. Oh, God. Having herself kneecapped as an informer. The age-old lament of parents came to his mind: *Where did we go wrong?*

He hardly knew where to begin. "Em, that's not the situation here, sweetheart." This isn't Belfast where you'd be in fear of losing your kneecap. Or worse. "Nobody would ever think of you as a tout, Normie. If there's something wrong, you can tell me." She merely shook her head, then looked fearfully at the door. Brennan decided against keeping her in any longer, lest someone out there think she was indeed telling tales. He opened the door and said, in a voice surplus to requirements, "Thank you, Normie. I'll get that book back to you this week."

He had a free hour then, so he took himself off to the auditorium where he could sit at the piano and pick out a few chords for a piece he was composing. But the music that came to him was much too dark for a hymn of praise; it was more in the line of *De profundis clamavi ad Te, Domine.* Out of the depths I have cried to Thee, O Lord. So, he gave it up for the time being.

He was passing by the study room at the back of the choir school when he looked in and saw the least likely person to be found studying. And in fact he wasn't studying at all. Richard Robertson, his class's designated comedian, was standing by the window, looking out. It was a warm day, and the window was open. Richard turned and gave a little jolt when he saw Father Burke in the doorway.

"You're studying for your air currents exam, Richard? Bird calls maybe?"

Normally, Richard would have come back with a quip to top Brennan's lame remarks. But he put his finger to his mouth for silence. He stayed at the window, and Brennan had the impression that Richard was inviting him to look, without saying so. Brennan walked in and joined him. The window looked out over the back of the school, where only three students were gathered.

"I'm going to beat the shit out of that fucker," Richard said, then, realizing what he had just said and to whom, he said, "Shit! Sorry about the language, but . . ."

It was Brennan's turn to signal for silence. When he had taken in what was going on, he said *sotto voce*, "You won't have to, Richard. I'll deal with him."

What he had heard was Chad Soames needling Kim and Normie. "Why did you put that stuff in your hair, Kimmie? You were turning into a real hot blond. Now you're trying to look like this little dweeb." He pointed at Normie, then put his fingers around his eyes to mimic eyeglasses, and said, "She probably can't even see your hair, so you fucked up your hair for nothing. Go back to blond, trust me. And by this time next year —" Now he was making a "shapely female" shape with his hands "— your phone will be ringing off the wall with guys wanting to you-know-what you. And," he said to Normie, "she won't even bother taking any more calls from *you*. You're gonna be left behind in her dust."

"Shut up, Chad-dick!" Kim responded. "You're such an idiot!"

Normie loyally echoed, "Yeah!"

Soames turned to Normie and said, "You won't have to worry about anybody phoning *you*, Not-Normal, unless it's some dork who's only after you for your *science* notes."

And there it was, presumably. Normie was at the top of the class in science and math, and everything else when he thought of it, with the exception of the visual arts. And Chadwick, to put it charitably — and Brennan was in no state to be charitable — was far down in the standings. But, somehow, Soames thought he had other charms that could compensate for that and win the heart of Kim Kennedy. The little bastard was so deluded that he thought humiliating Kim's friend, driving a wedge between the two girls, would get him time alone with Kim. And perhaps would blunt any critical opinions Normie might be sharing with Kim on the subject of Chadwick L. Soames.

The kid was still out there, playing his part to perfection. He leaned into Normie's face and said, "You're gonna end up being the skinny old maid like they have in the movies, in your house all alone, eating cans of cat food!"

"Leave her alone, you moron! She is my best friend, and she's the best person in this whole school!" said Kim. "And if I ever find out you rooted through my gym bag again, I'm going to get my father after you. You *perv!*"

What was this? What had the little creep been doing? Brennan turned to Richard. "How long has this been going on?"

Young Richard looked wretched standing there. He said, "I don't want to be a rat."

"You're not a rat. Unless that little scene out there was the first such episode, which apparently it isn't, you didn't tell. And even if you had, I would look upon you as a fella sticking up for his friends, Normie and Kim."

The poor kid then said, "I should have said something about it! He's got the hots for Kim and he always makes fun of Normie, to break them up. To break up their friendship. I don't know why. Just because he's a jerk."

Brennan didn't want to ask but had no choice. "What's this about the gym bag?"

Richard looked away and said, in a voice Brennan could hardly hear, "He went through Kim's stuff and stole one of her . . . a bit of her underwear."

"What?!"

"I know, I know. He's a little perv. Kim didn't tell me this. One of the other girls did. She wanted me to beat the shit out of him. And I have to tell you I've been thinking of doing exactly that." He glanced at Brennan and looked away again. "But now I've just —"

"This conversation never happened, as they say in the fillums. And that little gouger," he said, indicating Soames, "is out of here. He is about to become a nonperson at this institution."

"What? Can you do that? His old man is rolling in money. He donates thousands to the school!"

"I don't care if his old man is Donald Trump."

"Who's Donald Trump?"

"He's an arsehole in New York with all kinds of money. And absolutely no taste. Doesn't know how to act."

"Oh. Never heard of him."

"You probably never will."

"So, you're going to expel Chad Soames?!"

"Just watch me."

Brennan had no doubt whatsoever about Richard Robertson's credibility, but he would prefer to bolster his case against Chadwick Soames with something more than the word of one of the other students, no matter how credible. If Soames had taken something from Kim, Brennan reasoned that the kid might not have run the risk of bringing the item home, where it might be discovered by his parents. Or by the maid cleaning his room. Nor was he likely to take the chance of the other kids finding something in his homeroom desk. So, what Brennan wanted now was access to Soames's locker. It would be unseemly for a priest and choirmaster to go at the locker with an axe, so he would haul the kid in and have him open it in Brennan's presence.

Decision made, he turned and stalked from the room, down the corridor, out the door, and into the backyard.

The three students turned at the sound of his approach. Normie's eyes were wide with consternation, as were Kim's. Soames tried for insolence, but the fear was there.

"You! Come with me?"

"Why should I?"

"Because I'm a bigger bully than you are. Now move."

"What are you going to do, give me the strap?"

"Get into the school."

"But —"

"Move."

Chadwick sighed and rolled his eyes at the tedium of it all, but again Brennan could see the fear. Could practically smell it on him.

When they entered the building, the kid crossed his arms and looked up at Brennan, as if to say *Now what?*

Brennan gave him the *now what* in two words: "Your locker."

And if Soames had looked fearful before, he was petrified now. "There's nothing in my locker!"

"Good. That will speed things up. Get moving."

"No, I —"

"Now."

Brennan could see the kid's hands shaking as he walked. When they got to the locker, Brennan said, "Open it."

"No! I can't. I . . . forget the combination."

"You've remembered it several times a day, every day, and you're going to remember it now."

"I . . . some other guys got in it!"

"Sure, they did. Now open the locker. I can have the fella come up from the maintenance room and take it apart with a crowbar. Either way, I'm going to see what's in it."

Soames finally realized he had no choice. With trembling hands, he worked the combination and removed the lock. Brennan looked in and saw the usual jumble of gym clothes — not washed any time recently, he noted with disgust — and notebooks, papers, sports gear. Brennan began pulling the items out, and Soames again said, "Some other guys got in it!"

Brennan didn't bother to inquire what the *other guys* had done; he would know soon enough. And he did. There in a plastic grocery bag were the underthings, top and bottom, of a young girl. He turned and gave Soames a look that pinned him to the opposite wall and hinted at the imminent arrival of a firing squad.

"Those guys put that stuff in there!"

Brennan ignored that, turned to the locker, and placed the grocery bag — the evidence — on the top shelf. Then, "Pack your bag. You and your grubby belongings are out of here."

"What do you mean?" The kid's voice was little more than a squeak.

"I mean I'm giving you the boot."

"What is this? I'm being suspended for a little joke?"

"You're not being suspended; you're being expelled. And your behaviour here was not a joke."

"You're kicking me out? You can't do that! My old man'll kill —"

"Kill who? Me? Or you?"

Brennan moved closer to him, loomed over him, stood there till the bag was packed.

"To my office. Now."

The Soames heir tried again for a pose of indifference, tried to saunter along as if none of this bothered him in the least.

When they got to the door of Brennan's office, the outcast turned and said, "This is crazy! My old man's the chairman of the board of this place; that means he's the boss! He gives a lot of money to this school! And to your church! Do you think he's going to keep the donations rolling in if his son gets kicked out of here? You'll be begging him to bring me back here!"

"You don't know me very well, do you, Soames?"

Brennan propelled his former student into the office, where Brennan looked up the Soames's phone number and called to let the mother know that Chad was about to leave the building. As it turned out, the mother wasn't home, and the family's maid took the call. Right, Brennan remembered then, Vivian and Langston Soames had gone away to Florida. Would Father Burke like to leave a message? Oh, he was sure that, directly or indirectly, the parents would get the message. He merely told the maid that Chadwick was on his way home.

The little fucker was pretty humble by the time Brennan had loaded him into his car and pulled up in front of the garish suburban home of the family Soames. The attention-craving vulgarity of this place nearly did Brennan's head in, with its pastiche of architectural styles and its entrance nearly obscured by the triple garage thrust out towards the street. Brennan didn't waste any words on the final parting. Chadwick got out, slammed the car door, and was gone. Everyone at the school knew that his parents thought their brat was a gifted student who, if he applied himself, would outshine all the others in the class, and that the advanced, demanding curriculum at Saint Bernadette's would put him in a good position when it came time to compete for admission to Harvard or Yale. They were in for what Brennan guessed was probably not their first — and would not be their last — disappointment in relation to their offspring.

†

When Brennan got back to the parish house, he went up to his room and turned on one of his most beloved CDs, Kiri Te Kanawa singing Mozart. She had just reached the "Veritas Domini" when the phone rang.

"Brennan! It is Fried Habler calling. I am in Toronto."

"Ah, Fried. *Guten Tag*."

"*Guten Tag*, Brennan. I did not know whether it is you I should be calling or the police. But I do not like to involve myself in police business. Must be a hangover — a holdover? — from growing up in the East German state. You can pass this information along to the authorities, if you think that is best."

"What is it, Fried?"

"When Edelgard told me about her enthusiasm for seeing *Don Giovanni* at the Vienna State Opera, I made arrangements for her to have a very good seat, in the second row on the aisle. I told my colleague, Johannes Distel, that she would be there two nights in a row. When I spoke to Edelgard — Meika — here in Nova Scotia, she told me she likes to see a performance twice, once for the overall excitement of it and then again to concentrate more on the details of the music. So, I got that seat for her. But she did not use it. She was not there. I know this because Distel called me about another matter, in fact about his hopes to succeed me at U of T and Dal when my term is up. We talked about that, about *Tristan* in Toronto, and about *Don Giovanni*, and that is when he mentioned to me that nobody turned up for that seat. On either night. The reason I think there is something not quite right about this is that I was one of the speakers at a Dalhousie University alumni event a couple of days after she returned from Europe. I had not seen her since she came back — in fact, I never saw her again at all — but I noticed her husband there. He is a graduate of Dalhousie. So, I approached him and asked him how his wife enjoyed the opera in Vienna, and he told me she enjoyed it very much. He thanked me for arranging the tickets. But, well, as I say . . ."

"She told him she enjoyed it, but in fact she wasn't there at all."

"Correct. Her plan was to go from Vienna to Milan for *Traviata* at La Scala. Unfortunately, I have no way of finding out whether she went to Milan or not."

"I appreciate your letting me know, Fried."

"I realize that you may feel compelled to inform the police about this. If so, do not hesitate to give them my name."

"Thank you. One way or the other, I'll have to pass this along.

Who knows what they'll do about it, now that they have Lieutenant-Colonel MacNair charged with the killing."

Brennan wasn't sure what to do with the news. Go to the police? Or go to the lawyer who was representing the local man charged with the murder? Of course, as he had acknowledged to himself all along, with a sense of shame, he hoped MacNair was in fact guilty of the crime. But if there was some kind of intrigue surrounding Meika's trip to Europe, some motive on her part for being in one place and pretending to be someplace else, this led some credence to the notion that there was a European angle to the whole affair. A German angle, most likely, in light of the strange postcard she received shortly before the hurried transatlantic flight. Where should he go with the new information? The police had their man and would not be impressed with the mere fact that she had not been in her seat in the opera house. Monty, on the other hand, would be keen to hear anything that might suggest an alternative to his client as the guilty party.

Monty

As much as Monty considered Brennan's notion of a German angle to the killing of Meika Keller a bit too fanciful — and downright strange, coming from a man who was anything but fanciful himself — Monty could not help but be interested in the fact that Meika Keller had lied about her time in Europe. The decision to take the trip was abrupt. When she returned, she was preoccupied about something and told her husband it was that her pictures had not turned out, when in fact she may not have taken any pictures at all. Now, in a brief but most welcome phone call from Brennan, Monty had heard that she had not shown up to take her reserved seat at the Mozart opera in Vienna. She had lied about that, too.

Monty gave some thought again to the postcard. The sender of the card wrote a seemingly innocuous message saying "good for you" and expressing envy of Meika's talents. The photo on the card was far from innocuous: the former headquarters of the much-feared secret police, the Stasi. How to account for the difference in mood between the message and the image? The fact that she took off to Europe — to Germany? — soon after receiving the card was surely significant. What, Monty wondered, if the card was not meant to be creepy or threatening at all? What if it was from an old friend, or lover, in the spirit of "Remember what we had to put up with? That's over now." Did Meika take it as an invitation? Or even if it was not an invitation, did it prompt in her the desire to see someone there again? Whatever was going on, it presented Monty with a good handful of dust to throw in the eyes of the judge and jury to raise a reasonable doubt about the guilt of Alban MacNair.

Now, as a matter of strategy, where should he go from here? He was not under any duty to disclose the details of his defence to the Crown. The Crown was obligated to disclose its evidence to the defence but there was no equal, reciprocal obligation. This was an example of the law acknowledging the overwhelming power of the state, and the presumption of innocence for the individual facing that power as a defendant. If Monty did disclose the new information, he ran the risk of finding out, and having the Crown find out, that there was a perfectly good explanation, that there was nothing in Europe that had a bearing on the death of Meika Keller, and his reasonable doubt arguments would thus be destroyed. But if there was something to it, and an investigation turned up somebody from Europe as a plausible suspect, this could mean the charges against MacNair would be dismissed. So, in the end, he decided to hand the information over to the Crown, to Bill MacEwen, and let him provide it to the police.

MacEwen did not sound overly impressed, or overly concerned, about the vacant opera seats. "Except, as a good Scotsman, I deplorrre the idea of expensive seats going unoccupied!" But he assured Monty he would look into it. "Her passport will show which countries she visited on the trip."

CHAPTER XVIII

Monty

The month of March started off with a massive snowstorm. By the time Monty's street was plowed and he made it into the office, he had missed two phone calls from clients who could not get into the centre of the city in the snow. But he had an insurance investigator waiting for him, with a report about a plaintiff in a motor vehicle accident case. Monty was representing the insurer for the defendant. The plaintiff claimed that he could not return to work because he couldn't sit, stand, bend, or lift. Now here was the investigator with a surveillance video showing the plaintiff bending over the left rear wheel of his truck, removing it, hefting it up, biffing it into bed of the truck, and then replacing it with another wheel. Monty took the videotape, thanked the investigator, and went into his office. The same old stories over and over — enough to induce a coma in a lawyer who seen it all a thousand times before. What pissed him off more than the dishonesty was the contrast between the malingerers and the people who had suffered real and devastating injuries, people who deserved to be handsomely compensated. He swept the faker's file aside and turned to *R. v. MacNair.*

The discovery that Hubert Rendell had lied to the police when he claimed he had slept through the night of his wife's death, that he had made at least one angry call trying to track her down, made Monty curious, to say the least, about Rendell. Monty knew very little about the naval commander, and what little he had heard was the stuff of hagiography; the bereaved husband was nothing short of a saint. Well, it now sounded as if he had a temper and wasn't above embarrassing himself by phoning another man, demanding to know whether his wife was with him. It was time to learn a bit more about Rendell. Monty could not go to Rendell's fellow officers looking for dirt, or even make inquiries about him. It would hardly enhance the reputation of the legal profession to have a lawyer defending the accused killer of a man's wife going about with the obvious intention of casting suspicion on the bereaved husband. But was there a more subtle way he could ferret out some information?

You couldn't spend your entire life in a big Navy town like Halifax without making the acquaintance of a few naval officers and men. And women. In fact, a few years ago, one of Monty's old girlfriends had gone out in a ship, *Nipigon*, which was the first warship to take part in NATO exercises with a mixed crew of women and men. But, although Monty was on cordial terms with her, he couldn't quite see himself taking advantage of their relationship in this way. Asking someone to snoop around above and below decks for information on a high-ranking officer could bring grief upon the head of the person doing the snooping. The client list at Stratton Sommers of course contained the names of several members of the military as well. And then there were Monty's dad's old buddies on land, at sea, and in the air. He couldn't think of anyone who, as far as he knew, worked in any kind of records office. No such luck. He'd have to settle for someone who would be willing to ask around.

Without drawing attention to himself or herself. The name he came up with was Doug Sawyer. Monty was a bluesman, a member of a group called Functus. Doug had started out with the blues, in another band, but later went country. He still played steel guitar with the Darn Barn Doors now and then, when he wasn't out on patrol duty with the Navy. He and Monty had known each other for decades, and Monty decided to give him a call. It was a delicate matter, and Monty explained it as best he could over the phone: in order to give his client the best representation possible, he had to know if there was anything about the victim's husband that might be related to the case.

Sawyer could read through the lines, but he said he'd be willing to help. "As long as it doesn't require me to sneak in under the radar and break into anybody's pers files." Monty assured him that he didn't expect anything of that nature, while at the same time saying to himself that he wished such a thing were possible. "It shouldn't be hard to get a casual conversation going these days about Commodore Hubert Rendell," Sawyer said.

"True enough," Monty agreed. "It goes without saying, Doug, but I can't stop myself from saying it anyway. This little project is utterly confidential."

Doug laughed, as well he might. "You're telling me? You think I want anyone to know I've been working undercover for the lawyer representing the man charged with killing the wife of the commodore?"

Doug Sawyer had never been shy about speaking his mind.

"I take your point, Doug. And I'm very grateful for your help."

Sawyer was sitting in Monty's office three days later, his coat dusted white from another snowfall.

"Well, as you might imagine, Monty, Commodore Hubert Rendell has an exemplary record."

"Well, that's pretty well what we'd have expected."

"Yes."

Sawyer was quiet for a moment and then said, "There was one thing."

"Oh?"

"Old complaint. Nine years ago."

"What was the complaint?"

"It was filed by a woman. A lieutenant. We have something called a Redress of Grievance procedure, but I'm not sure that it went that far, you know, whether the process was actually started, or she let it be known that she had a grievance and she might go forward with it. I didn't want to grill the person who mentioned this to me."

Monty tried not to look too keen. "No, I understand. What did she say happened?"

"Said he acted inappropriately towards her."

"In what way?"

"My 'informant' didn't have the details. Just that she felt his behaviour, or his attitude, might be holding her back from promotion."

"I see."

"And that's all she wrote."

"Do you have a name for me?"

Sawyer hesitated, and Monty was loath to try and drag it from him. But eventually it came out: "Lieutenant Diane Borowitz."

"Where could I find Lieutenant Borowitz these days?"

"Jesus, whatever you do, don't tell her you got this from me."

"No, of course I won't."

"You'll find her at the dockyard. She's task group staff."

"Where was this incident, or behaviour, supposed to have happened?"

"Here in Halifax. Summer of 1987, so it must have been just after the commodore got back from Europe."

"Oh, he was in Europe?"

"Well, the North Sea. He was serving in HMCS *Algonquin* when she took part in NATO exercises there." Sawyer laughed. "Maybe the boys enjoyed some time in the ports of northern Europe, and old Hubert was still a little wound up when he got home!"

It was rare for Brennan to receive a personal letter in the mail, unless it was from his family in New York. But on Monday, March 4, he found an envelope with his name and address handwritten and a post office box shown as the return address. He took the envelope upstairs to his room and opened it. Mail delivery must have been delayed by the weather, because by the time the letter reached Brennan, he barely had time to do what was asked of him. The message was brief: "Father Burke, could you meet me at Perks at one thirty p.m. on Monday. There is something I would like to discuss with you." It was signed "Lt-Col. A.J. MacNair." Today was Monday. Why in the world would MacNair want to see Father Burke?

Brennan felt like a spook in a John le Carré novel, all the more because his identity was all but obscured by a high collar and scarf and a peaked tweed cap pulled down over his eyes to keep out the blowing snow. He slipped and slid his way to the coffee shop on Lower Water Street, arriving ten minutes before the appointed time. MacNair was in place ahead of him. Brennan stamped his feet to get the snow off and walked to meet his contact. He recognized him from his newspaper photo, although today he was in civvies — jeans and a sweater, with a heavy winter parka hanging on the back of his chair. Brennan joined MacNair at the table. Did not call him by name.

"Coffee for you, Father?"

"I'll have a cup of tea. Thank you."

MacNair ordered the tea and coffee, paid for them, and brought them to the table. Brennan made no attempt at small talk. Whatever this was about, idle chatter was not the order of the day.

MacNair was of the same mind. "I have of course heard the talk about Meika asking to see you the night of her death. As you can imagine in the situation I'm in, I have searched out every detail, every rumour, relating to this tragedy. I did not kill her, Father. It is important for you to understand that." Brennan merely nodded, said nothing. "I believe, and perhaps you do as well, that she took her own life."

Brennan did not express what should have been obvious: that the last thing he wanted to consider was that the woman had taken her own life. The grim possibility that she was murdered by the man sitting across from him in the coffee shop was Brennan's selfish, shameful, unconscionable hope.

"So," MacNair continued, "as a man facing life imprisonment for a murder I did not commit, I wonder whether you have any information that might help me."

"Well, you seem to be in the know about the fact that I failed to meet her as I had promised to do, a failure I will regret to the end of my days. I do know that something was troubling her, but I have no idea at all what it was." What he did know, now — or at least suspected — was that MacNair's motive in seeing him was to suss out whether Meika had said anything to Brennan that might be incriminating for MacNair. Was Brennan sitting across from a killer, who hoped to use the priest's relationship with the victim in his defence? Brennan was on his guard, but he would see the meeting through.

"You say she was troubled. That makes it even more imperative that I hear about any little detail," MacNair said, "no matter how trifling it might seem, about Meika's conversation, her demeanour, that night. Or any other time you saw her at the university or at the church. I realize that if it was a confession, you wouldn't be able to tell me, according to Catholic doctrine, but some other conversation . . . ?"

"That's right, but I can tell you this much. There was no confession, or even a request for a confession. If she was seeking the sacrament of reconciliation, she did not tip her hand to me about that when we had our brief encounter at Saint Mary's."

"If I've heard about your encounter with her, you've no doubt heard about mine."

Brennan had read and heard about the voices raised outside the Atlantic School of Theology the night before the body was found.

"I can't emphasize this enough, Father Burke. I had an argument with Meika that night, but when I left her, she was alive and well. Not happy, but not injured in any way."

"Why was she unhappy, Lieutenant-Colonel? You have asked me that question. But it seems to me that you have the answer."

"I know something she was upset about, yes. But I don't know whether that is what she hoped to confide in you."

MacNair took a sip of black coffee and looked around the room. He drew out a pack of smokes and offered the pack to Brennan. Brennan thanked him, took a cigarette, and they both lit up. MacNair inhaled, waited a few seconds, turned his head, and blew out the smoke. When Brennan remained silent, MacNair said, "We had an argument. It was just a personal matter."

That was stating the obvious, Brennan thought; what else could it be but personal?

"The sort of thing that can develop between people who have known each other a long time. We raised our voices, made fools of ourselves, I guess, if any of the good citizens of Francklyn Street heard us, but she walked away under her own steam. I didn't hurt her."

Brennan, like the police, found it hard to see the combination of events that night as coincidental: a shouting match near the shore, a big emotional row between the two of them, and Meika found dead in the water hours later. But the Army officer was hardly going to cop to that. "What do you think happened to her then?"

"You know what I think, Father Burke."

"She killed herself over you."

This brought MacNair forward in his seat. He mashed his cigarette in the ashtray and said, "No! She killed herself because of her own unhappiness. It was her own state of mind that drove her into the water!"

The man was overwrought. Little wonder. But Brennan decided to use that if he could. "The news reports about you said you served in Germany with the military. Did you ever meet her over there?"

"'East is east and west is west,' Father Burke. 'And never the twain shall meet.' Don't you know that expression?"

"Kipling. I believe it goes on to say, 'Till earth and sky stand presently at God's great judgment seat.'"

Brennan had not expected MacNair to be rattled by his recitation but something about it hit a nerve, because MacNair shot back, "Leave it to a priest to spin this around to Judgment Day. Well, I'll have you know that I have nothing to answer for on that day or any other day. Forget about Germany, forget about murder. I'm not responsible for the actions of a woman unhinged by whatever was going on in her own head. I was hoping you might have something that could shed some more light on that, but apparently you don't. I'm sorry to have wasted your time, Father Burke." And with that he got up and walked out into the blinding snow.

Monty

"Lieutenant Borowitz, thank you for agreeing to speak with me. You may want to put the run to me when you hear what I have to say, but I'll give it a try."

"That doesn't inspire a great deal of confidence, Mr. Collins."

Diane Borowitz was a tall, fit-looking woman in her late thirties, with short dark curls under a grey woollen tuque. She had agreed to meet him but far from her place of work at the dockyard on the shore of Halifax Harbour. She suggested the Chickenburger, a popular eatery in Bedford. It was about a fifteen-minute drive from the city, if you took the scenic route along the Bedford Highway, and Monty drove out there at lunch time on Wednesday.

"No. Well, as I said to you on the phone, I'm a lawyer working on a case here in Halifax. I am in fact representing the man who is charged in the death of Meika Keller."

The Navy lieutenant stiffened and she looked wary, as well she might. She didn't speak.

"Lieutenant-Colonel MacNair, as I'm sure you know, is the man who's been arrested."

"Right. But I don't know MacNair, except to say hello in passing. And I did not know Commodore Rendell's wife at all. Saw her, but I don't recall ever being introduced. I have spent much of my career on the West Coast, at Esquimalt, so I'm not as plugged in to the social scene here as others would be."

"I understand."

"So, I don't see how I can be of any help to you."

"Well, I'll explain. First of all, what can I get you?" He looked over at the counter.

"I was thinking of sushi with a spinach and goat cheese salad on the side."

Monty laughed. "Would you like fries with your chickenburger?"

"Naturally. And a large glass of orange pop."

"I'll have the same."

He returned with their orders, and they took their first bites. After what he hoped was a decent interval, he got to the point. "What I'm hoping, Lieutenant, is that you'll tell me something about Hubert Rendell."

That wary look again. On his way out to Bedford in the car, Monty had tried to come up with a cover story that would disguise the true reason for his interest, that is, his interest in trying to cast suspicion on the bereaved husband of the victim. He tried out his story on Lieutenant Borowitz. "In putting together a defence for my client, I am trying to find out as much as I can about the backgrounds of the key people in Ms. Keller's life. Any conflicts she might have had, her husband might have had, any history she had with other people in her time in Halifax."

The lieutenant didn't look any more convinced than Monty himself would have looked, upon hearing such a yarn. "How is it you think I can help you, since I had only a passing acquaintance with the people involved?"

"Well, I know you worked with the commodore."

"*Worked with* would not be an accurate description. He was, and is, senior to me in rank."

"I'll be open with you."

"Yes, I'd appreciate that."

"In my conversations over the past few days, I heard that there was an incident. Or a complaint that you filed against the commodore."

"You're fishing around to see if he's the type who would kill his wife."

"I don't know if I'd go as far as that."

She gave him a look that said she'd been around the block — around the world in a series of Iroquois-class destroyers, more likely — and knew exactly how far the accused man's lawyer would go in cobbling together a defence. Finally, she said, "I'm not going to get up on the stand and say Rendell strikes me as a killer."

"No, no, I'd hardly expect that."

"Wouldn't do much for my career."

"It could be a black mark against you, for sure."

"I'm no fan of Hubert Rendell. But if you repeat that, I'll deny it."

"Fair enough. Can you tell me what the complaint was about?"

"Again, I have no intention of testifying or giving a statement."

"All right. I understand."

"This was years ago. Back in 1987. I think he had just returned from the operation off the coast of Europe. The North Sea. I ended up alone with him outside the Fleet Club. Or he contrived to get me alone."

Here it comes, thought Monty. Now it was Rendell's turn to get a woman alone and show himself to be less than an officer and a gentleman.

"I had to be really careful how I handled it. Couldn't just walk away from him or tell him to eff off, because he'd use it against me whenever I came up for promotion."

"Right. So . . . what did he do?"

"He had obviously been listening to Wardroom gossip about me, if he thought I would . . . let's just say he had the wrong idea about me."

"And? What did he do? Or try to do?"

"He accused me of behaving inappropriately."

He accused *her*? "Really. In what way?"

"He said I'd been flirting with, or coming on to — or however he put it — one of our men here, the commander of one of our ships. I won't name the man, and I hadn't been *flirting* with him. Rendell got it into his head that I was some kind of home wrecker, and he would not stand for that sort of behaviour on his watch! It was bullshit. Me and this man, we were friendly, that was all. In fact, I was just as friendly with his wife as I was with him. His wife was great fun, and we used to joke around together. Rendell was way off base, making an accusation like that. He's a bit of a stick-in-the-mud, bit of a prude. I was offended by the accusation, and on the spur of the moment, I made the complaint about him and his inappropriate slander against me. When I cooled off, I wished I hadn't bothered to make a report. It's the kind of thing that happens, and you just let it roll off your back. Which I should have done." She folded her arms and gave Monty a tight little smile. "So, there you have it. Not much there to blacken his character, if that's what you were hoping to do!"

Not much indeed. He thanked Lieutenant Borowitz, apologized for taking up her time, and stood when she rose to leave. He went back to the counter and ordered a bagful of chickenburgers for the family, and drove around the Bedford Basin to the centre of the city. What had he gained from that encounter? Only more evidence that Commodore Hubert Rendell was a straight arrow. He expected those under his command to live up to the same standards. But what, Monty wondered, what might he do if someone close to him fell below those standards? What if he thought there was a home wrecker operating on his own patch?

CHAPTER XIX

Brennan

"I'm thinking the answer to all this lies in Germany." Brennan was on the phone to his brother Terry after another night haunted by Meika Keller. It wasn't that Brennan was hearing voices from the grave, not even Meika Keller's. What he was seeing, over and over, was her blanched face, her lightless eyes staring up at him from the waters of the Atlantic Ocean. And it was driving him to go to whatever lengths he had to in order to assuage his guilt, to solve the question of her death.

"The postcard," Terry said.

"Right. Patrick filled you in. Meika got that card and then, only a few days later, she took off for Europe. Now I hear from Fried Habler that she didn't show up two nights in a row for a Mozart opera in Vienna, yet her husband told Fried that she had enjoyed the opera."

"And? Why do I get the feeling you've a scheme in the works?"

"Long association with me makes you suspicious. Rightly so. But it's hard not to see significance in a homemade postcard showing the headquarters of the secret state police, and an unplanned trip right after she gets it."

"But if it was a threat of some kind, why would she drop everything and head over there?"

"On the surface, it doesn't make sense. But we don't know what might have been going on beneath the surface. Back in 1974 she made her escape at a checkpoint, and she was shot at."

"They fired on everybody who tried to flee, didn't they? But I have an idea. And don't make me regret this, Bren! If you think there was something from her East German past that came back to haunt her, something or someone, there's a guy I could talk to over there."

"Oh?"

"Old Air Force buddy of mine. Fella by the name of Russ. We flew together during my time in the service. Now he's stationed in Germany. I see him once in a while when I have a layover. I'm flying to Zurich tomorrow night. That doesn't give you much time for planning. My next flight to Frankfurt is Monday of next week. Russ is still at the old U.S. embassy in Bonn. With the move of the capital from Bonn to Berlin, the U.S. has two operations going, one still in Bonn, the other in Berlin. The German Ministry of Defence is in Bonn and so is Russ. Coincidence? You don't have to be James Bond to suspect a military intelligence angle to his assignment."

"And he'll talk to you?"

"Maybe, as long as we don't tag-team him. If he's going to say anything, it will be to me. Two of us will make him twitchy."

"Understandably."

"So, if you're thinking of a road trip, or a sky trip, or a space trip for the pair of us, you'll have to keep yourself entertained in a beer garden or a cathedral while I meet with him. Now obviously he's not going to know anything specific about Meika Keller. Or Edelgard Whoever-she-was. But he may be able to tell me where to look for information. General info about people who escaped or, well, I don't know what. But I can try."

Brennan was anxious to get over to Germany, anxious to try to unearth the origins of the Stasi postcard. He would be more than happy to get a flight for tomorrow night and meet up with Terry this week. But the coming week was his school's March break, so the later timing would be good. And he thought it would be more practical — more politic — to coordinate his excursion with Bishop Cronin's trip to Toronto for meetings with the Canadian Conference of Catholic Bishops. He would be leaving this weekend and would be away for several days. With Cronin out of the way when Brennan left town, the only person he had to provide with notice was his beloved pastor, Monsignor Michael O'Flaherty.

"Father Drohan and I will cover for you, lad," O'Flaherty assured him. "Sure, it's only an extension of your pastoral duties."

"God love you, Michael."

And then Brennan thought of Fried Habler again. Was there any bit of information he could offer to an amateur spy going over to the newly unified Germany in search of clues to a mysterious death in Halifax? Stated that way, it seemed unlikely that Habler could assist. But Brennan had never been to the eastern, formerly walled-off, part of Germany, so even the most basic information would be helpful. He called Habler and received a cordial invitation to drop by the house. So, Brennan stopped in at the Clyde Street Liquor Store and got a six pack, three German and three Irish, and knocked on the door of the little shingled house up the street.

"Welcome, Brennan, welcome! And God bless you for thinking of a singer all alone in his house with a parched throat! This is exactly what the conductor ordered."

Brennan went inside and they cracked open their choice of cans, Habler's Irish and Brennan's German, and Habler poured them into steins. They chatted about an upcoming opera recital by the music students at Dalhousie University.

Then Brennan said, "I have an excursion planned."

"Oh? Where are you going?"

"Berlin."

"Oh!"

"I know I may regret it. I know I may come away no wiser than I am now — and I admit wisdom is not my strong suit these days — but that postcard suggests a German angle to this whole affair. And if that is the case, I want to know what that angle is. Of course, I'm not daft enough to believe the answer will fall into my lap, but I won't rest until I've at least made the effort."

Habler was sitting back, nodding his head. Nodding in agreement? Or in an effort to humour a man with a barmy scheme that would almost certainly go kaput?

"What do you think, Fried?"

"Brennan, I don't know what to say. I understand completely your suspicion that the card is significant. A card showing the headquarters of the Stasi! The secret police who spied on everyone and kept millions of records! You may be interested to hear that the old records have been preserved, or many of them anyway. Back in 1989, during the dying days of the East German regime, some women in the city of Erfurt noticed dark smoke coming from the Stasi building in that city. The women knew the place was heated with gas, which makes white smoke. They concluded that the Stasi were burning papers in there. So, a bunch of citizens got together and occupied the building to prevent destruction of any more records. The military prosecutor was called in, and it all ended up with committees being formed, buildings being occupied in other cities, including Berlin, and records being preserved. After reunification, the government created the BStU, the Stasi Records Agency, and the position of Federal Commissioner for the Stasi Records. Four years ago, the files were opened to the public, and the Records Agency administers this process. So, people can see what the former government kept on file about them." Habler leaned forward with an amused look on his face. "That is not even to mention the samples they kept of people's sweat and body odours! Ah, I see that makes you — what is the word? Not sleazy . . ."

"Queasy may be the word you're searching for, Fried, and you are absolutely correct. What kind of world are we living in when government authorities . . ."

Habler was shaking his head. "You have no idea what things were like, Brennan. Here, we both need another beer." He got up, refilled the glasses, and handed one to his guest. "There were files on some six million people, over one-third of the population of East Germany. Brennan, you may be amused to hear what they are doing now. There was much shredding of records as you might imagine. And here is an example of our famed German efficiency! Bags of shredded documents are being painstakingly reassembled! This will take years, as there are thousands of these bags, and tens of millions of pages."

"My God. You couldn't make this stuff up. And if you did . . ."

"Nobody would believe you."

"Hard not to see a message of some kind in the choice of building on the card. Have you any idea, Fried, why someone would send a message like this to Meika Keller?"

"I have no idea at all. I'm sorry."

"I suspect I won't know any more after travelling to Berlin than I do now, but I feel compelled to make the effort."

"Well, if you do go, I know a family that has a small hotel. It's in the Alexanderplatz part of the city, which was of course formerly in East Berlin. Not far from the BStU office building, as a matter of fact, which is on Karl Liebknecht Strasse. This is not the Stasi headquarters itself, of course; the old headquarters block is where the actual records are kept in the archive. If you wish to see that frightening complex of buildings, you would take the U-Bahn, the underground train, to Magdalenenstrasse station. The hotel is the Gasthaus Pfeiffer. Shall I write all of that out for you?"

"No, just say it all again. I'll remember." So Habler repeated the information, and Brennan thanked him.

They talked about travel and history, and then Brennan brought the conversation back — rather abruptly, he knew — to the death of Meika Keller.

"The night she died . . . you weren't home that night when the phone rang, were you, Fried?"

"I was!"

"There's no harm in admitting you were out. The police are hardly going to be looking at you for the killing. And neither am I!"

"I can think of someone who would like to blame me. Well, I don't mean to make him sound unscroob— no, what is the word? A man who will do anything to achieve his goal."

"Unscrupulous?"

"That is the word."

"Who do you have in mind?"

"I am talking about the lawyer, Monty Collins. He would be happy to find another suspect, someone else besides this man MacNair. But I know Mr. Collins is not unscrupulous. Still, if it is believed that I was out and yet I told the police I was in . . ."

"It would look as if you had something to hide."

"Yes, it would. But I was here at home. I really was."

"So, how did you miss the telephone jingle-jangling beside your head while you were in bed?"

"I . . . was afraid it was my wife."

"But the timing of the call, it was around midnight. Would your wife be calling at five in the morning, German time?"

"She was in Toronto." There was a shamefaced look about him now.

"What is it, Fried? Why did you not want to speak to your wife? Maybe you weren't the only one reclining in your bed when the phone started clanging in your ears?"

"No, no! I was not in bed."

"Go on."

Habler sighed, polished off his beer, and put the stein on the coffee table. "I was not the only man that night who did not want a call from a wife. I was out at the Split Crow. Do you know that bar? I learned the history of it when I was there. Sailors have been drinking in that place for more than two hundred years. It may have started out in a different location, but I do know this: it was originally named the Spread Eagle, named after the double eagle symbol from Germany. And people looked at the image and began calling it the Split Crow! I met up with a group of people and drank rum with them, and it turned into a crazy party. And, well, I invited them all back here. And there were a couple of women . . . So, if I picked up the phone and my wife heard the voices . . ."

"Does your wife tend to doubt you?"

"Well, no, not usually. But if she found out I lied to the police? I am often away from home and she makes jokes about opera 'divas' and fans and all of that, but she is not entirely joking. She knows I work very closely with beautiful and talented women. And then this. With the . . . ladies. And the sailors and . . ."

"Sailors? Let's back up here, Fried. Why don't you start at the beginning?"

"Yes, all right. I was in the Split Crow. I had been passing by and heard music, rock music being played, and I felt tempted to go in for a drink and for some company. Some entertainment. And the place was crowded, no seat for me at a table, so I stood at the bar and ordered a drink. I heard someone speaking Dutch, which I understand, so I turned around and saw a group at a table. There were a couple of girls there and, I realized, some sailors from the Netherlands. There was a Dutch Navy ship in the harbour, visiting for official business of some kind. NATO or whatever it might have been. So, the sailors were drinking with the girls, who gave me the impression they were, well, prostitutes. And the men were telling jokes that went over the girls' heads because they could not understand the language. So, I joined in and translated but just made up most of the translations in what I thought was a humorous way. The sailors obviously thought so, too, because they invited me to join them. We all had some drinks and then, feeling grand about myself, I invited everyone back here to my house where I would be the host of the party. And the Dutchmen brought bottles of liquor, and the girls came with them. Someone had a red kerchief and put it around one of my lights, and there were jokes about this being Amsterdam jurisdiction so everything was tolerated. And all this foolishness. I launched into the score of *Così Fan Tutte*. You know what that means."

Brennan did. The title of the opera meant "Thus do they all" or "They're all like that," "they" meaning women.

"So, I did a very *opera buffa* version of some of the selections and then I began composing and . . ." Habler stopped speaking and appeared to be a bit flustered.

"And? Is something the matter, Fried?"

"No, no, it's just that there was something about composing. Did someone say Edelgard herself — Meika — had been composing?"

"What?"

"No, it was Mr. Collins. I remember now. When he was here, he asked if there had been some composing going on, and he meant Meika, but I thought at first he knew about the night of drunkenness here that night, and . . ."

"Meika composing?"

"No, never mind. It was something Mr. Collins had heard, but I don't know any more. Anyway, as I was telling you, I began composing magnificent operatic works on the spot. Correction: make that schlock. I grabbed one of the girls by the hand and made up an aria about her. I think I called it 'Lady of the Fleet,' or maybe it was 'Beauty Below the Decks,' or something. And there were some off-colour lines, terrible schmaltzy melodies, and bad, bad vocalizing on my part. I was in fact bellowing like a fourth-rate opera wannabe type of person. I pity my poor neighbours if they could hear me! My guests were nearly losing control of themselves, they were laughing so much. I made a complete fool of myself. I was a drunken, pathetic buffoon.

"One of the sailors took one of the women into the other bedroom here. I myself would have been too drunk to perform as a man in a bedroom! I don't know if you have ever been in that embarrassing situation yourself, Father Burke!"

"Don't ask!"

"Right, so unable to do anything else, not that I would — my dear wife need not fear on that score —"

"Right. But still and all, to tell the police —"

"I was not about to tell the police what really went on here that night! Or get the Dutch sailors or the women in trouble. So that is why I claimed I was home drinking all alone and then passing out and sleeping all through that outrageous night."

"Still, being unmasked as a bit of a buffoon beats being suspected of murder, now, Fried."

"But I am not suspected!"

"I'm sure you're right."

"But, Brennan, if the *politzei* are suspicious of me, I will certainly admit making a jackass of myself. And being unable to misbehave with the women!"

CHAPTER XX

Brennan

Terry Burke departed New York for Frankfurt the night of Monday, March 11, and took a connecting flight to Bonn. The following night, Brennan flew from Halifax to London and got a connecting flight in the morning from Heathrow to Berlin. He arrived in time to get settled in the Gasthaus Pfeiffer. He was exhausted from the long flight over the Atlantic; he had never been able to sleep on a plane. So he lay down on his hotel bed and debated whether to sleep or go out. It was raining quite heavily, so that offered an incentive to lose part of the day sleeping. He awoke refreshed, had a quick shower and a sandwich, and he made it to the late-afternoon Mass at Saint Hedwig's Cathedral. The hotel and the cathedral were located in what had been, for over forty years, East Berlin. The plan was for Terry to see his pal in Bonn, then fly to Berlin, and meet Brennan at the church.

Saint Hedwig's was modeled on the Pantheon in Rome, and after the Mass, Brennan had an opportunity to read the history of its martyred priest, Father Bernhard Lichtenberg. After Kristallnacht, the pogrom unleashed against Jewish synagogues and businesses in 1938, Lichtenberg began praying regularly for the Jews of Germany. He protested directly to Herman Göring about the concentration camps and took various Nazi officials to task over the persecution of the Jews and the killing of the sick and the mentally ill. Eventually, he was arrested by the Nazis and sent to the concentration camp at Dachau. He died on the way there. Brennan was on his knees in prayer and contemplation when Terry arrived with his carry-on bag in tow. Brennan handed him a brochure about the church and about Father Lichtenberg and whispered, "There is history in every paving stone in this country."

"I never doubted it. And I suspect the fella Russ has lined up for us has had some tense moments during that history. We're meeting him at one thirty tomorrow at a café on the river."

"Good plan. We'll see a bit of the city today." It was grey and cool but the rain had stopped, not a bad day for walking about. "You're not a regular visitor to Berlin, as far as I know."

"No, my German flights are generally to Frankfurt and Munich."

They left the cathedral and walked to Alexanderplatz so Terry could drop off his suitcase at their hotel. On the way, Brennan pointed to the most obvious landmark, the Berlin Television Tower. Brennan had heard it described as the tallest structure in all of Germany, but he had heard something else about it as well. "Keep an eye on the silver globe at the top of the tower. It has a nickname or two. Ulbricht Cathedral, named after the former party leader and head of state Walter Ulbricht. Or something that would resonate more with the likes of us, the Pope's Revenge. When the sun shines on it a certain way, the reflection takes the shape of a cross."

"That must have gone down well with the nonbelievers running things here."

"They wrote it off as a plus sign for their version of hard-arsed socialism. But we know different."

They stopped in at the hotel and then headed out for a stroll about the city. They noticed that every time they stopped at an intersection, nobody but nobody — young, old, male, female — crossed against a red light even if there was no traffic in sight. So, the Burkes decided to blend in with the custom and mores of the city and stood with unaccustomed patience until the light turned and gave them permission to cross.

Berlin was the loophole through which people had escaped from the East German state, because Berlin was within and surrounded by the East German territory. Brennan had seen varying figures for the number of people who had in the early years fled the people's republic for the West, figures ranging from two million to over three million. Something had to be done to close that loophole. Hence *die Berliner Mauer*, the Berlin Wall, built in 1961. West Berlin was separated from East Berlin and was blocked off entirely from the rest of East Germany by a wall of concrete blocks, wire mesh fencing, and anti-vehicle trenches, with machine gun posts and searchlights. There were more than three hundred watchtowers. The wall was patrolled by East German border guards day and night. Several thousand people managed to escape, but several thousand others were captured. Well over a hundred were either shot to death, or died in other ways, while trying to escape. But the wall came down in 1989, and the Berlin through which Brennan and Terry strolled was one undivided city, but a city of many styles.

"Intimidation architecture at its height," Brennan observed as they came upon the edifice that had been home to Hermann Göring's Air Ministry during the days of the Nazi regime. The structure epitomized the fascist style, massive and symmetrical with sharp square edges and row upon row of windows. Like other buildings constructed during the Third Reich, it was designed to impress and intimidate the masses. It was so enormous that Göring could have landed his airplanes on it. Little wonder it was a comfortable fit for the Soviet administration after the war and subsequently for the East German regime. There were a great many square modern buildings but also examples of the older styles, like the domed and elaborately decorated Berlin Cathedral and the Greek-classical Brandenburg gate. Brennan and Terry also saw the ruins of the imperial church of Kaiser Wilhelm II, with its bomb-damaged tower still standing as a reminder of the destruction of war.

Given the impetus for the trip to Berlin, Brennan intended to take a look at the office building Fried Habler had told him about, which was located close to their hotel. So, when he and Terry made their way back to Alexanderplatz, they walked the short distance to Karl Liebknecht Strasse and stood before the large modern rectangle of a building that was home to the Stasi Records Agency.

"Must be quite the operation, in a big building like this."

"I would think so, given that the state was spying on millions of its citizens. Habler said the original records are still kept in archives in the old Stasi headquarters, which of course is the building shown on the postcard sent to Meika. We'll make a point of going to see that before we leave town."

"So, Bren, was that postcard sent to Meika to say, 'They have a file on you'?"

"Or was it 'We have a file on you'?"

"Someone from the old Stasi days tormenting her, you mean."

"Could be. We just don't know."

"If she saw the postcard as a threat of some kind, why would she hop on a plane and fly over here? Or maybe it was from an old friend, and the image was meant to say, 'Look what we went through together. But that's over and done now.' Though, if that was the case, why would she lie about coming here to Berlin? Where was it she claimed she went?"

"Milan and Vienna."

"And she didn't show up for the opera in Vienna. And you think she came here."

"I imagine so, in reaction to whatever message she read into that card."

They stood looking at the building, and then Terry moved a little closer to his brother. He spoke in a quiet voice. "Brennan, don't turn your head. Stand the way you are now. But I was looking in the glass here and I saw the reflection of a man I think I spotted earlier near the hotel. Didn't think anything of it at the time, but . . ."

"You're not telling me we're being followed."

"Probably not. Who over here would know about us?"

"Well, your pal Russ, for one."

Terry laughed. "It's not Russ."

"And the fellow he has us meeting at the café?"

"Jäger. He'd have no reason to follow us; he'll be seeing us tomorrow. It may just be my old military training. Seeing enemies all around me!"

"Maybe so."

"But take a casual look in the window, see if there's a man wearing a short grey coat and a dark wool cap, black-framed eyeglasses. And if you see him walking, he has a bit of a lurch to the right side."

Brennan turned nonchalantly towards the glass and looked in the reflection. "I don't see anybody like that."

"No? He's gone. All right, let's get on with our sightseeing."

They walked all over the city, stopping for a stein of Pils or Kölsch from time to time. They had supper at a lively biergarten, suitably closed in for the season, where Brennan had a selection of *Meeresfrüchte*, seafood, and Terry had the *Hackefleisch*, ground meat. They hit the sack early to make up for all the travelling; they wanted to be sharp for the next day's assignation.

The next morning, Thursday, Brennan took the opportunity to attend another Mass in German, so he donned his clerical collar and headed out. After that, he and Terry took in a couple of museums offering a painfully honest take on German history, and then it was time to meet their contact, one Jäger, after what was traditionally the main meal of the day, *Mittagessen*. Lunch. Terry followed the directions he had been given to a café on the banks of the river Spree, and they seated themselves by the window. The sun was shining off the river, and the view was lovely. Terry said, "This guy Russ has arranged for us to meet, he's German but he was 'in the thick of things' in the American sector in West Berlin during much of the Cold War. Sounded to me as if he was a spook of some kind working for the U.S., though Russ didn't spell it out."

"Well, let's hope he can give us some idea where to start. In the meantime, let's eat."

Terry ordered schnitzel with a serving of German potato salad to start things off. Brennan started with Bavarian potato soup with bacon and pretzel croutons in it. He looked across at his brother and laughed. "You can take the lads out of Ireland, but you can't take Ireland out of the lads."

"Sure, what would we do without our spuds? Sheila gave me hell on a trip to Italy one time. I ordered potato pizza. 'You're in Italy, for the love of God, Terry. Can't you order something besides potatoes?' Affecting the attitude of a sophisticate, I told her I wanted to see how they *did them* in Italy. Did them to perfection, needless to say."

When Brennan's main course arrived, there was another story. The *maulthaschen* was a serving of dumplings stuffed with sausage, bread, onions, and herbs. Putting the plate down and eyeing Brennan's collar, the waitress said, "I don't know if I should tell you this, Father, but this was always a favourite during Lent; people could keep eating meat, because it was hidden in the pasta dough!" Brennan laughed and said he was doing the same thing, given that they were in the midst of Lent now. He savoured his first bite and called across to her that it was *köstlich*, which didn't mean costly but delicious. As was the Bavarian beer that accompanied the meal.

Brennan noticed a distinguished-looking grey-haired man in a suit and tie coming in the door and looking around. Brennan stood, and the man noted his clerical attire and approached the table. "I am Jäger." Terry rose then, and they all shook hands.

"What can we get for you, Herr Jäger?"

"I have had lunch with my wife, but I would certainly enjoy a beer — a Helles — and a *Donauwelle*."

"Please order whatever you like," Terry said. "We really appreciate your meeting us here."

"Here in the former *Deutsche Demokratische Republik*."

They engaged in small talk about the city until the waitress brought Jäger his beer and *Donauwelle*. It had layers of cake, white and chocolate, with cherries stuffed in it and chocolate glaze over the top. Brennan made a mental note to have a taste of this before he left the city. But business first. After taking a bite of his dessert and a sip of beer, Jäger got to the purpose of the encounter.

"The facts as they have been given to me are these: a woman named Meika Keller, originally called Edelgard Vogt-Becker, got out of this country in 1974, lately lived in Canada, received a postcard from this city depicting the headquarters of the Stasi. Shortly after receiving this postcard, she embarked on an unscheduled trip to Europe. She stated that she would be attending the opera in Vienna, but she did not attend. She died in suspicious circumstances shortly after her return to Canada. There is a question whether her death was a suicide or a homicide."

"That sums it up, yes," Brennan agreed.

"There are two men who would have some knowledge for you. Knowledge at the ground level, you might say. The man I recommend is Gerhardt Fischer. How many days are you in Berlin?"

"Only two more days after this."

"That is a pity. This contact, who would be most useful, is away in Den Haag right now on business. I doubt Fischer will return before your departure. That leaves us only Willy Horst Lehmann. I almost hesitate to recommend him to you. He is a low sort of person. But he has the advantage of being available. He is a humble waiter or, more accurately I suppose, a bartender. But he poses as a man of mystery, trying to create an air of intrigue about himself. It is true that he does have a past. He has not always been pouring whisky down the throats of the alcoholics six nights a week."

"How would we get close to him and induce him to talk to us? Get him out from behind the bar, I mean."

"Are you Scottish?"

"Em, no."

"I thought from your voice, perhaps . . ." He directed his question to Brennan.

"No," Brennan replied, "but why are you asking?"

Jäger laughed and said, "Willy is fascinated with Scotland, the bagpipes, all the music, and the bonnie lassies with red hair, and he has always nurtured an ambition to travel there. We used to make jokes that he would have served Erich Mielke on a platter with an apple in his mouth if the Scots had wanted him."

"Mielke? Head of the Stasi?"

"For more than thirty terrifying years. Famed for many things. With regard to those who attempted to *flee the republic*, he instructed his men in this way, 'When you shoot, you must shoot so that the guy you hit doesn't get away but stays here with us.' And so indeed many stayed, dead or alive. Even now, here in Berlin, the reference to certain streets will have people twitching. Magdalenenstrasse, Normannenstrasse, Ruschestrasse — that is where the enormous complex is located, the Stasi headquarters and associated buildings. Something like a million square feet of office space! Perhaps you have not seen it?"

"Not yet, but we intend to go and have a look."

"As for Willy Lehmann, you will find him at a very different place of employment, a bar called the Geggie. The street is Schiffbauerdamm. There is usually a band that plays Irish and Scottish music. But I warn you: Willy drinks a good part of the profits there, at least on the nights when the owner of the place is not present, and Willy cannot hold his liquor. His capacity is two glasses of beer. That is all. After that, he is of no good to anyone."

Brennan could see the ghost of a smile on his brother's face as Terry contemplated the advantage of this weakness in their target.

"How will we recognize him?"

Another laugh from Jäger. "He will be the only large, blond-haired German man behind the bar wearing a tam-o'-shanter on his head!"

They were all laughing then.

"You said he's a bit of a low character. And a drinker." Brennan didn't look at Terry when he said it. "Would a person like that have been given information, trusted with it? In other words, would he know anything?"

"He has some knowledge. A totalitarian state needs people on the ground. It is estimated that, at the time the regime collapsed, there were nearly a hundred ninety thousand people working not as employees of the secret police but as unofficial informers. They were called the IMs, *Inoffizieller Mitarbeiters*. These were civilians, regular people. Over all the years of the East German state, there may have been over half a million snitches in that category. And there was another whole world of informers, even less official than the unofficials! People in factories, universities, political organizations, cultural institutions giving information on their co-workers. Superintendents in apartment buildings keeping records of who came in to see whom. So, everywhere, you had people informing on their close friends, family members, lovers, neighbours. Schoolchildren informing on classmates. These ordinary citizens would report on anyone who said anything that offended the party line, or who spoke of escaping to the West, and those people were imprisoned or had their lives or careers destroyed. Do not forget the *Volkspolizei* as well, the national police force. Anyone walking the streets of eastern Germany today wonders about every person he meets. Was he, was she, one of the spies?"

"And this Willy was one of them."

"He was one of those assigned to keep an eye on East German citizens who, for whatever reason, were in West Berlin. He was at this work in the 1970s. Find a way to make him speak to you. You might tell him, 'Ve haff vays of making you talk . . .'" Jäger smiled and said, "I have seen those movies, too!" Brennan and Terry laughed along with him. Then Jäger rose, thanked them for their hospitality, wished them luck, and said, "See what Lehmann has to say."

CHAPTER XXI

Piet

On Thursday, March 14, Detective-Sergeants Van den Brink and Young drove the roughly two hundred sixty kilometres from Halifax, Nova Scotia, to Moncton, New Brunswick. They pulled up at the Moncton Flight Centre on the outskirts of the city, in Dieppe. Ailsa's friend Shauna had arranged for a Moncton police officer, who was a neighbour of Shauna and her husband, to meet them outside the club. Constable Ray Comeau introduced himself, and they had a quick look at the cluster of light aircraft gleaming in the sun.

"Makes you want to take to the skies, eh?" said a man behind them. They turned, and Albert Glendenning introduced himself as the man who had the day-to-day running of the centre. He invited them inside and offered them seats in a large meeting room.

"Thanks for seeing us, Albert," Ailsa said. "As Ray explained to you, we are interested in an incident that occurred here in 1985. Your flights were grounded for a day, as we understand it."

"Right."

"What happened?"

"First of all, let me make it clear that there was nothing wrong with any of our planes. Or with our facilities or any of our personnel. We run a tight ship here, if I may mix my metaphors a bit. Safety is our priority. What happened was we had a little reception for some of the people who'd attended the big do in Moncton with the Chief of the Defence Staff. Some of those guys came out here, and we had snacks and soft drinks, tea, and coffee for them. And a few of the people, those with accreditation to fly, were going to take up a Cessna or a Piper Malibu and have a short little flight over the city. Out to the beach, that sort of thing. These were of course civilian airplanes. This isn't an Air Force base. Not anymore."

"It used to be a base?" Piet asked.

"You wouldn't know it to look around now," Albert said, "but this was a big RCAF operation during the Second World War and for years afterwards. There were dozens of buildings, including a hospital, barracks, mess halls. A training centre for fliers from all over the Commonwealth."

"I never heard about all this."

"That's because you've never chatted with the old ladies here who were young during the war! Brings a big smile to my mother's face every time it comes up in conversation. She has fond memories of the men in uniform who thronged the city streets in wartime. She calls them the 'dashing airmen,' and they came from England, Australia, all over. The Moncton Flying Club — that's what we used to be called — was a big part of it. Flight training school. But those days are long gone. So, when the brass came down from Ottawa, they didn't come out here for the main event. The ceremony was in the city. And they dropped in to Number Five and the Wing."

Piet's face must again have betrayed his confusion.

"Number Five Supply Depot and the Air Force Association Wing, you know, chapter of the association. But they honoured us with a visit afterwards, and we put on a little reception for them. And, as I say, a few of our planes, two or three of them, were reserved for later that afternoon, early evening. There were a couple of the men who had been hitting the sauce earlier; you can be sure they weren't getting anywhere close to an airplane!"

"Do you have any names for us? People who attended, the guys who were drunk?"

Glendenning shook his head. "No idea."

"All right, so then what happened?"

"This is going to sound weird, because it may have been entirely harmless. You're going to laugh. But we found a mug of tea with cold medicine, allergy medicine, in it! Not exactly Baron von Richthofen buzzing our airfield or shooting down our planes!"

"No, not exactly." Piet laughed.

"We didn't know whether somebody just had a cold, and this is the way he takes his medication, or whether . . . well, that particular medication puts you to sleep. You know the old warning, 'Do not operate heavy machinery while using this product.' There's a good reason for that. We could not let anyone take a plane up if he was under the influence of a drug that would make him drowsy, or even fall asleep, while he was up there."

"How did you discover the drug in the tea?"

"One of our staff was cleaning the glasses and mugs off the table and noticed the powder from a capsule, not completely absorbed in the tea. The club did not use coffee whiteners, the powdered stuff, so that wasn't it. And it looked as if whoever had the tea drank only a couple of sips from it. Changed his mind about taking the medication in the middle of the day, or . . ."

"Or?"

"Or it was somebody else who slipped the capsule or capsules into the tea. And it didn't taste right to the tea drinker."

"Was there anything to point to that scenario?"

"I wasn't working here at the time. I only started here two years ago. But what I was told was that our people went outside and asked everyone whether he had left a cup of tea unfinished. It sounded like a stupid question, I'm sure. But nobody owned up. Nobody said, 'Yeah, I have a cold.' Or 'I'm allergic, and I put a bit of medicine in my tea and decided not to finish it.' Or some of the people out there didn't hear the question. Who knows? Anyway, out of what may have been an excess of caution, our people made up a story about bad weather coming in and ordered that all planes be grounded for the day."

Glendenning looked a little sheepish telling the story, but then he said, "We had Department of National Defence officials here, and we had a couple of drunks who got a little belligerent about politics, defence policy or whatever it was. It made one of our management people nervous enough that he kept the tea and had it taken somewhere to be analyzed. He didn't tell anybody till the analysis was completed sometime later. And if it had turned out to be a fairly harmless dose, he likely would never have mentioned it again. Would have felt foolish about doing it. But it turned out he was right to be concerned. There was the equivalent of nearly three capsules of the medication in the tea. So, whether it was somebody being careless with his own meds or, uh, one guy doctoring another guy's tea, it was a good thing that we did not permit any flights that day."

Piet and Ailsa were silent for a moment, taking this in. Then Ailsa said, "So, to ask the obvious questions: any idea who did it? And who was meant to drink it?" Glendenning shook his head. "Is there a log, or a register, showing who was to take out which planes?"

"Nothing from back that far."

And then the Moncton cop, making no attempt to hide his displeasure, asked, "But the records existed at the time. Did anybody remember who was to take the planes up? It must have been a topic of conversation, surely."

"As I said, I wasn't here then. The man who was in charge then died a few years ago. Of natural causes!" Glendenning looked embarrassed. "The way things were organized then, the manager at the time, the man who has since died, would have been in charge of the records. I think he may have done a clean-up job. From what I heard, he made it clear that nobody was to mention the incident."

Constable Comeau asked, "Was this reported to us? This *incident*, which could have been attempted murder?"

"Again, the former manager. It would have been his decision to, well, inform the authorities or not. But the Flight Centre did the right thing, kept everybody out of the cockpits, and all planes on the ground."

Nobody spoke for a long moment. Then Ailsa said, "As Ray told you, we have a man charged with murder in Halifax."

"Yes, I know."

"Does that name mean anything to you, Lieutenant-Colonel Alban MacNair?"

"Never heard of him until I read about the charges in the paper. And then Ray told me MacNair had been posted to Gagetown at the time of the DND visit, and that he'd been stopped by the Mounties west of the city. Other than that, I don't know anything. I wish I could be more helpful."

"No need to apologize, Albert," Ailsa assured him. "We wanted to check, just in case."

†

Ailsa had arranged for them to meet her friend Shauna for a fast-food lunch. The local copper came along with them. They talked about the bizarre event at the flying club and then moved on to other subjects of conversation. Constable Comeau asked after Shauna's husband, the Mountie, and they chatted about other people they knew. Comeau said the Moncton city police were on edge because they'd been hearing rumours that the force was going to be disbanded and replaced by the RCMP. "So, put in a good word with Keith for me, and maybe they'll take me on!" Shauna tried to maintain the light-hearted tone and assured Ray Comeau that he'd look wonderful in the Mounties' red dress uniform. They all said goodbye shortly after that, and Piet and Ailsa got into their car for the drive home to Halifax.

As soon as they were on the road, Ailsa said, "So. Was somebody targeted for murder? Or was somebody innocently taking too strong a dose of medication, a person who had no intention of getting into the cockpit of a plane that day?"

"That's the sanest way to look at it. But let's look at the most extreme case. If somebody had a grudge against the military, the unification of the forces, for instance, would he go so far as to murder a high-ranking officer or defence official? And if he did, wouldn't there be a more efficient way to do it? Soldiers are trained in the art of killing, after all."

"Which may be exactly why he tried it this way instead of shooting the man in the heart with an Army-issue weapon! This could look like an accident, carelessness on the part of the victim himself. And who knows? Maybe it wasn't even planned. MacNair sees Colonel Blimp there, and MacNair's out of his mind on booze, and he's got some cold medication on him and does something really stupid on the spur of the moment."

"All we have relating to MacNair, Ailsa, is a roadside stop half an hour from here late that night. And he was taken to the RCMP detachment and he blew under point zero eight. So, he wasn't piss drunk."

"Of course, that could have been the amount left in his system after being on a bender earlier in the day, and maybe the night before."

"Could have been. We just don't know. He did have a souvenir of some kind in his car, a keepsake given out to those who attended the event at the club."

Ailsa looked over at her partner. "I wouldn't like to trot this case out in front of a prosecutor! But what we may have here — *may* have

— is one death, and one intended death, that were meant to look like suicide."

Monty

Monty was sitting in his office on Thursday morning, staring in disbelief at the file on his desk. After more than two decades as a criminal lawyer, he should have been beyond surprise by now. But this guy . . . The client was charged with stealing a car. He and two women had just been in the office. It went like this:

Client: "I don't know nothing about it."

Monty: "But a witness named Josephine and another named Phyllis say they saw you with the car. Who is Josephine?"

One of the women put up her hand. "I'm Josephine." The client's mother.

"I'm Phyllis," said the other. His grandmother.

Still, the client would not admit he had the car.

Monty: "If they testify against you, it won't go well for you."

Client: "What if they don't testify?"

Monty: "The Crown will subpoena them."

Client: "So, what if they don't testify?"

Monty: "They could be put in jail."

Client: "How long would they have to stay in jail?" His own mother and grandmother.

But that wasn't the only charge against this client. He was also charged with a stabbing.

Client: "I wasn't there."

Monty: "Where were you?"

Client: "Home."

Monty to client's mother: "Was he home?"

Mother: "Yeah. Except when he went out."

Monty: "What time did he go out?"

Mother: "Uh, what time did the guy get stabbed?"

So, it was with relief that Monty took a call from Bill MacEwen from the Crown's office about the Keller case. "Morning, Bill."

"Morning, Monty. I spoke with Hubert Rendell about Meika not attending the opera in Vienna. Poor devil wasn't too happy hearing that."

"I'm sure, after everything else he's had to deal with. Now another deception."

"Right. And now it's worse. Her passport is missing."

This was getting better all the time. For Alban MacNair, not for the dead woman's husband.

MacEwen continued, "Hubert said she always kept the passport with her other papers in a desk drawer in their study. And the way he said it, I had no doubt that she always kept her papers in order in the same place. It's not there. And it's not anywhere else in the house either, or in her car or her office. I don't even like to think of the poor guy's increasingly frantic search for the damn thing."

"No. He's had a rough go of it. And now the case has opened up. The implication is that wherever she went, and I think we can assume for now it was Germany, she didn't want anyone to know about it. The question is why."

"She wasn't killed in Germany, Monty. Or Austria or Italy."

"If she even went to those latter two places."

"It happened here."

"All right. Thanks, Bill. Talk later."

Getting rid of a passport: that spoke volumes to Monty. She wanted to hide whatever information the passport contained about her travels, and she wasn't planning to travel again any time soon. Wasn't planning to go on living? Was that too much of a stretch in favour of Monty's theory of the case?

CHAPTER XXII

Brennan

The massive state security complex in Berlin-Lichtenberg would have been overwhelming even if it had not housed such a sinister organization as the *Ministerium für Staatssicherheit*. There were more than thirty buildings that made up the Stasi headquarters: big, ugly concrete blocks with long rows of windows that had looked out upon the terrified population. Walking around the enormous square in this eastern borough of the city, Brennan could well believe that the Stasi had over a million square feet of office space here.

"Gives you a whole new perspective, eh, Terry? Seeing this in person. And knowing that this is what L, the sender of the postcard, wanted Meika to see."

"Christ. I'd give the secret police whatever they wanted, confess to anything and everything, just to stay out of there," Terry said.

"True enough. I need architectural therapy of a quite different kind."

"I hear you."

So, Brennan spent the rest of Thursday afternoon visiting various historic churches in Berlin, and Terry went off to the Luftwaffe Museum, which, as its name indicated, was devoted to German aircraft. When they met up again, they had a fine supper at their hotel. Terry was bubbling over like a little boy about the planes he had seen, and he showed Brennan a sheaf of postcards depicting *Messerschmitts* and *Junkers* and *Heinkels*, and Terry's new favourite, the *Focke-Wulf 190*, nicknamed the *Würger* or Butcher Bird. Brennan caught the enthusiasm — his enthusiasm, like his brother's, was for the airplanes themselves and not the use to which they had been put — and hoped he might have time to go out there himself before he left the city. At supper, they limited themselves to one glass of wine each, in order to stay sharp for their assignation with the informer and spy Willy Horst Lehmann.

"When should we head over to the bar to meet Willy, Brennan?"

"We'll leave it till later. We want him when his tongue's been loosened a bit by drink. In the meantime, let's go out for a nighttime walkabout."

"Berlin by night. Sounds good."

They left the hotel and were immediately enveloped in a thick, chilling fog. Undeterred, they headed roughly west. They passed a brutal-looking rectangle of a building, tall, awkward, and featureless except for a colourful mosaic of socialist life, which banded the structure at the third and fourth floors. But there was much more to behold of an architectural nature on Karl Marx Allee. Designed as the socialist showpiece of Berlin, the wide, impressive boulevard was originally named for Stalin. Lining the avenue were luxurious apartment buildings in the socialist "wedding cake" style, with columns, balustrades, and recessed balconies.

"Workers' living quarters," Brennan said to Terry, pointing at the magnificent houses.

"Somehow I suspect some were more equal than others, and only the most elevated of the equal got to live in there." Terry affected a

Hogan's Heroes accent. "Only those in favour with the party were permitted to party there."

"I suspect you're right. But pleasing to the eye for those of us outside."

They walked the entire length of Karl Marx Allee to the square known as Frankfurter Tor, then turned back. After a few minutes, Brennan looked behind him and saw a car some distance away down the avenue, parked at the side of the street with its lights extinguished. It was a taxi, and it seemed to him that he had seen the same car near Alexanderplatz when they started out, a light-coloured Mercedes with a slight crumple in the roof as if something had fallen on it. But there were thousands of taxis in Berlin and many of them looked alike, and many no doubt got battered in the line of duty. So, he chided himself for conjuring up images reminiscent of the East Berlin he imagined from the recent past. He said nothing to Terry, and they continued on their way. They turned into Lichtenberger Strasse and found themselves on a street called Singer Strasse, which delighted Brennan with his love of music. It was in that leafy little neighbourhood with its warren of criss-crossing streets that Brennan noticed Terry glancing in the direction of the car. It was idling at the curb, lights out, and it was partly hidden by a delivery van parked on the street. Or was Terry just looking around, like any visitor to the city? Was Brennan the victim of his own overactive imagination? He made a point of looking all about him, trying to get a good view of the car while he did so. Yes, the same cream-coloured, old model Mercedes. The angle did not permit him to see the flaw in the roof, if it was there, but it appeared to be the same car.

"Eyeing that cab, are you, Bren?"

So maybe he wasn't alone in his fantasies. "I noticed it. What are you thinking?"

"I'm thinking that taxi has been on the same zigzag trail you and I have been on for the better part of an hour. Now that we're off the main drag, do you see a line of taxis or other traffic following this same route through the city?"

"You're right. It's not exactly a high-traffic area. But . . ."

"But nothing. Here's what we're going to do. I'm going to put on a little pantomime, as if we are going to split up for now, and I'll point you up the street. Then I'll turn around. Play along with me."

"I will. See if it has a dent in the roof."

"Noted."

With that, Terry made a show of looking at his watch under a street-light. Then he raised his arm and pointed in the direction opposite to where the taxi was sitting, directing Brennan to some destination ahead of them. Terry then turned and started walking towards the block where the car sat idling. He gave Brennan a little goodbye wave as he did so. Brennan commenced walking towards the imaginary point indicated by his brother. A few seconds later, he heard an engine rev up, and he turned to see the taxi, lights now on, reversing around the corner into a side street, and then pulling out and taking off, leaving Terry in its smoky wake.

"The plot thickens," Brennan said when Terry was at his side again. "Did you get a look at him? Was he alone or was there a passenger?"

"Passenger in the back seat, but all I saw was the shape of a man. Didn't catch any details, unfortunately. Well, no details of the cabbie or his passenger, but I was able to see that it was a Freundlich Taxi car, and he had the number seventeen in his windshield. Information I can use later when I hire a Freundlich taxi on a pretext."

"Or when I do. *Ich spreche Deutsch*, after all."

"I imagine many of the taxi drivers here have some English."

"*Roma locuta est; causa finite est.*"

"I may not know any German beyond *Noch ein Bier, bitte, Fräulein*, but you can't fool an old altar boy with that famous bit of Latin. Rome has spoken; the case is closed. Very well, Father. I defer to a higher power."

"And rightly so. But for now, our mission is to get to the Geggie bar and meet our man Willy."

They found their way to Schiffbauerdamm, which was a long street running alongside the river Spree. And there was the Geggie. They went inside. It wasn't half bad as a pub. The wallpaper was tartan, and there were portraits of Robbie Burns, William Wallace, and Robert the Bruce on the walls and a set of bagpipes hanging over the bar. But the place wasn't overly tatty, and it had a fine selection of whiskies and German beers. And Guinness on tap as well. Terry and Brennan ordered pints of stout and glasses of whisky from a lovely young dark-haired woman and stood at the bar surveying the room for their target. No sign of a large Teutonic man in Scottish headgear, but they would wait and hope that the man was working his regular shift. Jäger said he worked six nights a week, so there was hope. And it wasn't long before their man emerged from a room behind the long mahogany bar and began pouring beer from the taps. And, bless him, he was instantly recognizable with a red-and-green tartan tam on his big blond head. When the beer had settled, he hoisted his tray and carried the eight large steins to a table at the back of the room. Back there were microphone stands and an assortment of musical instruments propped up on shelves or hanging on hooks on the wall, including a couple of bodhrans, tin whistles, and a mandolin.

Then came the bad news. One of the barmen walked over to the performance area and made an announcement. Brennan translated the news for Terry. "I am sorry to announce to you that the Auld Reekie Rockers, the band for this evening, will not be coming." There were groans and protests throughout the crowd. "We are told that they have been detained at Heathrow Airport for reasons nobody has explained, and they will not be here. But we will play for you many recordings of Irish and Scottish music. So, drink up and enjoy your evening." He raised an imaginary glass and toasted the crowd, "*Prost und sláinte!*"

Nobody was more despondent than Willy in the tam, and Brennan was alarmed to hear him say to the young woman behind the bar, "What a shitty night for me! I worked the early shift precisely so I could stop working and sit and listen to the band; now they are not coming!" He looked at his watch.

Brennan thought fast; he didn't want to lose his quarry because of a lack of musical entertainment. He looked to his brother and translated what he had just heard from Willy. Then, "You've always been the barroom bon vivant of the family. Get up off your arse and earn your pint of porter. Tell him a tale. Make something up to keep him here."

"Thy will be done, Father."

Terry caught the eye of the young one at the bar, leaned over, and tried to communicate with her by way of sign language. He pointed to himself and the stage area, and the barmaid laughed and said, "I speak English." So, Terry repeated his story, and the young woman's eyes lit up. "Really?"

"Really," Terry assured him. "And my brother, too," he said, pointing his glass at Brennan.

Terry got up, walked to the end of the room, and took one of the tin whistles down off the wall. He grabbed a napkin off a table and gave the instrument a thorough wipe — Burkean fastidiousness coming through — and tested it for tuning. He put it back and tried another, repeated the process, and was obviously satisfied. He had the attention of everyone in the room.

"*Guten Abend*, everyone. Unfortunately, that's the extent of my German," he said in a conveniently acquired northside Dublin accent. "My name is Terry Burke. I can't possibly replace the band you were hoping to hear, but I can play a few tunes for yez, if you'd like." And he played a few jigs and reels on the whistle. The punters were delighted, Brennan saw, Willy Horst Lehmann among them, and they demanded more. Lehmann poured himself a beer and plunked himself down at a table, with several people he obviously knew, and turned his attention to Terry's performance.

"Now I'll sing yez a song that's well loved in Ireland, though I think it came originally from Scotland. My wife, Heather, from Inverness insists that it's all about *her*!" He did a lovely rendition of "Will Ye Go, Lassie, Go," with its lines about the bloomin' heather. A young woman at Lehmann's table asked if he would sing it again, so she and her man could dance. Terry obliged them, and several couples got up and waltzed.

"I need to sit and wet my throat now," he said after the song, "but my brother will be happy to take over. Amn't I right, Brennan?"

Lehmann and his companions offered Terry a seat at their table, introduced themselves, and ordered a round. Good. The Burkes wanted Lehmann on the batter and loosened up. Brennan tapped a finger on one of the bodhrans and announced that he would be singing "Foggy Dew."

Terry got up and whispered in his ear, "Are you going to say *Huns* or change the words?"

"Feck, I don't know." He'd heard a more *sensitive* version of the song in which Britannia's *Huns* became Britannia's *sons*. But he wasn't one for softening lyrics or passages of literature. Or Scripture, for that matter. He would go with the original. Taking the bodhran in his hands, he beat the rhythm to the old song about Ireland's 1916 Rising against the British Empire and sang it as if Britannia's Huns had just sailed in through the Dublin fog the week before. He, too, was treated to enthusiastic applause. After a sappy rendition of "Auld Lang Syne," Brennan insinuated himself at the table with his brother and the betammed Willy, and he listened as Terry boasted about the fact that the checkpoint scenes in the great 1965 film *The Spy Who Came In from the Cold* were filmed in a cobblestoned square in Dublin across from his favourite bar. Terry ordered a round and then went on to recount blood-curdling tales of the bold IRA in Ireland and Terry's own, not entirely fictional, role in the Troubles some years before. He was the family *seanchaí* — storyteller — and he had a rapt audience in the Geggie bar, Berlin. Most of the audience seemed to understand, so Brennan concluded that they had enough English to follow along; either that, or they were doing a good job of bluffing. Terry wound up with some colourful fictions about Heather, his fictional wife from the Highlands.

Once the Burke brothers were in like Flynn with the crowd at the table, and after they had rebuffed the barmaid's offer of payment for their melodic services, it was time to get their intelligence source on track and quietened down. Brennan gave Terry the eye. "Get to work" was the message. How was he going to introduce the subject of Meika Keller if this visit to the Geggie was just a happy coincidence? Brennan was confident that his brother was up to the job, and he hoped the rising level of alcohol in Willy's blood would do the rest.

After some inconsequential chatting about Germany, Terry said, "You know, Willy, my brother here is not very happy with me."

"Not happy?" The big, blond Scotophile glanced at Brennan. "Why?"

"Because we are supposed to be in Leipzig now. Brennan is a priest. Father Burke. Though you might not know it to look at him now!" Terry pointed to Brennan's stein of beer, and Willy gave a little laugh.

Brennan said, "It's so good. How can I resist?" He had decided early in the evening not to speak any German; you learn much more from people if you don't let on how much you already know.

"So," Terry improvised, "Brennan called me in Dublin and said he wanted to take a trip over from Canada to Leipzig. And not for a happy occasion, I'm sorry to say. One of the people in his parish died. She was originally from Leipzig; she left there many years ago and married a Canadian. Her family in Canada know very little — well, they know nothing at all — about whatever members of her family might still be here in Germany. The woman died in what we will call mysterious circumstances. Nobody knows whether it was an accident or . . . something else!"

Terry had succeeded in capturing Willy's interest, and then he strayed a bit from the main narrative. "I jumped at the chance to come over here and meet my brother, so I flew in to Berlin and we met here. And we will be going to Leipzig. But call me an old Gael, I guess. Whenever I see a bar with a Guinness sign or a notice that there is going to be Irish or Scottish music, I can't help myself; I just have to come in and have a pint. Or two. And a wee dram of Scotch. If there's a session on — music, that is — all the better. And if there's no music, well, as you've seen, I'll make my own!"

"And that's a good thing," Willy said, his words a bit slurred. "Your music was excellent!"

"Thank you. And I'll also tell you that this is not the first bar I have been in today. I was surprised to find that there are several Irish bars here, as well as this wee bit of Scotland."

"Oh, yes. I can tell you all of them. And one can hear Irish and Scottish music very often."

"Great. So, what are the names of some of the others? I've been to Finnegan's."

Father Burke butted in then. "Terry. The *craic* is mighty in this bar and in the others, too, I'm sure. And I appreciate being able to raise a jar or two with you. But we have to get to Leipzig and try to find Edelgard's family and give them the sad news."

"I know, I know, Brennan. I understand."

"And maybe if we are able to track them down, they'll be able to tell us whether they know anything about her that might, well, explain her death."

"But how could they know that if they haven't seen her for years, Brennan?"

"Now we don't know that for sure. She had a trip to Germany not long ago. Why would she not have visited some family members while she was here? And if she did, maybe they know if something was troubling her, something that might have caused her to . . . to take her own life." Brennan turned his attention to Willy then, as if he had momentarily forgotten him. "I'm sorry to bring this kind of unhappiness to the table here, Willy. It's just that it's on my mind. Edelgard was a wonderful woman. She and I had some lovely conversations about music at my church, and for her to die so suddenly . . ."

"This woman Edelgard. She was from Leipzig, you say?"

"Yes. Edelgard Vogt-Becker. Unfortunately, we don't know any more than that about her past life here in Germany." But Willy did, if Jäger's information was correct. "We may have to start with the telephone directory once we get to Leipzig."

"I know something about Edelgard Vogt-Becker," Willy said, leaning towards the Burkes and speaking in a quiet voice.

"Really!" Brennan said. "Are you from Leipzig?"

"No, I have lived all my life here in Berlin. But sometimes when people came from the East, I . . . Let me tell you something confidential." His voice was even softer now, a slurred baritone. "I played what you might call a double game here in the days of the Democratic Republic." In other words, the undemocratic republic of East Germany.

Terry, for his part, played to perfection the role of a mind-boggled tourist. "We have to hear this!"

Willy took a big gulp of beer and said, "I led the authorities of the DDR — in English for you, the GDR — to believe I was working for them, even though I was living in the French sector of the city. What they never knew was that I was using my skills to assist the West."

"A dangerous game you were playing!" said a breathless Terry.

"Oh, yes."

"What kind of work were you doing?"

"My official role was to meet or to watch those who crossed into West Berlin, to make sure they returned to the East when their time was up or their task completed. And of course I was required to carry out this work to the best of my ability. But sometimes I found ways to help a person stay over longer. Or I could arrange for them to get some 'welcome money,' some extra Deutsche Marks; people coming to the West were restricted in how much currency they were permitted to bring with them."

"It's great that you were able to help people in that way."

"I did what I could. Of course, I was living in the West with the permission of the DDR authorities because I was working for them. Undercover, naturally. But being in the West meant I had contacts with important persons who were grateful for information I was able to provide about important officials in the East."

"It's a wonder you weren't caught and thrown into prison!"

"Oh, yes, I lived in fear."

"So what years were you doing this work?"

"Long time. From the late 1960s all through the 1970s."

"We know Edelgard crossed over in 1974."

"Yes, it would have been in one of the years around then."

"And you knew of her? Did you meet her?"

"I did. She was one of many, but I remember her."

Brennan thought of another name then. "How about Rolf Antonio Baumann?"

"Who is Baumann?" Lehmann asked.

"Just another name that came up in this. Sorry to interrupt, Willy. Please tell us what you remember about Edelgard."

"Edelgard, yes. She came over, and I turned a blind eye when she did not go back."

"Did not go back to the East."

"No wonder," Terry said. "She would have been shot at! Again!"

"Shot?"

"Well, they fired at her. Just missed her. She barely got out alive."

Willy stared at Terry, then said, "When was this shooting?"

What was this, Brennan wondered. How did this fellow miss the shooting? But of course he may not have literally watched every person who came over. He couldn't be at every possible crossing point.

Terry replied to his question. "I'm talking about her escape across the border, when she was fired on by the guards."

Willy was shaking his head by this time. "There were no bullets flying when she came across the border. The only time she would have been shot at was if they caught her after she failed to return!"

Wait a minute, what was going on here? Brennan got into the conversation. "She escaped, she was able to evade the gunfire, she fell and hurt herself but kept running. This we know. Then, after that, when did you come into contact with her?"

"There were no shots fired. Why would there be? She had permission to cross over. She was to meet someone, receive information from him, and take it back to the East. I was supposed to make sure she returned."

"She crossed with permission?" She had not in fact escaped? Is that what they were hearing? "How would she have received permission?"

"I told you. She was to cross over at the Bornholmer Strasse checkpoint, the most northerly of the crossings in the city, to meet someone from the West. From America, I believe, even though where she crossed would bring her into the French sector. She was to get certain information from this man, important secret information, and bring it back to the DDR."

Brennan avoided looking at his brother. To Willy, he said, "And did she get the information?"

"Yes, she did."

"How do you know?"

"Because I was very good at my work! I knew where the meeting place was, in a church over in the Wedding district of the city. I waited there and I followed her after she met with him. The contact took place during a funeral at the church. The man who died was a well-known musician, so it would be crowded, not just a family event, and it would not look out of place to have strangers there. I was instructed to go to the churchyard to wait and follow her when she came out. When she appeared, she was carrying an envelope. She stopped to put it in her bag. It was a large envelope and did not fit in, so it stuck up out of the top of the bag. She walked away. And I followed."

"Who was this man from the West that she met?"

Willy put his hands up in a *do not ask me* gesture. "I cannot say."

Could not or would not? Perhaps this was an instance of the legend-building that Herr Jäger had described as part of Willy Horst Lehmann's character; Willy was making it sound as if he knew who this mystery man was, when in fact perhaps he hadn't a clue.

"All right," Brennan said. "Now, about the child."

"Child?"

"Was her daughter with her at the church?"

Willy looked momentarily confused. Then he said, as if to himself, "That must be what she did."

"What?"

"She must have handed the child over to her contact."

"Why do you say that?"

"Is it not obvious? I did not see her until she was coming out of the funeral, so I did not see a child. But if she arrived with a child and left without one, that must mean she had a plan for the American to take over the sheltering of the daughter. She would have wanted the girl to be safe for the new life in the West. And, I suppose, safe while she completed her assignment."

Brennan tried to picture the young mother handing over her little girl to someone after crossing the border. When did she see her again? How much time did Meika have with Helga? Brennan knew the child had survived the crossing into West Berlin but died before the two of them could make it out of Germany for North America.

"So, she left the church with an envelope in her bag. Then what happened?"

"Then she was supposed to return to the bridge, the Bösebrücke, and cross back into the East and take the envelope to certain parties who were waiting for it."

"Can you tell us who she was supposed to deliver it to?"

"Official persons, that's all I will say."

"What did she look like back then? I'm trying to picture the scene." That was Terry. Good thinking on his part, trying to determine whether Willy had really seen her. If Lehmann was put out by the question, he didn't let on, just launched into a description of Edelgard as she had been twenty-two years before. And the description matched closely enough to the woman Brennan had known that he was confident they were talking about the same person.

"What happened after the funeral?"

"She walked to the post office which was a few blocks from the church, and she went inside. She came out a few minutes after that. Without the envelope."

"What did she do? Mail it, drop it in a box?" Terry laughed as he said it.

"I cannot imagine that she would have done that! The post office officials would have seen the address in the DDR, so they would have opened it. And if it contained sensitive information for the East, it would have been turned over to the authorities there in the West. She may have had a contact waiting for her in the post office. Good place to pass an envelope from one hand to another without raising suspicions! All I know is that she emerged from the post office without the envelope."

"Then?"

"And then I walked away. I turned a blind eye to where she went after. If she did not return as she was supposed to, I would tell my superiors that I was distracted by an emergency and lost sight of Miss Vogt-Becker."

"You let her stay in the West, if that's what she had it in mind to do."

"That is correct."

So much for the story that Edelgard Vogt-Becker, a.k.a. Meika Keller, had escaped from East Berlin in a hail of gunfire.

CHAPTER XXIII

Brennan

First thing Friday morning, Brennan and Terry went to see the famed Checkpoint Charlie, the Allied sentry post at the edge of the wall in the American sector of Berlin, the scene of a tense sixteen-hour standoff between American and Soviet tanks and so many other momentous events of the Cold War. From there, they walked west to Niederkirchnerstrasse, where they'd made arrangements to meet up again with the man known to them only as Jäger. Jäger had suggested this spot, where they could view one of the remaining portions of *die Mauer*. The wall. It was about three and a half metres high, with a large pipe running along the top of it. Jäger was there waiting, and he explained that this was a late 1970s modification of the earlier construction. Much of the concrete was covered with graffiti now. Brennan lit up a cigarette, offered one to Jäger, and lit that for him, too.

"Did you find Lehmann at the Geggie bar?"

"We did," Terry said.

"And was he able to provide you with any information?"

"He told us a story. Here's what he said, and you can tell us what you make of it." He recounted the version of events relayed by Willy and waited for Jäger's critique.

"Willy Horst Lehmann no more turned a blind eye to refugees from the East than I would turn a blind eye to, well, that lovely Fräulein walking along the wall there." They turned to see an attractive young woman passing by in a stylish black hat and coat. Jäger took a deep drag of his cigarette and expelled the smoke. *"Er hat keine Eier in der Hose."* Brennan had to laugh; the phrase meant "He has no eggs in his trousers." Jäger continued on the theme. "He does not have the balls to play a double game. Anyone who did that was risking torture and death; Willy was not up to that standard. His work for the Stasi was to spy on those few East German citizens who had been allowed to go to the West, temporarily, for some permissible reason. If it looked as if the person was going to try to defect to the West, Willy was to either corral the person back across the border or report all the details to the Stasi. If your friend vanished from sight, it was because she outwitted him. It was a failure on his part. I can just see him now, facing the prospect of facing his superiors. *Nun ist die Kacke am Dampfen!*" The shit is steaming now.

Brennan spoke up then. "And if our friend crossed the border from East to West with permission . . ."

"Yes?"

"That meant she was in favour with the East German authorities."

"Absolutely. Otherwise she would never have been allowed to cross over. Whatever she was going to do in the West, it was with the blessing, or at the instigation, of those in power in the Soviet sector."

Brennan and his brother exchanged a look. The image they had of Meika Keller, the former Edelgard Vogt-Becker, was crumbling bit by bit like, well, like *die Berliner Mauer* itself.

"I made some inquiries after our meeting yesterday, and I was given the name of a man in Leipzig. I am told that he works fourteen hours a day going through the old Stasi records. His name is Manfred Peter Steiff. I will be doing some business there next week, and I could speak to him if you wish. In case there is any more useful information about Edelgard Vogt-Becker of Leipzig."

"Sure, Mr. Jäger," Terry said. "Thanks."

"Steiff may be willing to search through the indexes and see what is there. She existed," Jäger said, smiling, "so there will be a record of her. This is Germany, after all! Even records that were shredded in the days of the collapse of the old regime are being painstakingly reassembled." He inhaled one last breath of nicotine, then threw his cigarette onto the pavement, crushed it with his shoe, and then bent over and picked it up. He took it to a trash bin on the side of the street. Brennan made a mental note to do the same.

"Gentlemen, I must leave you now. I wish you the best for your search."

The Burkes expressed their thanks and watched as their Berlin contact walked away along the remnant of the wall that had exemplified, and caused, so much grief in his country.

Now the brothers had somebody else they wanted to track down: the mysterious taxi driver who, with a lone passenger in his back seat, had followed Brennan and Terry through the dimly lit streets of nighttime Berlin.

"God go with you, Father."

"Thank you, Brother."

So, Brennan made some inquiries and found out where the Freundlich Taxi company had its stand, close to the Schönhauser Allee railway station. In civilian dress, he caught a bus to the station in the Prenzlauer Berg area of the city. He found the taxi stand easily enough and walked into the shabby little building with the company name above the door. He waited until the dispatcher looked up and noted his presence. In German, he said to the man, "Excuse me. I was a passenger in one of your cars last night, and I think I dropped a little gold pendant I bought for my daughter. It was loose in my pocket and I've been unable to find it. I'm thinking perhaps it slipped out and fell on the floor or between the cushions of the seats, I really don't know. All I know is that I was in cab number seventeen. If you could call that cab for me, I would be most grateful, and I am in no hurry at all."

The man at the desk said, "There is nothing to say you lost this item of jewellery in one of our cabs; you may have lost it elsewhere." Unstated but obvious was "since you are obviously a careless man."

Brennan smiled the smile of one who has been careless before and doubtlessly will be again. "It's worth a try, if you would be so kind."

So, the man put a call out to number seventeen, and Brennan thanked him and said he'd wait outside. About twenty minutes passed before the cab pulled in. As soon as Brennan saw it, he turned so his face would not be visible to the driver. When the car drew even with him, he opened the passenger side back door and got in. The driver looked in the rear-view mirror, and the recognition was instant. The man lowered his head so they were no longer facing each other via the mirror.

There was no point in pussyfooting around. Brennan said, "I am here for some information, and I will be happy to compensate you for your time and assistance."

"I have no information."

"How do you know that, when I haven't asked my question yet? Here it is: you had a passenger last night and you were stopped on Karl Marx Allee and then on Singer Strasse at eight twenty-five. I want to know who that passenger was, and why you and he were following me and the man I was with."

"I do not ask my passengers why they are going here or there, doing this or that. I drive them where they ask me to go, and they get out and pay the fare and goodbye."

"The man must have come up with some kind of story. He had you creeping along and then stopping at the side of the street. And then when my friend starting walking in your direction, your passenger instructed you to reverse and get away from there. You must have asked him why he was acting so strangely."

"I don't know."

At that point, Brennan put on a B-movie act and opened his wallet, revealing a wad of Deutsche Mark notes inside, from blue-violet tens to blue-green twenties to brown-yellow fifties. He said, "It is important to me to know who has been following me."

The driver's eyes were on the money, but all he said was "I don't know who the man was. He did not give me a name."

That had the ring of truth. Whatever the man's motive, it was not a noble one, and he would hardly have revealed his identity to the cab driver. "What were his instructions to you?" This time, Brennan pulled two twenty-Mark notes from his wallet and held them in his hand. Again, the driver's eyes followed the money.

"He asked me to take him to Alexanderplatz and park down the block from the hotel called Gasthaus Pfeiffer and wait for two men to come out. It was more than forty minutes before y— the men came out. The meter was running all this time of course, but he was not concerned about that. I demanded payment for my time up to that point, and he paid without argument. He told me to stay back until the men were almost out of sight and then to move forward while he kept them in view. And that is how it went, creeping ahead, pulling over, turning into side streets. He did not tell me where he thought the men were going, just to keep following and stay out of sight. That is all."

Brennan said, "Thank you," and handed him the bank notes. The driver eyed the door in the obvious hope that Brennan would get out and leave him in peace, but Brennan had not finished. "What did the man look like?" Another note made its way halfway out of the wallet.

"Big. Rather old, I think, but it was dark. And he had a wool hat pulled down over his forehead and his ears. I cannot do any better in describing him."

"Was he German?"

"You know, it was strange. He spoke German to me but badly."

"So not a German then?"

"That's what was odd. His German was bad in a way that sounded as if he wanted it to sound bad, as if he was trying to pass as a foreigner."

"Oh?"

"Yes, speaking with a strong accent so I would think he was English or something like that."

"English, that's how he sounded? From England or . . ."

"From England, yes. But only pretending. I have had English people in my cab and this man did not pull it off successfully. And now I must return to work."

"One more bit of information. Do you know where he is staying?"

"He did not call me to come to his . . . any place. He came to the taxi stand."

"If I were a taxi driver and a passenger put me in a strange situation like that, I would be curious. Worried even. I might try to do some more following, to see where he went."

Once again, Brennan pulled some banknotes from his wallet. His conscience pricked him at that point, using the man's obvious need for additional income for Brennan's own needs. But the show must go on.

"I saw him walk down Pieterbraunstrasse and turn and stop. That is a dead-end street, and I did not see him come out from there again. There are hotels in Pieterbraunstrasse. Three of them. He may have been staying in one of them. I do not know."

"Very well. Thank you." Brennan gave him a ten and got out of the car. It pulled away even faster than it had the night before.

Brennan briefed Terry on the conversation when he returned to their hotel room.

"So, what do you think, Bren? It's a German who's been tailing us? Or is it a Brit?"

"Can't imagine what interest an Englishman would have in us."

"Unless we were in, say, Belfast or Derry in an entirely different context. But not here in Berlin surely. So, it looks as if we have a German spy to contend with."

"And the fellow tried to ham it up in order to sound if he was an *Ausländer*, a foreigner. Well, we've all heard people putting on accents of one kind or another. Somebody trying to sound like an English toff."

"Or walk into a bar in the United States of America on Saint Patrick's Day and hear the excruciating efforts to imitate our native speech, begob and begorrah!"

"Gives me a thirst for a dhrop of the craythur, so it does."

"Sure, we'll have time for a drop but not until we have completed our mission, a mission for which we have had no training."

"To unmask a spy in post-Communist East Berlin."

"So, Brennan, how does a citizen of this country know we're here, and why is he tailing us? Who knows we're here? Who tipped off a local and hired him to spy on us? I'm sure we can leave out anyone on my end. Nobody in New York knows anything about the imbroglio in Halifax, and our efforts to straighten it out. So, how many of your acquaintances in Halifax are in the know about your mission here?"

"It's not exactly classified information. Michael O'Flaherty knows about it, of course. And there'd have been no way he could avoid telling Mrs. Kelly. So, a well-known fact around the church. I told Fried Habler. Word could certainly get around."

CHAPTER XXIV

Brennan

It was just past eleven o'clock in the morning when the brothers selected their watching post at the dead end of Pieterbraunstrasse. They stood in the shadows of a tall, featureless office block, a space that afforded them a view of the three small hotels that fronted on the street. According to the Freundlich taxi driver, the man who hired him was likely staying in one of those hotels. There was a small, grassy park at the top of Pieterbraunstrasse.

"Don't you feel a right gobshite, Brennan?"

"I do, Ter, but what else can we do but lurk in the shadows and see if our spy emerges into the light?"

"And us playing at being spies ourselves."

"Right."

By the time they'd been in place for half an hour, they were feeling the chill of the clear mid-March day, and the boredom was weighing heavily on them both. And of course they had no idea when, or even if, their man would come out of the hotel. Or return to it if he was elsewhere. Terry offered to make a run for snacks and cold drinks, and Brennan saw no reason not to let him go even though he would want any confrontation to involve the two of them against the one dubious individual whose motives they intended to uncover. But when Terry came back, he hadn't missed a thing. A few tourists had come and gone but not the target of their investigation.

"It's nearly noon, Brennan. He may have checked out already."

"He may have. Let's eat."

They ate their snacks, consumed their beverages, and Brennan had a smoke. The time dragged on. Another hour passed. Terry expressed his restlessness again. "Maybe he had lunch in the hotel and went down for a nap, exhausted from the stress of all the spying he did yesterday and last night. Or he's out somewhere for the day and won't be back until dark. The pair of us will fall asleep on our feet, or we'll freeze our bollocks off, before he comes in or goes out."

"I know, I know. This is probably a complete waste of time, time that we'll never get back again, but it's the only lead we have. There's no plan B, so if —"

Brennan's attention was caught by a middle-aged woman and a man coming out of the hotel farthest from them. The man reached over and took the handle of her suitcase and began walking down the street with a bag in each hand. "No, not our man. There's nothing off about his gait; he's walking perfectly." A taxi drove up, and the couple got in. The car reversed and headed off. Brennan turned away and started to speak again when Terry's gaze sharpened.

He spoke in a low voice. "Bren, look."

Brennan returned his attention to the same hotel and saw a white-haired man come out, pulling a wheeled bag behind him. He looked at his watch and peered down the street where the taxi had just driven away.

"Our man had glasses on him," Brennan whispered.

"Yeah, he had a hat and glasses, but he was stout like that, the fellow we saw walking in the afternoon. And — look at that, the way he's walking. It's him."

The man had started off in the direction of the busier streets.

"He's got his bag. Looks as if he's going to the airport. May be planning to hail a taxi. It's now or never, Brennan."

"Let's go."

They took off at a clip and did not slow down until they were a few feet behind their target, Brennan on the left, Terry on the right.

Brennan reached out for the handle of the suitcase, then realized the man would think he was being robbed and he might shout for the police. So, he walked up beside him and said to him in German, "Keep walking to the end of this street and turn into that little park on the left." The man whipped around and looked at him, and the recognition was instant. "That's right. This is no street mugging. You're going to answer our questions."

The man let go of the handle and brought his right fist around to hit Brennan. Brennan drew back, and Terry grabbed the man from the other side and said, "You're coming with us."

Brennan took up the conversation in German. "Don't even think about drawing attention to yourself. Take hold of the bag again and keep pulling it. You can't get away, so keep moving."

Up close, it was obvious that the man was muscular and strong but well into old age, with his white hair and a face lined as if he had spent a lot of time in the sun. He must have been seventy-five at least. Brennan slowed the pace to accommodate the man's pained walking. Not another word was spoken until they got him into the little park with a few tall trees, empty garden plots, and benches. Brennan brought the three of them to a bench that was nearly hidden behind some thick tree trunks; it was barely visible from the street. "Sit," he commanded, and the man let go of his suitcase and dropped onto the bench with a muffled cry of pain. Terry sat on one side and twisted around to prevent their captive from getting away. Brennan adopted the same posture on the other side.

"All right. You obviously know who we are. So, who are you? Explain yourself."

When the words came, they were not German. Nor were they British-accented English. It was a Canadian voice, and Brennan thought then that he looked vaguely familiar. The man tried to bluff them by saying he had no idea what they were talking about or why they had waylaid him. But his heart wasn't in it; the threats to bring the law down on them sounded hollow, Brennan suspected, even to the man himself.

"What is your name?" The man merely shook his head. "We'll know everything we need to know about you before this is over. So, get on with it. Why were you following us? Don't waste our time denying it. "

"I have a plane to catch. I —"

Terry said, "The sooner you come clean with us, the quicker you get to the airport. And the cheaper it is for you to get out of Germany, without having to pay for a missed flight and whatever you can scrabble together to replace it."

Their prisoner seemed to relax into his seat, and Brennan made the mistake of relaxing in synch with him. Instantly, the man was on his feet, suitcase forgotten. He was surprisingly fast for a man with a limp, and he headed for the edge of the park. But he was no match for his captors. Brennan caught up and shoved him to the ground, pinning him there with both arms. Terry stood over him, hands out, ready for whatever move the man might make next.

"The Ides of March have come," Terry told him.

"Is that a threat, or are you merely giving me the date?"

"It was your destiny to meet with us. You have no options here." .

Reality set in at last. Brennan could tell from the hopeless expression on the fellow's face that he had surrendered to the inevitable. That was borne out when a young couple came by, jogging through the park. "Help you there?" That much German he understood, or intuited. This was his chance, but he didn't take it. In English, he said, "I'm all right. Thank you."

Terry smiled at them. "Thanks! We'll get him sorted." And the couple went on their way.

Brennan helped the man to his feet and over to the bench again. He grimaced with pain as he dropped onto the bench. "Twisted my knee getting off the plane," he said. Making conversation now? Or making them think he wasn't mobile enough to risk another attempt to flee? Terry and Brennan sat even closer to him this time, making another attempt next to impossible. By this time, there was no belligerence left; the man seemed to have collapsed in on himself. His demeanour was one of sadness, even despair.

"I'll talk to him," the man said to Terry, while pointing at Brennan.

"You'll talk to both of us. If you think you can take us on separately —"

"No. I'll talk to him because I know who he is. He's a priest. Father Burke. And I have a confession to make."

What?! "This is a bit sudden, isn't it?" Brennan asked him. "Seconds ago, you were denying you knew us. Now you want to make a confession?"

"I've been living with this far too long. Being here in Germany again, it . . . I'm a Catholic. Not a very faithful one for much of my life, but it's never gone away. So, if I can speak to you alone . . ."

"I'll go off over there," Terry said. "Speak quietly and I won't be able to hear. But I can get to you in seconds flat."

So, Terry moved off and leaned against a tree, ready to spring at a moment's notice. Brennan sat on the bench waiting for whatever was to come.

"Bless me, Father, for I have sinned. Do they still say that?"

Brennan nodded. "Sometimes they do."

"And it's still the case that the priest can't repeat anything he hears in a confession?"

"Of course. Anything you say to me is covered by the seal of the confessional."

The man stared into Brennan's eyes, searching for a sign, something that would give him confidence in Brennan's word. He seemed to find it, because he nodded and took a deep breath.

"Take your time and get it out," Brennan said. "My brother there is a pilot; he can smooth things over for you at the airport."

"All right, then. This isn't easy. It all arises out of my own guilt, something I've been living with ever since it happened. I've never told a soul, and it's eating away at me. My wife thinks I'm sick. I'm not: I'm guilty. And I have to get it off my chest. I doubt I can ever get it off my conscience."

The story had an unexpected beginning. "It was 1943. I was flying bombers out of England during the war. I was a bomb aimer, part of those thousand-bomber night raids over Germany when we blasted the hell out of German cities. We were fighting Hitler. Our cause was honourable. The courage I witnessed in our men was almost indescribable. Especially in the early years when we were losing men and aircraft at a horrifying rate. We had young men who had been shot down, managed to escape, some of them badly injured, and made their way back to England against incredible odds, and what did they do? Sit around at the base or in the bars and tell their war stories and thank the heavens above that they wouldn't have to do that again? No, they climbed aboard their planes and set out again. And again. Some of these fellows were twenty-one, twenty-two years of age. That's what our boys were made of. And that's what we were. Just boys."

Ireland had been neutral during the war, not surprising perhaps, given that the country had just emerged from its War of Independence against Britain eighteen years before. The Second World War was known in Ireland as the "Emergency." But Brennan, like so many of his young friends in Dublin, had heard the stories about the airmen of World War II and was in awe of their courage and daring exploits.

And he had always cringed when their children, growing up in peace and prosperity, got into typical parent-child disputes and sneered at them, "What do *you* know, old man?" Here was one of those men who had lived it and was now reliving it more than fifty years later.

Brennan heard footsteps and turned in their direction; two young businessmen were cutting through the park, one of them showing a sheaf of papers to the other and explaining their contents. When they had gone by, Brennan's captive returned to this story.

"My luck ran out over northern Germany in July of 1943. I was part of Six Group, of RAF Bomber Command. You may know about our airmen flying with the Brits."

Brennan nodded but did not want to interrupt the flow.

"I remember this as if it was yesterday, that warm summer night, being transported out to the airfield, to our Lancaster, having one last cigarette with the other six crewmen before we boarded. Our tail gunner, Mackie, pissed on the tail wheel. They all did that before a raid. Good luck somehow, never quite figured that out! And we got on board and lumbered along the runway and up into the sky with our hundred-foot wingspan and four big Merlin engines — and our thousands of pounds of bombs. Imagine that we were just one of hundreds of bombers making their way across the channel in the night sky. You've seen the newsreels, the war movies, but you probably can't really picture what it would be like to look up and see waves of massive bomber aircraft flying over your city."

Brennan couldn't help but think how much Terry would appreciate hearing this story, but he never would. Seal of the confessional. Brennan could not so much as hint at it.

"On this particular night I was dropping our bombs on the city of Hamburg. We knew we were targeting densely populated areas. Of course we knew. The objective was to destroy the German workforce and to destroy the people's morale. To make Hitler's war so cataclysmic that the Germans would give up and surrender. So it was us and the Brits, the Commonwealth, bombing them by night, the Yanks by day. Shortly after dumping our load, we turned and commenced our return flight to England. But a German fighter got us. Ironic, isn't it? We gave the Luftwaffe something honourable to fight for! Not Hitler now, not glory, but their cities, their homes, their families. Anyway, we were hit, we were on fire, and I managed to be the first to parachute out. I was one of only two of our crew who survived. The other fellow jumped later. That was Mackie. He spent the rest of the war in a P.O.W. camp. I landed with nothing more than a few scrapes and bruises. I thought, 'How in the hell am I going to get out of here?' I was in the countryside, fields and pastures. I started walking. Of course I was in Air Force kit, what else? So, nobody was going to take me for a local. But after I'd been out there for an hour or so, I saw a farmer. He was outside staring at the smoke coming from the burning city. I figured he'd kill me, but I had to take the risk. I couldn't survive without food and shelter. And God bless him, he took me in. Got the wife out of bed. He and the wife were terrified. They weren't unsympathetic, it was clear — of course they wouldn't yet have known just how much destruction had been visited that night on Hamburg. Anyway, there were no swastikas or anything in the house, so I figured they might not have been fans of the Führer. And it turns out they weren't. They fed me and stashed me in the cellar of the farmhouse. Gave me shelter for three days.

"Then early one morning, my heart nearly stopped; there was a strange man standing at the foot of the cellar stairs. But he was a friend of the family, a member of the underground. A Communist. His name was Dieter. He had been in the resistance against Hitler since the 1930s. The farmer's wife gave me civilian clothing to wear, typical work clothes for a farmer. And my resistance man said he'd try to get me out."

Brennan marvelled as the storyteller's voice grew younger and stronger as he told his painful tale. Stronger, in spite of the circumstances he was in, here in a Berlin park fifty-three years later.

"But there was something Dieter wanted me to see. He took me into what was left of Hamburg. An old city, a trading centre since the time of Charlemagne in the early ninth century. Huge swaths of it were now just rubble. What I saw that day has seared itself into my memory, and my conscience, and will haunt me until the day I die. You know what we called it? Operation Gomorrah! This was beyond destruction of ports or shipbuilding facilities. This was firebombing of the centre of the city, heavily populated working-class areas. Many people had come into the area after the previous nights' bombing raids by our boys. More than forty thousand people were killed in the bombings. Hundreds of thousands, perhaps a million, survivors fled, leaving the city to the rats and the flies."

The man's voice was tinged with bitterness now. "This wasn't a case of some civilian casualties as *collateral damage* in attacks on military targets. This was the deliberate, strategic bombing of cities. Where the population was clustered. Terrorism, wouldn't you say? Hamburg of course was one of the many places destroyed by our campaign. Dresden, Lubeck, Cologne. Our cause was just, yes; we were fighting Hitler. We were fighting a fascist, racist dictator, a mass murderer, who had started the war and overrun much of Europe. But this was the mass murder of civilians by the Allies, including Canada. And I had been a part of it.

"My contact, my rescuer, wanted me to see it, smell it, feel it. We walked through the devastated streets, still smoking from the inferno, some fires still blazing, and saw human beings who had been *roasted*, turned brown and shrunken to only a third of their size! And Dieter would point to each of the grotesque remains, saying, 'Not Hitler, not Hitler.'

"Then — it seemed like a lifetime later, and in a sense it was — he took me to a safe house out on the coast. After some terrifying moments, including another bombing raid from across the channel, he put me in touch with another man, another member of the resistance, and he arranged for me to go to Denmark, and I was eventually able to get to neutral Sweden. And then, long story, I made it to England.

"So, Father Burke, I never got over my guilt about the firebombing of Hamburg. Never got over . . . Do you know what I saw, Father? I saw a puddle of greenish-brownish liquid on the ground with bones sticking out of it. Large bones, and a set of smaller ones up next to it. A child with its mother. Or father. Impossible to tell. These were human beings who had melted! This was what happened in the firestorm that raged through the city of Hamburg."

Brennan struggled to take in what he had just heard. Finally, he managed to say, "I can hardly imagine what you witnessed there. But there is no question in my mind that you are remorseful, and you were carrying out the orders, the policy, of the commanders back in London, so your confession here today —"

"Oh, you haven't heard anything yet. My confession goes way beyond what I did in '43."

What on earth was Father Burke going to hear next? "All right. Take your time."

Brennan glanced over at Terry. He was still leaning against the tree, his arms crossed over his chest. Brennan knew that his brother was practically vibrating with impatience. He was not a man to be standing still — after all, he spent much of his time flying through the sky at five hundred miles per hour — and not a man to be missing out on the conversation. But he would have to wait until the scene played itself out.

The elder airman peered about him, at the park, the trees, the buildings beyond, as if fearing that even today it would not do to be overheard. "I owe my life to the man who led me to safety in 1943. Dieter. And he tried to save other lives, countless lives, through his resistance to the Nazis. Probably didn't succeed. Futile resistance, you might say, but he tried. Sure, he was a Communist, but so were a lot of the people in the underground. I told Dieter that someday, somehow, I would repay him for what he had done for me. And that 'someday' came in 1974."

Brennan gave a start at the reference to the date. It was of course the year Meika Keller had crossed over from East Berlin to the West.

"The Canadian military had bases here in Germany, as you probably know. At Lahr and Baden-Soellingen. It wasn't unusual to be posted over here, to the Air Force base at Baden. If I hadn't been given the posting, I may have requested it; I don't know. But when I got here, I made a point of following up snatches of information I'd heard over the years about Dieter. Intelligence reports, briefings we were given about the East German regime. He had worked his way up to a fairly powerful position in military intelligence. But, by the 1970s, it sounded as if he was falling out of favour. I thought maybe because he was too much of a humanitarian, too soft for the regime. Or at least that's what I wanted to think. And that inspired me again to try to repay him for saving me from torture and death at the hands of the Nazis. And perhaps at the same time boost the fortunes of a decent man in the East German regime.

"So I decided to pass some information across the border, information I knew would reach him as an intelligence officer working in Berlin. And with it, I inserted a little memento that he would recognize. Nothing that identified me to anyone else, God knows, but a photo I found of a street corner in Hamburg, where we saw some of those roasted human bodies. That, and the fact that the information came from Canada, would telegraph to him that it was from me."

In spite of himself, Brennan interrupted the confession and started to ask, "What sort of information . . ."

The man leaned in and said in a voice Brennan could barely hear, "I handed over information about Canada's war-fighting capabilities at that time. Specifically, our nuclear capabilities."

There was no screen separating priest from penitent here on a park bench in Berlin, and no filter that could have hidden the priest's shock at the penitent's revelation.

"Yes, you may well be jolted by that news, Father. We tend to forget that good old Canada had nukes on our soil for twenty years; of course, we were deploying them for the Yanks. At home and in West Germany. And I can understand your dismay upon hearing that a loyal Canadian would give up such sensitive information to the other side."

A cloud passed over the sun then, and Brennan heard a clacking noise above the place where they were seated. Their heads jerked up at the sound, but it was merely the bare branches of the trees rattling in the wind. The man resumed speaking.

"I was able to obtain and compile classified information about our Voodoo jet fighters and the Genie rockets they would carry, rockets armed with nuclear warheads. You know where they were stored, don't you?"

Brennan of course had no idea. He was far out of his depth here.

"No, you didn't grow up in the Maritimes, did you?"

Brennan shook his head.

"Next province over from Nova Scotia. Well, I'm sure you know the provinces. We had American nuclear weapons at the base in Chatham, New Brunswick. For years. So, I gave over a bit of information about that. And about the arrangement Canada had with the U.S. about this whole system. I eased my conscience somewhat by telling myself that the Soviets would have had much of this information already, maybe all of it. But I could still make a gift of it to Dieter. Can't remember now whether I included the information about the bomb the Yanks blew up over the Saint Lawrence River!"

Brennan couldn't help himself. "They what?!" As if this confession wasn't already overwhelming, what was he hearing now? The Americans detonated a bomb in Canada?

"You heard me correctly, Father. It was in 1950. One of the B-50 bombers developed engine trouble while the American crew was flying one of the bombs from Goose Bay, Labrador, back to the States. Standard procedure in a case like that was to release the bomb having set it to air burst. So that's what they did. Middle of the afternoon, the thing blew up in the air over the river, not far from the town of Rivière-du-Loup in Québec."

"I can't believe I've never heard of this." Did Terry know, he wondered. But he couldn't ask him, at least not in connection with this man's confession.

"There was no plutonium core in it, so it was not a nuclear explosion as such, but it scattered uranium all over the place. Here we are forty-six years later, and our government has never admitted it happened. That kind of thing stretched my loyalty to my country and to our closest ally, let me tell you. So, I provided bits of intelligence to my East German rescuer. And he of course would have passed the stuff along to his Soviet masters." The man looked Brennan in the eye and said, "Doesn't get any worse than that, does it, Father? Bet you never heard a confession like this one before, eh?"

Passing nuclear secrets to the Union of Soviet Socialist Republics, one of two superpowers that had stockpiles of weapons nobody should ever have had. Brennan almost felt he should be groping beneath the park bench for listening devices.

"But you know what would have been worse?" the man said, and Brennan shook his head. "Something on a much smaller, more human scale. Information about spies, agents in the field, individuals working on the ground to gather intelligence from the Warsaw Pact countries. I may strike you as a man who would do absolutely anything, but I would never have done that. In my view at the time, the more knowledge that could be shared about the kind of weapons that threatened life on this planet — the more they knew about us, and the more we knew about them — the safer we would be. I wasn't in Japan when the U.S. unleashed the world's first and so far *only* atomic strikes, setting those two cities ablaze. But I saw what our bombs and incendiary devices did to the people and the city of Hamburg. I knew all about the death and destruction we rained down upon Dresden, a city that was called the Florence of the Elbe for its beauty and culture.

"All right, I've been sitting here justifying what I did, explaining why I did it. But of course it was wrong, immoral, illegal, and treacherous. I was a traitor to my service, to my country, the country I love. I am a traitor to some of the great airmen, the true heroes I served with or met during the war, all of whom risked their lives over and over for the Allied cause and ended up prisoners of war in Stalag Luft Three. The P.O.W. camp that was the scene of the Great Escape. I betrayed men of that calibre. I betrayed the men in my crew, Mackie and the five who died. But I felt that I owed my life to Dieter and I convinced myself that the decency he showed to me in 1943 might work to influence the regime he worked for, to become more humane and less totalitarian. And if receiving secret information might raise his profile, so to speak, well . . . You wouldn't expect such naivety from a man who had seen what I had seen in the Second World War, would you?"

"You've left me nearly speechless here . . . I don't know who you are, but you do look familiar."

The man shook his head. That was not to be part of the confession. "Here I sit, the unnamed traitor. I could be shot for this!"

"Shot? People don't get shot in Canada," Brennan protested. "There's no death penalty there."

"It's still on the books for military crimes, Father. You never hear about it. There hasn't been a military execution since 1945, and I took some comfort from that when I hatched this plot in '74. But the death penalty is still on the books in the *National Defence Act*. Even if they didn't take me before a firing squad, I could spend the remaining years of my life in prison. I would not be able to bear that."

He looked utterly exhausted, as if he had lived the whole thing all over again and had begun a life sentence in prison. Brennan stayed quiet, letting him collect his thoughts.

"And of course you're wondering how all this brought me to Germany now. I came all the way over here to spy on you! Because, and I think you know where this is going —"

Brennan thought back to what he had heard from Willy Horst Lehmann, and he knew exactly where his, Brennan's, investigation and the park bench penitent's story coincided: at a border crossing between East and West Berlin in 1974. He said to the man beside him, "The person who carried your secrets across the border . . ."

"Edelgard Vogt-Becker, known to you as Meika Keller." Edelgard, agent of the totalitarian regime in Germany. "The word was out in Halifax that there was a missed meeting or something between you and Meika Keller the night she died, and then I heard that you were coming here. I didn't have to be a detective, or an intelligence officer, to figure out that you were here to find out what had led to her death. I was petrified that you might find out what I had done. Then I had my work cut out for me, calling hotels in the city asking for Father Burke! In the midst of all my terror and nerves, I also felt like a fool." He pointed to his eyes. "I wear contact lenses — I'd never meet the vision requirement for the Air Force now! — so I went to a pharmacy here and purchased a cheap pair of reading glasses. I put those on and dragged a hat down over my head, trying to alter my appearance in case you had seen me around Halifax. But it soon became clear, as it should have been from the outset, that I wasn't going to be able to find out anything you had discovered. Stupid plan, irrational. So I gave it up, checked out, and started for the airport. And here we are. Anyway, now you know. Last thing I expected to do was confess the very things I was terrified that you'd uncover!"

"I . . ." It wasn't often that Brennan was left without words, but he had no idea what to say. He looked across the way to Terry, whose eyes were fixed on him. He was out of earshot, but he wouldn't have missed the fact that something extraordinary was happening.

Brennan and the airman sat in silence for a few minutes, then Brennan asked, "How did you meet Edelgard in the first place?"

The man shook his head. "It doesn't really matter, does it? But, as you can imagine, I have been following the news about her death. I did not kill her! Considering what I just confessed, Father, you may be sure I would have confessed to that if I had done it."

Brennan had a gut feeling that the man was telling the truth. So, in spite of all that had happened, he was no further ahead with respect to the woman's death. But given the life she had been leading here in Germany, there may have been more than one person who would have benefitted from her death. Or had her guilt driven her to suicide after all?

The man beside him slumped down on the bench, as if depleted of all form and substance.

Brennan had not scanned his mind for theology fitting the kinds of matters this man had confessed, for where his actions would fit, if at all, in the catalogue of sins recognized by the Church. But no matter. "Are you sorry for the things you did?" The question was banal, rhetorical; Brennan knew the man was filled with remorse.

"Oh, yes. The guilt has been eating away at me. Not just the fear of being found out, but the immorality of it all."

Brennan made the sign of the cross over him then and pronounced the words of absolution. *"Ego te absolvo a peccatis tuis in nomine Patris et Filii et Spiritus Sancti, amen."*

It was obvious from the man's haunted face that he had taken very little consolation from the sacrament.

CHAPTER XXV

Brennan

Brennan landed back in Halifax on Sunday afternoon, and his only desire was to push from his mind all the disturbing information he had collected in Germany. He longed to collapse in bed and catch up on his sleep. But he had reckoned without Sunday being the seventeenth of March. Saint Patrick's Day.

The calls came in from various devotees of the great saint, and Brennan's half-hearted pleas that he was shattered after his travels met with "Sure you're shattered, but you've the rest of the week to sleep. So, you'll join us in lifting a glass or two to our patron saint." What else could he do? He went out skulling pints with the lads. Again.

It was another excruciating Monday morning, for the usual reason combined with the effects of jet lag and the fact that, in spite of all the unwelcome news he had received in Germany about Meika Keller and the unsettling confession in the park in Berlin, Brennan had not solved the question of Meika's death.

But he dragged himself out of bed, had a shower and a shave, and managed to have a quick breakfast downstairs without being annoyed by any other resident of the building. He felt as if he might be able to keep the breakfast down and not hurl it up twenty minutes later, as had so often happened in the past. He returned to his room and made an effort to concentrate on his choir school and his music. He sat listening to a recording of the magnificent eight-part *Tulerunt Dominum meum* by Josquin des Prez. "They have taken my Lord away." He was making notations and trying to scope out how to get his choir of students to master the eight-part harmony. Well, the answer was obvious: bring in the choir of men and boys from the church, and combine forces. That decided, he let himself be subsumed by the music. Music of the starry heavens. If he lost everything else in life but was left the music of the Renaissance, he would be at peace. He could feel all his cares floating away on the tide of the ethereal harmonies.

A knock at the door. Go away, whoever you are.

"Father! Father! Are you in there?"

Oh, Christ, that one pestering him. He got up and snapped off the music, lest it be compromised by her very presence. He opened the door.

"Good. I thought you were in there, when I heard all that noise."

"Noise? You consider Renaissance polyphony *noise*, Mrs. Kelly?"

"I may not know music, but I know what I like."

And I know what I don't like. But Brennan, striving, however unsuccessfully, to imitate patience on a monument, remained silent and waited to learn the reason for this interruption. And it wasn't long in coming.

"His Grace is here! And he looks like he's on the warpath!"

"Oh, well, we'd best let him alone then. Don't want to add to his troubles."

He made to shut the door, and he could see the panic in her eyes. She didn't want to miss this. "No! Wait!"

"Yes?" he said, all innocence.

"He wants to see you!"

"Ah. Why didn't you say so?"

"Should I send him up here?"

"Why not? Why keep the poor man waiting downstairs?"

"I just . . . I wanted to make sure . . ."

"Yes, I'm sure you did."

She turned and flapped away down the hall, and Brennan waited for yet another visit from his bishop.

And here he was. "Brennan."

"Come in, Bishop. Have a seat. Will you have a cup of tea?"

"No." When they were seated across from one another at the table, Bishop Cronin said, "You don't look all that well, Brennan."

"I couldn't be better, Your Grace."

"There is more than one way to interpret that statement."

"True."

Brennan waited for him to start giving out about Brennan being away from the parish for four days. But no, it was something else that had brought the bishop to his door.

"I just had Vivian and Langston Soames running up one side of me and down the other."

"Yes, I suppose you did."

"Ranting and roaring that this church and this diocese would never see another cent of their money unless you apologize and readmit young Soames to the school. You know they gave us a donation of twenty-five thousand dollars this year?"

"I don't do the accounts here, Dennis."

"Obviously. But now that you know . . ."

"Now that I know what?"

"How generous the Soames family has been."

"And now they won't be."

"Amn't I just saying that?"

"They could hand me a million dollars a year, and I still like to think I wouldn't, to quote Yeats, 'fumble in a greasy till, and add the halfpence to the pence.' I wouldn't take that little prick Soames back into the school."

"As you said, you don't do the accounts here, Brennan."

"And I'm not amenable to bribes."

"I'm going to pretend I didn't hear that."

"That remark wasn't directed at you, Dennis. It was directed at the Soames family, if they think they can use their cash to buy their way into our good graces. As far as I'm concerned, Chadwick Soames is a product, like all of us, of his upbringing. Langston and Vivian Soames have a lot to answer for, having raised an arrogant, heartless bully like young Chadwick. And expecting the rest of us to put up with him. Or maybe he has a personality disorder that can't be attributed to his upbringing. I don't know what accounts for his behaviour, but I know this much: our other students should not have to put up with the likes of him."

"What is he supposed to have done?"

"What he *did* was bully two of the other students in the school."

"Is this something the two students told you?"

"I saw it with my own eyes. But if the two girls had told me about it, I would have taken their word for it without question."

"Who are the girls?

"Kim Kennedy and Normie Collins."

The bishop nodded. He knew both families and was obviously satisfied that neither girl was a spinner of tales.

"And I know that wasn't the first instance. I think, looking back at Normie being upset on a number of occasions, that it had been going on for quite some time. And I don't think Kim Kennedy dyeing her hair red was just a coincidence."

"I'm not following you there, Brennan."

"Wouldn't expect you to. The way I see it, Chadwick Soames was fixated on Kim. He was, in his own awkward way, making a play for her. Sexually. And there was also an incidence of theft, articles of clothing stolen from Kim's gym bag." He gave the bishop what he hoped was a significant look.

The bishop caught it and said, "Oh, God. Do I want to hear this?"

"I'd say not. But I saw the personal items myself, in his locker. As for Kim, she is very attached to her friendship with Normie, and I have little doubt that Normie has made it clear exactly what she thinks of Chadwick Soames. And Normie outperforms Chadwick by a mile on all their schoolwork. She's brilliant; the Soames kid isn't. So, the whole thing works itself out with Soames trying to hurt and belittle Normie to make Kim look down on her. Of course part of the attraction of Kim is her lovely golden hair. And Chadwick mocks Normie about her red curls. And that's why Kim coloured her hair red. To be in solidarity with her best friend. At least, that's what I make of it."

"Any point in talking to the kid?"

"No, though I'm sure there are some who would say that if he's made to understand how hurtful his behaviour is, he'll stop. He'll stop, in your hole. A lecture, a *sensitivity session*, would only cause him to take revenge on the girls later on. I think he's capable of much worse; that's the feeling I get off him."

Brennan waited to see how quickly the bishop would dismiss his analysis, but Dennis Cronin surprised him. "Yes, unfortunately, I think you're right. He's a nasty piece of work. Even the few times I've seen him, I've had that impression. These two young girls probably aren't his first or only victims. Let his parents take him off somewhere else, get him off our turf."

"Them and their money."

"Feck 'em."

"You're a mensch, Dennis. I've always known it."

✝

When Cronin had departed, Brennan sent up a prayer of thanks for the gift of a man the calibre of Dennis Cronin as archbishop of

Halifax. He listened to the eight-part Renaissance masterpiece with even more reverence than before. A few minutes after the last exquisite note, the telephone rang.

"Brennan, a belated *Beannachtaí na Féile Pádraig ort.*" It was Terry on the line from his home in New York.

"Same to you. Have you been taking lessons in the old tongue?"

"Only what I heard from the lads at O'Malley's."

"It's a start."

"And now some news."

"Do I want to hear any more news?"

"That remains to be seen, I suppose, depending on whatever the news was that you gathered in that park in Berlin!"

Brennan had of course maintained the secret of the confessional; all he'd told Terry as they walked back to their hotel was that he had heard something that might be connected with Meika Keller's death. And that Brennan was ninety-nine percent certain that the man in the park had not killed her. Brennan didn't say that if in fact the man was the killer, the matter would likely never be resolved for the police, the public, or, most painfully, for Commodore Rendell and his family.

Now Terry said, "I heard from Jäger in Berlin. I now know his first name is Erich. And he heard from his man in Leipzig."

"Steiff, I think was the name he gave us?"

"Right. Apparently, he has some information about Edelgard's family."

Brennan felt a stab of anxiety; none of the unwelcome information he had gathered so far had furthered his stated goal of finding out what happened to Edelgard Vogt-Becker, a.k.a. Meika Keller, let alone his shameful goal of relieving himself of guilt. Did he want to know whatever it was that this man had to say about the dead woman's family? But of course he had to know.

"Did Jäger give any hints about what this fellow has to say?"

"Nope. Either he doesn't know or, from long practice, he's not giving details over the phone. I suspect it's the first. His contact probably didn't go on about it; likely just said, 'I have some information if your friends want to get in touch.' Which I'm assuming you do."

"Have to see it through now that we've started. So, I'd better get over there. Again."

"We've all heard of the *Flying Nun*. I guess you're the priestly equivalent. Soon you'll have your own TV show."

"I can't think of anything worse."

"This from a man who preaches on the scorching fires of hell!"

"Terrence, have you ever heard me preach about hell?"

"Well, no, now that I think of it."

"But if I did, I might use having my own TV show as a particularly ghastly version of hell. Now, back to the subject at hand. I'll look into flight connections from here to Leipzig. Sooner the better."

"I'm not scheduled for Germany this week at all, but if you can wait, I'm flying to Zurich a week from tomorrow."

Brennan didn't want to wait — he was anxious to find out whatever was in the Vogt-Becker family file in Leipzig — but that impatience was outweighed by the idea of his brother as his pilot and as a convivial presence during the visit. "Sure, I'll wait for you."

Piet

Piet Van den Brink was just about to make a Tim Hortons coffee run on Monday morning when a call came in from a man named Darren Fullerton. Fullerton had something to tell him about the Keller case, and Piet arranged to see him at his home on the Herring Cove Road. Piet gave the word to Ailsa, and they headed out along the suburban road until they came to the given address, a small bungalow clad in green vinyl siding. A black Chevy Blazer sat in the driveway, new body work on the rear left fender. Fullerton met them at the door and invited them to have a seat in the living room. The place was filled with overstuffed chairs; everything was shabby and worn but clean.

Darren Fullerton was in his early twenties with a pale complexion and longish light-brown hair; he looked as if he'd had a rough night. He said, "My mother's over at my aunt's and there's nobody else here, so I thought this would be a good time to, you know, give you the information."

"Right," Piet said. "What have you got to tell us, Mr. Fullerton?"

"I go out with Lauren Rendell."

"Oh, yes."

"And this one night, I kind of, well, I'd had a few too many and I passed out at Lauren's. In her room, like."

"When was this?"

"Woulda been the first week of February, couple of days before her mum died. It was one of the days Lauren had to get up early because they were doing renovations at the bar where she works, and she was helping them out. And I was still there and I wasn't supposed to be there."

"Weren't supposed to be there . . . ?"

"They didn't like her going out with me."

"Oh? Why's that?"

Fullerton jerked his head from side to side, apparently to indicate his modest surroundings. "He's a commodore. My old man wasn't. I don't know where my father is, but wherever he is, he's not top brass in the Navy. Or in anything else. My mum works in a drycleaner's. The Rendells thought Lauren should be going out with a *man in uniform* but not a Burger King uniform like I wear. They didn't tell me this; they're too polite for that. But I know. I'm going to do something better, see about trade school, but for now . . ."

"I see. How do you and Lauren get on?"

"Great! She doesn't think I'm not good enough for her."

"I understand. So, what happened on the day you're telling us about?"

"Okay, so, I passed out in Lauren's bed and she got up and left for work next morning, and I wasn't supposed to be, you know, staying with her. The parents were home, so I decided to wait till they left and then sneak out of the house. Her brother, Curtis, has his own place, so it was only them. So, I was there listening till I'd hear them leave. And I heard them having a fight. Or arguing, I mean."

The detectives stayed silent, waiting.

"The reason I'm telling you this now is that Lauren told me last night that you guys were asking about a letter that her mum got from Germany. And she doesn't know I called you. I'll be in shit if she finds out."

"A letter?"

"Or no, just a postcard. It came from Germany, which I know because I heard him going on about it. Lauren's dad. He wasn't hollering or anything, but you could tell he was pissed off. I remember him saying, 'If this was from some stranger over there, he would have signed his name. He just used his initial, which tells me you know perfectly well who it is. So, who in the hell sent you a postcard from Berlin, Meika? And why was it tucked away under your summer clothes?'

"And she said back to him, 'What were you doing looking through my clothes?' And he was like, 'Never mind that. There's a bigger issue here.' Something like that, anyway. And then it was 'Where in the hell did you go when you were over there? Did you see this guy? Is that why you took off and flew to Europe on a sudden whim?'

"And then I heard some banging around, but I don't think it was anything violent. Not like he was hitting her or anything, just drawers being slammed. And then I heard her stalking out of the room, and she said, 'I will not be interrogated, Hubert!' And she was gone. And he did some more banging around, looking for things maybe, and then he left for work, and I hightailed it out of there."

"Thank you for telling us, Darren."

"Yeah, well, I knew I should. I didn't even tell Lauren; didn't want her to, you know, remember her mum and dad fighting, and her mum dead now."

"Had you ever heard them arguing before?"

He shook his head. "This was the only time. And it may not be important. I mean, I don't think Rendell killed her! I'm not saying that; it's just, well, I don't know. That postcard got him royally pissed off."

As they headed to the car, Piet and Ailsa exchanged glances. "So," Ailsa said, "what do we have here? An innocent man who didn't want to be remembered for quarrelling with his dearly beloved? An innocent man who knew the argument about the card could distract us from concentrating on the real killer? Or something else?"

"Probably the first. He didn't kill her, but he knows it would look bad for him if we learned that he was harsh with her about that message from the old country. But still . . . Do you know something that bothers me about this, Ailsa?"

"What?"

"That a Canadian soldier committed this murder. I was born less than ten years after the end of the war. My family has always revered the Canadian Army. You may think I'm being too sentimental here, but the Canadian Army's role in the liberation of the Netherlands has never been forgotten. And it's painful for me to have Lieutenant-Colonel Alban MacNair charged with this."

"You're not being sentimental at all, Piet. I have an uncle who served in the war, and he was there for the liberation of Holland. He's been over there for some of the commemorations, and he's been overwhelmed by the way he and his fellow veterans are treated by the Dutch. I don't like it either, the colonel being charged, but you and I have been around long enough to have seen fine, upstanding citizens convicted of very serious crimes."

Piet knew this all too well. Still, was it possible that MacNair was not the killer after all? Not much better, though, if it was a commander of Canada's Navy. There was of course no evidence to connect Commodore Hubert Rendell to the death of his wife. But this did not look good for him, being caught in bad humour with his wife

— being "royally pissed off" — over something he had told the police he had never seen. Piet had to let it drop for now. It would hardly look good for *him*, the lead investigator, if he was seen to be investigating the grieving husband of the murder victim after arresting another man for the killing.

CHAPTER XXVI

Brennan

After the bishop departed, and Brennan had ended his phone call with Terry, he was just about to immerse himself in Renaissance music once again, when he heard a timid knock on his door. He opened it to find Normie Collins standing there with a sheaf of papers tucked under her left arm.

"Hello, Normie. How are things? Come on in." He smiled at her. "How did you get past security?"

She looked alarmed then, and he hastened to reassure her. "Mrs. Kelly, I meant."

"Oh. Ha ha. I knocked but she didn't come to the door, so I just walked in. Is that okay?"

"Of course it is."

"I hope I'm not disturbing you too much, Father."

"Not at all."

"I was just wondering if I could borrow the music for the *Requiem*, the beautiful one by Fauré. I, uh, want to practise it at home."

"Certainly. Let me have a look. Have a seat there."

She sat down, and he went over to the table where he had his music stacked and sifted through in search of the piece. "Ah, here it is."

He handed it to her, and she said, "I just want to look through the 'Pie Jesu' and ask you something."

"Sure. Take your time."

She peered at the pages and then said, "Right. It starts with a B flat and then goes up to E flat. I get it mixed up with the other one."

"The Lloyd Webber version?"

"Yeah, that one."

"The Webber goes up a semitone, or half tone." He sang the first two bars for her. "Now here's the Fauré." And he sang that one.

"Thank you! I have it now."

"Any time, Normie."

"Father, what is a 'flameout'?"

Brennan knew from long experience with children that sometimes their questions seemed to come out of nowhere. He answered as if it was the most natural question in the world. "I think it originally meant the failure of an engine on a plane. But people use it to describe a complete and very obvious failure."

"Oh."

"Why are you asking, Normie?"

"No reason."

The child fell silent then. Brennan waited. But the conversation was steered in another direction. "I wonder how Pebbledash is. Do you remember the kitty that me and Timmy rescued?"

"I do, *go deimhin*."

"What's guh divvin mean?"

"It means indeed, or for sure."

"I hope Timmy is taking good care of him. He loves the kitty, but, well, you know Timmy."

Timmy was a boy they had met in Belfast, a member of a family connected with the events that had spun out of control during the ill-fated trip to Ireland. Timmy and Normie had rescued the kitten from the clutches of some lads over there, who would never be taking the cup for kindness to small animals. Timmy Flanagan was a little ball of fire, full to the brim with personality.

"Pebbledash is in good hands. Have no doubt of it, Normie."

"Yeah, I know." She paused and then, as if it had just occurred to her, "'Spectacular' means really good, right?"

"Sure. It means amazing, striking, brilliant."

"Right. And 'Irish' is good. We know that!"

"Ah sure, it's not so bad."

"Ha ha."

"So, who's the spectacular Irish flameout, Normie?"

You didn't have to be psychic like, well, like little Normie here to know who had been written off with that particular label. And who had done the writing off. She looked distinctly uncomfortable, the poor little pet, and Brennan sent up a *mea culpa* for putting her on the spot.

She made an effort to be convincing. "I don't know who it was," she claimed, her big hazel eyes wide and unblinking, like those of a politician when he wants to look as if he's not lying about the brown envelope in his pocket stuffed with cash. "But it was somebody he liked."

He being Monty. *Liked* could be up for debate these days.

"Someone who's not doing all that well, perhaps."

"Yeah, maybe. I don't know."

"What would you suggest for such a person, Normie?"

"To cut down on the booze." It was all Brennan could do to keep a straight face. "I mean, if that was the problem. But that may not be it at all, since I don't know who they were talking about."

"Well, you and I know somebody who might be said to be a little too fond of the drink, don't we?"

This was met by an attempt at innocent surprise. "You mean you, Brennan? I mean Father?"

"I do mean myself. And 'Brennan' is fine. I'm such a regular around your house, I wouldn't dream of standing on formality. We'd better keep it at 'Father' out there in the corridors, though. Wouldn't want Richard Robertson to start calling me 'Hey, dude.'"

She laughed at that. Then she got back to business. "So. Say you sometimes drink a little too much . . ."

"Guilty."

"Ha. You should get Daddy to defend you in court!"

If only. "Oh, I'd have to admit to the judge that, yes, I do take a drink."

She looked away from him then, and Brennan could see her struggling to come up with the appropriate response. Finally, she gave him a little smile. The smile of an empathetic counsellor. "It's not just one drink, though, is it?"

"You've got me there."

"You're not the only one. I like to drink, too. I love it!"

"Oh, is that right, Normie?"

"Red wine especially! I had three glasses one time when Mum and Dad had people over for dinner. I snuck the last glass without them seeing."

"Did you now? How did you feel afterwards?"

"I threw up! So, I know what you are going through."

God bless you and keep you, Normie. May you never, ever have to experience some of the things I have gone through. He didn't say it aloud.

"And I have another addiction, too," she said. "Chocolate. If I had my way, I would always, always have a chocolate bar on the go. Morning, noon, and night. And I especially love to *drink* it. But I know it's bad for me if I have too much, and it will make me fat and that will give people like . . . mean people . . . even more reasons to laugh at me."

Brennan had a vision of himself pounding the face off whoever might have the misfortune to laugh at Normie Collins.

"Now, about drinking too much, it says in the b . . . or, where did I hear this? I can't remember. The CBC maybe."

God love her. She had done some research on this, read a book on it, and didn't want him to know. He felt as if his heart would burst with love for this young girl with her book and her determination to redeem him. He battened down his emotions and played along. "Was there something on the radio about easing off the drink?"

"It wasn't exactly easing off. It was more like . . . quitting altogether. That's what it said, what somebody said. On the radio. And they said you do it one day at a time; you just worry about whatever day you're in, don't drink at all that day, and not worry about the next day or the next year."

All the Alcoholics Anonymous meetings in the world — though he tended to veer away from the A word — all the meetings or AA partners in the world would not be able to convince Brennan Burke to give the stuff up completely. It was a social thing, wasn't it? Enjoying a few scoops with pals in a convivial setting, having a few laughs, enjoying the *craic*, all that.

True, in the wake of his arrest and the beatings he had suffered at the hands of a bigoted, sectarian police force in Belfast, he had come to rely on the stuff far too regularly. Relied on it while he was in prison, and still relied on it now. What obsessed him in the wee hours of the night was not the physical pain he had endured but the knowledge that another man, a fellow human being, could look him in the eye and then inflict that kind of savagery upon him.

But he would put that behind him. And he hoped to God that in all the revelations about Meika Keller, he would uncover something that would ease his conscience and banish his nighttime visions of her accusing face.

Even with all this, though, there was no need to give up the drink altogether. No need to overreact by posing as a teetotaller.

The little *ban-drui* — female druid — was reading his mind. "They said it's important to not have any at all."

None at all! He knew fellas who didn't even start counting until after the sixth pint. Anything below that "wasn't drinking." But that was hardly what his little therapist meant. Better just to go along. "I should be able to do that, eh? For a . . . period of time? With a few special prayers to help me along!"

"Honest? Are you going to do it?" He could hardly bear to see the delight, and the hope, in her flushed little face. She looked as if she had been promised a pony for Christmas.

"Sure," he claimed with the poker face for which he was renowned. Then he said, "Normie, you are the kindest, most thoughtful person I have ever known."

"Really?"

"Really. I thank you from the bottom of my heart for being so concerned about me. On Sunday, I'll do the *Missa de Angelis*."

"The Mass of the Angels!"

"And I'll dedicate it to you."

"Oh, that would be great. I —"

The phone rang and Brennan excused himself to pick it up. "Hello."

"Brennan, *conas atá tú?*"

"Go maith, Paddy, go maith. Agus tú féin?"

"Fine altogether."

"I have young Miss Collins here with me. You remember Normie."

"I certainly do. How is she?"

"Why don't you ask her yourself?" And he handed the phone to Normie. "It's my brother Patrick."

"Oh!"

Brennan knew she was fond of Pat, having met him on a couple of occasions before. And he knew the feeling was mutual.

"How are you? Oh, not too much new here."

Now there was discretion for you; nobody would ever be able to accuse Normie Collins of being a gossip. She chatted with Patrick for a bit and then said, "You know what? I decided what I'm going to be when I grow up. You'll never guess. No, wait, you probably will. A psychiatrist! Do you really think so?"

Patrick most likely did think so, and Brennan did, too. She would make a wonderfully caring, conscientious psychiatrist.

"I like helping people with their problems." The dear little thing looked guiltily at Brennan. "I mean, I *will* like helping people. I've never helped anybody yet. At all, for anything. Well, yes, maybe. Some little thing some time. I don't remember. I should go now so you can talk to your brother. It costs money to call long distance. Okay, good. Thank you!"

She gave the phone back to Brennan and signalled that she would be leaving him to have his conversation. He mouthed the words, "Thank you, angel." And she smiled and was gone.

Brennan filled his brother in on the eventful few weeks since they had seen each other last. Then, "So, Bren, you had a visit from little Normie. She's not in trouble with the principal, I hope!" He was laughing as he said it; he knew the chance of Normie being in trouble was about equal to one of their family winning the Irish Sweeps.

In a rare moment of candour — rare indeed — Brennan decided to be candid. "The little sweetheart came up here on a pretext of wanting to borrow the score of the Fauré *Requiem*. We are doing a couple of pieces from it, but that's not the real reason she came up here."

"Oh?"

"She came up to, em, be my psychiatrist."

"Well!"

"She's concerned about . . . my fondness for the drink. Would you like to interject here, Doc?"

"Not at all. Carry on."

"And the most endearing part of it all was that she'd obviously researched the subject. She'd found a book on, let's say, alcohol problems. And some information from AA. But she didn't want me to know it; wanted me to think she'd just happened to hear something

285

on CBC Radio. I don't think I've ever felt —" Brennan suddenly found himself unable to speak. Patrick didn't rush him. After a few moments of silence, Brennan came clean with his long-distance shrink. "I don't think I've ever felt such a rush of love for anyone in my entire life."

CHAPTER XXVII

Brennan

The following week, Brennan was treated to one of those infrequent opportunities that thrilled him to the core: after taking a flight to New York, he was soaring over the Atlantic in a plane flown by his younger brother. He thought of little Dominic Collins and how delighted he would be in this situation, and Brennan promised himself he would arrange a cockpit adventure for the little lad someday soon. And of course he thought of Normie Collins, and how he had not — not *yet* — acted upon his promise to her, to go off the drink. This wouldn't be a good time to try to wean himself off it, not with the trip to Germany with Terry, and the stress and anxiety over the Meika Keller situation. If he tried now and failed to stay off the stuff, that would only compound his feeling of failure and might even lead to more drinking. So, he would put it off for a bit. For now, it was the Burke brothers on the 747 from New York to Zurich. Terry's voice came over the PA system; he introduced himself and welcomed everyone aboard. He said his brother Brennan was on the plane and remarked that if anyone found the time a bit long on the transatlantic flight, they should ask Brennan about their family's first voyage across the Atlantic to New York. The ship was an old tub, the sea was stormy, and the trip took the better part of a week. This got a laugh from the passengers and from Brennan as well, though he remembered the long, sickening voyage to exile from their beloved home in Ireland. It was still the stuff of nightmares for him, and he put it out of his mind; he looked forward to the eight-hour flight to European shores.

They caught a connecting flight to Leipzig and checked into a small hotel in the city centre. Captain Terry Burke was of course well accustomed to being wide awake all night and showed no sign of needing a rest in the morning, so Brennan was determined to put aside his jet lag and keep up with his brother. He called the number provided by their contact in Berlin and spoke to the man doing research in the government files, Manfred Peter Steiff. Steiff asked him to call again later in the day, and they would arrange a meeting. Brennan thanked him and headed down to the lobby with Terry. They obtained a map of the city and set out for a bit of sightseeing. Brennan's first destination was the church where one of his musical idols, Johann Sebastian Bach, had been cantor and choirmaster in the 1700s.

It was a bright cool day with a bit of a breeze. The walk through the centre of the city was, to Brennan, architectural Himmel. Leipzig was renowned for block after block of magnificent buildings spanning the centuries and architectural styles. There were elaborately decorated facades everywhere, and Brennan nearly brought on whiplash for himself, gazing up, down, and around him. Then it was musical heaven. Bach's church, Thomaskirche, was built in the twelfth century; hundreds of years of renovations had culminated in a new Gothic–style building with a stained-glass window dedicated to Bach and a statue of Mendelssohn outside. And the church boasted something that was particularly close to Brennan's heart: there had been a Saint Thomas boy choir here for eight hundred years. Civilization was rich and deep-rooted in this country; Brennan wondered, as he and countless others so often did, how such a highly accomplished and cultured civilization had given way to two forms of murderous totalitarianism in the twentieth century. He also knew that Germany had turned its back on its brutal past and was now one of the most progressive societies in the world.

But it was the darker history of the city that Brennan had to contend with on this trip. Leipzig was the hometown of the woman he had failed so utterly, and Leipzig had been on the wrong side of the border when Germany was divided following World War II. This city had been in Soviet-controlled East Germany. They stopped for a beer across from the church at the Johann S pub. Brennan pushed thoughts of Normie out of his mind as he sipped his Pils and consulted his map. "I'd rather not ask any of the locals where the Stasi headquarters was."

"Don't blame you."

"But I did some research and I think this is where we'll find it. They call it *der Runde Ecke*, the Round Corner." He pointed to the map.

"Are we meeting our contact at the headquarters?"

"No, I'm to ring him later. But I want to see it. We're here to meet somebody about secret police files and, well, I want to see where that element of sordid history was centred."

They drained their beer steins, paid up, and walked to the local headquarters of the infamous secret police. The building was constructed of light-coloured stone; the corner facing them was round and it had a curved balustrade with carved figures upon it. It was topped by a terracotta-coloured roof and a modified turret above the corner. It was a far cry from the brutal, intimidating complex in Berlin, a complex befitting a sinister state apparatus. The Leipzig HQ would in fact have made a lovely postcard. But now that Brennan knew what he knew, he suspected that there was significance in the choice of the menacing Stasi building in Berlin, rather than a picturesque scene from Leipzig.

When they returned to their hotel, Brennan made his call, and Manfred Peter Steiff said he would meet them at Auerbach's Keller that evening. He could not give them a time, but he would be there eventually.

"We'll go early," Terry suggested. "Treat ourselves to a meal and some more of that magnificent German beer."

"I thought you were trying to be a good influence on me, Terrence."

"I am. I'll show you, by example, the pitfalls of excessive drinking. I'll demonstrate what a lowly, babbling wretch a man becomes when he lets beer and liquor rule his life. You'll never touch a *dhrop* of anything but Communion wine again."

God help me, if Communion wine is to be my only libation. All he said was "May God and Patrick and all the saints bless you for your sacrifice."

"Now where is this place?"

"It's in an arcade called the Mädler Passage off Grimmaische Strasse," Brennan said, peering at his map.

"You're a better man than I, brother Bren," Terry said. "I can read a map, but I'd never be able to get my tongue around all those clashing esses and esches."

"That dooms you from ever learning Irish, my lad."

They left the hotel and attracted disapproving looks from their fellow pedestrians when, with no traffic in sight, they crossed against the red light. Nobody joined them in this flagrant flouting of the rules. They reached the cobblestoned market square, and Brennan was enthralled yet again with the great and varied architecture all around them. Soon enough, they arrived at the Mädler Passage.

"Here we are. Auerbach's Keller."

"Maybe yer one took her name from this place."

"Doubt it. Keller just means cellar. A common name and a common word. But there's nothing ordinary about this spot. It was opened as a wine bar in the 1500s. I've read about it. Well, I'm sure you have, too, Terry, when you studied Goethe's *Faust*. He set some of the play in this very building."

"I'm boycotting *Faust*."

"Are you now? And why would that be?"

"Because Gerta set it here instead of in O'Malley's bar in New York."

"I understand you, but many wouldn't."

Brennan was reminded of a performance in New York not at O'Malley's but at the Metropolitan Opera. It was *Faust*, the Gounod opera, and it was brilliant. He wondered whether Fried Habler had ever sung the lead, had ever been Faust. But it was more entertaining to picture the exuberant German as Mephistopheles, agent of the devil. That was bass-baritone, though, so probably wouldn't happen. All this brought to mind Habler's claim that he had been home asleep the night Meika Keller died, so deeply asleep that he had not heard the phone ring when Hubert Rendell called looking for his wife. Brennan knew Monty had spoken to Habler, and, thinking about it now, Brennan wondered whether Monty had ever had the opera singer in his sights as a possible suspect. The story that he had slept through the phone call had never been credible and of course it wasn't true. Habler had later admitted to Brennan that he hadn't answered the phone because he was afraid it was his wife calling. There was an unholy racket going on in his house when the call had come through. He had been spending a raucous evening, an evening of *opera buffa*, with a group of sailors and ladies of the night, and the cover-up had been motivated by nothing more sinister than Habler's fear of his wife finding out.

What would Brennan say to Habler the next time they met? The singer, Meika's old friend from their school days here in Leipzig, would be anxious to know what Brennan had discovered on his visits to Germany. Some of it of course could never be revealed. Secrets of the confessional. Would he want to disillusion Habler about his friend by revealing what he had learned from Willy Horst Lehmann? And what other revelations would be in store when Brennan and his brother sat down with the contact tonight?

He and Terry went inside and toured the various rooms. "Look at this place!" Brennan exclaimed. "Vaulted ceilings, painted columns, food and wine. The divil be damned; I'm here for the night."

They had a fine meal and lingered over a bottle of Riesling. They started a bit of a party with a man and woman at the table beside them. The couple appeared to be in their fifties, and Brennan heard them speaking English to the young waitress, who was studying the language on her own while attending college part-time. During his brief spells here in Germany, he had been struck by how many Germans spoke English and spoke it well. Linguistic imperialism by the English-speaking countries, one might say. And, as an Irishman, he understood why one might say it. But for Brennan, it was more a case of the European countries being proficient in teaching several languages to their students. Unlike in the U.S.A., where he had spent most of his life and where there seemed to be little effort, and little enthusiasm, for teaching anything but English.

The couple in Auerbach's had two bottles of wine on their table, and Terry got the conversation going by saying he was a mere tourist and hadn't realized that wine was to be paired with itself. The people weren't in the least offended, and they gave Terry a bit of a lesson on German wines and where the vineyards were. They introduced themselves as Heinz and Margrit. It wasn't long before comments were made about the difference between the atmosphere in Leipzig now and before. Before the wall came down and Germany was unified.

"We all heard stories," Terry said, "about how bad it was here. And I know that fundamentally it was true. But there was an overlay of propaganda, as you might expect, particularly in the United States. Those nasty commies and all that."

The man laughed and said, "*Ja*, there was a lot of that. But the truth is that things were terrible here." He looked around him. "We like to believe that the walls no longer have ears to listen and record every word we say. It is hard for us to break away from old habits, when we were afraid that someone at the table beside us was spying and reporting back to the Stasi everything we said. The *Staatssicherheit*. State security, secret police. Well, you have heard of the Stasi."

"Oh, yeah," Terry acknowledged.

"Speaking to you here, or speaking to this young lady, would have made us suspects in the eyes of the authorities. Any person who had friends or contacts in the West was under suspicion. Anyone suspected of wanting to leave for the West could be imprisoned. It was a crime to try to leave the country."

"But if this was the best system in history, the workers' paradise, why would anyone want to leave?"

"They never gave us the answer to that question!"

His wife piped up. "Nobody was brave enough to ask such a question."

"I know I did not have that courage," her husband admitted. "There were listening devices on our telephones; our letters were opened. There was even a system of, well, this will sound comical to you . . ."

"Don't tell them, Heinz!" the wife urged him.

"Yes, I will tell them." Again, he looked around the place, then appeared sheepish about doing so. "Not used to the new regime yet even though more than five years have gone by now. Anyway, the Stasi had a procedure for capturing the personal scent of people!"

"My mind refuses to go in that direction," Brennan said.

His brother laughed. "There is no personal scent permissible to my brother other than soap. And maybe the faint smell of whiskey in the mouth."

"If it was soap or anything else," Heinz said, "the Stasi tried to capture it. When people were brought to headquarters for an interview, or interrogation, a piece of cloth was on the chair underneath the person's rear end." Heinz must have seen something in Brennan's expression because he said, "It is unbelievable, I agree with you, but it is true. Then these cloths were saved in jars. If the Stasi intercepted a letter or found other incriminating documents or items, sniffer dogs were brought in to see if the paper smelled like the cloth from under the person's body!"

"Jesus the Christ, who could come up with an idea like that?"

Heinz merely raised his hands and looked around him: these people, this culture, came up with the idea all on their own.

"And," he continued, "that was not even the worst thing. The worst was the informers, those who were Stasi themselves and those who were not but operated as civilian informers. My sister was sent to prison for three years! All she did was make inquiries about emigrating. An informer of course — someone my sister thought was her friend — told the authorities about her inquiries. In order to subdue the population, the Stasi used blackmail, imprisonment, torture, and murder. Some say there were ten thousand informers here in Leipzig alone! You were afraid to trust anyone, and I mean anyone at all."

"Like those at the other end of this room," Margrit said. Her eyes went to a table of men at the far wall.

Exactly, Brennan thought. All around you today were people who had, only a few short years ago, been betraying their friends and family to the monstrous state of East Germany. If you lived here, you would be suspicious of everyone you met.

"After everything we went through during the World War," Margrit said, "after everything our country did under the fascists, we were then under the boot of a regime that declared itself to be anti-fascist. The wall which you know as the Berlin Wall was formally called the Anti-Fascist Protective Wall. So, the West was fascist and we here in East Germany were free, happy citizens of the true democracy. I still cannot believe I am free to say that!"

Margrit and Heinz finished their meal and wine and paid their bill. Brennan and Terry stood and shook their hands, wishing them well.

A few minutes later, Brennan saw a tall thin balding man in wire-rimmed spectacles come into the restaurant. He looked around and seemed to register every one of the patrons in turn. His eyes lingered on the group of men Margrit had pointed out against the far wall. Then he walked towards Brennan and Terry and said, "Are you the Burkes who have just arrived from New York?"

"Yes. I'm Terry, and this is my brother Brennan. More formally known as Father Burke."

"I am pleased to meet you. I am Manfred Peter Steiff. Shall I join you?"

"Please do."

"What can we get for you, Herr Steiff?"

"I shall have a Pils if you will be having some yourselves."

So they ordered three Pils, and Terry thanked him for agreeing to see them. "Brennan here is a priest working now in Canada, in the city of Halifax, and Edelgard Vogt-Becker was a member of his parish. Her name in Canada was Meika Keller."

"Yes, I have found her in the files."

"Anything you can tell us will be appreciated," Brennan told him.

"Vogt-Becker showed great promise in the sport of volleyball."

Brennan's surprise must have been evident in his face because Steiff said, "You did not know this?"

"No, Herr Steiff. This is news to me, but then everything we've been hearing about her is news to us."

"I see."

"I know she was a highly regarded professor of physics."

"An intelligent girl. She did very well in her studies."

"And I know from meeting her in Halifax that she had a great interest in music."

"That is correct. That is in her files as well. But it was her talent for sport that marked her for future success in the DDR. And that was what enabled her to go to West Berlin in 1974. Permission was rarely given, as I'm sure you have heard. But the state was putting resources into volleyball for women. There was an East German team in the Olympics in Canada in 1976. They did not do all that well. Better in

1980. But I am getting ahead of things. There was a volleyball tournament in West Berlin in 1974, and Vogt-Becker was an assistant coach. So, she was to go with the team. Here is a photograph taken of her before she left."

Steiff reached into his pocket and took out an envelope. He extracted a small black-and-white photo of Edelgard, head only, stamped June 23, 1973. Her fair hair was pulled back to reveal a pretty, strong-featured face. There could not have been more of a contrast between the face of this young, vital woman and the death mask that haunted Brennan's nights. Not surprisingly, she had not smiled for the official state photographer. She had a scar over her left eyebrow. The scar she claimed had resulted from her fall at the checkpoint as she dodged the bullets from the border guard.

"But she had another job to do as well," Steiff said. "Someone from the West — one of the Western democracies, I mean — had offered to provide sensitive information to the East German Ministry of Defence. Because Vogt-Becker was such a loyal citizen, and such a helper to the authorities from time to time, she was given the assignment of receiving the information and bringing it back to the East, where it would be passed on to the headquarters of the ministry, in Strausberg, outside Berlin."

Another confirmation that the woman he had known and admired in Halifax had been a loyal citizen and helper to the authorities in the totalitarian East German state.

"I have the impression that this information is disconcerting to you, Father Burke."

"There's no denying it, Herr Steiff. I hardly know where to begin with my questions. Well, first of all, one name has come up. Do the records show anything about a man named Rolf Antonio Baumann?"

"Of course. He was her husband."

"Ah."

"Perhaps a great romantic love or perhaps something more practical. Married couples were eligible to get apartments, loans of money.

The DDR promoted marriage and children with almost the same zeal as does the Roman Catholic Church!"

Brennan laughed and said, "I had no idea we were on the same side."

"Here is a photograph." Steiff produced a picture of a young man with a long narrow face, thick dark hair, and dark eyes. He stared straight at the camera, unsmiling. The photo had the appearance of a mug shot.

"So, yes, this was the husband. And, in the end, the hostage."

"Oh, God. What now?"

"I see you are a man with a conscience, Father Burke. These revelations disturb you."

"I don't like what I'm hearing, but I've come a long way to hear it."

"Right. Of course, when she defected, when she did not return to the East, her husband was held in custody as a hostage. As an incentive for her to come home. But she never did."

"How . . . how long was he held hostage?"

Steiff raised his eyebrows and took a sip of his beer, then said, "How long did she stay away?"

"Jesus," Terry muttered.

Brennan said, with trepidation, "Where was he held?"

"In prison."

"God help him. Please don't tell me they kept him in prison from 1974 to the collapse of the East German state in 1990."

"No. But only because he did not survive that long. Conditions were harsh. He died in 1982."

And she had entered his name in the Book of the Names of the Dead in, when was it? In 1993. Had she just learned of his death then, or was it her first opportunity to write in his name, because she had only recently joined the Church? And was she the one who had crossed out his name? Almost certainly, given the relationship between the two. But why? Brennan didn't know, but he did come to one conclusion: if she had died by suicide, it was highly unlikely that she did it because of Rolf's death. She had known since 1993 or maybe much longer. However she dealt with that in the privacy of her own conscience, it was almost certainly something more recent that accounted for her death.

"Baumann and Vogt-Becker relocated to Berlin after their marriage, but the Baumann family lived at this address here in Leipzig. It is one of the *Plattenbauten* — concrete slab buildings — constructed during the DDR era." Steiff took a small notebook out of his jacket pocket, wrote on a page, tore it out, and gave it to Brennan. The address was Strasse des 18 Oktober. "But I do not have up-to-date information about how many of them, if any, are still in that place. His sister, perhaps. She never married." Steiff looked at his papers again and said, "I have her daughter's address as well."

"Baumann's sister's daughter."

"No. I apologize for my lack of precision. I meant the daughter of Edelgard Vogt-Becker."

"Edelgard's daughter?" There was another one? Something else Brennan was hearing for the first time. He said, "So, she had another child."

"What do you mean another child? There was only one child of the marriage."

"There must be some mistake, then. Her daughter, Helga, died before Edelgard could get her out of Germany."

"Why do you say that, Father Burke?"

"Well, what we know is that she brought the little girl with her across the border into West Berlin, the plan being to emigrate from there to — at the time, I think the plan was to go to the United States. And there is some suggestion that she handed the child over to . . . to someone she met in West Berlin, but the child was ill and then . . ."

Steiff was looking at Brennan with something akin to pity. "You say you *know* this. How do you know it?"

Brennan didn't bother to reply, didn't admit that this was another part of the legend around Meika Keller that had just been blasted to smithereens.

"You're telling us Helga is alive," Brennan muttered.

"That's what I'm telling you, yes."

"Do you have any information about her?"

"Why don't you go and see for yourself? I can give you her address in Berlin."

"Oh!" Brennan was still reeling from the news that she was alive; now he might actually meet her? He could not begin to imagine the conversation.

"She is in the northeastern part of the city. Marzahn." Steiff wrote the address down and handed the page to Brennan. "It is another of the *Plattenbauten*. Socialist slab housing."

Brennan sat across the table from Steiff in the richly decorated Auerbach's Keller, holding the addresses of the dead woman's in-laws and of the daughter who had not died after escaping East Berlin with her mother in 1974. He pondered the events surrounding Edelgard's escape — or, more accurately, her defection. Willy Horst Lehmann said that Edelgard had met with the man who had the secrets — secrets, Brennan now knew, about the nukes kept in the province of New Brunswick — and that she then went into a post office, came out without the papers, and that was the last Willy had seen of her. Brennan said to Steiff now, "Erich Jäger may have told you that we contacted a man named Willy in Berlin."

"Yes."

"We were not entirely convinced by his description of what happened, or his role in it."

"Permit me to guess. He claimed to be a hero of the resistance, ostensibly working for the Stasi but really risking his life to usher people into freedom in the West. Am I correct?"

"You are. That's the story he peddles about himself."

"He is not the only one who now denies being a tool of the secret police. According to the file, he had some explaining to do after she got away from him. This was very important, sensitive information she was to bring back across the border, information about the capabilities of certain segments of the NATO forces. She had been instructed to bring the material back and hand it personally to a particular individual in East Berlin. Instead, she took it into a post office in West Berlin and left it with some contact she had arranged on her own. Very insecure. She put important information, and important persons, at risk."

Terry chimed in then, "Not very good tradecraft for a pack of spies."

"Spies! Nobody was Kim Philby here! They were low-level persons, she a girl who provided the occasional bit of information to the Stasi about her friends and acquaintances in order to stay on the right side of the authorities. Her courier from the post office, who knows? And the man from the West, again we don't know. A low-level cypher clerk? A little man with a grudge to settle? Not someone from MI6 or the CIA!

"So," Steiff continued, "the envelope eventually arrived. Who knows how many eyes may have looked it over on its way to the DDR Ministry of Defence? As for Vogt-Becker, she somehow managed to disappear."

"Lehmann claims he saw her come out of the post office without the envelope. And, he says, he merely walked away after that. Let her go."

"So ein Misthaufen!"

Brennan had to laugh; it meant "What a pile of crap!"

"Lehmann lost sight of her," Steiff said. "He failed in his duties. She was clever enough to get away. Our information now is that the person who gave the secret documents also helped her to defect to the West. Which does not seem to make sense. Whose side was this man on? Giving important information about his country's armed forces to the Eastern bloc, but also assisting an East bloc defector to get to the West. Whatever the case, it seems she was able to obtain papers that got her into the United States or Canada. There must have been a couple of name changes, because the record ends when she leaves this country."

Steiff rose from his seat and said, "I have no way of knowing of course whether the NATO countries ever became aware of this breach of security. That becomes more likely with time, now that Germany is united and the entire country is an ally of the West. I would not want to be that man, the man who passed the information over, never knowing whether or when the authorities in his country might be tipped off about what he did."

Images of the park bench confession came to Brennan's mind, the guilt and fear of the man who had made his painful admissions.

"I suspect," Steiff said now, "that the file is never closed on treason!"

Brennan and Terry expressed their gratitude to Manfred Peter Steiff, paid the bill, and walked out into the Mädler Passage.

"Jesus," Terry said, "yer man Steiff certainly gave us enough to stew about. That whole story about the daughter, Helga, dying. Imagine a mother making that up about her own little kid."

"Between him and Willy Lehmann, they've cut the heart out of everything I thought I had known about Meika Keller."

"I wonder whether the mystery figure who passed the secrets and smuggled her out of Germany was ever unmasked as a traitor. Or whether he is still alive." Terry eyed Brennan as they walked along, wondering no doubt whether what they had just heard had any relation to what Father Burke had heard in that park in Berlin. "You don't have to be an old Air Force veteran like me to know that an offence like that would never be forgiven. Or forgotten. This must be a dirty cloud hanging over his head every time he walks out his front door in the morning."

"And for twenty-two years, the man, whoever he is, has known that Meika Keller knows about it. Knew about it. That may be how she managed to get to the West, pressured him into procuring a false passport or something, helping her emigrate. I wonder if he thought of her as a shadow that still followed him everywhere he went."

"Blackmailing him, maybe, Brennan?"

"Maybe not, but the threat of blackmail would always have been there."

"Until now."

"Until now."

"And he had something on her as well. He knew she did not make a hero's escape from East Berlin. She was in fact a Stasi snitch, very much in favour with the regime for the services she had rendered unto it."

"True enough, Terry." Conversations on this subject always made Brennan uneasy. "How do we know we wouldn't have done the same things if we had lived here during those times? After all, hundreds of thousands of people ended up being unofficial informers, not employed by the state but passing over information about their fellow citizens. We would all like to think *we* wouldn't have gone along with that, *we* wouldn't have collaborated with the Stasi. Or with the Gestapo. But think of the terror people lived with. Would any one of us be so terrified that we would weaken and go along to keep ourselves or our families safe?"

"I hear you. It's easy for us to look back and say we'd be above it all. We wouldn't tattle on our friends. We wouldn't sneak the last crust of bread into our own mouths instead of giving it to our children. But for those who had to live with those horrors day after day?"

"You never know, I suppose, until you live it."

Brennan stopped to light up a smoke. He looked around him and marvelled at how beautiful the city was at night, the great city that had once been home to Edelgard Vogt-Becker. "Maybe that's how things stood for twenty-two years, each of them, she and her contact, having dangerous or shameful information about the other. Each of them petrified that the other would talk."

"Exactly. We're still no further ahead about that postcard, though, are we, Bren? Who sent her a deceptively mild message on the back of a card that depicted the headquarters of the Stasi?"

"Maybe somebody she turned in to the secret police, someone she informed on. But why then did she dash over here with a cover story about going to the opera in Austria? It doesn't make sense, Terry."

"And she met her death in Canada, not here."

"Right."

"Was it Canada she arrived in directly from Germany, Bren, do you know? Or did she make her way through some other countries first?"

"As far as I know she came to Canada. Toronto, I think it was, and then on to Halifax."

"And there's a member of the Canadian Army charged with her murder. Now, what are you going to do? Call the Halifax Police tip line?"

Brennan shuddered. It was bred into the Burkes down through centuries of conflict with colonial powers that a Burke did not inform on anyone, ever, to the police. But the police hadn't a clue about the history of what had really happened here, that a veteran of the Second World War had handed over highly sensitive military information to the East German regime and that Meika Keller was the go-between. Brennan had to tread carefully; he could not disclose anything to his brother, let alone the police, that might reflect back on the airman's confession.

"One thing is indisputable," he said. "Alban MacNair had a row with Meika hours before she died. Did that have something to do with all this, with the trip we're assuming she took here to Germany?" Not likely, given what he had heard in Berlin. And of course MacNair was not of World War II vintage. Brennan was leaning towards the idea that there was something personal behind the quarrel Meika had with the Army officer. "Nothing I've heard suggests that MacNair left the province of Nova Scotia in the weeks before Meika Keller's death. Maybe," he said lightly, "it was a lover's tiff between the two of them."

Terry was eyeing him with the skepticism Brennan might have expected. "You know more about this than you can tell me. I can appreciate that, *Father*. But are you being a bit fanciful now?"

"What I can tell you in all honesty, *my son*, is that I am no further ahead about what or who caused the woman's death than I was before I left Halifax. I can also reiterate to you that I am virtually certain that the man we encountered in Berlin is not the killer."

Terry searched his brother's face for any sign that Brennan was dissembling; he appeared satisfied that he was not.

"Bear with me now, Terry. I keep coming back to this question: what if the postcard wasn't something menacing at all, but a note from somebody who had shared some experience with Meika? And the Stasi had a particular significance for the two of them, something they both survived. Well, the secret police had significance of course for every man, woman, and child in East Germany."

"And every sniffer dog."

"Don't remind me."

"But, Bren, I'd find that card menacing. No two ways about it. The headquarters —torture chambers, no doubt — of the secret police. And Fried Habler told you that people can now go in and see the files the Stasi had on them. That would frighten the hell out of me, if I had something to hide. Yet, when this person reconnected with Meika, she flew over to see him. Or her. Let's go with 'him' for now. But what about the reference to talent — 'I wish I had your talent'?"

"Perhaps the words meant exactly what they said, or perhaps they meant something else, something understood by the sender of the card and by Meika herself."

"A lot of *maybes* and *perhaps* here. And I hate to leave it like that. Guess I was a little optimistic hoping it would all be wrapped up before I take off." Terry would be flying back to New York the next morning. "I'd say I hope you come up with more information, but every new door you open leads you into someplace even darker than the last."

CHAPTER XXVIII

Piet

Piet was in the station on Wednesday taking a call from a news reporter he knew; the reporter was trying to get a comment from Piet about the upcoming merger of the Halifax police with the departments in Dartmouth and Bedford. As of April 1996, Piet would be a member of a regional police force, not just a Halifax force. This was part and parcel of the amalgamation of the city with the surrounding municipalities. He was not about to get himself in hot water by going on the record with a journalist about the changes. Before he could end the call, Constable Fraser came by and placed a slip of paper on his desk.

When Piet hung up the phone, he read the message: *Phone RCMP Cpl Broussard re Lt-Col MacNair*. What has MacNair done now, Piet wondered, killed somebody else? Fled the jurisdiction?

"What's he done now?" he called out to Fraser.

"Got himself killed, sir."

"*Goede hemel!*" He got up and walked over to Ailsa Young. "MacNair's dead. Just heard it from the RCMP."

"What the —" Her eyes were wide with astonishment.

"Don't know yet. Have to track down Gilles Broussard."

Piet knew Corporal Gilles Broussard and was anxious to hear what he had to say. It took a few calls to track him down, but he finally got through. Broussard was out at the cottage owned by the MacNair family on the south shore of the province.

"Just wanted to put you in the loop, Piet, given your involvement with MacNair in the Keller case. We're out at MacNair's cottage, and a neighbour has positively identified MacNair as our victim here. The Ident investigators have just arrived, and they've cordoned the place off. So, no point in coming out here yet. I'll let you know when we've released the scene, and you can come out and have a look."

Piet had a great many questions, but he didn't want to keep Corporal Broussard on the phone while the investigation was getting underway, so he thanked him and let him get back to work. Piet buried himself in other cases, but his mind kept wandering to the startling news he had heard from the RCMP. Finally, late that afternoon, he got a call from Broussard, telling him that the crime scene work had been completed, and the Mountie would wait for Piet at the cottage. He provided directions, and Piet thanked him, gave the eye to Ailsa, and the two detectives headed out.

They drove along the south shore of the province on the Saint Margaret's Bay Road, with the land to the right of them and the Atlantic Ocean to their left. It felt as if winter had returned. The wind was strong and chilling, the sea was rough, and the waves splashed up onto the shore. They eventually pulled into a dirt driveway, oceanside, where several RCMP vehicles were parked in front of a wood-shingled cottage, white with green shutters. There wasn't room for Piet and Ailsa's car, so they availed themselves of the property next door, where there was no sign of life. MacNair's cottage was situated on a lawn that sloped down to a rocky beach. Occasionally, the surf smashed against the rocks and sent spray up as far as the vehicles parked in front of the building. There were five brightly painted Adirondack chairs on the lawn facing the water. The sides of the cottage were bordered by evergreen trees, offering a degree of privacy from the few other buildings along the road.

The detectives got out of their car and walked up to the door, where they were met by Corporal Broussard. The Mountie was of medium height, slight of build; his hair and eyes were of the same dark brown. He put his hand out to Piet and his partner, and they all shook hands. "Thanks for letting us know, Gilles. What's the story?"

"Head injury. Definitely Alban MacNair. He was knocked off his feet and smashed the back of his head on a storage trunk on the floor. Somebody tried to choke him before he went down. Or at least that's how it looks from the marks on his throat. Couple of punches to the face as well. Come have a look. Body's been removed, but you can see the location."

Piet and Ailsa walked into the living room, where there was a large blue metal storage trunk, or locker, and blood on the pine boards of the floor.

"Back of his head smashed against that," the Mountie said, pointing to the sharp metal corner of the trunk. Then he turned and pointed to a back room. "Quart of rye in the kitchen, less than an inch left in it, and two glasses."

"The glasses . . ."

"One of them wiped clean of prints. The other has prints, probably MacNair's, but we'll let you know as soon as that can be confirmed."

Piet nodded and stated the obvious. "Somebody he knew, drinking together."

"A neighbour down the road, Bob Donaldson, came by this morning to see if MacNair wanted to do some fishing. Walked in. Door's never locked, he said, whenever MacNair is here. Said MacNair comes out, used to come out, by himself for some peace and quiet, and a bit of fishing. So, the neighbour knocks and walks in this morning, at around eight o'clock, and finds the body. Calls it in right away."

"Did he have any idea when MacNair came out here?'

"Said he drove by late yesterday afternoon and there was no sign of MacNair. No lights, no car, so that might mean he didn't arrive till evening. We'll check to see what time he left work."

"How about vehicles?"

"The Volvo out front is MacNair's. Well, you'd be familiar with the car. The Ident investigators of course photographed the area all around here. We didn't notice any other tire tracks but the ground is frozen hard, so they might not have shown up. Even our own tracks aren't obvious out there."

"All right, Gilles. Thanks again for filling us in."

"No problem. We'll let you know whatever we find out."

When they were back in their car and on the road to Halifax, Piet turned to his partner and said, "So. Where do we go with this?"

"My first reaction would be Emscote Drive. But it's not our investigation."

"Let's cruise by anyway, see if there's any action."

So, they drove to the south end of the city and along Emscote Drive. The lights were on in the house, but there was no sign of Hubert Rendell's Toyota Camry. They knew he was usually home by this time in the early evening, and when he was there, his car was in the driveway. "That looks like him," Ailsa said. "I can see in through the window. He just walked into the living room."

"Well, let's hope he gets to sit and relax for a bit, because I suspect he'll be getting some uninvited guests before too long."

"Right. So, let's clear off before they arrive. Don't want to be seen encroaching on the Mounties' investigation."

"No indeed. Though I imagine Gilles Broussard will consult with us from time to time."

†

And two days later, the RCMP officer did just that. Corporal Broussard called Piet and they arranged to meet at the Tim Hortons at Young and Robie Streets. They greeted each other, and then Broussard gave Piet an account of the interview with Commodore Rendell.

"We pulled up to the house and Rendell opened the door and he appeared startled to see us. Or he put on a good show of being startled. Of course, even if he had nothing to do with MacNair's death, he'd react seeing us at the door, after what happened to his wife. He'd be wondering, 'What now?' But anyway, he invited us in, and we all sat in the living room looking out over the water. The Northwest Arm there. Rendell stayed quiet. Waiting for us to explain ourselves.

"We had several options. We decided on the least courteous but maybe the most effective. 'Commodore Rendell, there has been a new development in the case. And so we have to ask you — and we'll be asking others as well.— where you were yesterday and last night?'

"He was wary when we arrived; he was alarmed now. 'What on earth do you mean? What is going on?'

"'Just give us the information please, sir.'

"He told us he was at work that day, as always. He had dinner at the Wardroom and then he came home. He was home all night. Questioned why he had to give an account of himself. But I just asked him, 'Where is your car, sir?'

"And he had an instant of hesitation, then, 'My daughter has it.'

"When we asked if anyone was at home with him that night, he said, 'No, I didn't have any minders.' His daughter lives with him, but she was out. Didn't know what time she came home, because he was asleep. So, an alibi that can't be corroborated. Like his alibi for the time of his wife's death, for that matter.

"'That takes care of me,' Rendell said. 'Now, why don't you explain yourselves? Why are you here treating me like a criminal?'

"So, I broke the news. If it was news. 'Lieutenant-Colonel MacNair was killed last night.'

"'What?!' The shock sure looked genuine to me. Of course, you've seen it over and over yourselves, a person guilty of something like this pretending surprise, even practising pretending surprise for the moment when we'd show up at the door. I told him MacNair was found dead in his cottage.

"'Good heavens!' he said, and 'Well, I won't pretend to be in mourning.' And he made a remark, something about divine retribution. 'And of course you think I did it.'

"We told him we hadn't come to any conclusions, this early in the investigation. But we have to follow any and all leads. 'And you can understand why we had to speak to you.'

"He said he understood that, but he hadn't done it. Hadn't killed MacNair. 'Almost wish I had,' he told us then. 'Somebody else did the job for me.'

"So, I said, 'Are you suggesting —'

"He interrupted me, saying, 'Did I hire a hitman? No.'

"We said we'd leave it at that for now, and he asked us how MacNair had died. 'Maybe the bastard killed himself? Committed suicide out of remorse for the suicide he staged in order to murder my wife?'

"And I told him MacNair's death was not a suicide. How did we know that? I assured him that we knew."

"So, Gilles," Piet asked, "what was your impression when you talked to him?"

"His shock and his denial did seem real. But, then again, they would. If he did it, he's been planning it ever since MacNair was charged with Meika Keller's death, or at least ever since MacNair was released on bail. We know MacNair's family is away in Boston for a wake and a funeral because he applied for an exemption to his bail conditions and was turned down flat. So, family away, and he apparently goes out to the cottage in the spring to fix things up and do a bit of fishing. And Rendell of course had time to plan the face he'd present to us when we inevitably turned up on his doorstep.

"When we left him, we drove up the street a ways and sat out there, watching the house to see if he made any panicked moves. He didn't leave the place, but a Chevy Blazer pulled up near the house — not right in front of it — and a young girl got out, went up to Rendell's house, and went inside."

"A Blazer? That's what we saw at the daughter's boyfriend's place. Darren Fullerton, Herring Cove Road. He goes out with Lauren, and apparently the Rendells weren't all that happy with her choice of a mate."

"So, there goes the story that the daughter had Rendell's Toyota."

CHAPTER XXIX

Brennan

Brennan pulled his Leipzig city map from his pocket, consulted it, and then faced into the wind. Yes, he was going in the right direction for Strasse des 18 Oktober and the big slab of concrete containing the flat where the Baumann family lived. He walked up to the tower block and pressed the buzzer for apartment 609. No answer. He pressed it again. Finally, a voice croaked out, *"Was wollen Sie?"* What do you want? The tone suggested that whatever he wanted, he wasn't going to get it.

Brennan replied in German, "Are you Mrs. Baumann?"

Again, silence. He repeated his question.

"This is not Mrs. Baumann."

"May I come up and speak to you for a minute?"

"Who are you?"

Brennan identified himself and said he was looking for a member, any member, of the family of the late Rolf Baumann. The woman did not answer, but he heard a click at the interior door, and he seized upon the chance to open it. He headed to the elevator, pressed the button, and waited. And waited. He was not one of those who believed that pressing a lift button over and over again increased the likelihood of the thing arriving. He gave it about two minutes and then went for the stairs. He smelled smoke and stale beer and overcooked food on his climb to the sixth floor and then came out in an unlighted corridor. When he reached number 609, he placed himself within view of the little hole that was placed in apartment doors so residents could look out. What was it called? All the words he could come up with sounded creepy: peephole, spyhole . . . He returned his attention to the task at hand and rapped on the door. He heard the shuffling of feet, and the woman's voice called out, "Who's there?" He identified himself again, and she opened the door a crack. Her face bore the ravages of a hard life, and he suspected that although she looked to be in her seventies, she may well have been younger.

"Please forgive the interruption. As I explained, I am looking for the Baumann family. I won't take up much of your time."

"Indeed you will not. Because there are no Baumanns here. They lost this apartment through their own actions, and it was given to me and my own family."

"Oh. What do you mean when you say they lost it, if you don't mind my asking?"

She clearly didn't mind at all. Her face virtually lit up as she started in on the Baumanns. "Criminals they are, not good citizens. They have spent time in institutions, every last one of them. They do not need an apartment; they need a jail!"

Brennan heard a door open behind him to his left, but nobody came out.

The woman in 609 terminated their brief meeting with "You have wasted your time coming all this way looking for those people. Goodbye." She shut the door in his face and that was that. But a ray of light behind him widened as the door to number 612 opened, and a man emerged.

"Excuse me, sir. I heard you. Easy enough to do when she left you standing out in the hallway. I heard you asking about the Baumann family. Would you like to come inside?"

"Sure. Thank you."

The man was tall and reedy with greying-blond hair brushed to the side. He held the door open, and Brennan preceded him into a modestly furnished flat, with a sitting room to the right and a galley kitchen to the left. The man introduced himself as Reiner, and he called out, "Klara! We have a visitor!"

A heavy-set woman with tightly curled brown hair came out of one of the rooms and nodded to Brennan.

"We have tea made. Would you like a cup?" Reiner asked, and Brennan said he would, thank you very much.

Reiner turned and went into the kitchen, reached up to a cupboard, brought out a cup and saucer, and filled it with tea. "Milk or lemon?"

"Milk for me, please."

The three of them went into the sitting room and made themselves comfortable. "I heard you asking that old crow about the Baumanns and I heard her slandering them. That is typical behaviour of that woman. Boasting to you that she was given the apartment and the Baumanns were put out of it."

"That's not the case, I take it?"

"Well, it is. But what she left out was the date when she and her husband were given the rights to the place. It was in 1983." Reiner gave Brennan a significant look.

"In the time of the old regime," Brennan said.

"Yes. The Baumanns were not in favour with the authorities then. That pair were." He jerked his head in the direction of the apartment across the hall. "So . . . you are looking for these people for . . . ?"

"Sorry. I should have explained." And he did, but without all the details. "A woman I believe was related to the Baumann family died recently in Canada where I am living now. As far as I know, she was married to Rolf Baumann."

"Ah. The one —" he switched to English "— the one that got away!" Reverting to German, he said, "I never met her. That was before I moved in here. And, from what I know, she and Rolf Baumann moved to Berlin not long after their marriage. So, I know little, I know nothing, about them. Except that she went over to the West, and Rolf was left behind to bear the consequences. There was a sister. She lived here for a number of years, but of course she had to go when the apartment was given over to the current occupant. I don't know where the sister would be now."

"Are there other members of the family still here in Leipzig?"

"The parents are long dead. They were not strong people, and life was very hard here. Well, you probably know that. The only one who is known to be thriving is the brother. Ernst Alfred Baumann. Now old Gerda there, she calls the Baumanns criminals. While it is true that Ernst Alfred has some rackets going, that he lives on the other side of the law, we might say, one can understand that a man is sometimes forced by circumstances to do things that are a little, shall we say, shady."

Klara gave her husband what Brennan interpreted as a warning look, but he either missed it or chose to ignore it. "There has been, as you might imagine, a period of adjustment here. The ground has shifted beneath our feet, you might say. Going from a state-run economy to a capitalist one provides great opportunities for some, for those who are risk-takers, who take naturally to the role of traders, business people, entrepreneurs. And you could say Ernst Alfred Baumann is an entrepreneur. One of the new class of businessmen, risk-takers, men who understand and take advantage of the system of the *free market*." Reiner took a sip of his tea and continued, "There are some who say he is in league with similar elements in Russia. Some of the things they do cross the line of legality."

"Was he close to his brother, Rolf, do you know?"

"I am sorry, I did not know them when Rolf was still living. If one can call it 'living' in the prisons we had here. And it would be difficult to get that information. Ernst would be a hard man to find, because he frequently crosses borders for his business interests. And frequently changes residence. So, I doubt I can help you there."

"No, I don't suppose I'll be able to track him down. And if I do, I'd better hold onto my wallet."

"Oh, no, you would have nothing to fear from E.A. Baumann. He would not steal from you, and he would not cause you harm. He might try to talk you into making an investment, but he really is not a bad man. Just someone who sees plenty of opportunities in the new Germany and knows how to work the system. I say, good for him!"

His wife gave him a look again and said to Brennan, "My husband has not shut his mouth since the Stasi went away." She raised her arms and wiggled her fingers as if to illustrate something dispersing into the air.

"She is correct. After all those decades of fear, yes, I talk all the time!"

"Your mouth never stops. But, now, isn't it time for us to go and work in the free market out there? We both work at a hotel in the city centre," she explained. "We start in half an hour from now. And he yaps so much to the guests when they arrive at the desk that they should be given a discount, because they spend so little time in their rooms!"

Brennan thanked them for their hospitality and wished them well. He could see no point in trying to track down Meika Keller's late husband's entrepreneurial — piratical? — brother. That left him with one person to try to see. He was not looking forward to an encounter with the dead woman's daughter.

†

Brennan was in bed in his hotel room, just about asleep, when the phone rang and he picked it up.

"Brennan, I don't like to ring you this late your time, but I thought you should know this." It was Monsignor O'Flaherty.

"What is it, Michael?" Brennan braced himself for whatever it was.

"Lieutenant-Colonel MacNair is dead."

"What?"

He heard a voice in the background, and he thought he heard "killed himself."

"What's that, Michael? Who is there?"

"Em, it's Mrs. Kelly here in the kitchen with me, Brennan. She's saying she thinks MacNair killed himself, because . . . what's that, Mrs. Kelly? Sorry, Brennan, just a minute. Her idea is that he killed himself because . . . No, Mrs. Kelly."

Christ, wouldn't you know she'd get in on this. Likely she materialized out of the mist just as Michael spoke his first words into the phone. Brennan well knew that in Mrs. Kelly's expert opinion, the evidence pointed at one man, and it wasn't Lieutenant-Colonel MacNair. The errant Father Burke was the culprit after failing to meet with Meika Keller the night of, or before, her death in the water. Good thing Kelly didn't know that MacNair had asked to meet with Brennan — how long ago now? — more than three weeks ago. Imagine the theory she'd put together then.

Michael said again, "No, Mrs. Kelly. The police charged the lieutenant-colonel with murder; they must have had evidence against him. And now the Mounties say this death, too, is a homicide. They're not saying why they think so. You know how they are, keeping details to themselves. It's the Mounties investigating; the killing took place outside of Halifax, out at MacNair's family cottage."

"You know who they're going to suspect now!" The housekeeper's voice came through loud and clear along the transatlantic line. She obviously had her beak right up against the telephone.

"Who, Mrs. Kelly?" asked the ever-patient Monsignor O'Flaherty.

"The commodore! Because he probably thinks the lieutenant-colonel really killed his wife. But I know the commodore would never do anything like this!"

How she knew the mind of the man in charge of the Canadian Fleet so well was not explained.

"Is that the doorbell?" Michael O'Flaherty asked, out of the blue. Then, in a hushed voice, "I'm sorry, Brennan. To be passing along this disturbing news. And to have made the mistake of calling from the kitchen, rather than in the privacy of my own room! She shuffled in as soon as she heard me say your name. Here she is now. Nobody at the door. As you might have guessed. The blessings of God on you, Brennan."

Brennan tried to process the stunning news he had just heard. Somebody killed MacNair, and Mrs. Kelly was not far off the mark in thinking suspicion would fall on the grieving husband of Meika Keller. But Brennan's investigations in Germany had uncovered things about Meika Keller — Edelgard Vogt-Becker — that were not known in Halifax. Or, at least, Brennan was not aware if these facts were known there. From everything he had heard, it was an accepted fact that Meika had made a hero's escape from East Berlin, mother and daughter running away from the checkpoint with bullets whizzing past them. That legend had not survived Brennan's visits to Berlin and Leipzig. And Brennan had met a man who had passed secrets to the East German regime, passed secrets to Meika to send along to an apparatchik of that regime. So, what now accounted for the murder of Alban MacNair? Revenge by Commodore Hubert Rendell for the death of his wife? Revenge by someone else aggrieved by MacNair's actions, personal or political? Or was it something else altogether, a spectre risen out of MacNair's own past?

CHAPTER XXX

Piet

Piet Van den Brink was far from satisfied with what he had heard from the Mounties about their interview with Commodore Rendell. But it wasn't his place to be satisfied; it wasn't Piet's investigation. And his dissatisfaction was not with the investigators in any way; it was with the answers Rendell had given when questioned. As far as Piet knew, there was no evidence as yet that Rendell had been at MacNair's cottage, let alone that he had battered him or smashed his head against the corner of a metal trunk. But if anyone had a motive for a violent encounter with MacNair, it was the husband of the woman MacNair had killed.

So, when Piet got a call from RCMP Corporal Gilles Broussard inviting him to meet again at Tims at Young and Robie, Piet dropped everything else he was doing and made a beeline for the coffee shop. The two cops got their double doubles and found a table. After a bit of small talk, they got to the subject at hand.

"Piet, we spoke to Commodore Rendell again. Went to his house yesterday evening. This time, his car — silver Toyota Camry — was in the driveway. We decided to have a look before knocking on his door. First thing we noticed was dried salt spray on the body of the car. You don't get that when you're parked in the driveway of a house on the Northwest Arm in the city of Halifax. No crashing surf in the Arm that would splash up to Emscote Drive. So, he had been out to the shore. We went up to the house, knocked, and he was there. 'Still at it, Corporal?' he asked. I said, 'Yes, sir, we are.' And could we have a word with him? He stood aside and let us in, and we all sat in the living room. He perched himself on the edge of his chair and waited for us to begin.

"I have a copy of the transcript of the interview. Easier for you to just read it than have me act it out for you. Here it is. Take your time."

Piet put down his coffee cup and took the papers in his hands. The transcript showed that Rendell had been questioned by Corporals Broussard and McKenna. A few notes had been pencilled in on the margins. Piet began to read.

"Have you been out driving in the country, sir?"

"The country?"

"Yes. Outside the city."

"Is that a crime now?"

"If you'd just answer the question, sir, this will go a lot easier."

"For you, maybe."

"Sir, where were you in your car in the last couple of days outside the city?"

"I wasn't anywhere committing murder, I can assure you."

"Where did you get the salt spray on your car?"

(R. hesitates, looks disturbed.) "I was out in Lawrencetown Beach visiting a friend."

"When was that, sir?"

"The night of Tuesday, March twenty-sixth."

Piet looked up at Broussard. "Contradicting the story he gave you the first time, that he had not left home that night."

"Right."

Piet returned to the transcript.

"What time were you out there?"

"I don't know. Left here at nine or so."

"And you returned when?"

"Late. I don't know what time it was."

"How did you get there?"

"Well, I drove, for Christ's sake. Didn't you say I have salt spray on the car? The waves were huge along the road there."

"Your car was not here when we spoke to you last time. Wednesday evening."

(R., no reply.)

"Sir? When we spoke to you that night, we were present here on Emscote for some time after we talked. We saw a young woman get out of an old Chevy Blazer and let herself into this house. Was that —"

"I left it out there."

"Sorry, what was that?"

"My car. I left it out at my friend's place."

"Why was that, sir?"

"Guess. You're the investigators."

"Why don't you just tell us?"

"I was drinking."

Piet looked up again and said to Broussard, "Why was he so hesitant to admit he'd been drinking and *not* driving? Being a good citizen!"

"Finish reading and then I'll fill you in."

Piet resumed reading.

"When did you start drinking?"

"Oh, when I was fifteen or so."

"And on Tuesday night?"

"I had a drink before I went out there."

"We're not here to charge you with an impaired driving offence."

"No, you're here to charge me with murder."

"You can easily clear yourself of suspicion if you can account for your movements, Commodore Rendell. What is the name of the person you went to visit?"

"Petty Officer J.C. Lesage."

"And what happened? Did he drive you home?"

"Yes, in the wee hours. Two o'clock or something."

"And how did you get your car back?"

"My son drove me out there to retrieve it."

"All right. What's the petty officer's address?"

(R. writes out address, gives it to Cpl. B.)

"Out in Lawrencetown, I see."

(Cpl. McKenna) "If you'll excuse me for a minute, sir."

The transcript ended there. Piet said, "McKenna went out to check the alibi, I assume?"

"That's right. Got the number, made the call, and the lieutenant denied that Rendell had been there."

"Shit."

"Yeah. The petty officer is a she, by the way."

"So, what's happening now?"

"We've taken Rendell in for questioning."

"Right."

"So, I just wanted to get your impressions of the commodore from your time with him."

"Honestly, Gilles, up to this moment I would have given him a pass. I really felt he had nothing to do with his wife's death. I have to tell you, though, that there were some hinky aspects to all this." Piet told the Mountie about the scene described by the daughter's boyfriend, Rendell flipping out over the postcard and asking where his wife had really gone during her trip to Europe. "And maybe he had good reason to be suspicious. She had tickets to the opera in Vienna, and the Crown lawyer told me she never showed up. Yet she claimed she had enjoyed the opera. Or at least Rendell told us she did."

"Whoa! That certainly puts a new spin on things."

"Yeah, but I still didn't figure him for her death. We had MacNair for that."

"And why would Rendell take it out on MacNair in a fit of rage, if Rendell had killed her himself?"

"Maybe you've hit on it right there, Gilles. Rendell knew his wife and MacNair were getting it on, and he finally snapped and killed him. Same old motive, as old as time."

CHAPTER XXXI

Monty

You never know, when you hang out a shingle advertising yourself as a criminal defence lawyer, who might appear on your doorstep. But the events of Monday, April 1, were extraordinary even after a quarter of a century in the business, even after all the surprises in the Keller-MacNair case.

Monty was sitting in his office in the morning, reading the news stories about the amalgamation of his city with the city of Dartmouth, the town of Bedford, and the county of Halifax. The police were now one regional force. As usual with a plan like this, some people were gratified and some were outraged. He was reading some of the comments, from both ends of the spectrum, when his secretary popped in to say that someone was here to see him. Lieutenant-General John Joseph Patriquin. Sure, send him in. The retired Air Force officer — and hero of the Sinai Desert — had been ready and willing to provide glowing testimony about Monty's lately deceased client, Alban

MacNair. What did Patriquin want to see Monty about now? He rose from his seat to welcome the old flyer when he walked into the office. The man seemed to have aged twenty years since Monty had seen him last. Despite his stocky build, he looked weak now. Stooped over. He had lost the confident air he'd had when they'd met before.

"Good morning, sir. Have a seat. Would you like a coffee?"

"No. Yes, yes, sure, a coffee."

"Cream? Sugar?"

"No, thanks. Black is fine."

Monty picked up the phone and asked the receptionist to bring two cups of black.

"So, what can I do for you today, John?"

Patriquin turned and looked behind him, then back at Monty, and was about to speak when Darlene came in with the coffee. She smiled at both men, gave them each a cup, and left the room. Patriquin got up and closed the door behind her.

"They're looking at Rendell for the murder of MacNair. They took him in for questioning."

"Yes, I know."

Patriquin started to speak, stopped, and cleared his throat and began again. "Rendell is . . ."

"Rendell is?"

"Innocent. Didn't kill MacNair."

"What? How do you know this, John?"

"How in the hell could I know it?"

"You were with Rendell that night? Is that it? You're his alibi?" Monty didn't give voice to the other possibility.

"No, that's not it."

Monty was getting uneasy with the conversation. "Please explain what you mean, sir."

"Anything MacNair told you is protected by your oath of confidentiality, am I correct?"

"Solicitor-client privilege, yes."

"And now that he's dead?"

Jesus, what was Monty to infer from this? "Yes," he replied.

"And the same privilege would cover me if I was your client, true?"

"True, but we don't have a solicitor-client relationship, at least not yet, unless . . ."

"I want you to represent me."

"Represent you for?"

"I killed MacNair."

Monty tried to hide his astonishment. He'd had long years of practice in court, maintaining a deadpan expression, obscuring his reaction to the unexpected and the unwelcome.

"So, I want you to represent me."

Monty made an effort to stay on track, though his mind was reeling. "I wouldn't feel right about it, John. How would it look to MacNair's family if I represented him and then the man who killed him? And whatever happened between you and MacNair before . . . his death would undoubtedly be traumatic for the family to hear. But I'll get you someone who will do a stellar job for you, give you the best defence possible."

"No need, Mr. Collins. I intend to plead guilty. No sensitive information has to come out. All we're talking about here is some effective plea bargaining."

"Well, I'll have to think about this."

"I don't know what MacNair told you to explain that shouting match between him and Meika the night before she died." He put his hand up to ward off Monty's objections. "I know you're not going to tell me. But he probably came up with some boy and girl story, forbidden love or some nonsense like that."

Monty made no reply. He remembered MacNair's claim that Meika Keller had been chasing him, putting pressure on him for a commitment.

"If he told you something like that, it was bullshit. If there was anything like that between them, it was long ago. When he met her in

Germany. And even then, I doubt it. But back to the matter at hand. I would claim self-defence, except that I don't want a trial."

"Why not, if it was self-defence?"

"Because I can't take the chance that my history with MacNair will come out. And if I was fortunate enough to be acquitted at trial, suspicion would fall again on Rendell. I ask you again: is our conversation covered by lawyer-client confidentiality?"

Monty made his decision. For now, at least, Patriquin was his client. The privilege would attach and remain in place. "Yes, it is."

"I went out to MacNair's house in Armdale but he wasn't there. Family was away. I figured he'd gone out to his cottage, as he often does. He was plastered; been drinking for hours. I knew he'd given up the stuff; hadn't been drinking in years. He sometimes got crazy when he was drunk. And that's the way he was Tuesday night. I took a drink, too. We got into an argument and it escalated. Got to the stage where we were standing chest to chest, shouting at one another. We threw a couple of punches. He gave me a shove. I got my balance and put my hands around his throat. He wrenched my hands off, and I backed away. Then I came at him and knocked him on his back. He hit his head on the corner of a metal trunk there on the living room floor. I thought, Jesus Christ! He was dying before my very eyes. I thought I could get away with it. I wiped any place that would have had my prints. Left no traces in that cottage. Nobody saw my car parked a hundred yards away.

"I did worry that the police would look to Hubert Rendell, and sure enough that's what they've done. I told myself that they wouldn't be able to charge him because there is no evidence against him. Because he didn't do it; he wasn't there. I can't have an innocent man, a grieving husband, charged with the killing I did myself. So here I am, trying to figure out what I might say to get my own conviction down to manslaughter, or second-degree murder. It isn't first degree; I didn't go out there with the intention of doing him in. But as for now, I don't know what my strategy would be because I sure as hell cannot reveal the real reason."

Patriquin was pale, trembling.

"John, should we be calling a doctor?"

Patriquin shook his head, then said, "Did MacNair tell you anything . . . about me? I know you can't tell me specifics."

"That's right." Was this why Patriquin had come to Monty, to find out whatever MacNair might have told him? "But if you want me to represent you, you'll have to explain what was behind all this, so I don't end up misleading the court, however unintentionally. Or getting sandbagged by the Crown." In fact, though, Monty would almost certainly have to bow out and procure another lawyer to handle the plea.

Patriquin gripped his coffee cup in both hands, took a long sip, and looked down at the desk. "MacNair and I were acquainted here in Halifax, him a much younger serviceman, of course. In 1974, we were both here on leave from our postings in West Germany, and we ended up having a few drinks together at RA Park. And he started going on about how much he hated the fact that the government had stripped us of our separate identities as Air Force, Navy, and Army. He hated unification, and so did I. And sitting there, I had a flash of inspiration. Alban MacNair would be my courier."

Monty stared at him.

"I . . . I owe my life to someone over there."

"Over where?"

Patriquin cleared his throat and said, "Germany."

Monty waited him out.

"It's a long story and a long-ago story. From the war. The second war. A man saved my life. I'm not going to get into that part of it. But I always felt I owed him. And I was pissed off at our leaders here, the politicians, the military. And I came up with a way to provide something for the man in Germany and to embarrass our Department of National Defence, if it should ever come out that the other side had the information."

"The other side being the East Germans? The Soviets?"

"The East Germans, yes. I had already done my research on how to locate the man who saved me, by that time serving in the bureaucracy in Berlin. So, I began working on MacNair. He was pissed off enough that he'd be more than happy to stick it to the brass in Ottawa."

There was something missing in this tale, Monty knew.

"Why, John, would the East Germans care about the unification of our forces? Or any ill-conceived decisions along these lines made by the politicians in Ottawa?"

"I . . . I gave them a bit of other information."

"Oh?"

"Just stuff that they could find out for themselves. Hell, they probably knew anyway, given their espionage capabilities."

"What sort of information are we talking about here?"

"We're not, Mr. Collins. We're not talking about it. Trust me that I didn't give them anything that would put any of our own spies in danger, our people behind the Iron Curtain. Nothing like that."

Monty knew there was a wealth of information that a high-ranking officer in the Air Force could pass over to the other side, which would have nothing to do with spies on the ground. What was it? Details of Canada's military personnel, equipment, weapons?

"But —" he began.

"I'm not saying anything more about it, Mr. Collins. Haven't I just admitted killing a man? Isn't that enough for now? That's why I'm here. So, 1974. I told MacNair I had put together a package in such a way that it would look as if it was compiled by someone at the top in Ottawa. And would be profoundly embarrassing to the government and the Chief of the Defence Staff if it ever got out; it would look as if the leak had come from the very top. I put a little something in that my contact over there would recognize as coming from me, but nobody else would catch that."

"What made you think that your contact or anyone else working in the East Bloc would ever let slip what they had learned? I don't recall anything about our government being humiliated in that way."

Patriquin shrugged. "We handed it over. What they did with it was out of our hands."

Monty knew he wasn't getting the whole story, or even the real story. And he likely never would. His concern should be the fight out at MacNair's cottage, which resulted in the lieutenant-colonel dying on the floor of his living room.

"All right," he said, "so you put together this information. What role did MacNair play in this?"

"We returned to our bases in West Germany, me at Baden-Soellingen and him at Lahr. MacNair would travel from Lahr to West Berlin, and somebody would cross over from the East and pick up the envelope."

"And," Monty asked, knowing the answer in advance, "who was the person who crossed over to pick up the envelope?"

"You know perfectly well who it was."

Monty remembered MacNair's reaction to Monty's question about how he first met Meika Keller; had he known her in Germany? And how MacNair had laughed off the suggestion, had told Monty to look at a map and see how far Canadian Forces Base Lahr was from Berlin. He answered his own question: "Meika Keller."

"Right. And she wanted to get out of Germany. The two of us helped her defect and get resettled in this country. Long story there, but we got her out. And from that day on, we were all vulnerable to blackmail. We all lived in a state of fear, each of us terrified one of the others would tell. We lived in a situation of Mutually Assured Destruction, you might say."

"Christ!"

"Yeah. Oh, it eased off for a while there. When nothing happened over the years, we all relaxed a bit. But when MacNair found out she'd received some kind of message from Berlin and then bolted for Europe, he must have experienced a terrifying wave of fear, same as I did. That's what the two of them would have been arguing about that night by the Arm."

And, Monty figured, that explained the nine panicked phone calls. He remembered, too, the story MacNair had told him when Monty questioned him about the postcard; MacNair said she had been composing an opera, and the postcard must have been connected with that. Monty now saw that as a fiction made up, perhaps on the spot, to deflect speculation about the card.

"But what we'd all heard about Meika Keller escaping to West Berlin, getting past the checkpoint . . ."

"Ha! That was a legend she built up around herself. She was so completely trusted by the regime over there that they let her go over and get the papers. It was timed with a volleyball tournament in West Berlin; she was a talented athlete. She fooled them, though, and defected to the West. And, it has to be said, became a model citizen of this country. Loving wife and stepmother, esteemed professor of physics, tireless worker for charity. Driven by guilt? Or was it her good side permitted to come out at last? I'd say the latter, wouldn't you?" He paused for a few seconds and then said, "She had a discreditable past, but mightn't we all have acted as she did, in those circumstances? And once she had the freedom to do whatever she pleased, she chose to lead an exemplary life."

Patriquin's expression hardened. "But then she flies off to Europe, I think we can assume to Germany, and comes back. And next thing we know, she's dead. And Alban MacNair gets arrested for the murder."

Monty wondered whether Patriquin assumed MacNair had killed her. He kept that to himself.

"And I was spooked. Aside from the fact that the woman had died, and MacNair was facing life in prison, I was worried about my own ass. Would MacNair get so rattled that he might let something slip? That he'd met her in Germany and handed over secrets that I had procured? I was afraid MacNair might try to make himself a hero, claiming he got her out of East Berlin, and that he'd never hurt her after taking such a risk for her. Would this lead to the other information coming out? And if convicted, would he even offer to trade information — deflecting the attention onto me — for a more lenient sentence for the murder?

"I nearly went out of my mind worrying about it all. I'd wake up at three in the morning, bathed in sweat, with visions of being paraded in front of the officers and men with a noose around my neck, or being put up against a wall to be shot by a firing squad!"

"Noose? Firing squad? John, there's been nobody executed in this country since two men were hanged for murder in 1962, and . . ."

"And the death penalty was abolished for criminal offences twenty years ago. But it's still there in the *National Defence Act*, isn't it, for military crimes. Spying or passing intelligence to an enemy!"

"When was the last execution of a member of the forces, though, John? There weren't any during the Second World War, as far as I know."

"There was one in 1945, July, so the European war was over. The Army always tried to keep it under wraps. There were no other executions during the war and none since. But look what happened in more recent times. That young fellow a few years ago in Newfoundland caught trying to sell information to the Soviets. Info about our — or, the Americans' — underwater surveillance capabilities, how Soviet submarines could be tracked. Sensitive stuff. He was a civilian, not a member of the forces, so he wasn't tried under the *National Defence Act* but some other law, I can't remember now. But the young guy had had a tragic background, family trauma and all that, and he still got sentenced to nine years in prison. What would a court do with me?!"

"I know the *Criminal Code*, John, but I'm not familiar with the limitation periods, if indeed there are any, under the *National Defence Act* or any other act that might come into play here, but I—"

"Let's assume I'm in the category of *they can come for me any time*. But prosecution or not, I'd still be unmasked as a traitor!"

"But, John, if you plan to admit to the killing of MacNair . . ."

"My desperate hope is that we can get it down to manslaughter.

A drunken argument. Without admitting what the argument was about. After all, the two other people involved in the scheme are dead now. And the only other people who've been told are bound by the secrecy . . . When I learned that somebody well known to you flew over there, over to Germany, to try to put things together, I . . ."

"You what?"

Patriquin was flustered and said, "Never mind, never mind. Water under the bridge now." Once again, he held up a hand to discourage any questions. "Even without considering the length of the sentence I might get, I'd rather go down for an unintended death than for betraying my service, betraying my country."

Monty didn't know where to begin to react to all of this. And then there was more.

"There was something else, something I'd dismissed when I heard it years ago. As I say, MacNair was a big drinker, and sometimes he'd absolutely lose it. Go out of control. He quit drinking some years ago. And now I think I know why. I have friends in Moncton, former Air Force guys and others who like to fly. They hang out at the Moncton Flight Centre. Years ago, I got a call from one of them. And he told me something so effing incredible that I thought he must have been making it up. Except maybe he wasn't. Back in the 1980s, there was a big do in Moncton, brass coming down from headquarters to rally the troops. I was up there for it, and so was MacNair. There was a reception for some of the defence guys out at the Flight Centre. No liquor, just some bakery stuff, tea, coffee, soft drinks. I was planning to take out one of the Pipers right after the reception. But they grounded all the planes, didn't tell us why. What I heard from a buddy of mine up there was that one of the mugs of tea had some kind of sleeping pills, or nighttime cold medicine, in it, something that makes you drowsy, puts you to sleep. One of the staff at the Flight Centre found this, passed the word up the line, and they wouldn't let anybody take a plane out. They weren't sure who had been drinking the tea. Or —" Patriquin paused and looked intently at Monty "— or whether the tea was doctored by somebody, to be consumed by somebody else."

Once again, Monty was left reeling.

"Could have been disastrous, somebody up there at the controls and the guy falls asleep. My buddy called me a couple of weeks ago, told me two Halifax cops went up there asking about it. Why? Because they'd received information that Alban MacNair had been stopped for the breathalyzer up there in New Brunswick late that night."

Monty opened his mouth to speak but had no idea what to say.

"Yeah, I know, it's a stretch, and it all sounds too wacky to be believed. That was the first time I'd heard any possible connection between Alban and the tea. I don't think I drank very much of it, if it was my mug, because I was anxious to get up in the air. But I do remember that Alban was drunk at the event in Moncton. And sometimes when he got like that, he was a freakin' hothead. The pressure, the guilt about his past, I don't know. Did he slip a drug into my tea before I was scheduled to go up in one of the planes? Had he been plagued with the same visions late at night, visions of a firing squad, and this drove him to do something that crazy?

"When I went out to his cottage on Tuesday, I brought this up. And I asked him why he quit drinking so soon after that trip to Moncton. And why he was back on the sauce now. I accused him of trying to kill me. He laughed — hysterically, I'd say — there was something about the look on his face. I think he actually did plan it, on the spur of the moment when he was blitzed. And he sobered up and swore off the booze, till all the new pressures built up inside him.

"We started arguing and I got wild at him and he got wild at me. I ended up killing him. I did not intend to. But would he have killed me? I think he would have. We both had information that could put the other away for life. Or worse."

Monty was, to borrow a word from Brennan Burke, gobsmacked. Whatever had built up between MacNair and Patriquin over the years had ended in the two men raging at each other, and one of them dead. And the other disgraced, headed to prison for murder or man-slaughter for what could be the rest of his life. Monty didn't know what information had been given over to the East Germans. But it was almost certainly something more serious than embarrassing information about military policy in Ottawa. Whatever it was, it was something that amounted to disloyalty to the Canadian Armed Forces. To Canada itself. And perhaps to its role with the NATO mission in Europe.

As the lawyer who had represented Lieutenant-Colonel MacNair and who had won the trust of MacNair's family, he could not possibly go on record as the solicitor for Lieutenant-General John Joseph Patriquin. He explained this to Patriquin, assured him that he would never reveal to anyone what had been revealed in his office that day, and said he would arrange other counsel for him before the day was out.

It was impossible to see the dashing airman, the hero of the Sinai, in the diminished figure who shuffled out of Monty's office to go home, a home that might soon be forsaken for a prison cell.

When Monty was once again alone, he sat back in his chair and chastised himself for underestimating Brennan Burke, something he had learned early on never to do. Burke hadn't been crazy after all. There was indeed a German angle to this case.

CHAPTER XXXII

Brennan

Terry had left for New York, and Brennan had only two days left himself before he would take a flight from Berlin to London and from there to Halifax. He took a last look at Leipzig, taking in the splendour of the architecture, the steeply pitched front-facing gables, the ornately carved exteriors of the buildings, and then boarded a train for Berlin. The trip took an hour and a quarter, and then he was in a taxi — not a Freundlich taxi but not un-freundlich at all — on his way to Marzahn in the northeast part of the city. He had no idea what he would say to Meika Keller's daughter, but he could not bring himself to leave the country without having a word, a consoling word he hoped, with the daughter of the woman whose death had set all these events in motion.

When he got to Marzahn, he found himself surrounded by massive grey high-rise buildings, constructed of concrete slabs like so many other brutalist apartment blocks slapped up in so many cities in the middle of the century. Helga Baumann's place was in one of them, in Märkische Allee. He found the right apartment, and after a bit of understandable reluctance on her part, she opened the door to apartment 306. Facing him in the doorway was a short thin woman with lank light-brown hair to her shoulders and expressionless dark eyes. She appeared to be in her mid-thirties, but that could not be right. If Brennan remembered correctly, Meika said her daughter was only five years old at the time Meika left East Germany. If at least that much of the story was true, Helga would be twenty-seven now. What he could see of the apartment reflected the worn look of the tenant herself. Maroon-coloured curtains sagged over the windows, a white fake-leather sofa was soiled and split, and dirty dishes were stacked on the kitchen counter.

Brennan addressed her in German. "Fräulein Baumann, I am Father Brennan Burke. I am here from Canada, and I wondered if I might . . ."

"What do you want?"

"I knew your mother in Canada."

What little expression the young woman had mustered died away; she was perfectly still.

"Would it be all right if I come inside?" Brennan continued to speak German.

"Only for a few minutes. I have someone coming here in a little while." But she stepped aside and Brennan went in. She pointed to the soiled white sofa, but he chose a cleaner-looking hard-back wooden chair. She took the other wooden chair and sat facing him.

"Well?"

"I am a priest in Halifax, Nova Scotia, and your mother —"

"Oh! I hope you gave her a lovely icon of the Madonna and Child, the very emblem of her life."

"I'm sorry to have to say this, Helga —"

"My name is Leni now. I never liked Helga. It was my grandmother's name. As a child, I liked the name Leni. So, that is who I am now."

"Yes, Leni. I am sorry to tell you that your mother died. She drowned."

The news hit Leni like a blow to the heart. She didn't speak. Brennan decided that this was not the time to unload more of the bad news on her, so he just sat quietly in the chair.

Then her demeanour changed. The tears came, followed by loud, uncontrollable sobs. After a couple of minutes, she put her hands to her face and tried furiously to scrub away the tears. "I am pathetic."

"Leni, what is pathetic about crying over the death of your mother?"

"My mother who abandoned me? Left me here to my fate, while she went off to her successful and happy life in America? In Canada?"

"Please tell me," he said, "so I'll understand."

"You don't have time to hear such a long story."

"I have time."

Her eyes searched his face, as if wondering whether she could hope to find understanding there. Finally, she began. "I had just turned five years old. I remember with the clarity of a motion picture the day she left. The three of us were in our apartment: her, my father, and me. She sat me down across from her at the kitchen table and reached over and took my hand. 'Little one, I am going away for a while.' I asked her why she was going. She just said, 'To play.' So, of course I said I wanted to go, too. I wanted to go with her and we would play together. I didn't know whether she meant play a game, like volleyball, or play music. I have no idea why she did not give me the details; maybe she reasoned that the more I knew about it, the more I would want to go with her. I remember her hand trembling. I, as children do, caught the mood and I got up and ran around the table and held my arms up. She stood and picked me up and clasped me to her.

"I said, 'Mutti, why can't I go with you?' and she was crying, too, and then she put me down and turned away. She went into the sitting room, and my father went in after her. And do you know what she whispered to him? Thinking I couldn't hear?"

Brennan shook his head no.

"She said, 'Helga cannot make the journey with me because she does not have the talent.'" Her eyes blazed across at Brennan. "She could not take me with her — and we now know she was leaving me forever — because I had *no talent!*"

Leni was trembling with rage. Rage and grief. Brennan could not imagine what to say in the face of such pain.

"Then she came back in, picked me up, kissed me, and put me down again. She turned to my father, and I could not see whatever look she gave him. But I saw his face. He was staring at her, as if he had been struck by lightning. She had her travel bag by the door. She picked it up and walked out."

"Leni, I had no idea. I am so sorry."

"Oh, I believe you, that you had no idea. I think she never even mentioned to you or maybe to anyone else in her new life that she had a daughter left behind in the German *Democratic* Republic." Brennan did not reveal to Leni the story her mother had told, that she had got her daughter out in that daring escape, and that the child died of illness before they could leave Europe. "That was the defining moment of my life. I was a no-talent child, abandoned by my mother for that very reason."

"That is terrible, Leni. I wish there was something I could do for you." He realized how inane that sounded; he just did not know what to say.

"Are you a time traveller, Father Burke? They say that a thousand ages in God's sight are but an evening gone. You're a man of God. You want to do something for me? Take me back to 1974 and make my mother stay with me. And wipe out those hateful words she said, that curse she left on me. Because it was not long before that judgment came to haunt me. When my mother did not come back, and did not come back still, my father saw the writing on the wall. She had fled, and he would be the one to pay the price. The state would take him as a hostage and hold him in prison until she returned. So, he worked fast, trying to get me into a good school. A school that concentrated on the arts and music, because he knew I loved music. Even though I had no talent! But I refused to cooperate, for that very reason. I wanted to go to that school. I used to see the other girls coming home with their flutes and violins in their cases. I had always wanted to go there, but now that I knew I could not possibly make the grade, that I would make a fool of myself at that school and be laughed at, I threw a tantrum and refused to go in and talk to the head of the school. I made such a fuss that he never got me in the door before the Stasi came for him.

"So, I became a ward of the state, and the state had a place for me. A children's home, one of many in this country. There was nothing special about me or my suffering during my long years there. Thousands of us were humiliated, beaten, and abused. It was an education system — I mean, a *re*-education system — designed to achieve one of the most important goals of a totalitarian state: the destruction of the individual."

Brennan sat there helpless, outraged at what had been done to a little girl left alone, left to the mercy of a merciless state.

"Any feelings we children might have had of self-worth, any little spark of personality, or any attempts to assert ourselves as free individuals were destroyed. We were to become automatons, merely products of and supporters of the socialist state. First we had a fascist state, then we had the anti-fascist state. Hard for their victims to tell the difference."

"Leni, it's unbearable hearing what you went through."

"Me and thousands of others. And those of us who were considered 'anti-social' got the worst treatment of all. I gained a reputation as a troublemaker. One of my fellow inmates, someone I thought of as my friend, informed the director of the home that I had been writing and singing protest songs, satires about the home and the state. All dissent was to be crushed. So, they doubled their efforts to re-educate, reform, brainwash me from thinking for myself. One of the caretakers, though, was friendly to me. Paid special attention to me, even invited me to his home on a weekend."

Brennan's reply was a cautious "Oh?"

The look she gave him was enough; he knew the kind of thing that had probably happened to her on her weekend with the friendly caretaker.

"I tried to kill myself," she said, as if saying she had tried to learn Greek. "I twisted up one of my shirts and used it to hang myself. But, as you can see, I failed. No talent even for suicide." Brennan found the words for suicide interesting in German. *Selbstmord*, self-murder, was virtually identical to the Latin origin of "suicide." What Leni said was *Freitod*, free death.

"You must think I am very selfish, Father Burke."

"What? Of course not. Why would you say that, Leni?"

"Talking on and on about me, me, me. Poor little Leni with all her pains and sorrows."

"You suffered immense pain and sorrow. Why wouldn't you recount what you endured?"

"Ha! I must have ingested some of that anti-individualist group-think after all, apologizing for talking about myself, thinking that my little life is of no importance."

"Your life is of infinite importance, Leni."

She looked away from him, and her body began shaking again. He did not know what to do. He wanted to embrace and comfort her, but the intimacy might be unwelcome, might bring back even more of the horrific memories of how she was treated. Brennan stayed where he was, irresolute.

Finally, he said, "You sent her a postcard."

"Yes, I did."

"You used the word 'talent' when writing to your mother."

"Of course I did. I wrote that at least I had the talent to read. And in case that word had not stayed in her mind the way it had been burned into mine, I put in another word she would recognize. *Schlingel.*"

Brennan knew it meant a scallywag, a rascal, a scoundrel.

"She always called me that, in an affectionate way. Ah, the good old days, Father! Anyway, when she arrived here, I explained how I had tracked her down. I had been told that there was a story in the newspaper about her, living with a new name in Canada, and I read it and found her that way. I had already searched and found references to her in the records, the Stasi files, which are now available for people to examine."

"And that's why you sent her a card with a photo of the Stasi complex."

"Exactly. So, she came to me here after I sent the card. She must have done some research, too, perhaps with her old contacts in the Stasi!"

"Your mother was a committed Communist, then, a true believer. Supporter of the East German regime."

"No," she said in a voice he could barely hear, "it was worse than that."

"What do you mean?"

"I mean that from everything I learned about her — learned from family members, people who knew her — she wasn't a supporter of the regime. She despised it."

"But if she informed on people and was allowed to cross over . . ."

"She wasn't a supporter. She did not have that excuse. But she did it anyway. She went along. Went along with something evil that she didn't support, didn't believe in. To me, that is worse."

Yes. Brennan understood. It was one thing to act according to a deeply held conviction, however misguided. It was another thing altogether to willingly cooperate with a regime, or with an individual, that one despised.

"So," he said to Leni, "she came to see you."

"She arrived at my door. I opened it and it took a second for me to recognize her, and then there was no doubt. I knew it was her. She said, 'I know you must hate me,' and I said, 'Oh, did you spend years studying psychology along with physics?' Then, 'Come into my home, see how the no-talent daughter lives.'

"And it was clear to me that she knew exactly what I meant. She started in right away, explaining what she had meant by the 'no talent' remark. What she said to my father was that she could not take me with her because she would have to tell a good many lies to convince the authorities that she was coming back. She did not know what kind of stories she might have to invent if she ran into any trouble with the authorities here, if someone questioned her permission to leave, or with East German spies operating on the other side of the wall. She was afraid of what I might say to blow her cover, so to speak. So, what she said to my father was that she could not take me because I 'had no talent to deceive.' And I heard only the first part of that — and had to live with it for the rest of my life. And she began to weep, my mother did. She told me, 'I don't know how I'll be able to live with myself knowing . . .'

"'You have lived very well all these years, knowing you deserted your only child, so you could have a good life for yourself. And you knew how things were here, and how they would be for me. A young girl left on her own to survive. Confined and abused in a state institution.'

"She was shaking by this time. And pleading with me to understand. She said her plan had always been to send for me, have me taken to the West. And I think my father was to come separately, afterwards. I'm not sure. But I laughed in her face. 'How did you expect to do this? A defector asking the state to bundle up her little girl and bring her across the wall, please? A state that imprisoned people for merely talking about going to the West?!' She said she had a friend here, a Lutheran church minister. He was a liberal, an opponent of the regime. And he had contacts on the other side of the wall. She said he had succeeded in getting a couple of people out. So, somehow she contacted him. And he said he would try to help her. But of course my father was shut up in prison, so in order to find out where I was, the minister had to ask questions. And I don't know how it went, whether his questions raised suspicions about him, or whether the Stasi were listening to his conversations, or there was an informer. I don't know, and I don't think she knew either. But word came back to the minister: they told him I was dead. My mother repeated that to me: 'They said you had died!'

"'And you believed them,' I said to her.

"And she looked even more miserable then, but I did not back off. I said to her, 'Did you not suspect that maybe they lied to the minister, made up that story to punish you?'"

How dreadful for all of them, Brennan said to himself. He remembered then what Commodore Rendell had said. Rendell had heard that, during her first couple of years in Canada, Meika had never mentioned her daughter. Then, by the time Rendell had met her, she had begun telling the story of the harrowing escape from the checkpoint, mother and child hand in hand, and how the child had not survived long enough to make the journey to North America. Meika would have been devastated when she heard that her daughter had died after being left in the East. And then, in case word got out that there had been a daughter, she came up with the alternative version of reality, in which she portrayed herself as a heroic mother trying to get her child to safety, rather than a mother who had left her husband and child behind when she got herself out of East Germany.

Brennan sat there looking at Leni but could not for the life of him come up with an appropriate response.

"And then," said Leni, "I told her, 'Now I have to pick up my own daughter at her kindergarten.' You will be interested to know, Father Burke, that it is run by a church here. Lutheran church. Not the same one my mother's friend was at. I think that minister was arrested and imprisoned for *anti-social conduct*. Yet another person punished for having a conscience. Anyway, this other church operates the kindergarten, and my little girl loves attending it. My mother said she would love to meet her granddaughter. But I said no. I know I wounded her when I said that, because she knew there was no reason she could not have come with me to collect Imke. I was being cruel. We both knew it. Revenge, I suppose it was. So, I told her to leave. And my parting words were 'I hope you will have a long, long life, Mutti, and that you will think of me every day of it.'"

They sat without speaking for several minutes. Then Brennan heard footsteps outside in the corridor. "I told you when you first arrived that someone is coming here soon. And she is here now. My daughter, from kindergarten. I take turns with another of the parents here, collecting our children at the end of the morning." Leni got up and opened the door.

"Mutti! Look what I made today!"

"Hello, my little love!"

Brennan watched as Leni lifted a little girl into her arms and kissed her cheek. Leni was transformed; she looked like a different person altogether, her face animated and almost joyful. She thanked the person who brought Imke home and drew the child inside and closed the door. Imke was around three or four years old, petite, with bright blue eyes and blond hair in elaborate braids. When she caught sight of Brennan, her eyes grew wide and she moved closer to her mother.

"We have a visitor, Imke."

Imke looked up at Leni and whispered, "Who is that?"

"This is Father Burke. He is here from way across the Atlantic Ocean, in Canada."

"Hello, Imke," Brennan said in his softest voice and pointed to a paper in her hand. He stayed seated so as not to tower over her. "What do you have there?"

"It's a castle," she said shyly. "I made it in kindergarten today. And see the letters I printed on it? That's my name!" She thrust the crayoned picture of a castle up so he could admire it.

"That's a beautiful castle. My first name is Brennan."

"You are burning!"

He knew his name sounded like the German for the verb to burn. "You'll have to ask my mother why she gave me such a name! You have a lovely name yourself, though."

"Thank you. I like it!"

As she began to fill her mother in on all the activities she had enjoyed that day, her shyness eased. She recounted how one of the boys had to be spoken to because he had used a bad word, and another child had climbed up to the cabinet where the snacks were kept, and he wasn't allowed to have one until tomorrow. Watching the young mother with her daughter, one would never suspect that Leni had endured such a horrendous past.

"I'm going into my room to do something. Don't come in!"

"All right, we won't." Leni laughed as the child skipped into her room and shut the door behind her. "You can see that she is happy. I am planning to take Imke and leave this country. I know things are better here now, but for me there are too many reminders of my past. Wherever I walk here in Berlin, I wonder about every person I meet in the streets. Did he inform on someone, get the person imprisoned or tortured? Was he one of the guards at the prison where my father was kept until the end of his life? I want a new start for myself, and the sooner we go, the less of a painful break it will be for her. I am learning English, but I am not good enough yet to try to speak it with you. Imke is learning it, too; she knows it quite well. We may go to England, or America."

His reaction was immediate. "Have you ever thought of Canada?"

She laughed. "No, I never thought of it, because we hear so much about the United States and England."

"I could help you come to Canada."

She looked at him without her usual cynicism; what he saw in her face was hope. But then, "I do not want to go where my mother was, where people knew her."

"You wouldn't have to see them. Halifax is not a huge city, but there are enough places to live and work that you wouldn't have to worry about crossing their path if you didn't want to. And there are lovely small towns nearby with a strong German heritage, one of them being Mahone Bay, another being Lunenburg."

"That would be, I don't know, comforting I suppose. There is a university in your city, as I know from the news I heard about *her*."

"There are several, along with community colleges, trade schools, art school, all kinds of opportunities."

"I did well in maths and science, and I always wished to train as an engineer."

"There you go. Dalhousie University has an excellent engineering program."

"But that's where *she* worked."

"No, actually, she taught at another university, Saint Mary's."

Imke emerged from her room then and gave her mother a questioning look. "Are we going away?"

"The walls have ears," Leni said, "but they always have had, here in Berlin." To Imke, she said, "I was telling Father Burke that you are very good at speaking English."

"I know a song, and it's in English! Mutti doesn't know it. It's about raindrops and kittens. And strudel!"

"Oh, that sounds wonderful. Would you like to sing it for me?"

She retreated to her mother's side again. Had Brennan's reputation as a tough audience for music accompanied him to Germany?

"I want somebody to sing it with me."

Brennan didn't think that should be him, but he had an idea. Surely "My Favourite Things" was known to someone known to him in Halifax. What time was it? Twenty past one in Germany, so twenty past eight in Halifax. She would be getting ready for school; well, if she was late one day out of the year, Brennan would see to it that the infraction was not entered in her permanent record. "I know a girl who would love to sing with you."

"You do?"

"Yes. I have a music school in Canada."

"A school for music?" She looked as if she had just won the lead role in *The Sound of Music*.

He dialled the Collins home number and waited. The MacNeil answered. "Hello?"

"Morning, sunshine. Hope I didn't wake you."

"Did I blast a string of obscenities into the phone, or did I merely say 'hello'?"

"Grand. I didn't wake you. I shall be able to return to Halifax without fear of reprisal."

"I make no promises. Where are you?"

"Just another day in Berlin for me."

"Is everything all right?"

"Well, that would depend on —"

"Don't launch into a philosophical treatise, Brennan. Just reassure me that you are safe and sound, of body if not of mind."

"I am. Now I have a young girl here —"

"A girl! Should I even ask?"

"Just ask Normie, if you would, to come to the phone and sing a song with Imke."

"Of course. Why ever didn't you say so?"

So, he greeted a puzzled Normie, gave her a short explanation, and passed the phone to Imke. She spoke hesitantly into the phone in English and then launched into the song. The animation in her face told him that Normie was playing her part. He took out a few Deutsche Marks and placed them on a nearby table. "For the phone call," he whispered to Leni. He waved off her protests. When the singing wound down, he gently took the phone, thanked Normie, and said he would see her soon. Imke danced off into her room, singing "Edelweiss."

Brennan turned his attention to Leni and the nascent idea of emigration from Germany. "It's a hell of a lot for you to consider. But if after giving it some serious thought, you'd like to go for it, I'll do everything

348

I can to smooth the way." He reached into his pocket and took out a pack of cigarettes. He smiled at her and said, "This is all I have for your first immigration papers." He wrote out his address and phone number on the top of the package, tore it off, and handed it to her.

"Thank you. You are being very good to us."

"You are more than welcome, Leni." Now there was another question he had to ask. "Em, would it be the two of you, or . . . ?"

Leni laughed. "Is there a man, you're asking? Well, there was, obviously. But he found a better location on the other side of the city, and a better class of person to share it with."

"I'm sorry."

"We are better off without him."

Brennan was forced to examine his conscience: am I doing this for her or for me? Both, he knew, but if Leni and her little girl could make a fresh start in a new city, they would benefit greatly from it.

As Brennan was standing at the door, about to take his leave, he saw that there were tears in Leni's eyes. "Tell me something, Father. Maybe something from the Bible, or from the poets, something that will help me look past all that has happened to me, that will reassure me that I'll be the kind of mother I should be, for Imke."

It wasn't scripture that came to mind. It was a loose translation of Aeschylus:

"Even in our sleep, pain which cannot forget

Falls drop by drop upon the heart,

And in our own despite, against our will,

Comes wisdom to us by the awful grace of God."

She stared at him and then spoke softly. "I hope I'll have that wisdom someday. I hope my greatest fear never comes true. Do you know what that is? I have known fear, but this is the worst. I am afraid that somehow I will cause pain to my daughter, harm her in some way. If I hurt my daughter the way my mother hurt me, I could not live with myself."

Brennan's reply was quiet, sorrowful. "Neither could she."

CHAPTER XXXIII

Monty

Three days after Lieutenant-General Patriquin's astonishing admissions, and after Monty had set him up with Saul Green as his new counsel, Monty got a call from Bill MacEwen in the Crown's office.

"Couple of things, Monty."

"Okay, Bill, let's hear them."

"You may have heard that the Mounties had Commodore Rendell in for questioning."

"Oh, yeah, I heard."

"Well, Rendell is off the hook. He had a couple of drinks and then drove out to Lawrencetown Beach to visit a friend, someone in the Navy. A woman named Lesage. This was the night MacNair was killed, but it wasn't the only night Rendell had been out to Lawrencetown recently. Anyway, after first denying he'd left his own house, he changed his story and said he'd been out to this Lesage's place. But he'd been worried before this that if anybody knew he'd been visiting this woman, people would think he had a mistress, and he might have had a hand in his wife's death. So he told Petty Officer Lesage to deny he'd been there if anyone ever asked. When the RCMP got in touch with her, she was a good soldier — well, a good sailor — and lied and said Rendell hadn't been there. It all got straightened out — comedy of errors kind of thing — apparently he and Lesage are, after all, just friends. Her romantic interests lie elsewhere. So, his alibi stands up."

Monty was well aware that Rendell's alibi would stand up, given that he had heard in person from the man who really was responsible for MacNair's death. When it came time for the plea bargaining, the Crown lawyer would know the identity of the man who had killed MacNair, but he would never know why. But this was Bill MacEwen's day, and he had not quite finished.

"Monty, have you ever gone wreck diving in the harbour here?"

"Can't say as I have, Bill."

"Well, as I'm sure you know, there are thousands of wrecked ships and boats along the coastline of this province, scads of them in and around Halifax Harbour. Some date back to the 1800s and even earlier."

"Oh, yes, I know about the wrecks, but I've never gone down to see them close up. Pretty spooky, I imagine."

"And cold. Especially at this time of year. But there's many a hardy soul who goes down there in scuba gear, even in the early weeks of spring. Quite the tourist attraction for the dive community."

"The Dive Community — that'd be a good name for a bar."

"Good place for you to have savoured a celebratory drink. If it wasn't too late, which sadly it is."

"What are you getting at, Bill?"

"If Alban MacNair hadn't been whacked, we would have been dropping the charges against him."

"*What?*"

"Couple of cold-water divers, Americans, were down there in the water out beyond Point Pleasant. They'd been there in the summer looking at a wreck and wanted to go down again and take some more pictures. This time, they saw something that hadn't been there before. Old wooden rowboat with the oars fastened in, some rocks in it for ballast, and a couple of holes in the hull and couple of boards wrenched loose enough to let water in. In other words, deliberately sunk."

"Jesus."

"Little metal plaque on the stern, with the name *Lumberyard Leviathan*. Bit of humour there. A little homemade rowboat, old and not in the best of shape, and the police traced it to a couple by the name of Pemberton. They live in the south end, right on the shore on Chain Rock Drive."

On the western edge of Point Pleasant Park. Close to the home of Meika Keller and Hubert Rendell.

"The Pembertons are away for an extended vacation in Cuba, but the police got in touch with their son here, and he went over to the parents' place and looked in the shed. Saw that the boat was gone. Also missing were a crowbar and a hand-powered drill and bits. Taken along to make sure the hull of the boat could be pierced or wrenched open. All this leaves Alban MacNair out of the picture. We would not have been able to make a case that he got her into a tiny boat, rowed her out to the depths, pushed her off, then sank the boat, and swam back to shore in water that is barely one degree centigrade. Nor can we picture him taking another boat out and following her. She was an athletic woman. She could have rowed away from him, back to shore. And if he had a gun, why not just shoot her? That would have been quicker and would not have left him possibly on view with a boat to deal with in the winter. We don't see any of that happening. She did it herself. We don't know why, but we know this much: we could no longer have made a case against Lieutenant-Colonel MacNair."

"Jesus, Bill, this gets more bizarre by the day." Monty couldn't let on to the Crown attorney what he had learned about Meika Keller, or the conspiracy she entered into with Alban MacNair and John Joseph Patriquin. Did a guilty conscience finally catch up with her?

Why now, after twenty-two years? Was there something about that postcard that had pushed her over the edge?

"So," Bill said, "poor MacNair was innocent after all. But somebody out there is guilty of beating MacNair and pushing him to his death."

Bill would know soon enough who was guilty, Monty reflected. As soon as Saul Green and Lieutenant-General Patriquin worked out their strategy for a plea bargain.

"So there you have it, Monty. Stay tuned."

"I will. Thanks for letting me know, Bill."

Monty remembered Brennan Burke's little jest: "Maybe she took a ship out and scuttled 'er." That's exactly what she did, according to the prosecutor. A boat, not a Navy ship. For whatever reason — guilt? fear of exposure? — Meika Keller took her neighbour's rowboat out of the shed, loaded some tools into it, dragged it down to the shore, added some ballast in the form of heavy rocks, and rowed it around to the southern tip of the peninsula and out into the Atlantic. And scuttled the boat. Why do all that work? Why not just tip it over? So she wouldn't be tempted in her panic to climb back onto the hull if it was still afloat? Once the boat went under, she was on her own in the frigid waters of the ocean. Death was a virtual certainty. And it was obviously well planned. She did not come up with this scheme spontaneously after her midnight altercation with MacNair. Late that afternoon, she had approached Father Burke and asked to speak to him at ten that night. Whatever drove her to this desperate act, she knew all about it before going to — trying to — see her priest. If and when Brennan Burke learned of this, Monty could not imagine how heavily the knowledge would weigh on him.

CHAPTER XXXIV

Monty

Monty was sitting in Saint Bernadette's church the evening of Holy Thursday. There were a few choral pieces before the Mass would begin; the men's and boys' choir was up in the loft with the children's choir from the school. The men and boys were doing "Ubi Caritas" and their magnificent singing earned Monty a malevolent look from his wife beside him in the pew. Yes, he should be up there. And he would be; he had to get past all the awkwardness with Burke and take his place in the tenor section where he belonged. Then the children's choir sang a piece he didn't recognize, but it was something from the Renaissance, possibly Palestrina. As always, the children's voices blended beautifully, and their intonation was perfect. After that, Monty and Maura were in for a surprise: they heard the voices of two young girls, an alto and a soprano, singing in German. It was "Maria Wiegenlied." Mary's lullaby. The voices were heartbreakingly beautiful, and it was time for another look passing between husband and wife, father and mother. The alto voice was Normie's, the soprano Kim Kennedy's.

That's when Monty remembered something he had overheard the day before. He had come home early from the office and heard Normie and Kim chatting, their voices coming up from the den. Monty had cracked up when he heard Kim say in a wonderfully accurate imitation of the Irish voice of their choirmaster, "Burke will be pissed. Can't you hear him? Sure d'yez think it's feckin' Christmas?"

His daughter laughed but said, "Yeah, but I really want to sing it for her. And nobody in the church will catch on it's about Christmas, 'cause it'll all be in German."

The rest of the conversation went something like this:

"What was her name again?"

"Imke."

"That's a cute name."

"Yeah, I really like it. I only talked to her for a few minutes on the phone, but I know she is so sweet! I helped her with her English for a song, and I told her I'd sing one in German for her. And she said 'Maria Wiegenlied.' It's a lullaby. She loves it, but her mum is too shy to sing it for her; her mum says she's no good — the mum is no good — at singing. So, me and you will sing it, and if Father Burke says we're good, we'll phone Imke in Germany and sing it to her!"

That was the conversation as far as Monty could recall. Then the girls must have heard his footsteps above them, because they fell silent. He of course wondered who Imke was — a relative of one of the visiting scholars at the Schola Cantorum? — but he didn't hear anything more and hadn't thought about it again until now. Apparently, Burke hadn't been "pissed" after all, if he'd permitted the song on Holy Thursday.

Speaking of Burke, here he was now in the procession, walking up the aisle to begin the Mass. Maura shook her head and whispered to Monty, "He looks like one of the Irish Republican prisoners on hunger strike. Either that or one of those God-haunted saints who starved themselves in the desert."

He did indeed look haunted, thin and exhausted, but he "said a beautiful Mass," as Monty's aunts would say, and at the end when he sang the Gregorian chant, "Pange Lingua," his baritone voice was as rich and inspiring as ever.

And that brought it all back to Monty: the brilliant talent that came blazing through, despite everything Brennan Burke had endured. Monty felt, like a knife in his gut, the painful memory of dismissing Brennan as a spectacular Irish flameout. Now here he was, walking down the aisle in his vestments after the beautiful ceremony. How did Brennan manage to keep it together? There was the pain of his all-too-human failure to meet Meika Keller the night when she was planning to end her life. And that wasn't by any means the only thing weighing on Brennan's mind, Monty was sure. He had come home to Halifax after his harrowing experience in Belfast to find his choir school in the hands of an occupying force, a crowd of bean counters more interested in the ringing of a cash register than the ringing tones of a heavenly choir. At least there was some good news on that front: W. Langston Soames, who had installed himself as the school's chairman of the board, had resigned in a huff, taking his bags of gold with him. Good riddance.

But there was no getting away from the events that had precipitated Brennan's woes and his excessive — even by Burkean standards — drinking. And there was no getting away from the role Monty himself had played, and tried to downplay, in what had befallen Brennan in Ireland. Monty had laughed off the warning he had been given late at night on a Belfast street, just as he had more recently laughed off Brennan's insistence that the motive for Meika Keller's death lay in her German past. The warning in Ireland was to tell Monty that certain legal work he was doing could "hurt" certain people he knew in Belfast, including his friend Father Burke. The reason Monty had laughed was that, as far as he knew, the only risky endeavour Brennan had taken part in was his undeniably droll impersonation of an American tourist in order to disguise himself and get close to and identify a man in an East Belfast bar, a man suspected of committing an atrocity decades before. But there had in fact been more going on than Monty realized. And to say Burke had been hurt as a consequence was a gross understatement. It all came back to Monty now in a wave of pain and guilt. He remembered how horrified he'd been when he read the news out of Belfast, the stories of the fallout from his own legal case over there; Monty had felt as if he himself were one of the Belfast gunmen, that he had fired a bullet into the heart of his friend. So, now, with Father Burke greeting his congregation at the back of the church, what could Monty possibly say?

"Feel like a beer and a night of down and dirty blues at the Shag?"

An elderly woman standing next to Monty gaped at him in horror. No way to speak to a priest of God on Holy Thursday; Monty could see her point.

The priest of God leaned towards Monty and said, *sotto voce*, "All I want in this world is to fall into my bed, sink into a dreamless sleep, and not regain consciousness until three o'clock tomorrow." Tomorrow being Good Friday. "Sitting in a smoky bar, guzzling beer, and hearing fellas sing about being all alone and out of work and riding a boxcar to the next parole violation is the last thing I need. So, the appeal is irresistible. See you there."

Brennan

Brennan walked into the Flying Stag, popularly known as the Flying Shag, after exchanging his priestly vestments for a pair of jeans and a faded T-shirt that bore the immortal words of Saint Augustine: *Da mihi castitatem . . . sed noli modo.* Give me chastity . . . but not yet. The Flying Shag was located in a down-at-heels strip mall in a suburb of Halifax; the other establishments were a laundromat, a cheque-cashing service, and a pawn shop. Monty and his blues band, Functus, were launching into one of their signature pieces, the Muddy Waters classic "You Can't Lose What You Ain't Never Had," when Brennan arrived. He saw some people he knew, regulars at blues night, and they invited him to join them. He lit up a smoke, caught the eye of the waiter, and ordered a round for the table.

Brennan had received a jolt that morning when he read the news: a decorated Air Force veteran by the name of Lieutenant-General John J. Patriquin had turned himself in, in connection with the death of Alban MacNair. If there had been any doubt in Brennan's mind, there was enough in the newspaper article about Patriquin's wartime exploits to identify him as the man who had followed Brennan and Terry to Germany and made his startling confession on a park bench in Berlin. Where MacNair fit into the picture, Brennan didn't know. But coming so soon after the Berlin episode, it would be a safe bet that MacNair had a role somewhere in the Keller-Patriquin drama. Brennan said a quick prayer, the latest of many, for Leni Baumann and her little daughter, Imke.

Then he returned to the present, to the Flying Shag bar, where Monty and the other members of Functus were wailing on about busted motors and busted lives, loneliness, failure, and heartbreak, the trials and tribulations of the bummed-out and the jilted, the boozers and the junkies. Brennan could sympathize with all of them. He lifted his glass of draft and poured a good few ounces down his throat. And then, looking at Monty, he thought inevitably of Normie. And he felt the remorse all over again. Guilt over his failure to keep his word to his little AA counsellor, who had staged such an endearing intervention to save him from himself. Guilt over his failure to meet Meika Keller and possibly save her from taking her own life.

He put his glass on the table, pushed it away.

The band took a break after a searing rendition of "St. James Infirmary Blues," and Monty came over to Brennan's table. They all made small talk for a few minutes, then the other people at the table got into a discussion about the impending bankruptcy of a dejected-looking man across the room.

Brennan said to Monty, "You're in fine voice tonight. Appropriate, I suppose. We're in the penitential season liturgically, and I'm listening to the blues. Fits the mood, no question."

"True enough."

Monty said no more for a few seconds, then, "I take it that, if you went back for a second trip to Germany, you learned some history there."

"I could have learned it — some of it — here in Halifax the night of February sixth, if only I'd honoured my commitment to meet with her . . ."

"But Brennan, it was a minor transgression, a mere instance of forgetting, something we all do every day. Who could have foreseen the consequences? It's not as if —" Monty looked down at the table "— you had any warning."

"The fact that she wanted to talk to me at ten o'clock at night should have been warning enough."

"Still, nothing that would have had bells tolling in your mind, giving an intimation of what she was about to do." Monty looked up then. "You know that it . . . it's been ruled a suicide."

"Oh, I had that sussed already."

"You found out in Germany."

Brennan nodded. "I tracked down her daughter."

"Her *daughter*?!" Monty looked poleaxed. "But . . ."

Brennan waved it off. "Later," he said. Then, "If only I'd met with Meika that night —"

"You couldn't have known." Then Monty looked Brennan directly in the eye and said, "I have no such excuse. I received a warning. One night in Belfast. An IRA man. He warned me that the case I was working on could cause harm to people I knew in Belfast — the people I knew in Belfast of course were members of your family." The words came out in a torrent, as if Monty was afraid that if he stopped, he'd never be able to get started again. "And the guy mentioned you. And I laughed it off. I made a joke. Because, Brennan, the only thing

I knew you had done was go into a bar posing as an American tourist, and that's the image that came to me. So, I laughed."

Brennan had heard that the warning had been dismissed with a laugh; that had eaten away at him while he sat in his cell in prison. Here, now, was the simple and understandable reason.

Monty continued, "I had no idea that there was another, well . . ."

"Exploit? Escapade? Ill-advised venture?"

"Action you had taken. Taken to protect your family. I only found out when it was obviously too late."

Too late by the time Brennan was behind bars.

"My case was a righteous one," Monty said.

"It was, I know that."

"But if I had heeded the warning and waited, waited till you had left the country . . . Christ, when I read about the fallout from all that, I just . . ." Monty took a deep breath and said, "Brennan, I'm sorry for my part in all that. For what I did. More sorry than you will ever know."

But, at last, Brennan did know. He could see it etched in his friend's face: deep regret, true remorse. He said to Monty, "You were only a bit player in all that, Monty, somewhere off stage without a script. I was the victim of my own misguided attempt to save a member of my family, and then I fell into the hands of a brutal police force and an unjust system of justice." Brennan fell silent for a moment, then said, "Do you remember the words? *Averte faciem tuam a peccatis meis, et omnes iniquitates meas dele?*"

"Is that my penance?"

"No, it's the *Miserere mei.*" The words meant "turn thy face from my sins, and put out all my misdeeds." But it wasn't Monty's penance.

"You'll be singing it tomorrow afternoon, if you are still a member of my choir."

"I am indeed. I . . . I've missed it."

"And it has missed you." He reached for his glass and then withdrew his hand. He summoned the waiter and said, "A Keith's for Monty here. And a ginger ale for me."

Monty raised his eyebrows, and Brennan gave him the official line. "It's nearly twelve, and you know what I turn into at midnight: a priest boozing it up on Good Friday." But that wasn't the reason. The reason was Normie, and her love and concern for the weak, flawed man — the flameout — who was her priest. He didn't know how long he'd last without the stuff. Months? Weeks? Days? But he would do his best for her, for as long as he was able. The beer and the ginger ale arrived, and he said to Monty, "I'll see you tomorrow."

"Tomorrow."

Brennan raised his glass to Monty, and Monty raised his. They clinked their glasses and drank together.

Acknowledgements

I would like to thank the following people for their kind assistance: Joe A. Cameron, Rhea McGarva, Joan Butcher, Bill McKillip, John Elliott, Peter O'Brien, and Kishan Persaud. Thanks as always to my astute and sharp-eyed editors, Cat London and Crissy Calhoun.

1996 was a period of change for Halifax, the police, and the military. I have done my best to use the titles, designations, and locations that were current during the months in which the story is set. The death penalty was not removed from the National Defence Act until 1998.

I would like to emphasize that the people I have thanked here gave me much-needed information for this story, but they are not responsible for the opinions or perspectives voiced by my characters! This is a work of fiction, and any liberties taken in the interest of story-telling, or errors committed, are mine alone.